NOT A MOURNING PERSON

GRIMDALE GRAVEYARD MYSTERIES, BOOK 4

STEFFANIE HOLMES

Not a Mourning Person

Was bringing three hot AF ghosts back to life a grave mistake?

All I wanted to do was kiss my ghost boyfriends, but instead, I broke the Veil between the worlds of the Living and the Dead. Whoops. Now, a horde of demons and hellbeasts are after us, and if I don't get control over my resurrection magic soon, we're in for some grave consequences.

Like the end of the world.

I'm creeping it real here – I'm terrified. There isn't enough coffee in all of Grimdale to fortify me for this battle.

What if the price of falling for three beautiful, spirited, impossible men is *worse* than death?

What if the only way to stop Grimdale from becoming a literal ghost town...

...is to give up my soul?

Bree and her ghostly men are back for their final spooky adventure in *Not a Mourning Person*, book 4 of this darkly humorous cozy fantasy series by bestselling author Steffanie Holmes. If you love a sarcastic heroine, hot, possessive and slightly unhinged ghostly men, a mystery to solve, and a little kooky, spooky lovin' to set your coffin a rockin', then quit ghouling around and start reading!

JOIN THE NEWSLETTER FOR UPDATES

Want a free bonus scene from Bree's school dance and Bree's playlist? Grab a free copy of *Cabinet of Curiosities* – a Steffanie Holmes compendium of short stories and bonus scenes – when you sign up for updates with the Steffanie Holmes newsletter.

http://www.steffanieholmes.com/newsletter

Every week in my newsletter I talk about the true-life hauntings, strange happenings, crumbling ruins, and creepy facts that inspire my stories. You'll also get newsletter-exclusive bonus scenes and updates. I love to talk to my readers, so come join us for some spooky fun :).

*For my dad
Who is my first hero*

...Yet in thy somber realm, a truth resides,
   That death, though feared, its purpose still provides,
   For life, in its fragility, finds worth,
   In moments seized, in deeds of noble birth.

With every toll of bell, a lesson speaks,
   To seize each day, though fortune's fate may tweak,
   For death, the great equalizer, shall claim,
   The lowly beggar and the noble's name.

So let us face our fate with steady grace,
   And meet our end with valor, not disgrace,
   For death, though fearsome, grants a chance to be,
   A legacy, an echo, through eternity.

—'Thou Comest A Thief', Edward the Poet Prince, 1644.

PROLOGUE
NINETY-TWO YEARS AGO

"Go on, darling. Put us out of our misery," Horace Van Wimple, the current home secretary of Britain, glares at her across the table. "You don't have a thing in that pretty little hand of yours that will beat me."

Van Wimple leans back in his chair, towards where a group of other men are gathered around the roaring fire, pouring more Scotch as they gossip about the latest Parliament sitting. Van Wimple wants the game over so he can join them.

The woman facing Van Wimple across the card table adjusts her pink jacket and takes a drag of her cigarette. She doesn't enjoy cigarettes, but she very much enjoys the way men like Van Wimple look at her when she smokes – as though she's a creature from a mythical story, one he cannot control and shouldn't try.

She shuffles the cards in her hand – the front ones to the back, the back ones to the front.

She has a pair of kings.

A good hand, but from the way Van Wimple so casually laid down the deed to his grand, crumbling house beside the enormous stack of money on the table, he must know he cannot lose.

Why else would Horace Van Wimple risk the beguiling Grimwood Manor? It's been in his family for generations. It was once owned by the notorious Poet Prince Edward, and it's the most beautiful building she's ever laid eyes upon. This house is everything she craves and everything that Horace Van Wimple doesn't deserve.

She wants the house so badly that her bones ache with craving. She doesn't know where this sensation has come from, but it's the most she's felt in years.

And Elsie is tired of running from her feelings.

Horace lifts his cigar cutter between his thumb and forefinger and cuts it above the shoulder with a satisfied *snap*. He blows a ring of smoke in her face. "Come on, love, we don't have all night."

Is he bluffing?

The other men in the room shift awkwardly. In the corner, three women – two of whom she presumes are prostitutes – drape themselves over the piano. One plays while the other two sing a popular song about long-lost love in low, sultry voices. More men buzz around them like drone bees around a honeypot, filling the ladies' drinks and rubbing their shoulders against the invisible cold. The curtains are drawn against the view – a pity, because the room looks out over a grand cemetery. Elsie loves the peace of the places of the dead, but the others declare the view morbid and unfit for their party.

Elsie's fiance, Gregory, looks up from the pianist's cleavage long enough to glare at her. He didn't want her to join tonight's gathering. After dinner, he'd suggested that she head upstairs to bed, as Horace's friends' wives all did, ascending the grand staircase like a parade of parakeets. She wanted to follow them, but she wouldn't give Gregory the satisfaction.

She wants to leave the party now. She wants to leave Gregory, run away to Italy, see the ruins, give herself a new name, wear her hair down and drink wine at breakfast every single day. But she can't.

Without Gregory, Elsie would be penniless. If he leaves her, her family won't accept her back, certainly not when they realise the state she's in.

Elsie's world has closed in around her – she is the same as the other wives – a pretty songbird in a cage. But Horace has presented her with another path to freedom.

So she remains at the table, debating her next move, as the deed to the house haunts her from atop the pile of coins and jewellery.

"Two of your pictures are the same!"

An unfamiliar, excited voice startles her, but she manages to hold her composure. She's had a lot of practice.

Elsie pretends the strap of her dress needs adjusting, and looks up at the ghost of a Roman centurion. For most of the night, he's remained in the corner of the room, his head in the liquor cabinet or swinging his sword at Horace. Now, he peers over her shoulder at her cards.

"You have two the same." He points to her kings. "Is that how you win the game? We had a game like this in Rome, only there were tiles with pictures of naughty nymphs on them, and you won when you dumped your wine on the other man's head."

She darts a glance over at Van Wimple, who has called over one of the possible-prostitutes to refill his glass. No one is watching her, so she hisses at the ghost. "I can only win the game if my cards have a higher value than his."

"You can see me! And talk to me! Oh, that's exciting! A Living hasn't been able to see me before. We're usually stuck with useless, rotten Living humans like Horace over there." The warrior shakes his head sadly. "He can't even swing a sword. Last night he was showing his friends one of his ancestor's blades and put a giant hole through the hallway tapestry. Most disrespectful. May Jupiter cut off his testicles and serve them as Christmas truffles. My name is Pax – Pax Drusus Maximus – and my job around here is to protect the house from Druids and annoy Edward."

Elsie doesn't know who Edward is, but Pax seems nice, for a ghost. He hasn't asked her for anything yet, which is usually what happens the moment a spirit realises that she can see them. For that reason – and because her parents threatened to have her committed if she continued to talk to invisible people – she taught herself to ignore ghosts.

But tonight, she's breaking her own rule. Pax Drusus Maximus might come in handy.

The Roman pats her shoulder, his touch a blast of warm air as his fingers sink partway into her skin. For a moment, she's assaulted by his memories – the warm pooling of Roman wine in her belly, the loud taunts and lewd jokes of her friends, the ache in her sword arm as she slices into a foe...

Elsie jerks her shoulder away. This new power is even more incentive to ignore ghosts. Elsie has also noticed that over the last few days, when she's near ghosts, they seem to be able to affect the Living World in small ways – knocking over a vase, or whispering something lewd in her husband's ear, as a dark-haired, handsome man in a billowing white silk shirt is doing at this moment. Elsie never had these abilities back in Sheffield, but something about Grimdale – and Horace's old house – has given her new abilities.

Despite herself, Elsie smiles at the centurion. Perhaps they could help each other. "I could get Horace out of your hair if you could help me win this game. Tell me what cards he has."

"Of course!" The centurion stomps off to the other side of

the room. He walks right through Gregory, sending him reeling. Elsie's lips quirk up into a smile, which she quickly hides. She wouldn't want to give Horace any ideas.

"Horace, old chap, there's a mighty chill in here." Gregory clutches his heart. "Elsie, perhaps we should get you to bed. I can finish your hand for you, darling. I'm sure that Horace doesn't mean to play so competitively with a woman. You know your constitution can't stand it. Horace, my wife is ill. She has these turns and I—"

"Horace and I were clear on the rules when we began." Elsie nods at Pax, who leans over Horace's shoulder and squints at his cards.

"He has a six, a five, and a three," Pax exclaims. "He also has two grumpy-looking women. They have not had a Roman soldier in their tents for quite some time."

A pair of queens. He has a pair of queens.

I'm winning.

"Thank you," she mouths to Pax. She twists the diamond ring from her finger and tosses it into the centre of the table. "I'm all in, Horace. You must show your hand."

"What are you doing, you absurd woman?" Gregory's face clouds over. "That engagement ring belonged to my father. It's worth thousands—"

"You'll have to get your disobedient fiancée some lesser bauble, old chap." Horace throws down his cards, a triumphant grin on his face. As Pax had told her, he has two queens, a three, a five, and a six. He reaches across the table to collect the pile of money.

"Perhaps you're being a bit premature." Elsie places her hand on the table. Horace's face clouds over as he takes in the two kings. Behind him, Gregory pales.

"She won!" The possible-prostitute squeals with delight. "She bloomin' won! Well done, duckie!"

Elsie catches the possible-prostitute's eye, and winks.

"Oh, she won? Jolly good show!" A handsome ghost wearing a Victorian frock coat claps from the corner. A wooden stick rests against his knee. She saw him earlier in the evening floating through the foyer and crashing into a table, knocking a vase to the floor, which is at least partly her fault. Elsie suspects he is blind. Ghosts retain their habits and abilities from their Living lives, so a blind ghost is completely normal.

A cheerful ghost, however, is not. But the ghosts in Grimdale seem mostly harmless.

Horace stares, mouth open, as Elsie reaches across the table and drags the pile of money towards her. Her fingers brush the deed, and her heart does a little skip.

I own this house. It's mine now. This house and its resident ghosts...

She glances down at the silver cords stretching from her heart and twining through the air around her. They dance and jerk, clearer than ever before, so bright and solid that she almost believes that she can touch them. The cords draw her chest tight. She feels so strange here, as though she is walking a tightrope, balanced precariously above the Realm of the Dead. If she's not careful, if she puts one foot wrong, she will fall in, and she won't be able to come back.

Elsie is ready to fall. At least falling is better than standing still.

Gregory tries to tear the money from her arms. "This was a friendly game, Horace. I'm certain that Elsie will give you back your house, and all will be right again—"

"Bah. She can have it." Horace glares at her as he tosses his still-burning cigar on the table and rises to his feet. His cheeks are red with rage and humiliation. "When you learn about the curse of this place, you'll wish you'd never set foot in Grimwood Manor."

"Ooooh, a curse!" The Roman grins. "By Jove's jaunty javelin, I hope it's a good one, with boils and frogs and a lightning strike up the wossit. Did you know I got a badge at Centurion Scouts for my cursing?"

GREGORY BEGGED her to return the house to Horace, but Elsie wasn't having it. She won Grimwood Manor fair and square. And she wanted it, talkative ghosts and all. She couldn't explain why she wanted it so much, but the house called to her, as if it had always been hers.

Horace, for his sins, seemed eager to part with the property, but his pride was such that he could not bear to be the victim in the story where he lost to another man's fiancée, and so while he signed over the paperwork to Elsie, he also cut Gregory out of his circle. This, in turn, made Gregory concede that Elsie was not the kind of meek, obedient future wife he wanted, and so he left her to follow the possible-prostitute to London.

Elsie waved him goodbye from the driveway of her new home.

Grimwood Manor. It's mine.

She returned to Sheffield and packed lightly, not having many possessions now that Gregory had given all the fine dresses he bought for her to his new mistress. She still had his diamond ring on her finger – a peace offering from Gregory so that she would not bother him for the needs of the child.

The child.

Elsie pats her swollen stomach. The baby would come any day now, and she is a woman alone, without a husband, living in a haunted house that she won from a politician in a poker game. She would never be accepted back into society. She would have to raise this child on her own.

That's exactly the way Elsie prefers things.

I'm alone at last. No parents or fiancé to tell me what to do or who to be. No more having to take care with my words and actions for fear of making people uncomfortable. I may not be able to travel, but I can live here with my baby and my ghosts and be perfectly content.

She picks up her tiny pink suitcase and ascends the grand stairs to the front door. She fits the key – *her* key – into the lock, pushes open the door, and steps over the threshold into her new home.

The first thing that strikes her is the *vastness* of the house. How the walls loom over her and the great empty entrance hall is too large for her pathetically small dreams. The house had felt grand and alive when she visited with Gregory, what with Horace's friends and staff bustling every which way. But now it is still and empty and silent, and she can't imagine ever having a life that will fill the space.

The second thing that strikes her is how the house calls to her, even now. She listens, and she imagines she hears it whispering her name on the draughts. The creaking floorboards and gurgling pipes echo *Elsie, Elsie...*

The third thing that strikes her is the Roman centurion flying down the staircase toward her.

"You came back," he cries. "I didn't expect you to come back. Most Livings stay away from us. We prefer it that way. Would you like to meet my friends?"

He sweeps his arm toward the upper landing. Two other ghosts stand on the staircase – three, if you count the ghost bat hanging from the chandelier, which Elsie most certainly does.

"It's a pleasure to meet you." The blind Victorian gives a deep bow, wincing as he puts his head through the balustrade.

"Pax tells us that you can see and talk to us. We're going to have such fun."

"I am pleased to hear you are taking over the job of custodian of my property," the other ghost tilts his haughty, aristocratic features towards her. "I have a long list of grievances which you are required to hear. One, the Roman has farted in my boudoir. Two, these two philistines have rejected my invitation to a weekly poetry reading. Three, I cannot locate my secret wine cellar, and I fear it lost forever. Four..."

Elsie nods to them as she passes by them on the staircase. She knows it's rude not to talk to them, but the house demands her presence. Her feet carry her to a room in the turret – the same dark-panelled gentleman's drawing room where she won the house from Horace. The room is bare now, save for an overturned card table and some mouse droppings in the corner.

The silver cords that enter Elsie's chest – the ones she can only see since she acquired the house – tug at her ribcage. Ignoring them is now physically painful, and she can't write off the pain as a symptom of her pregnancy. She steps deeper into the room.

"Elsie, you have come."

She startles, and whirls around. Although the room was empty, now a man stands beside the window, his face shrouded in shadow beneath a white hooded cloak. At least, Elsie assumes it's a man, judging by the deep voice and impossibly broad shoulders.

His voice is thunder rolling over the hills. Her name on his lips sounds like a death rattle.

A scythe rests against the wall of the room. The blade shimmers with a silvery glow. Beside the scythe, sitting on the windowsill and catching the glow of the late afternoon sun, is a crown made of tiny, bleached bones.

The stranger raises an arm, stretching impossibly thin and

bony fingers towards her. "Come. I have much to tell you. You do not recognise me, but I am your ancestor, your blood. You must begin your studies immediately. I have seen my death. It is the blessing and the curse of our kind. You must prepare to take up my crown."

Her hand flies to her throat. Her whole body screams at her to run, but she's so heavy with child that she knows he will quickly overpower her. *I must protect my child.* It takes her several tries to make a sound, but when she does, her voice is strong and clear. "Excuse me, sir, but I think you have the wrong house. Do you have family nearby? Do you need me to call a constable?"

As she speaks, she backs towards the door, her eyes never leaving the stranger.

Her escape is cut off by the ghosts poking their heads into the room. "Who's your friend?" asks Pax Drusus Maximus. "I like his blade. It has a jaunty curve. But does he know how to use it?"

The stranger inclines his head toward them, and his laughter falls like rain as he says. "Come closer, my friend, and you may find out."

He can see the ghosts.

Elsie's fear freezes her feet to the floor. Her hands fly to her belly. *I must protect my child.*

Lightning crashes outside the window. Moments ago, it had been sunny out.

"He's not a ghost, is he?" the blind Victorian's voice wavers.

"You need not be afraid." The stranger's voice rumbles in her veins. "You and your babe are safe in this house. Do you sense your powers growing? Can you see the souls of those close to you as their lives spiral about like fireflies dancing in the moonlight?"

Else gasps, touching her fingers to her heart, where thin,

gossamer silver threads tug and pull. They spiral through the air, becoming more solid the nearer they get to the stranger. Three of them double back to enter the chests of the ghosts, while others spill out the window, and one enters back into her own stomach. She grazes the edge with her finger, and her baby stirs.

The stranger tilts his head, regarding her. "Tell me, Elsie, do you feel close to death in this house, as though you are visiting a long-lost friend?"

Yes, that's exactly what it feels like.

"Centuries ago, my predecessor placed here a gateway to our realm. That is why the house calls you." The stranger glides to the windowsill, lifting the crown in pale, bony fingers. "I have chosen you to succeed me. Only those with our power can wear the crown, and only those with a gentle heart and a will of iron can walk the pathway."

"It's not a very pretty crown," the aristocratic-looking ghost remarks. "Where are the jewels? And the fur trim? That crown looks like what's left after a particularly overzealous feast."

"I...I don't understand..."

Lightning flashes again. As the world outside explodes with white light, the stranger disappears. A moment later, he is right in front of her. The lightning cracks again, casting flickering light across his shadowed features. In that moment, she sees the edge of his face beneath his white hood – not a man's face at all, but that of a gleaming skull.

Elsie screams.

The man touches his bony hand – his *bones* – to the side of her head. The cold of his knucklebones presses against her skin.

Elsie's scream cuts off.

She *sees*.

She sees death.

Not just the side of it that she's familiar with – the forlorn spirits who have lost their way and still walk the earth – but the other parts of death. The weight of inevitability crushes her lungs. She no longer feels safe inside her fragile, breakable human body.

A great wave of grief swells up inside her chest. Grief so powerful that it carries upon itself the entire world – the grief of all the children who must live without parents, the parents who lost children, all the lovers separated by the great chasm of eternity. All the hearts broken and the promises unkept.

She sees the pathway that the stranger wants her to walk alongside him, a path he has trod countless times. She sees Grimwood Manor lit by ghostly lights, a waystation along a long and treacherous route.

And she sees *him* – the stranger – wrapped in his white shroud, walking amongst the lost and the grieving, swinging his scythe over his shoulder. She sees him lay his bony hand upon those left behind, and him walking with those who must leave too soon. She sees endless silver cords on spindles, unfurling wildly until eventually they are snipped off. She sees the stranger's own cord – not silver like the others, but the deep, cold black of space – unwinding on its spindle, weaving a tapestry of sorrow and nearly at its end.

She tears her face from his cold touch. "I don't want this. Choose someone else."

The stranger shakes his head. The bones on his crown rattle. "I cannot unchoose. It is in your blood. Look."

Elsie glances down where he is pointing. A new cord unfurls from her chest – the same nightmare black as his. She tries to grasp it in her fingers, to pull it out, to throw it away, but her hands go right through it.

"Take it back." Elsie glares at the stranger. "I know you can do it. I've seen what you can do. What you *are*. I wouldn't have come to this house if you hadn't called me here. You *tricked* me."

"I am many things, but I am no trickster. You came because you are ready to begin our work." The stranger nods towards the doorway, where the three ghosts are still watching. "They have been trapped here for many centuries. They are so near the pathway, but they can't find their way without you. They have forgotten what it means to die. They need your help. Will you deny them?"

"I...I..."

"Do not be frightened." His voice is so soft, even as he tears apart her universe. He points to the black cord that grows from his chest. "I have plenty of time left. Your child will have a safe, loving home as you learn your duties."

My child...

Lightning forks across the window, and the stranger disappears. Elsie collapses to her knees, her hands flying to her belly. The sky outside the window clears, and the sun shines.

Elsie sobs.

"There, there," the centurion pats her shoulder. "You don't have to be afraid. He ran away, probably because he was afraid of my sword. If he comes back, I'll make you a delightful musical instrument out of his ribcage."

But despite his words, the fear clenches in Elsie's gut. She's not afraid of the ghosts – she's seen more than enough of them in her lifetime, and these three look mostly harmless (and rather handsome).

Her fear is for the child moving in her belly.

What would his life be like if she did what the stranger wanted?

What about *her* life? The life she had wrought from nothing?

I'm not ready to give myself to Death yet.

Elsie sits back on her heels and glances around the room. She was born and raised in a big house like Grimwood, with parents who wanted their daughter to be *demure* and *proper*.

They never knew what to do with their strange child who talked to shadows and told tall stories about ghosts. Her parents brought doctors from all over to cure her maladies, but they could find no medical explanation for the things Elsie saw. When Gregory came in search of a wife and didn't seem worried about Elsie's eccentricities as long as he could have her name, they pushed for a quick engagement. Elsie was to go from their home in Sheffield to Gregory's estate without a moment to *live* in between. They intended to shutter her away, where her eccentricities would not reflect poorly on them. And now that she has ruined their plans by pushing Gregory away and having his child out of wedlock, they have simply washed their hands of her.

She tried so hard to be good and proper and normal – to be the perfect daughter, the ideal wife. And it bored her to desolation.

Grimwood Manor was her glimmer of hope, her chance for the life that her gender and station denied her. And she's not ready to give it up, not even for all the stranger had promised.

My child will not have that life. No one will ever tell them that they are broken.

How can she be what the stranger asks of her and also be a mother? How can she carry the grief of the world and walk that pathway over and over, *and* raise a child to believe in hope and grace and love?

The walls of Grimwood loom over her. She sees inside them now, deep beneath the foundations of this house, to the secrets it hides. The gateway. The path of souls.

Grimwood is not a home, and it never will be.

If her child is brought up in this house, with its ghosts in the walls and this...this *monster* waiting in the wings, he or she would be just as crazy as their mother.

These walls are no longer the symbols of her freedom, but a prison that ensures her child will forever remain a pariah.

Elsie's hand flies to Gregory's ring on her finger. She'd have enough money from the sale of the bauble to book passage to Europe, maybe find a little house there in Italy or Malta or on the French Riviera. She could rent Grimwood Manor to tenants who didn't see ghosts, keep it in case she needed to return to the doorway. But the rent from such a fine house would give her a modest income.

"Are you hurt?" the centurion asks. "Is it your baby? Don't worry, we've seen several babes born within these walls. We can talk you through it. Perhaps if I remain close to you, I can even cut the cord myself."

If you leave, the stranger's voice echoes inside her skull, *their souls will forget you. They will not remember that they once had a chance for the future they'd been deprived of. They will remain trapped here until you or your successor decides to set them free.*

"I don't care," she hisses.

She owes no loyalty to ghosts.

Elsie's plan forms. They would travel far from England, far from fashionable society and from the stranger with the bone crown. It would be a different life to what she's used to, a *difficult* life, but preferable to remaining inside Grimwood's gilded cage and taking on the task the stranger had given her.

She could *live.*

"I'm sorry," she whispers to the ghosts as she rises to her feet. "I can't help you. But you won't remember me anyway. I have to go."

"Wait, where are you going?" The centurion's booming voice follows her as she lurches down the stairs. "There aren't any Druids nearby, I promise. I've frightened them all away."

"You can't leave yet," the aristocratic one snaps. "I haven't read you the sonnet I've written about your epic card game."

You can run from me, Elsie, but the crown will always call to you. When the time comes, we will walk the pathway together.

"I'm not walking the path with you!"

Elsie's heart sinks into her heels as she leaps down the porch steps and runs as fast as she can away from Grimwood Manor.

PROLOGUE
EARLIER

The Ripper jerks his blade from the body of a priest. The man's face contorts one final time before he drops upon the marble floor. He doesn't move. Red mist leaks from the wound, curling around Jack like a whip.

Black-clad bodies litter the throne room. The Order of the Noble Death. They'd known as soon he did it, of course. They listen along the pathway, although those of them on earth cannot walk it. Instead, they sent their most desperate magicians, their most loyal soldiers, along the more *traditional* route, each hoping to claim the crown for themselves.

He laid waste to their ranks.

He doesn't want them to send word back that he failed, lest they tether him to their will again.

Jack's face twists into a smile. It takes more effort than he recalls, the muscles of his human form slow, sluggish. He steps back to admire the chaos he has wrought.

"You missed one," a voice clucks from behind him. "In the corner."

Well, the almost-silence.

Jack loved every glorious moment he spent on earth, but he

hadn't heeded the warnings from the other beasts. Those who visit the Living World may find they bring something of it back with them. Some unwanted remnant of humanity that burrows deep into a monster's soul and plants a little seed. They say that monsters who come back from the Living World are never the same. They reek of the stench of humanity.

Jack's unwanted remnant is the infernal shade who dogs his steps. He took her life, and because of some ancient rule, this means that he cannot kill her again here, even with his modified blade. This makes her brazen. She uses her witch powers to pollute his every thought, trying to stop his hand from ripping and slaying, forcing the black chasm that might have once been his heart to beat once more. She mocks him when he fails and ruins his triumphs.

She is worse than his human mother. But unlike his mother, he cannot get rid of her with his knife.

In this rare instance, their goals are in tandem, so she doesn't stop Jack as he steps over corpses to arrive at the still-twitching priest. He's a young man – too young for the grisly task he has been set. But the Order likes them young. They can be moulded like clay into soldiers for immortality.

Jack reaches down and brushes a strand of hair from the boy's face. The boy peers up at him, eyes wide. "Please…" he whispers. "I must have it. Otherwise, I'm—"

"—dead. That's right, old chap. You are dead. Twice dead, in fact."

Jack cups his hands over the sides of the boy's head.

He twists.

Air rushes from the boy's throat. The air is a remnant from the boy's life – there is no air here, not the kind the boy is used to. Jack drops the body on the floor. It makes a dull *THUMP* that echoes in the vast room. He kicks the body as he steps over it and strides toward the dais. Toward the prize he has won.

The body lies prone upon the steps of the dais, where she has lain for some time. The Crown of Bones still rests upon her head, and she clasps her sceptre in cold, bony fingers. Jack reaches forward to pull it free, but his hands bounce, propelled by some invisible force.

He reaches again, but he cannot touch the sceptre.

Jack yells his outrage. He swings his legs and kicks the fallen Lady. Her bones rattle as she absorbs the blow, but he does no damage. He can't hurt her while she still wears the crown.

"Why isn't it working?"

The foul creature behind him – the witch clinging tenaciously to his bones and sinew despite all his efforts to extricate her – cackles uproariously. "You didn't think it would be that easy, did you? Oh, you did. Poor lamb. You've gone to all this trouble for *nothing*."

"Tell me what you know, witch," he growls. He can't hurt her, but when she is inside him like this, she can feel his pain. He drags his knife down his arm, drawing a thin line of red mist. She hisses as the pain touches her.

She snuggles back into the darker recesses of his mind. "That's for me to know, and you to never find out."

Jack smirks. Unfortunately for the witch, if her fingers are inside his mind, then he is also inside her, and while she can obscure some of her thoughts from him, she has forgotten the fallibility of her human mind. Tell a human not to think about a pink elephant, and watch their brain immediately fill with images of a pink elephant. The witch is trying not to think about what she wants to hide from him, but instead, she calls up the memory.

Now Jack is inside the witch's shop – the same shop where he was sent as the messenger of the Order. Only, in this memory, he *is* the witch, and he and the ghost of the old crone who hangs out there are friends, of a sort. Jack is explaining to the crone that he has been given a task by another witch. He must watch over the entrance to the pathway.

"Only blood can access the doorway and wear the crown," he explains through the witch's lips. "But if there is no blood, the crown is there for the taking. I swore an oath to my friend that I would keep the doorway safe, that I would keep *her* safe."

Jack smiles. The witch curses as she dissolves the memory.

"You're too late." The grin spreads wide across his face.

Now he knows exactly what he needs.

He understands why the Order of the Noble Death sent him to Grimdale to get rid of Bree Mortimer. If she is gone, they can claim it as their own.

Once she is gone, the crown could be his...except that he is not a Lazarus. Only a Lazarus can wear the crown.

And Jack knows exactly where to find one.

I

AMBROSE

"**C**an you still see Bree and Edward?" I ask Pax, my fingers gripping his arm tight enough to make an ordinary man wince. But Pax is practically superhuman, and all he does is increase the pace of his march through the house, dragging me along behind him.

Hinges creak as Pax shoves the back door open. "I can't even see to the end of the garden. The world is completely shrouded in darkness. It's so gloomy, I wouldn't be able to see the moonlight glinting off a Druid's naked buttocks."

My heart twists as the sense of wrongness in my gut worsens. *We have to find Bree.* "We have to get to the cemetery."

"How? It's impossible to find our way in this darkness. I cannot even see the security lights around the cemetery fence—"

I grab his hand. "We don't need light to find our way. I know the paths as well as I know my way around Bree's body. We'll find them. Come on!"

2

EDWARD

"You mean to tell me that I've been alive all of ten minutes and I'm already dying again?" I shake my head. "No, that simply won't do. I'm not having it. This prince demands to *live*."

I'm *not* going back to being a ghost – or something worse. Not now that I've tasted Brianna for the first time. One cannot taste heaven and then be sent to hell.

"The Ripper isn't exactly going to care about your princely orders. So let's try and move this together." Brianna shoves her shoulder against the flagstone. I crowd into the top of the staircase and thrust my shoulder alongside hers. The air up here already tastes strange, sulphuric – not the way I remember air tasting.

Red mist seeps around the stone as we grunt and shove and sweat.

It doesn't move an inch.

The Ripper's laughter echoes down the stairwell. It rings in my newly Living ears, harsh and painful.

How is the Ripper back again?

Brianna holds up her magical rectangle. She has it turned

on to a bright light that illuminates the graceful planes of her face. Her honey gaze meets mine. Her eyes are wide with terror. The red mist curls around us. My throat scratches and I start to cough. I try to wet my throat with saliva but it doesn't help. My nostrils close and my eyes water, but it's too painful for me to enjoy these Living sensations.

"I guess the good news is that we're not going to suffocate slowly to death." Brianna grips my shoulders as she too breaks down in a coughing fit. "He's going to do us in much quicker than that."

"The Ripper has trapped us in here so he can toy with us," I choke out. "The way Moon plays with a field mouse before she snaps its neck."

"Thanks for that delightful visual. We can't stay here." Brianna tugs me back down the stairs. We cough and splutter as we stagger down the steps, moving out of the red mist.

"Argh!" Brianna's foot slips out from beneath her. I try to grab her, but she topples forward and drags me with her. We bump and jolt down the steps, landing in a tangled heap at the bottom.

Oof.

"Eeeeeeooooo, it hurts. It hurts." I flap my arm, trying to shake off the horrible sensation. I thought I left pain behind me now that people can no longer walk through me, but I'd forgotten how awful it was to knock your elbow against a hard surface.

"Ow." Brianna picks herself off me, rubbing her hip.

"You're bleeding." I frown at the smudge of dark blood across her palm, visible in the square of light from her magical rectangle.

"Yes, I cut myself on—" Brianna's face transforms into a grin as she holds up an object. "Edward, look what we have. The crowbar!"

The faint light from her magical rectangle glints off the end of the curved bar she used to pry up the flagstones.

"What good is that?" I scoff. I don't understand how a peasant's tool could possibly get us out of this situation.

"Are you kidding? This little invention has a hundred uses – mainly, getting into tiny gaps between things and making them larger. It can also stave in a skull in a pinch."

"You spend far too much time with Pax."

"Thank you," Brianna grins, clutching the metal implement to her chest. What did she call it, the Bar of Crows? "It can't stop the red mist, but it might be able to get us out of here."

Brianna aims the light of her magical rectangle deeper into the cellar. I follow her as she darts between the rows of my finest vintage, using her light to scour the walls and roof – looking for what, I still don't entirely understand. But I will follow Brianna to the end of our days, which might be coming much sooner than either of us hoped.

My fingers brush the bottles as we run by, and memories rush me all at once – flashes of the raucous parties, poetry readings, and romantic entanglements that made up my life before Brianna. I long to have the time to peruse those shelves and rediscover the treasures I stored here.

But that can wait until after we've defeated the bloodthirsty murderer. *Again*.

More memories battle inside my skull – memories of Hugh, who didn't kill me after all. Pieces of my life in the days before my death fall into place. I remember Hugh jokingly begging me to return to court as a representative "for all rakes, wastrels, and degenerates." I remember him telling me that if I died before him, he would bury me with my greatest treasure, like a Pharaoh. I remember writing an offensive letter to him as a joke and reading it aloud at one of my parties, and him swearing to get me back.

That's what Brianna and Ambrose found – one of Hugh's little jokes. His only crime was stealing my poem, and he guilted himself over that far more than I ever could. He *was* my friend. I had a friend. A *real* friend, and now I am alive again, and I have Brianna, and—

"Edward, hurry!"

"Right, yes! I'm behind you." I shake myself free of the memories and hurry after Brianna. If I want to enjoy my second life, I need to help us escape *now*.

As a prince, I never had to run in my life, except for one time when I accidentally let my father's hunting dog free of its chain. But I've also never been chased by a ball of angry red mist. I sprint toward Brianna's voice. My newly Living legs and lungs aren't fond of the notion. I shan't think I'll try running again.

The cellar stretches for quite a distance. My breath huffs from my burning throat. I find Brianna on the far end, the edges of her perfect features illuminated by the light of her magic rectangle. She's feeling the stone wall with her long fingers the way she caressed me only minutes ago.

I am jealous of the wall. Now that I am Living, I don't want to be anywhere except inside her.

"Can you feel that?" Brianna nods toward the ceiling. "There's a cool breeze blowing down on us. It's faint, but I think there might be another way out of the cellar. I'm going to try to loosen these stones."

"Excellent. And I shall compose a sonnet to honour your victory—"

"It would be more helpful if you could just hold the light."

"Oh, yes. I can do that." I'm not used to being helpful. I didn't realise there was actually a job I could do. I scramble to pick up the magic rectangle from her. I suppose I should get used to thinking of it as a 'phone,' since everyone Living has one. Now that I'm Living too, I might have to get one of my own...*if* we get out of here alive.

Brianna shows me the button that turns the light off and on, and I angle it for her while she tries to wedge the metal bar between two of the stones. My eyes weep from the sting of the red mist as it creeps across the ceiling toward us, or perhaps it is simply from the joy of finally being able to touch her.

"The mortar is old," Brianna murmurs as she hacks at the stone with the Bar of Crows. "It's all flaking off. I think we might have a shot at this."

"Um, Brianna..."

I glance back over my shoulder, which is a mistake. Red mist curls out of the staircase on the other end of the cellar and coagulates in the aisle between the wine racks. Even from this distance, the sulphur smell makes my eyes water. I shouldn't be able to see it in the gloom, but the mist glows as if it is on fire.

I'm a deviant prince, not a scholar of weather, but I'm certain the mist isn't supposed to glow *red*.

The Ripper's laughter grows louder and more cruel. My ears ring as his laughter pounds against the inside of my skull. How does he laugh *inside* my head? Terror clutches at my limbs as before my eyes, the red mist moves and shifts and starts to form the shape of the Ripper.

He's coming into the cellar as mist. He's locked us inside here with him.

Flecks of stone and dust rain down on my head as Brianna works.

"Brianna..."

"Edward, I'm a little busy."

"You can't hide from me, Little Lazarus," the Ripper rasps, his voice booming inside my skull. Brianna makes a whimpering noise, but keeps working. "Now that the Veil is broken, all the monsters that your kind has banished will come for you. And oh, the fun we'll have."

She hasn't seen this. She needs to see.

I reach up and tug on Brianna's arm. She snaps her head up and swallows a scream when she sees the outline of the Ripper, the mists swirling around him, giving his body form and substance.

"Shit. I didn't know he could do that." Brianna lets out a sound that's half laugh, half sob. "I guess he's not human anymore."

The Ripper's laugh tears through the cellar like a maelstrom, rattling the glass bottles in their rusted racks. "Nothing can be human again after returning through the hole in the Veil. You will learn this soon, Lazarus."

Brianna's fingers tighten around the Bar of Crows. Her pretty features arrange themselves into a look of grim determination. I've seen this look on her before, and it terrifies me because it means that Brianna is not going to bury her head in the sand and run. She's going to *fight*.

"Edward, hold him off!"

"With what? A sonnet?" I had fencing lessons in my father's court, like any proper prince, but I was hopeless. He declared me a useless wastrel after I accidentally sliced through a priceless tapestry, and I was allowed to swap my fencing foil for painting lessons. Now, I wish I'd paid more attention. I've never dueled with an enemy in my life, unless you count late-night tussles with Hugh that usually ended with us kissing.

Somehow, I doubt the Ripper is here to spend the night in my boudoir.

"I don't know – use your imagination," Brianna shouts, her voice trembling with fear and resolve. "I've almost got this. I don't need the light. Go!"

Edward, it's your time to shine. You can prove that you're not completely useless.

The Ripper grins at me, and I want to curl up and die.

"Hey, Jack. Jacky boy." I step toward the Ripper. Red mist curls from his sleeves and from beneath his black top hat. He's almost completely solid now. "Fancy a drink?"

I pull a bottle at random from the shelf. A beautiful Latour I purchased because it was the Countess de Rothschild's favourite. Such a shameful waste.

I hurl the bottle at the Ripper.

It hits the side of his head and kind of...*hovers* there, suspended in the red mist that leaks from his eyes, nose, mouth, and the cuffs of his black coat.

Jack the Ripper laughs as the bottle sizzles, the cork pops out, and French wine pours all over both of us.

"Ah," he grins, as tendrils of red smoke wipe drips of wine from his cruel lips. "*Delicious.* This will make a lovely match for when I consume your lovely Lazarus."

"You'll have to go through me first, and that wasn't so pleasant for you last time."

"Ah, but I see you are Living once more. Good. Bones break more easily than souls." The Ripper advances on me, reeking of French wine. Curls of smoke reach out to graze my skin. I jerk my arm back as burning pain explodes over my skin.

It's too bad that we can't get the Ripper drunk because if he's anything like me, he'll fall out a window and that'll be the end of him.

Oh, but perhaps...

Jack lunges for me, his knife held high. But I'm well-practised at avoiding the excited slashes of Pax's sword whenever his favourite chef wins a Bake-Off challenge. I dart out of the way and scurry around to the absinthe shelves.

I bypass my French absinthes, which are too mild for this situation, and grab a bottle of the nastiest Eastern European green fairy – the stuff that Hugh and I used to gulp back well after the other revellers had tired of partying and fallen asleep. The bottle is covered in skull-and-crossbones and labels written in various foreign languages, warning that people have gone blind or keeled over dead from drinking too much.

Perfect.

I tug out the cork, marvelling at how my fingers work again. Touching things is such a sublime sensation. I hope I can get us out of this cellar so I can continue to touch Brianna in all the ways I've been denied...

Focus, Edward.

The stench of aniseed and hangovers slams me in the face. I'm still getting used to having all my senses back again. Absinthe smells much stronger and more disgusting than I remember.

"Oh, little prince, little prince, hiding away. Little prince, little prince, whom I shall filet..." The Ripper rounds the corner of the shelves. His eyes flicker briefly over me before he swivels toward Brianna. His knife swishes at his side.

"You're the one I want, Lazarus," he purrs, flicking his blade in his fingers like a circus performer. "And now that I'm free of my old masters, I can use you for your blood, your true purpose. But I'm going to have a little fun with your princeling, first. Perhaps I will slit him toes to nostrils and crawl inside his skin, the way he did to me. He'll be my very own puppet to do my bidding."

I don't have time to wonder what he means by Brianna's 'true purpose' because the Ripper flies at Brianna, his knife slashing through the air.

No!

She screams, flattening her back against the wall. My newly reborn heart hammers against my chest.

Rage fuels me as I fly after him. I *just* got my body back, and

I can be with Brianna. I won't allow this macabre remnant of history to take her away from me.

I am the Poet Prince Edward, slayer of sonnets, conqueror of boudoirs, the scourge of husbands throughout the British Empire, and not even this monster of the Veil will keep me from my Brianna.

"She is *mine*," I growl.

I grab the Ripper's wrist as he swings his blade. He's so strong that he doesn't even flinch. He continues to advance on Brianna, jerking me along behind him as he drags me through the shelves. My flailing legs catch a wooden cask of Dopff au Moulin, upending it. I cry out as the seal pops out and the precious liquid spills across the stone floor.

No. You will not take my woman and my wine from me.

Gritting my teeth against the pain as he drags me along, I lift the absinthe bottle over my head and pour it over the Ripper.

Much of it slops back at me. I yell as alcohol splashes in my eyes and the Ripper drags my new body over broken shards of glass. But I don't let go until I've emptied every last drop of absinthe over the Ripper's head.

Please, if any of Pax's gods are listening, let this work.

"What nonsense is this?" The Ripper turns to me with a scowl. Absinthe drips from the brim of his hat and dribbles down his nose. His skin sizzles where red mist and alcohol meet. *Please work please work please work...* "Do you think that your bar-room antics will save your little Lazarus? You have no concept of what I am or what I have done to come back for her... wait..."

He stops in his tracks, his lips smacking together. He grabs the bottle from my hands. My heartbeat pounds in my ears. Behind his shoulder, stone chunks cascade from the wall as Brianna attacks my cellar with her Bar of Crows.

The Ripper's tongue darts out, licking the sticky alcohol from his lips.

"It's delicious," he cries.

The red mist curling from his skin grows heavy like storm clouds as it absorbs the alcohol. It doesn't burn quite as much where it touches me.

The Ripper breathes in, his red eyes sparkling, and the mist becomes one with his skin.

But will it be enough? Will it...

The Ripper's eyes flash. His sharp features sag.

His lip wobbles.

The bottle falls from his fingers, smashing on the stones beside me.

"I see fairies!" the Ripper cries. He drops his knife from his other hand and waggles his fingers in front of his face. "Hundreds of tiny green fairies crawling all over me!"

Huzzah! It worked.

I am *quite* brilliant.

I untangle myself from the Ripper, who lets out a stream of ecstatic gibberish as the absinthe works its way into his body. He spins in lazy circles, his eyes blown out as he tries to catch the invisible sprites.

My feet slide in the alcohol-splattered flagstones, but I manage to make it to Brianna just as the Bar of Crows pops a large stone off the wall.

"Edward, look! I did it," she cries, turning out her hips to spread her legs invitingly. "Quick, kneel down and put your head between my legs."

"I'm not certain this is the time for amorous congress." I lick my lips. "But if my lady insists—"

"*Edward.* I meant for you to give me a boost."

Disappointed, I crouch down and push my head between her legs. She smells so beautiful, I long to linger in my new favourite spot forever, but my treat can wait until we get out of here alive.

I wrap my hands around Brianna's thighs and rise to my feet, bearing her weight on my shoulders (I can feel her weight! This is wonderful) as she scrambles into the narrow tunnel she'd uncovered. Brianna grunts as she hoists herself up and drags her legs through.

"It comes out in the base of the Witches' Monument," Brianna calls down to me. "No wonder Mr. Pitts is worried that the stone is falling over – it's got no foundation. Hold out your hand, Edward. I'll try and pull you up. Put my phone in your pocket. The light is useless. It's...it's strange and dark up here."

"I don't have any pockets. What use has a prince for a pocket when there are perfectly good servants to carry your ephemera—"

"Edward."

"Right, yes."

Brianna's hand thrusts down. I slide her phone into the waistband of my pantaloons and grab her fingers, bracing my feet against the stone walls as she lifts me from above. My arm screams in agony, and the stone scrapes against my chest, tearing my silk shirt and grazing my skin. The pain is quite exquisite.

"Edward!"

Brianna's fingers slip through mine, and I crash back through the hole. More beautiful pain jolts down my spine.

Behind me, the Ripper roars with fury. I don't look back but focus on the narrow, dark hole through which Brianna is dragging me. My feet and spare hand scramble for purchase on the rough stones.

"Run!" I yell. "I can take him."

"Don't be ridiculous. You're not Pax, and you're not leaving my sight. You can do this, you just have to push up from the ground!"

"Oh, yes. I suppose that makes sense."

I guess I'm so used to other people pulling my weight. Now that I have actual, *literal* weight, I can't expect Brianna to do all the work.

I scramble to my feet and hurl myself at the hole, just as Brianna tugs my arm with all her might. I go flying through the gap, scraping my already raw belly across stone before crashing into Brianna and sending both of us sprawling into the side of the Witches' Monument.

The pain is immediate and exquisite. I'd forgotten how breakable human bodies are.

I fumble around for Brianna. She's right, it *is* dark up here. And not simply the dark of night, for even on a grim, stormy night, the lights emanating from Grimwood Manor and from the security lights around the cemetery fence would illuminate our surroundings. But right now, I cannot see even the graves in front of me or Brianna's hand reaching for mine.

I reach for her, but my fingers glance off her. I try again, and clasp her hand. I don't want to lose her in this darkness.

"Edward, what is this?" she cries as we fumble our way in the gloom, heading in the direction I believe is the house. She trips over the edge of the path and I catch her before she brings us both down. "Why can't we see—"

Her words cut off with a strangled cry. For a moment, I don't know what's wrong, but then I hear it. Footsteps run along the concrete path toward us, and the *rap-rap-rap* of some unholy spectre as it comes for us.

"It's another beast of the Veil!" I cry out. "And we left our absinthe back in the cellar."

"No, it's not a monster!" Brianna cries. "It's Pax and Ambrose!"

3
PAX

Ambrose's puny fingers squeeze my wrist tight as he hurries down the garden path toward the cemetery.

At least, I assume we're heading toward the cemetery. I cannot see a thing.

This is worse than the time my general decided to unleash a swarm of wasps on the battlefield to disarm our enemy. My face swelled up so badly that I couldn't see out of my eyes for three days.

But our general didn't have the secret weapon I do – Ambrose. He moves through this dark world with the same purpose that he uses every day of his life. The darkness does not frighten him. His stick taps the ground, and he hears something in the echo of that tap that I do not – the way forward.

The way to our Bree.

We descend the stairs with alarming speed. "Duck your head," Ambrose instructs. He doesn't slow down as he drags me through the hole in the cemetery fence. I feel the bent metal clawing at my back, but we don't slow down. "I can hear something near the Witches' Monument."

Thunder cracks overhead as we hurry over the uneven

concrete path. The air tastes bitter, strange. The gods are displeased. They know that something wrong is happening tonight.

I curl my fingers around my sword.

The Ripper won't take Bree. He *won't.*

Ambrose stops. I crash into him, almost sending both of us tumbling over a grave. I don't know if we're at the Witches' Monument or not. I'm completely turned around in the gloom.

"Bree?" he calls out as we untangle ourselves. "Edward?"

"We're here, Ambrose," Bree calls back.

"Pax is with me."

"I'm ready to stab things!" I call out.

"No stabbing anything in the dark. I don't want anyone to accidentally end up with a gladius through the chest." Bree lets out a ragged breath. "I'm so happy to hear your voices."

My heart soars with relief. Bree is all right.

"I hope you've brought a magical priest and a basket of demon-banishing fruit," Edward says warily. "Because the Ripper is right below us."

I listen. I can make out the sound of someone crashing about beneath my feet.

"How is he below us? Did you already send him to Hades?" I start to slide my sword back into its scabbard. "I'm disappointed. I was looking forward to severing his head and sticking it on the spike on top of Edward's tomb."

"Don't you deface my tomb," Edward growls. "Or I will compose a forty-two-verse epic poem about your flatulence and recite it to you every night as you try to sleep."

"Oh yeah? Well, I'll crack your testicles into a pan and make a delicious omelette—"

"The Ripper's not quite in Hades yet, Pax," Bree interrupts, before I can detail my imaginary punishment. "He's in Edward's secret wine cellar, but he won't be for much longer."

Ambrose moves close to me. "He sure is crashing about down there. He sounds like Pax after he's spent the night sleeping with his head in the liquor cabinet."

"I resent that. I'm a very graceful drunk." I pound my fist against my chest.

"Edward got the Ripper drunk on absinthe," Bree says, her voice louder as we get closer to her. A familiar soft hand brushes my arm. "He brought us time to escape. Edward, can I have my phone, please? All we have to do is get his weapon off him and we'll banish him the way we did last time—"

"I don't think he's a revenant any longer," Ambrose says. "I think that he's something far worse."

I screw up my face, not understanding. "That may be so, but I have thought of something even more disturbing. How can Edward have Bree's magic rectangle?"

A faint beam of pale light appears beside me, but it barely illuminates the edge of Bree's features as she holds the magical object. "I don't know how I feel about my phone being warm from your crotch, Edward. But guys, Edward is—"

"Make way for the most powerful bitches," a gruff voice snaps from the gloom.

"Yoooohoooo, Bree?" Lottie calls out. "You're here, right? We can't see a thing!"

"We've come to save the day," Mary adds from somewhere behind my left shoulder. "As soon as we saw the giant doom cloud, we figured we'd head straight to the cause."

"How do you know I'm the cause?" Bree shoots back. "And what are you doing here, Agnes? You hate the cemetery."

A cold chill slams into my body as a ghost walks through me.

"Yes, well, it wasn't my idea to come here," Agnes grumbles. "And if it wasn't you, who turned out the lights? I just walked through the Roman and it was not an experience I'd like to repeat."

"Stay out of my organs!" I shout into the darkness. Bree's fingers clamp tighter around my arm.

"We saw the skies darkening over the cemetery," Mary says. "And we figured you could probably use some help."

"Did you know there's a dead body by the front gate?" Lottie adds.

Bree's fingers dig into my flesh. "What?"

"Yes. Sweet little Harriet Johnson. Her throat's been slit and her guts are all—"

My blood boils. Harriet Johnson worked at the village tearoom. She always gave me an extra pot of jam for my scones because she knows how much I love jam.

By Jupiter's jam-coated fingers, I will avenge your death, Harriet.

"Thank you, Lottie." Bree's voice cracks. "It was the Ripper. He still has his instinct to slash and rip. He must've killed her on his way in here to find us—"

"I did," a dark voice booms from right behind me, the words slurring, the fetid, aniseed stench of him dripping with malice. "And how nice of you to give me a whole bonny circle of victims, Lazarus. I'm going to enjoy carving up your friends one by one."

4

BREE

I swing my phone screen around just as the Ripper claws himself up out of the cellar. The pale light illuminates his twisted features as he lurches toward us, that dangerous blade flashing in the air.

"Bree, you can stop him," Mary calls out. "Find your power."

Find my power. Right, no problem. I try to go to the memory of painting the soapbox racer with my dad, but when I open my eyes to look for the lattice of cords, I can't see them.

Instead, hundreds of red-soaked tendrils hang from the dark clouds. No, not hundreds. Thousands. *Tens* of thousands. They're so thick that when I run my hand through them, I can't see the end of my arm. The cords feel like tar, gross and squishy in my fingers. I squeeze one in my fist, and my stomach lurches as an intense *wrongness* fills the air.

I don't know what these cords are, but if they're attached to souls, those souls are in *torment*.

"Yessssss," the Ripper hisses from the other side of me, closer to Edward. "Call them to you. Break open the Veil, Lazarus. We are so crowded down there. We want to be free."

"Bree!" Mary cries.

"I can't do it," I cry. "I can't touch my magic. Everything is wrong."

"Hmmmph, figures if you want something done, you have to do it yourself," Agnes huffs. "Aaaaaaiiiieeee!"

The Ripper hisses again. I don't know what's happening, but as I swing the phone around, I can just make out a thin shape fly through the air as Agnes leaps at the Ripper.

What is she doing?

The Ripper stabs at Agnes, but his blade goes right through her. Agnes flies inside him, the way Edward did last time. The Ripper sways unsteadily as Agnes rearranges herself inside his limbs, taking up residence in his body.

"He's drunk," the Ripper's lips croak. "But there's plenty of room in here. The bastard doesn't have a pesky soul to take up valuable real estate...aaaahh, no you don't!"

Agnes breaks off into a series of grunts and cries as the Ripper's body jerks erratically. He slaps himself across the cheeks, yanks his own hair, and shoves his fingers down his throat. Pax circles him, his sword raised, searching for the perfect opening. But the Ripper is still holding his deadly blade, the red mist curling from the tip, and I know that Pax won't want to risk hurting Agnes.

"Hurry," the Ripper gurgles. "I can't hold him much longer. He's more powerful than ever, and he's...he's...he's going to *eat* you, Little Lazarus."

Delightful.

"I will stop you. For Jupiter! For Bree!" With a war cry that shakes the earth and wakes the gods, Pax surges forward. His sword pierces the Ripper's chest and keeps going. The Ripper doesn't even flinch.

"Hey, that tickles..." the Ripper smirks, and I'm not even sure if that's Agnes or the monster speaking.

Pax jerks his arm back, sliding his sword out of the Ripper, who staggers a bit but remains upright, still fighting with Agnes for full control of his body.

Okay, so that didn't work.

"What do we do?" I cry, reaching for my power again. But it's no use, I can't do anything with the dark forest of red cords blocking me.

"Take that!"

A small parcel sails over my head.

What's that?

I whirl around, raising my phone. Mina stands in the path, her arm outstretched, a raven perched on her shoulder and her dog Oscar at her side. Her jaw is set in a determined line.

"Mina, what are you doing here?"

"I'll explain if we get out of this alive," she shouts back. "Get that charm!"

The little parcel lands near the Ripper's feet, bounces, and skids into the darkness on the edge of the path.

"Croak!" Quoth dives for it as the Ripper stumbles toward him. Agnes must be losing the battle over control of his body.

"Sorry," Mina calls out as Quoth scrabbles around in the darkness, hopping away from the Ripper's blows. "Blind girl aim."

Quoth grabs the object in his beak. The Ripper lunges, grabbing the bird, but Quoth beaks him and wriggles free.

"Croak!"

"Get back here, bird," the Ripper yells, wrestling control away from Agnes. "I'll poke your eyes out. I'll pluck every feather from your wings one by one and force you to eat them. I'll—"

But the Ripper doesn't finish his sentence because Quoth stuffs the little object into his mouth.

The Ripper's face explodes with a sickly green light. It's only then that I have enough visibility to recognise the object as the velvet bag of herbs from Vera's box. I left it with Mina so she could find out the ingredients from her friend Jo.

Hands clawing at the bag, the Ripper staggers backwards. His eyes fix on mine, and he flashes me one last triumphant glare before he vanishes with a vaguely comical *pop*.

Immediately, the gloom eases – not enough to see properly, but the red cords become less solid, and I can see the edges of the path and the graves and the Ripper's hat resting on the pale stone of the Witches' Monument.

"I think he's gone," Pax says. "The raven got rid of him. My friend Björn told me all about magical ravens. They are messengers of the gods—"

I'm not a messenger of the gods. I just play a lot of softball with some guys in my art school.

"Thank you, Quoth." I sag against Pax, relieved that at least the Ripper is gone for now.

"Agnes?" Lottie cries. "Where's Agnes?"

"She's not here?" My stomach tightens.

"Agnes? Are you under there?" Mary peers under the hat as Edward picks it gingerly off the ground.

"Walpurgis is gone, too," Lottie sobs. "He never leaves her side."

Dread settles in my chest. Agnes was inside the Ripper when he vanished. Does that mean that wherever we sent the Ripper, we've sent her there as well?

But there was no white light, no snapping of Agnes' cord. She didn't cross over like other ghosts I've seen and helped.

I call up my power again and search for her cord. With intense focus, I can just make out the twisting silvery cords of the ghosts and Mina and Quoth, and the blue-tinged silver of Ambrose, Edward, and Pax. But Agnes' silver cord has disappeared.

My hands feel around in the slimy red cords, sifting through them, pushing them apart. *She has to be here somewhere. She has to be...her soul can't just be gone...*

There!

Out of the corner of my eye, I catch a glimmer of silver. One of the red cords has a faint dusting of silver around the edge, nothing more. My fingers close around it, and I sense an old witch's magic barely clinging onto the sticky red tar.

Wherever she's gone with the Ripper, it's turned her cord – her *soul* – into this.

No, Agnes, I'm so sorry.

Lottie must sense what I'm seeing, because she wraps her arms around Mary and rests her head on her shoulder. "Agnes is gone," she wails. "We banished her beyond the Veil with the monster."

"Is that what happened?" I turn to Mina. "What was in that bag you threw? How did you know we were in trouble?"

"I didn't. Jo came over on her way to work on the autopsies for the victims of the Giant Vegetable Festival 'gas leak'," Mina holds up her fingers in air quotes. "She gave me her lab report on the velvet bag, including a complete ingredients list. I cross-referenced the ingredients with the various spell books in Nevermore's occult room and figured out that it's a banishment spell."

"We could have told you that." Mary bends over to inspect the bag. "We were the ones who gave Vera this spell. It's classic Agnes – herbology mixed with a little sadistic horror."

"Banishment spell? So the Ripper is gone?"

"Not permanently." Lottie frowns at the gloom-filled sky. "Not while the Veil is weak. He'll be back, and he won't be the only one."

"What do you mean, the Veil is weak? Is that what's gone wrong with the sky?" *And the cords?*

Ambrose swallows. "We can't know for certain, of course, but I believe the Veil has thinned over Grimdale. I think that Father Maxwell was trying to tell you that every time you bring someone back to life, it weakens the Veil. That's why that Soul-Eater was after him – he helped so many of his parishioners that it weakened the Veil around All Souls. I think until we know more, you shouldn't use resurrection magic."

"That's okay," I squeeze Edward's hand as I pull him close. "I have no reason to ever use my powers again. I have everyone I need."

Everyone turns to Edward, seeing him for the first time. Pax's eyes practically bug out of his head. He wraps Edward in a crushing bear hug. "Edward? You're Living again."

"Not for much longer if you don't allow me some air, Roman," Edward grumbles.

Pax sets down a rather squashed-looking Edward, who stumbles awkwardly towards Ambrose and takes his proffered hand, shaking it firmly. "After all these years, friend, at last we can do this for real."

"I'm honoured to meet you in the flesh." Ambrose squeezes Edward's hand warmly, then wraps him in his own, less spine-crushing hug. "If you might satisfy my professional, mystery-solving curiosity, what *was* your unfinished business?"

"I'll show you."

His fingers firmly knitted in mine once more, Edward heads back to the hole in the monument. He drops down and beckons everyone to follow him into his secret cellar. Pax helps lower everyone down the tiny hole, but doesn't come down himself. His shoulders won't fit.

"Behold, my unfinished business." Edward frowns as he kicks aside a large shard of broken glass. "Alas, the Ripper has damaged some of my vintage, but it was worth it to see that monster of the Veil drunk on terrible absinthe."

"Of course, Edward's unfinished business would be locating his beloved booze tunnel." Ambrose runs his fingers along the racks of bottles. "I can't believe I didn't think of it. For years he has grumbled that his friends must have drunk his cellar dry, since he didn't know where it was, and all this time it was right here beneath the cemetery."

"If these bottles were fancy and expensive when Edward was alive, that means they must be worth a fortune," Mina says. "We need to cover this place up, or Grimdale will be swarming with treasure hunters wanting to get rich from it, and if what Ambrose says is true and the Veil is thin..."

"...then we could be leading a bunch of people into the Ripper's clutches?" I shudder as I think of poor Harriet.

"Hmph. If they come seeking to steal from a prince of England, then I say good riddance." Edward plants his hands on his hips, looking more serious than I've ever seen him.

"Then we're going to have to hide the cellar until you figure out what you want to do with it. We all know that rightfully, this cellar belongs to Edward, but if the council finds this on their land, they won't give it back to him just because he claims to be the resurrected ghost of a long-dead debaucherous prince."

She's right. I didn't want to think about the wine now, not when we had the Ripper and the Veil to deal with, but practically, these wine bottles could enable Edward and the other ghosts to sustain themselves in the modern world, at least until we can figure out how the hell to get them IDs and jobs.

"It should be easy enough to put the mausoleum back into order and replace the key in the ticket office," I say. "But the base of the Witches' Monument is ruined. Perhaps if we spray paint something lewd on the monument and leave the crowbar there, Mr. Pitts will assume that it was some rowdy teenagers. We do sometimes get vandals in the cemetery."

"We can do that," Mina says. "And then what?"

"I have an idea." Edward grabs a bottle of something ancient off the shelves and holds it up, a wicked grin spreading across his lips. "Let us drink until everything seems rosy and golden."

5

EDWARD

We each stuff our arms full of as many bottles as we can carry and leave the cellar. The weight of the wine in my arms makes stabbing pains shoot between my shoulders. Despite the danger of our current predicament and the fact that an innocent woman has lost her life, I can't stop smiling. I can feel pain again. I can use my arms again!

I can taste wine. I can taste Brianna. How can I feel anything but joyous in this moment?

If the Ripper is going to bring our doom, and my newly reforged life is to be tragically cut short, then I intend to go out as Edward the Poet Prince, drunk and high with my head between my Brianna's legs, worshipping her beauty.

But before my party at the end of the world can begin, we must deal with the practical matters of covering up my cellar. The Ripper had already laid the flagstones in my tomb back into place and pushed the sarcophagus on top of the cellar entrance, which does ensure its invisibility but Mr Pitts will undoubtedly notice that it's not in its usual place a couple of feet to the right.

Pax helps Bree to shove the sarcophagus back into its original position, so my tomb will appear undisturbed.

I wait outside the mausoleum with the others while they take care of it, my newly Living arms aching under the weight of my booze. I stare up at the tomb, waiting for the familiar melancholy to wash over me at the sight of its resplendent cherubs and multiple dancing skeletons. But now that I'm alive, this monument to my demise holds none of the usual terror and unease. I have nothing to fear from my own earthly remains.

I get to live again. I get to do everything over.

Maybe in this life, I will finally do something that matters.

If I think about it too long, my head spins, and not in a 'enjoyed a little too much absinthe' kind of way. I am not supposed to exist. I'm not supposed to be alive, breathing this somewhat thick and gnarly air, or touching the hand of my dear friend Ambrose. I'm supposed to lie dead and alone in that tomb.

I won't be the man in that tomb again – the one who spent so much time feeling sorry for himself and longing for the love of a cold king that he didn't appreciate the family of misfits and artists who filled his days with joy.

I'll be an entirely different Edward. And that begins tonight.

Well, actually...I stare at the stricken faces of Ambrose and Bree's friends, and then down at the bottles in my hands, and amend my plans. New Edward's life begins tomorrow.

Tonight, what everyone needs is a good old-fashioned Poet Prince Edward night of debauchery.

Bree locks the metal gate of my tomb behind her. She turns to me, her honey eyes seeking me out immediately, as though checking that I'm still real, still with her. "We should call the police about Harriet's body, but we'd better deface the Witches' Monument first, so we're far from the cemetery when they arrive."

"I can help with that." Mina digs around in her purse and pulls out a bright pink cylinder. "Quoth entered a street art competition to beautify Argleton. He's painting a mural down at the old railway station with Earl Larson and some of his friends. I've got a stash of these in my bag."

"Perfect." Brianna tosses the can to me. "Would you like to do the honours?"

I stare down at the strange contraption. The pink cylinder is made of metal, and when I hold it up to shake it, the sound of a single tooth suspended inside clatters against the walls.

Creepy.

"It's called spray paint, Edward. You press down on the top and paint comes out." Brianna holds the cylinder up to the stone and presses my finger down. I jump as a forceful spray emits from the cylinder, leaving a pink dot on the stone.

"Now all you have to do is draw. You're the artist of the group. Paint something lewd."

"As you wish." Lewd is practically my middle name.

It takes me a few strokes to understand how to work the spray paint, but within minutes I've sketched a drawing that would make even my old friend the Countess de Rothschild blush.

"Edward, that's..." Brianna turns around and compares her derriere to the image. "That's quite good. Possibly *too* good for some random graffiti."

"It's what I have in mind for you this evening," I say. "I have been dreaming about all the things I'd like to do to you if I could ever truly touch you, and now my depraved imagination is truly free."

In the pale beam of light from her rectangle, I see Brianna turn her face away, and I know with a fizzing joy that spreads through my whole body that she is blushing. She is thinking of our encounter earlier in the cellar, and of all the other mischief we might have been able to get up to if we hadn't been so rudely interrupted.

Pax tilts his head to the side as he studies my painting, his mouth quirking up at the end. "I'm not sure that Living people bend that way."

I grin. "Wouldn't you like to find out, Roman?"

"Do you think Mr. Pitts will recognise your butt?" Mina asks with a smirk.

"Croak," says the raven.

"Arf," adds Oscar the dog.

Brianna hides her face behind her hand as she turns back to the others. "I'm *hoping* that Mr. Pitts hasn't paid that much attention to my butt. I think that he's secretly in love with Carla from the Friends of Grimdale Cemetery committee. Shall we?" Brianna picks up her bottles. "Pax has replaced as much of the broken stone at the base as will hide the entrance to the cellar. I think this place looks suitably trashed by disrespectful teens. Let's go home."

We stroll back to the house, moving slowly through the gloom. When we pass under the broken fence, the blackness thins a bit, and I can make out the edges of Grimwood Manor, some of the garden beds and Mike's strange statues, and Pax's pink horseless carriage (bicycle. It's called a bicycle. I need to remember this. Brianna had one, too. A bright red one that's now in the attic.) lying across our path. I kick it aside so that Ambrose doesn't trip on it.

I notice that the lights are off in the sitting room. Brianna's parents have gone to bed. Brianna pushes open the kitchen door and beckons us all inside. "Let's go to the guest lounge. It's far enough away from their room that they shouldn't hear us. Pax, can you fetch glasses? And do we have any party food?"

"I made Chigs' Raspberry and Chocolate Slices from *Bake-Off* season twelve," Pax says with a completely earnest expression as he dumps his bottles on top of mine and hurries to the pantry.

"Perfect. We'll see you in there." Brianna staggers down the hallway. I follow, carefully stepping around the old antique furniture covered in drop cloths and open paint pots Mike has left lying around. I don't want to lose another bottle.

Brianna kicks open the door with her foot and we all follow her inside. Everyone places their bottles on the table, and I start to sort them, placing the reds together and deciding which pinot noir will pair best with Raspberry and Chocolate Slices.

Mina lets Oscar out of his harness and slides out her phone. "Do you mind if I text Heathcliff and Morrie?" she asks. "They love a party. Well, Morrie does. Heathcliff loves an excuse to drink someone else's expensive alcohol and complain loudly about the government."

"Croak," adds the raven, nodding profusely.

"Of course, invite them! I couldn't imagine who I'd rather spend the end of humanity with than two of literature's greatest villains." Brianna picks up her own phone. "I'm going to invite Dani and Alice, if they're still awake."

"Should we really be partying?" Ambrose asks as he hangs by the doorway. "Is it wrong to celebrate while so many have died?"

"It's like Dad said, it's precisely why we *should* celebrate. We don't know what tomorrow will bring, but tonight we are alive, and Edward is with us, and *for once*, I want to be a normal, irresponsible twenty-something with my friends." Bree takes his arm and leads him over to the sofa. "Do you feel okay? You look a little pale."

"I think I am still recovering from dancing with the Soul-Eater." Ambrose sinks into the sofa.

I frown. Usually, Ambrose is the one whose enthusiasm for life cannot be tempered by the mediocre reality of existence, and yet tonight, he is not himself. I don't like to see him like this...like...well, like *me*.

Brianna's fingers clasp his. "Today I have fought a Soul-Eater, made a demon mark out of vegetables, brought my third boyfriend back to life, escaped a poisoned cellar, and banished Jack the Ripper back to hell, *again*. The sky is wrong, and I think the world might be ending. But Edward is alive, so let's party like a bunch of clueless, debauched princes."

"Hear, hear!" I pluck one of my favourite French tipples from the collection on the table and pop the cork. "To clueless debauchery!"

As I POUR wine into overflowing glasses, the party gets going in earnest. Bree connects her magic rectangle to the moving picture box's sound boxes, and loud, crunchy music fills the room. It's not the kind of accompaniment I'd usually choose for heavy drinking, poetical musings, and carnal happenings, but I do find myself stomping my foot along with the beat.

Ambrose eats five pieces of Pax's Raspberry and Chocolate Slices and perks up a little. Pax downs an entire bottle of Chianti in three gulps and pulls Brianna up to dance on the coffee table with him, but then the coffee table breaks and the pair of them collapse in drunken giggles on the floor.

Friends trickle into the room. Dani arrives with a slightly nervous-looking Alice, who does a double-take when she sees me. "I studied you at university. You're...you're..."

"The Poet Prince Edward," I swoop down into a low bow. "At your service."

Alice's face turns pale. She flops down onto the sofa. "I think I'm going to faint."

"Don't pass out before you taste this wine." I set a glass down on the table in front of her. "It came from a little family vineyard just outside of Florence. In 1622."

Alice picks up the glass. Her lip wobbles as she takes a deep gulp.

"Bree, when you said that ghosts are real I didn't think I'd be meeting actual famous dead people." Alice grips the stem of the glass so hard that her knuckles are going white. "No offence, Ambrose, but you were a bit obscure until your viral hit."

"No offence taken," Ambrose says as he sips his wine.

Mina's two other boyfriends arrive shortly after. Heathcliff dumps some shopping bags on the table. "I brought crisps."

"The perfect accompaniment to centuries-old wine," Morrie murmurs.

"Exactly." Heathcliff tosses a bundle of fabric at the raven. "Here, birdie. I brought your clothes, too."

"Croak." The raven catches the clothing in his talons and soars off into the hallway. A few moments later, the handsome Quoth walks back in, tosses his dark, silken hair over his shoulder, and accepts a glass of wine from me with paint-splattered fingers.

Honestly, with the number of beautiful people in this room, this party is not too dissimilar to previous debaucherous carousings from when I was the lord of Grimwood...if one ignores the drunk Roman in the corner drawing his sword after a particularly brutal argument with a lampshade.

And speaking of beautiful people...

"Is that the prince's stash?" Morrie's ice-blue eyes go huge as he takes in the table brimming with my bottles. Now *that* is a stunning example of the human form. In a different era, at a different party, I might have invited Morrie to my boudoir for a private poetry reading. But as he wraps Heathcliff in his sinewy arms and plants a soft kiss on his forehead, I find myself thinking only of one woman...

Brianna leaves the room briefly to welcome Hayes and Wilson, the two police officers who investigated the deaths of Albert and Vera. They're here because Dani called them to say that she was walking over to Grimwood when she found the body. They take a quick statement from everyone in the room, but it's clear they don't believe we had anything to do with it, especially not when I put on my princely charm and describe in great detail the two teenage derelicts I saw skulking around the cemetery. Ambrose and Mina aren't the only ones with a skill for telling stories.

It may perhaps also have helped that by now everyone at my party is so merry with drink that we couldn't navigate our way through the front garden without falling foul of a concrete squirrel, much less brutally stabbing a woman.

Hayes and Wilson make their notes and leave again, and Brianna lurches across the room toward me.

"There you are." Brianna holds out her empty wine glass. "I missed you."

"Well, now you have me, flesh and bone, and I'll never leave you."

Instead of filling her glass, I wrap her in my arms, twirling her and sweeping her around the room in time to the awful music. Her hands go around my waist, and she rests her head against my shoulder, those Champagne eyes peering up at me with such love and wonder that I feel utterly invincible.

This is the best party I've ever thrown.

And when the night winds down, and the glow of good wine still warms my veins, I pull Brianna against me again, marvelling at the way her body fits with mine, as if we were sculpted for each other. I could live for hundreds of years and never get tired of the feel of her, so warm and yielding and *real*.

My nose fills with pear and almonds, and my head spins, but not from alcohol – from the giddy joy that swells in my heart. Brianna gazes up at me, her eyes so trusting, and she wobbles on her tiptoes as she leans up to kiss me.

Her lips on mine are sweeter than any old wine. My hand cups her cheek, tilting her head back so I can drink deeper of her. No matter how many more months, days, or hours I have left on this earth to taste her, I will never sup my fill.

I break Brianna's sweet kiss to grab Pax by the collar and pull him into our embrace. He regards me with his bold stare, his jaw slack from drink but his icicle eyes clear and bright. A whim overtakes me, and I reach up and draw him to my lips, as well.

The roughness of his mouth after the softness of Brianna is a shock, but I tilt my own head back and welcome the duel of our tongues, the brash way the Roman fists my hair in his hand.

When Pax pulls back, we're both panting. And Brianna's eyes have blown out to three times their usual size.

"What is this?"

Pax shrugs. "A Roman is always happy to show his affection for his brother."

A slow smile spreads across my lips. "If the end of the world is truly upon us, I would have all of you in my bed tonight, blood and bone and flesh, until we are but dust."

"Yes," Brianna breathes. "Please."

I will never refuse a lady.

Pax lifts Brianna into his arms, burying his face into her neck, kissing along her collarbone as he heads toward the door. I follow behind, stopping only to peel Ambrose away from where he's locked in a deep, philosophical debate with the raven. I bend over him, enjoying the way the hairs on his skin rise as my lips tickle his neck. His hair has fallen free of its fastening and flies wildly about his face. I pull the silken locks to one side and whisper my command against his ear.

"I am taking Brianna and Pax to bed. Join us."

Ambrose makes a stuttering apology and allows me to lift him from the couch. I wrap an arm around his shoulder and we steady each other. His warmth against me only stirs my hunger deeper.

My brothers.

We have come so far from the early days of our forced cohabitation. We have been through fire and flame together, and now we are flesh and blood, resurrected not by a sanctimonious old saint but by our remarkable woman. I know with a certainty that shocks me that as precious as my second chance at life is to me, I'd give it up in a heartbeat if Pax or Ambrose needed me. So this is what it feels like to have brothers? To have a true family?

But the things I wish to do to both of them tonight are anything but brotherly.

"Edward, my head is positively spinning," Ambrose murmurs as we drunkenly stumble up the stairs, falling over each other.

"Wait until I get you to my boudoir. I have plans for you that will pop that head of your right off your shoulders. Poetically speaking, of course," I add in a hurry as his brow furrows in concern.

I drag him into my boudoir. Mike and Sylvie have just finished repainting the walls a bland white and they replaced the beautiful purple velvet bedding with grey linens. It's no longer a room fit for a king (Brianna rolls her eyes and calls it the 'greige-room' whenever she passes by), but it is the room where I have lain so many nights, dreaming the depraved, filthy thoughts that I can finally make real.

My heart thuds in my chest as I find Brianna and Pax already entwined together. His huge hands grasp her possessively as he crushes her mouth with his, and she clings to him as if his tree trunk of a torso is the only thing holding her upright.

At the sight of them, my sceptre stirs and lengthens.

"It seems that our friends have started without us," I purr at Ambrose as I draw him over to the bed.

Brianna's Champagne eyes meet mine, and she pulls back from Pax's kiss to reach out a hand to me. She clasps her fingers over mine, pulling me and Ambrose closer until the four of us are huddled together. Ambrose leans his head on my shoulder and Brianna touches her forehead to mine.

"All three of you..." She runs her fingers first down my cheek, then down Ambrose's. Pax towers over all of us, still holding her possessively, his pale eyes shot with need. "I can't believe you're here, and you're *real*."

"Is this what you want?" Ambrose says, a note of concern in his voice. "Our heads are filled with drink and fancies. Do you not wish to rest, to be ready for what the Ripper throws at us next?"

"That's for tomorrow, Ambrose. Tomorrow, I'll be afraid. Tomorrow, we'll make a plan. Tonight I want the three of you to love me as if it's our last night on earth." Brianna glances toward the windows. "Because I worry that it might be."

Pax's cold eyes meet mine. The Roman's features are unusually taut, stretched thin from too many nights without sleep, from holding his sword too tightly, as if his blade alone can save us all.

I cock a princely eyebrow at him, then turn back to Brianna. "And what if it is our last night? What if the last hurt we have to endure is dying in each other's arms. I for one am happy to go if it means our souls will share eternity together."

"Me too," Ambrose says quickly and softly, as if he cannot bear the thought of dying before the words are unsaid.

"The four of us will make Jupiter blush," Pax adds.

Brianna laughs her deep, throaty laugh, and I'm utterly overcome by her. For so many centuries, alone in this house even though it was never truly empty, alone in the prison of my mind, I have wished and dreamed and hoped for a love like this. I have planned in great detail the man I would be if only I had the chance, the way I might shower my lover with gifts and write them poems that made them blush and kiss them twice in case the first kiss didn't take. And then, Brianna comes along and I find all my plans crumbling to dust. I can't even compose a poem about her because poems are made of words that describe things, and she is indescribable. This need inside my heart is indescribable, the way it has become a living, breathing thing that claws at my insides. The want inside me is a distorted, festering thing, and only she can cut it free.

"Edward…"

I drop my forehead again to hers. "I've always loved you, Brianna. I loved you before you were even born. I might be the one who's haunted this house for six centuries, but I've *always* been haunted by you. You're why I write my poems, why I paint, why I seek every possible pleasure upon this earth – because I wish to drive you from my flesh, to make you real. But nothing I could ever imagine compares to the woman I hold in my arms. I feel as though I am lost in a dream, for surely nothing in my life could be so perfect, so made for me?"

"Oh, Edward." Her voice cracks. "I think you've always haunted me, too. I carried the three of you with me wherever I was. I wish…I wish you didn't have to live so many years alone. I wish I could have held you when your father treated you cruelly and made you see that you are worthy of love. I wish we could have had all this time together, because now I'm worried that we have so little left..."

"We have tonight, and that's all that matters."

I brush my lips to hers, slow and soft. Before, in the cellar, we were all over each other. But now, I want to savour every moment with her. I'm shaking with need of her, but I force myself to draw away. I nibble her bottom lip, dragging out a moan from her that pools heat in my belly as I pull her into a deep kiss that has her melting into me.

My muse.

The taste of her is like coming home. And before tonight, I never understood what that meant – *coming home.* I never had a home to return to. The palace had been a hellscape and the aching pass of time had turned Grimwood into my prison. But now, with her, and Pax, and Ambrose, walking these halls as a Living man, kissing her in this room where I have longed and yearned and dreamed, I know what it is to be *home.*

I wrap my fingers around Brianna's neck, pulling her head to mine as this kiss between us becomes an urgent, needy dance.

Brianna's fingers still clasp Ambrose. He moves closer, raising his other hand to her cheek, stroking her skin and mine, touching my hair, tangling us together until I don't know where she stops and I begin.

"Marvellous," he murmurs. "Simply a miracle."

Pax growls, and I can feel the hardness of his *verpa* against my thigh. I start to nudge us towards the bed, but the impatient Roman simply picks up all three of us and deposits us on the soft pillows.

Ohhhh, the pillows...

I lean back into the pile of softness and sigh happily. All the years I have 'slept' in this room (ghosts don't really sleep, we kind of exist in a liminal state between dreaming and remembering), I've never been able to feel the surface of the bed. Now I am wrapped in a fluffy cloud of happiness.

"With sheets of silk and pillows piled high," I murmur as I nuzzle myself deeper into the silken sheets. 'Twas a haven for the weary to lie. No lumps or bumps to disturb thy rest, just plush comfort, at its very best..."

"Are you composing a poem for the *bed*?" Brianna's lips curl back with amusement.

"A true artist finds inspiration everywhere."

"Can you find inspiration here?" Pax grabs the collar of my shirt, pulling me to him, and mashing his mouth against mine.

He's the opposite of Brianna, his skin rough with stubble, his tongue demanding, violent. He tastes like the battlefield, raw and bloody and beautiful. The weight of him against me, after so many centuries of not being able to truly touch him, brings a visceral pleasure that thunders through my body as he pins me against the pillows. I struggle to regain my control, my dominance, but that only makes the Roman drive the kiss deeper. His cold blue eyes crackle with flame, and I realise that maybe we had been dancing around this for far too long.

When he draws back, I find myself breathless, my chest heaving, my sceptre throbbing with want. And when my eyes meet Brianna's over the Roman's shoulder, and I see how much she enjoys watching us, I realise that she has done this. She has split us wide open and exposed the rough, broken edges of our hearts, and what happens next is all because of her.

Not one to be left out, Ambrose crawls up beside Brianna and brings his mouth to hers. I've never seen Ambrose kiss her like this before, hard and desperate and possessive, and my dark, broken heart swells at the sight of it. Pax breaks our kiss with a growl, and he tugs Brianna's legs from under her, pulling off her jeans and underwear and helping her to shrug off her t-shirt. His clothes follow soon afterwards, making a dull thump as they hit the armoire and drop into a messy pile on my floor.

"Please," Brianna cries, her sweet voice dripping with need. "I want somebody inside me, *now*."

"Edward?" Ambrose asks stiffly as he shrugs off his new, modern clothing – the shirt that pulls at his lean, sculpted shoulders, the trousers that invitingly hug his ass. It is just like Ambrose to offer her to me first, knowing that I have only just become Living and have only just begun to explore the wonders of her body.

"Not yet." I crawl back on the pillows, making myself a comfortable nest as I kick off my codpiece and pantaloons, allowing my sceptre to bounce free. "Your prince wishes to watch for a bit. Go on, peasants – dance for my amusement."

Pax rolls his eyes at me, but then his hunger overtakes him and he grabs Brianna by the hips, pulling her across the bed to impale her on his waiting cock. She gasps as the full length of him enters her in one thrust, but she is so wet and ready that her body can take the Roman's violence without regret.

Ambrose turns her face to his and takes her mouth once more, drinking in her little gasps and sighs. His long fingers stroke her her nipples, rolling and squeezing until they are hardened buds.

The sight of it, the beautiful wantonness of our love made flesh, has my fist clenching around my sceptre and my breath rushing ragged through my teeth.

Brianna slides off Pax's *verpa* and rolls over, motioning for Pax to move around to the other side of her, his enormous length inches from her lips. She runs her tongue over the tip, and Pax's eyes roll back in his head. Ambrose grips her thighs and pulls her back onto his cock, impaling her with a single deep thrust. Her mouth closes around Pax's waiting cock, stifling her cry as she takes that Roman dick deep.

My hand strokes my own length as I watch them greedily – my eyes first drawn to Ambrose, the sun-kissed muscles on his back sloping down to narrow hips and that firm ass that just begs to be spanked red, his usually neat hair all dishevelled and his lips bruised from kissing, his head tipped back as he takes Brianna with a fierce possessiveness borne of being pulled back from the void.

I then move to Pax, his eyes wide open, his fingers tangled in Brianna's hair as he fucks her mouth. The hard wall of muscles that is his body trembles and shudders, slamming the bed against the wall with every thrust.

But then my eyes are drawn away. To Brianna. Always, she is at the centre of my being. She lies back on the sheets, her long fingers bunching the fabric as she holds on. Her head tosses back, and her dark hair fans around her face like a halo. With a sigh that is like a little death, she arches her back and *surrenders*. She gives herself over completely to the sensations, to our worship of her, and I know that she has laid her fears and worries at the door to my boudoir.

I don't have to tie her down this time. Brianna is not going to run.

Brianna trembles through the final remnants of her orgasm, her eyes rolling back in her head.

I can't take it any longer. I kneel on the bed and stroke my fingers down her back, feeling her soft skin slick with sweat. I lean over her, careful not to disturb my brothers as they go about their most important task.

"Such a good girl," I murmur. "Such a good little ghostslut."

She shudders and jerks as the pleasure overtakes her once more. It's a glorious sight to behold – my Brianna, impaled between two cocks, taking them so deeply and loving every moment of it. I wish I could paint her like this, her hair in disarray, her skin slick and flushed, her eyes filled with love…

I forgot that I am Living again. I can hold a paintbrush once more. I *will* paint her, one day. If we have enough days left. But I don't need a painting to remember her by. I know that I will see this vision of her beauty every time I close my eyes.

Pax comes with a grunt, thrusting his hips with such violence that he throws Brianna back against the pillows. He draws out of her with a happy sigh and sags back onto the bed, lying with his huge arms behind his head and a dopey smile on his face. "It's your turn, Edward. I am utterly spent."

"Are you, really?" I raise an eyebrow. "What about our surprise for Brianna?"

He sits up with a jerk. "Yes, our surprise!"

"Of course," Ambrose agrees. "It's the perfect night for our surprise."

"What surprise?" Brianna lifts one eyebrow. Her lips purse with concern. "Please, no more ghost dates. I think we need a few more lessons on modern etiquette before we try another movie..."

"Do you trust me?" I ask Brianna as she lays her head against my chest, her ear pressed against my beating heart.

She laughs low in her throat. "That's a difficult question. Do I trust you to understand when I have big feelings and need a shoulder to cry on? Yes. A thousand times, yes. Do I trust you to empty the dishwasher or remember to feed Moon and Entwhistle? Probably not."

"Do you trust that I won't hurt you, that I will only do things to you that will bring you pleasure?"

Brianna's lips part a little. She stares up at me, her eyelids heavy. "I trust you, Edward. I trust you with my body. And my heart."

Her words make my throat close over. I swallow back the words I long to say, words that seek to form themselves into a poem. But this is not a moment for pretty words. I order Pax to retrieve the special box.

"What's this special box?"

"A little something Pax and Ambrose helped me put together when I was still a ghost," I say as Pax slides off the bed and runs to fetch it. "I thought that modern Living people had forgotten the more dark and depraved ways of pleasure, but then Ambrose informed me about the internet. Did you know that the internet is the most amazing thing?"

"I use it for reading about history," Ambrose says, leaning on his elbows and resting his head on one hand while he played with Brianna's hair with the other. "But Edward found new wonders."

"I bet he did." Brianna's smile lights all the dark corners of my heart. "Did Ambrose also explain that to procure such wonders from the internet, you need something called money?"

"Your prince is not so out of touch that he doesn't know what money is." I place my hands on my hips, offended. "Why, I've squandered more money than you will see in your lifetime."

Her laugh is infectious. "I believe it. But how did you pay for these items when you don't even have a bank account—"

"He used your credit card," Ambrose says quickly.

Brianna jerks upright. "You *what?*"

"It's all in the service of your pleasure. I think that you won't mind when you see what we got." I snap my fingers, and Pax jogs into the room, carrying the sparkly red box tied with a black velvet ribbon from a shop in London, which he places in front of Brianna.

She makes a face at me, but curiosity grabs hold of her and she lifts the lid of the box. My belly warms with heat and my sceptre stirs with fresh vigour when I see the flush creep across her cheeks as she pulls out my carefully-chosen items.

"Edward, these are...what are they?"

She touches a pink device with various attachments that I know would have made the Countess de Rothschild weep, before holding up a pair of cuffs, a blindfold, and some clamps that look like something that Hugh used to enjoy on his nipples. My sceptre jerks impatiently, just imagining using these things on her, on all three of them. I have so much to teach them all, and only one lifetime...

"We can try all these things when you're ready." I rummage in the box and draw out a small bottle of elixir. "But for tonight, this is all we need."

"What is it?" She reaches for the bottle, but I hold it just out of reach.

"You trust me, yes?"

"Yes. Damn you."

"Good. Now, move aside. I want Ambrose to lie down."

The Victorian obeys with enthusiasm, lying back on the bed, his hands behind his head, his cock standing proud, already slick from being inside her, a place I so desperately want to be. But this will be so much more enjoyable if it is drawn out.

"Lower yourself onto him," I instruct Brianna. "Go slow. We don't want him to come too soon."

Brianna rushes to obey. She straddles Ambrose and he grips her thighs, guiding her as she lowers her hips gently down on his, tossing her head back with ecstasy as he enters her.

I tsk. "What did I say about going slow?"

Ambrose groans as I lay my hands on them, forcing Brianna to slow her strokes. His chin juts out defiantly, but the sparkle in his eyes tells me that he loves this. He and Brianna are a lot alike in so many ways. They enjoy having me instruct them. They like being praised, so I offer them what I know will make them happy.

"That's it. Very good. Nice and slow. That's exactly how she likes it. Now, while I prepare Brianna, you can't come. You have to hold on, because this is as much a gift for you as it is for her. Can you do this?"

"I can," Ambrose says, but his words are a little strained. I understand – it's hard to hold yourself back when Brianna is riding you like a show pony.

I let them go at it while I move around behind Brianna. Pax reclines on the pillows as he grows hard again, his eyes fixed on me, his expression wary. There is something between us that pulls taut – it is not the same thing that I feel for Brianna, but it is the flush of something new, something charged, that we can explore slowly and gently. We have time. I *hope* that we have time.

But tonight, it is about her.

Our Brianna, who brought us back from death with nothing but her will and the magic in her veins, who loved us enough to reach for us through the Veil, who saved each of us, even when we did not know how badly we needed to be saved.

I open the elixir and squirt the liquid onto my fingers. As she slowly rides Ambrose, I rub the liquid between her cheeks, reaching around to stroke my fingers over her clit until she starts to squirm.

With my other hand, I tease her second entrance, running my wet finger around the rim, and pushing gently inside each time she slams her hips down on Ambrose. Brianna's body twists as she tries to see what I'm doing.

"You trust me, remember?"

"I do, but no one has ever..." her eyelashes flutter and she loses her words as Pax leans in and sucks on her nipple. "I don't want it to hurt."

"I'll only hurt you if you beg me." I gently nibble on her earlobe. "Maybe one day, my Brianna, you *will* beg me. But tonight, we are all three of us going to fill you. If you want us?"

Her body tenses up, but a slow smile creeps across her perfect lips. "Yes. I want you."

My heart leaps with happiness. Those three simple words – *I want you* – have the power to undo me. I have been adored, admired, despised, tolerated, but wanted in the simple way that a person wants family, home, peace, protection...I've never had that until now.

I stay where I am, gently stroking and teasing her rear entrance, while Ambrose and Pax drive her closer to the edge. I need her relaxed and willing. When I feel her muscles relaxing again, I push my finger a little deeper.

My breath hitches. She's so *tight*. I have tortured myself with this dream for so many months, and now it will come true.

Brianna lets out a little gasp, but she doesn't tell me to stop. Instead, she presses back against me.

That's all the encouragement a filthy prince needs.

As I add a second finger, delving deeper and making her ready for me, I can feel Ambrose's member pushing against the thin wall inside her, filling her alongside me. Brianna's body shudders. Her head is thrown back, her eyes closed, her lips falling open invitingly.

It is time.

I crawl closer, gripping myself in my fist, making sure I am coated in the slippery liquid. My lips graze her shoulder, tasting the salt of her sweat against her hot skin, feasting my senses on the smell and taste of her as I press myself to her entrance and *push*.

"Oh," she murmurs, and then again. "Oh, oh..."

Gently, gently, I move a little at a time, stopping to give her body a chance to adjust. Each time I stop, Ambrose strokes inside her, his movements rubbing against me, driving me even closer to the edge. Pax leans in and captures her mouth in his,

his hands cupping her cheeks and swallowing her delicious little moans.

I push in deeper and deeper, and she is so impossibly tight, holding me like a vise, my whole body trembles from the pleasure of it. Everything has disappeared now – the dangers we face, the house that holds us protectively, the rules and manners that hold us back from true pleasure.

All that exists are our bodies and hearts, moving as one.

Once I am inside her completely, Ambrose stills. I don't move, and Pax holds Brianna upright between us. Her head leans against his shoulder. We breathe. We watch each other. We revel in this soft, perfect moment.

"I can f-f-feel you, Edward," Ambrose gasps. "This is…"

"What did I tell you?" I grin. "I know my way around a boudoir. Now, my protégée, what do you propose we do next?"

Ambrose's cock twitches. I feel it.

I feel *everything*.

His lips curl back into a smile that's entirely too much like one of my own, full of mischief and promise.

Slowly, Ambrose draws himself out of Brianna, his mouth forming a silent O as he experiences the sensation of sliding out of her with the pressure of my cock against his, and only that thin wall of flesh separating us.

Then he lets out all the breath in his lungs and thrusts back in.

As he does this, I draw back, gritting my teeth because it feels so good, too good, and I want to prolong release as long as possible. I want to revel in the sensations, so new and so beautiful.

"This…this is…" Brianna gasps, but her words are torn away by her pleasure.

Soon, we fall into a rhythm, with Brianna between us. Pax holds her, kisses her, whispers things about old gods and going to war for her body, that she is the sword he will die upon. He keeps her with us so she doesn't float away. Her body trembles and convulses as she experiences orgasm after orgasm, and it is all I can do to hold on to my release so she can have all the pleasure she deserves.

Finally, I cannot take it anymore. Even this depraved prince has his limits. I pull out of her and release my seed over her naked back. Ambrose comes inside her and makes a face so comically delightful that I long to paint it, and the three of us collapse into a sweaty heap on top of Pax.

"That was…" Brianna falls into my arms. "You are…"

But the night is not done, and I have so very many ideas for what we can do with it. Words give way to moments, a symphony of touch and sensation. At some point, I'm kissing Pax, while he plunges so deep inside Brianna that she's choking on Ambrose's member, and I look over this scene before me and think that I may not have a kingdom, but there has never been a prince as lucky as I.

6

BREE

When I wake the next morning, my head pounding from a five-hundred-year-old wine-induced hangover, and my thighs aching from all the debaucherous things the four of us did in Edward's boudoir together, the sky over the village is still strange.

The darkness has spread even wider. I can see it through the open curtains creeping down Grimwood Crescent, obscuring the thatched roof and English rose arch of Honeysuckle House B&B.

My heart sinks. If Ambrose is right, and using my powers thins the Veil, then bringing Edward back last night looks to have done even more damage.

I think of Harriet, the Ripper's latest victim, who was killed simply because she was in the wrong place at the wrong time. Through the window, I can just make out the police tape flapping in the breeze as the forensics team gathers still more evidence. Hayes and Wilson seem to have believed our story about the kids we saw in the cemetery, but eventually they'll connect the murder weapon to Vera and Peggy's bodies, and they'll be back here to investigate a serial killer.

Little do they know, they're on the trail of the most elusive serial killer in British history.

Briefly, I think of giving them the information I learned from Abberline – the Ripper's true name. But that wouldn't be helpful. What *would* be helpful is for me to figure out how to repair the Veil and keep the Ripper and his Soul-Eater out of the Living World forever.

That makes me think of poor Agnes, trapped inside the Ripper within the Veil. I hope she's giving him killer indigestion. Thanks to her, the Ripper is back where he belongs, at least temporarily. But how long do we have before he returns?

And, most importantly, what does he want? My head pounds as I consider that if he wanted to, he could have simply walked up behind me and Edward when we were in the cellar and stabbed us. He didn't have to trap us, so why did he?

What did he say to me in the cellar?

You're the one I want, Lazarus. And now that I'm free of my old masters, I can use you for your true purpose.

What does he mean by my 'true purpose'? And why does it make me feel violently ill?

No, wait, that's just the hangover. Owwww.

"Good morning, Brianna." Edward's face appears amongst the sheets. His dark hair is rumpled against his face. He wraps his arms around me, pressing his face into my neck. I breathe in deep, savouring his scent and trying to push down the worries that threaten to overwhelm me.

Edward is alive, and in my arms, and as hopeless as everything seems right now, I will cling to that fact.

"My head doesn't think it's a good morning," I shoot back, rubbing my throbbing temples.

Why did I drink so much last night?

Oh, that's right. *Edward.*

He's an even *worse* influence now that he's Living.

And it doesn't help that old wine is the best wine. I'm forever ruined for £6.99 plonk now. From now on, I will only drink things with dusty French labels where the grapes were squashed by the calloused feet of Benedictine monks.

But not today. I groan, reaching for the bottle of painkillers one of the guests left on the bedside table. Today I will be drinking *nothing*.

Nothing but sweet, fortifying, soul-healing coffee.

"Are those magical make-better pills?" Edward asks hopefully, eyeing the bottle as I tip pills into my hand.

"Yes. Are you sure you want one?" I'm not sure how the body of someone who was technically last alive in the Enlightenment will react to modern medicine.

"Whenever I had a case of sore hair following an evening of revels, the royal physician recommended a tincture of raw eel and bitter almond." Edward held out his hand. "These honestly seem safer."

"Fair." I gulp down two pills and pass the water glass to Edward. He gulps down his pills and smiles sheepishly.

"Thank you. I'd rather forgotten how painful an evening of drinking could be."

"Let that be a lesson to you." I slide out of bed and fumble around for my discarded clothing. I really need coffee.

As I stagger into the square of dim light cast by the window, I notice Pax standing behind the curtain, his sword gripped tightly in his hand as he watches the silent, gloomy street below.

"Did you sleep?" I ask him.

He shakes his head, his gaze never leaving the window. "I must be ready. The Ripper will come back."

"You must *sleep*, Pax."

He merely turns back to the window, his gaze fixed on the strange, dark sky that has spread from the cemetery nearly to the end of the street. Lightning crackles on the edges of the dark cloud, even though it's the height of summer and the weather report is for clear skies.

My head is too full of bees to deal with Pax's hero complex, so I stagger into the hallway, heading in the vague direction of coffee. From the closed doorway of the guest room across the hall, I can hear Alice snoring loudly.

"Do you know where Mina and her guys ended up?" I ask Edward as we stagger down the hallway.

"They are sullying the room next to my boudoir," he grumbles. "If that raven gets out and does its business on my silken sheets…"

"Quoth won't crap in your boudoir unless you make a habit of quoting Poe's poetry at him. Besides," I squeeze his hand. "It doesn't have to be your boudoir any longer."

Edward's whole face lights up. The storm clouds in his eyes become clear and bright. Before he can make some kind of lewd suggestion, we step onto the first-floor landing and my fragile ears are assaulted by my mother's loud complaints.

"—people warned them for years about the pollution from that factory, but did the government listen? Oh, no, and now there's a giant black cloud over Grimdale and people have *died* and who knows what horrible chemicals we're all breathing in? And they're trying to say it's a gas leak…"

Mum scrubs the wall sconces so hard that she removes a layer of paint, but Dad has Uriah Heep blasting out of a portable speaker while he oils the balustrade on the grand staircase, and he seems relatively calm for a man living through the current apocalypse.

I suck in a breath. It's going to be a long day.

"Mum, Dad?" I hesitate on the staircase. "I want you to meet someone."

Mum wipes her hands on her overalls and peers up at me

with narrowed eyes. Dad turns down the music and beams at us. Stomach churning – and not all because of last night's indulgences – I sweep my arm out with a flourish just as Edward struts out from behind the grandfather clock. "This is Edward. He's another...foreign friend."

"I'm not foreign," Edward says in his haughty, put-out voice. "I'm as English as a country rose. Why, my family have ruled this fair nation since—"

"Edward got hit on the head during the kerfuffle at the Giant Vegetable Festival," I say quickly. "He's fine, mostly, but he thinks he's a seventeenth-century royal prince. I've just been playing along."

"Ah, of course. You know, a royal prince actually once owned this house. I think his name might even have been Edward." Dad stands up and shuffles his way up the stairs. "He was a bit of a ratbag."

"A man after my own dark and depraved heart," Edward beams. I elbow him in the ribs.

"Please, Mike, hold the balustrade," Mum scolds. For once, I agree with her. With every step, Dad looks like he's about to pitch over. The Parkinson's is getting worse. His brain struggles to tell if he's picked his feet up enough, so he does this weird shuffle.

"Then I'd get my hands all oily." Mike grins as he offers his hand to Edward, but at the last moment he retracts it and gives a deep bow instead. "A pleasure to meet you, Your Majesty."

"Oh, Mike, please." Sylvie fixes Edward with her signature stare. "You're dating my daughter, too, I presume? Well, I suppose you're welcome in this house as long as you make yourself useful."

"I can be useful," Edward declares. "Last night I very usefully supplied the alcohol for our little gathering, and there's plenty more where that came from. Also, should you require a sonnet for any occasion, or someone to throw a fabulous party, I am your man."

"We don't need any of that. I think there's been more than enough partying around here." Mum glares from me to Dad. "But we *do* need the drain in the laundry unblocked. Those blasted cats shed like you wouldn't believe. This way, follow me."

Mum leads a worried-looking Edward off toward the laundry. I fight a hysterical laugh as it bubbles up inside me. Sure, the Veil between the realm of the living and the dead may be thinning over Grimdale, and all kinds of monsters may be unleashed, but my parents have accepted my unconventional relationship with three ex-ghosts, and Mum is now making a royal prince clean the drains.

"Hey, Bree-bug, you look as if you had a rough night." Dad's back on the staircase again. He dips his brush in the oil. His hand trembles and it takes him a couple of goes to get the right amount. "There's a fresh pot of coffee in the kitchen. Your mother made it, so it's basically rocket fuel."

"Thanks, Dad." But as much as I desperately need coffee, I can't seem to make my legs move. Through the window at the end of the hallway, I can see the dark cloud shifting. Dad curses under his breath as he splashes oil on his overalls. His hands won't allow him to have the finish he's after.

I can't bear it anymore.

I'm done lying.

I am terrified and I need all the help I can get.

In the five years I was away from Grimdale, I missed my parents terribly – my mum's no-nonsense advice, my dad's unfettered optimism that everything turns out okay. But I had this annoying need to prove that I could make it in the world alone, without them, or the ghosts, or anyone else.

What did I get for my independence? Five years of working

in shitty pubs and cleaning hostel toilets, and a hole in my heart where my family should be.

This problem is so much bigger than me. I need my daddy, and I'm not ashamed to admit it.

I sit down on the top step, my head in my hands. "Dad, I can see ghosts."

He doesn't look up from his task. "Yes, of course. This old house is full of them."

My heart hammers against my chest. "I don't mean poetically. I *see* ghosts. All my life, I've seen dead people around the village. There are three ghosts who live in this house, and they used to be my best friends when I was a kid. Only now, they're—"

"Bree-bug, I *know*."

"Huh?"

"I've always known you could see ghosts." He carefully sets down his brush and leans back on his heels. "Your great-grandmother Elsie did, too, of course."

"She did?" I *knew* it.

"Well, you didn't get it from my side of the family." Dad thumps his chest with his fist, slathering oil across his overalls. "Not a supernatural bone in this body, I'm afraid."

"So Mum can—"

"No." Dad shakes his head so violently that he doesn't even notice he's flicked oil on the carpet. "No, no, no. Can you imagine if your mother could see ghosts? She'd be ordering them to carry sheets for the guests and to scare away the council inspector."

I smile, but it doesn't stick to my face. My father's easy laugh is throwing me off.

He *knows?*

All this time, I've been fretting about keeping my powers a secret, and he already knew?

I have so many questions. I don't even know where to begin. "Dad, I don't understand. How do you know I can see them? When did you figure it out? Why didn't you ever say anything to me?"

He talks while he spreads oil unevenly across the wood. "When you were a baby, you used to struggle to make eye contact with us sometimes. We'd hold your attention with a toy and then suddenly, you'd snap your head away, caught by something or someone we couldn't see. We had you checked out by every kind of specialist. They thought you might have a vision impairment, but I'd started to wonder even back then if you were looking at something...or someone...that we couldn't see."

"But what made you go from vision impairment to ghost whisperer?"

"From your great-grandmother Elsie. Your mother and grandfather love to tell stories about her, about how she could see ghosts and that Grimdale must be full of them because she never set foot in this house after she won it in that poker game."

"It was backgammon," I say, remembering Ambrose's insistence.

"I'm pretty sure it was poker."

"What do you mean, she didn't set foot in the house again?"

Dad shakes his head. "Grandfather Bert had a strange life with her. She rented out Grimwood to a string of hapless tenants while she and Bert travelled. I think you got your yen for adventure from her, too. She lived in Italy for a time, before moving to Austria, India, I think, and Egypt, and Greece, and then after Bert married and moved back to England, she spent several years on the island of Malta."

"So she didn't live in the house?" That must explain why none of the ghosts remember her being able to speak to them.

"According to your mother, something happened in Malta

that sent her back to Grimwood. Your mum and her parents went down to help her remodel several of the upstairs rooms, including your old bedroom. The family stayed here so that Bert could help repair the radiators. Sylvie says the whole week Elsie was jumpy, and she kept dragging the family out of the house on insane outings and playing loud doo-wop music at all hours of the night."

Probably to drive the ghosts away. It would certainly work on Edward.

Dad continues. "Unfortunately, she died before she got to move in and enjoy Grimwood. Apparently, she had a tumor that had gone unnoticed and untreated for a number of years. And there's something else, too. It was the strangest thing. I *swear* that Elsie came to the house once, when you were just a couple of years old. We'd just opened the B&B, and we were so excited to have our first guest in. When I opened the door for her, she was wearing a bright pink suit and carrying a pink suitcase, and she looked just like your great-grandmother's portrait."

I swallow. That sounds an awful lot like the Pink Woman in the dreams I've been having.

"It couldn't be her, since Elsie had been dead for at least fifteen years at that point," Dad says. "But I always wondered if—"

"The Pink Woman," a voice whispers behind me.

Dad and I whirl around. Ambrose stands at the bottom of the stairs, his fingers gripping the handle of his cane so hard that the knuckles are white.

"I didn't mean to eavesdrop," he says. "I was on my way to see about making Bree some breakfast, when I heard you mention the Pink Woman."

"How do you know about the Pink Woman, Ambrose?" Dad asks.

"I saw her in one of Bree's dreams."

Wait, he saw *her? But how can he see anything?* "Ambrose, what are you talking about?"

"I think you'd better explain yourself, lad." Dad sets the oil can down and glances in the direction of the laundry, where Mum had corralled Edward with a long list of chores. "Let's go into the guest lounge where we can talk in private."

I get up on shaking legs and go to Ambrose, looping my arm in his to help him navigate around the furniture and the piles of empty bottles and crisp packets we left behind in the guest lounge. I lead him to the sofa opposite Dad and plonk down beside him.

"What have you heard of our conversation?" I ask.

"Your father knows that you speak to ghosts," Ambrose says. "But I don't know if he understands who I am or—"

"Perhaps you'd better fill me in, Ambrose."

"Yes, well, I'll do my darnedest." Ambrose clears his throat. "But much of this story isn't mine to tell. I suppose you should know, first of all, that I *am* a traveller. Bree didn't lie about that. But I'm not from your time. I'm—"

"You're Ambrose Hulme." Dad leans back on the sofa, knitting his brow in understanding. "I saw a video on the Grimdale community page about you. You're the blind Victorian adventurer who is buried in the cemetery. But then how are you alive, flesh and blood, sitting on my ottoman?"

As quickly as I can, I explain everything. It all tumbles out in a rush, as if the words have been waiting on the end of my tongue to spill over. All my life, I've kept this secret from my parents, my family, from other kids. I thought that if they knew, they'd lock me away or have some doctor cut my head open or... or...anything except for my father's cool, delighted acceptance of my Lazarus powers.

"Ever since Bree returned to Grimdale, it's as if there's been magic in the air." Ambrose's voice rises with delight as he recounts portions of our tale. He's always been a storyteller. "We ghosts have been able to interact with the Living World, touch and manipulate objects. Sometimes, if I touch her, I see flashes of her memories. I actually see them...it's hard to explain, because I haven't seen things since I lost my sight, but I think because Bree remembers things visually and they're her memories, that's how I experience them, too. I might not have actually seen the woman, but I know that she was wearing pink. It's like a memory from when I had sight, only the memory isn't mine."

"What happened in this dream?"

"Well, in the dream, I was you, and I was on some kind of rug and she sat down beside me and was talking to me in this nice, soothing voice," Ambrose says. "I didn't think much of it at the time, but I felt like I'd met her before, although I can't remember where."

"You were at the infamous poker game?" Dad says. "Where Elsie won Grimwood from Horace Van Wimple?"

"You told me it was backgammon," I say.

"It *was* backgammon, and I was indeed there," Ambrose beams. "It was all so thrilling. We didn't like that Horace at all, so we were so pleased to see him gone, but the woman who won wasn't anything like the Pink Woman. I...I actually can't remember the woman who won at all. I can't recall her voice or her scent or anything. Isn't that odd? And you'd think that I'd be able to remember someone who could talk to ghosts. Actually, come to think of it, Pax may have said something to us that day about the Pink Woman being able to see us, but Edward and I thought he'd had his head in the liquor cabinet too long."

Dad looks confused. "Head in the...?"

"Never mind. It's a ghost thing." I was too excited by what Ambrose was saying to stop now. "I've seen her in my dreams, too. She said that she'd come a long way to find me, and she wanted to see if I had the gift she gave you. She said that it was a beautiful gift, but it's also a curse, and that she left me everything I need in her 'rose garden.' But how do I remember that if I was only a baby?"

"There was a second part to my dream, too," Ambrose says. "But it was dark and scary."

I sigh. "Of course it was. We should probably hear what it is, then."

"You were outside in the driveway, Bree, riding a red bicycle with bright silver ribbons. Mike was holding the back of the bike to keep you upright as you rode around and around the zodiac mosaic. Edward and Pax were watching you from the upstairs window, cheering you on. I wasn't there, I think I was watching a history show on the moving picture box with Sylvie.

"Mike let go of the back of your bicycle, and you're flying! You pedal as hard as you can and you ride straight out of the gate and you turn toward the graveyard. Mike, you chase her through the cemetery, and you say something like, 'Careful, Bree-bug. Don't go too fast. You'll wake up the ghosts!'"

"I remember this day," Dad says with a frown on his face.

"You pedal hard around a corner, and someone lurches at you from the shadows. A figure in a black cloak and hood. They reach for you, and Mike yells, 'Get away from her!' and you scream and fall and your head makes this awful crunch on the concrete."

"I remember this day, too." At least, parts of it. I hit my head pretty bad and the doctors said that I actually died for a couple of moments, and I would probably forget bits of the day. I remember riding my bike. I remember feeling like I was flying. I remember Dad scooping me up in his arms, and the drawn, worried expression on his face before everything went black. I remember that most vividly of all, because I'd never seen my dad worried like that before.

But I don't remember anything else Ambrose describes. I don't remember the robed figure or the accident. I don't remember Dad yelling.

This was always the day I thought I started seeing ghosts. That's what all the lore says. You have a near-death experience and suddenly you can see the dead. My whole life I thought that was the case…until Edward told me otherwise.

And now I learn that a black-robed figure was there on the day of the accident. That can't be a coincidence.

"Do you think the figure was someone from the Order?" I ask Ambrose.

"The Order?" Dad asks.

So *then* we have to break to explain to Dad about the order of crazy priests who are after me for using my powers. I tell him about Father Bryne but I leave out the bit where Ambrose accidentally kills him (much to Ambrose's obvious relief) and we bury him in Ralph Sommersby's grave.

"Did you see if the robed figure was wearing a spiky cross?" Ambrose asks Dad excitedly.

"Honestly, I was a little too busy panicking that some maniac was lurching after my daughter in a cemetery to notice the jewellery they were wearing."

Ambrose leaps to his feet, waving his stick around with such enthusiasm that he knocks over a couple of empty wine bottles. "I should tell Pax about this. And Edward, too, when he's finished with the drains. They'll want to know immediately. I can't believe they didn't see the hooded figure."

As Ambrose hurries off, his feet crunching over empty crisp packets, I settle into the sofa next to Dad, who pulls me under his arm for a hug.

"I should have known these three friends or yours were ex-ghosts," Dad says. "Pax was much too concerned with the movements of Druids to be a modern lad. And I suppose your friend helping Sylvie with the drain is actually…"

"The infamous Poet Prince Edward, who used to own this house, yes." I flush. "And I rushed out last night because I figured out the location of Edward's secret wine cellar, which was the unfinished business he needed to figure out to return to life. That's what all those empty wine bottles are about."

"I thought the labels looked hand-written, but I assumed they were some of Dani's mother's experiments." Dad glances out the window. "And I suppose this dark cloud over Grimdale has something to do with the ghosts, too? And the…er…gas leak from the Giant Vegetable Festival?"

"I don't exactly know what's happened, but there's this thing called the Veil. I think it's like a barrier that separates the Realm of the Living where we are from the Realm of the Death. I think directly on the other side of the Veil is some kind of waiting room where restless souls hang out. And some demons and Soul-Eaters and other nasty things. And there's some kind of system that decides where souls go next. We're guessing that my power means that I can reach into the Veil, which is why I can see and talk to ghosts, and sometimes bring them back. But I think that what's happened is that the Veil has thinned over Grimdale, and that means that those things can start coming out."

"How do we fix it?" Dad asks. "How do we repair the Veil?"

"I don't know. The priest, Father Maxwell, who came to the Giant Vegetable Festival, might be able to figure it out. But he was badly injured when we sent the Soul-Eater back, and I don't even know if he's conscious. Dad, I'm afraid. Everyone we love lives here. What if more things like the Soul-Eaters come back?"

"Then we get them out," Dad rubs his chin. "We convince as many people as possible to leave Grimdale. If the Soul-Eater shows up and there are no souls to eat, maybe it will go home again?"

As far as ideas go, it's better than anything that I can come up with with my hangover throbbing against my temples. "How are we going to do that?"

"Leave that to me." Dad rubs his fingers together. "I'm the leader of Grimdale's most successful pub quiz team. People may not believe the evidence of their own eyes that they're in danger, but they will believe someone in authority. Twenty minutes with the village rumour mill and I'll turn this place into a ghost town, no pun intended."

"But what about Mum? She won't leave, not with the house sale imminent and—"

"I'll take care of your mother."

"I don't think she'll fall for the 'Let's run off to Europe for a romantic getaway' again, especially since you just got back from Europe—"

"Oh, I'm not leaving with Sylvie. I'll probably have to rope your grandmother in to help me, but she owes me a favour after I repaired her water heater last year. I'll get your mother out of here by tomorrow, I promise."

"What do you mean, you'll get Mum out of here? You're going with her."

"I'm staying with you, Bree-bug." Dad squeezes my knee. His dark eyes sparkle with mischief. "I'm not going to miss the chance to help my daughter restore order to the world of the dead."

7

BREE

Dad is true to his word. The next morning, my grandmother calls with a clutter emergency, and Mum throws clothing and industrial cleaning products into her suitcases, writes us a to-do list the length of the Magna Carta, and rushes off up north to her rescue. Dad winks at me as we wave her off.

Maggie comes over to deliver a casserole for Dad, the 'poor, lonely bachelor,' and Dad casually mentions that Sylvie has decided to leave Grimdale because of her fears about the gas leak. He says that he overheard some government officials in black suits wandering around the village, frowning at each other and speaking into their phones about 'adverse health effects' and 'the cover-up.'

Maggie rushes out of Grimwood without even leaving reheating instructions for the casserole.

Two hours later, Maggie has gotten to everyone in the village. People are complaining of nausea and hallucinations. There's a steady stream of cars heading out of Grimdale, creating a traffic jam on the dual-carriageway for the first time in living memory.

Not everyone leaves, of course. But enough do. Enough that if a Danse Macabre begins on the village green, we won't have enough people left for a decent conga line.

Which is just as well, since the black cloud is now creeping toward the duck pond. Even the ducks have gone into hiding. Don't ever let anyone say that ducks are stupid.

Dad comes home after waving his pub quiz team goodbye at the train station. "Okay, Bree-bug, I've cleared out the village as best I can. The rest is up to you."

I wrap my arms around him. "Thank you, Dad. Thank you for believing in me, and for making this happen and keeping people safe. I promise I won't let you down."

"I never doubted you. So you have a plan?"

"Not even remotely, but I know where I can get one."

8

BREE

"Hello?" Father Maxwell taps the microphone attached to his headphones. "Can you hear me?"

"Yes. Can *you* hear *me*?"

The priest's face screws up in concern. He taps his screen. "Hello, Bree, are you there?"

"I'm here, Father. Have you got your volume on? Can you hear me now?"

"This reminds me of a seance I attended once," Ambrose says excitedly. "Everyone was yelling 'Can you hear me?' to the ghost of an old sea captain."

"The priest is on the moving picture box!" Pax booms.

"Ah, yes, I am." Father Maxwell sighs with relief. "There you are. Hello Pax, Bree, Ambrose. And I'm guessing the moody fellow in the corner is a recently resurrected Edward. I can hear you all now."

Father Maxwell leans back in his chair and steeples his fingers. He doesn't look as awful as he did when Björn dragged him out of Grimdale after we banished that Soul-Eater, but that's a low bar.

I'm happy that he's back with us again, but his eyes are swollen and haunted. He looks as if he can barely remain upright. But we can't wait for answers for Father Maxwell to be fighting fit again. Grimdale is in danger *now*.

"Hello again, Father. We have a problem." I turn the camera to the window, showing the grim cloud of darkness that hangs over the village.

He winces. "I'm so sorry, Bree. I'm afraid that I've brought evil to your doorstep in more ways than one. But I didn't know what else to do."

"You helped me when I needed it, and I'm happy to help you in return. But I need to know the truth. All of it. What exactly happened on the day of the Giant Vegetable Festival? How the hell were you being chased by a Soul-Eater in the first place?"

Father Maxwell sighs.

"It's as I told you, this demon has been closing in on me. When we Lazarii perform our resurrection magic, we reach through the Veil. Unlike when we help souls cross over, when we bring someone back who is supposed to make their journey to the Veil, we cause damage. The more we do it, the more it weakens the Veil — the barrier around us that separates the Living Realm from that of the Dead. And demons and monsters and corrupted souls...they sense these weak points. Sometimes, they can escape through them into the Living Realm. This is perhaps one reason the Order of the Noble Death seeks to control our magic. They don't want to risk having demons unleashed upon the earth."

I think about Jack the Ripper. "Except the ones they control."

"Precisely." He shakes his head. "Although not even the Order would risk raising a demon such as the Soul-Eater. This is all my fault. I could feel the Veil weakening around me, and I promised myself that I wouldn't touch my resurrection magic again. But a teenage boy brought his little sister to see me. She was dying of leukaemia. A *six-year-old* girl was dying, and I had the power to heal her. How could I refuse?"

How could he refuse? How could anyone refuse?

Cold panic seizes my chest as I realise exactly what having these powers means.

My whole life, I'll be confronted by impossible choices. If I'd known that bringing back the ghosts would bring monsters like the Soul-Eater to Earth and put the village and my family and friends and poor Harriet in danger, would I have done it? I don't think so, but I can't fault Father Maxwell for his decisions.

What would I do for the people I love?

I haven't been faced with that impossible choice...yet.

But I know the answer is...*everything*.

"Do you mean," I say slowly, making sure that I understand, "that every time I use my resurrection power I'm potentially attracting these demons? You don't think this was something you should have told me at the beginning?"

"Yes, I should have. But I am only a man, Bree, and I am so, so fallible. I have been in denial. For so long, I've known the Veil was weak. I've felt the Soul-Eater turn its gaze to me, sensed him closing in on me every time I brought someone back. But I've had years of helping my parishioners, and it's never been able to break through the Veil before. I thought I had time. I thought that if I kept searching, I'd find the answers in my books and stop this horror before it escaped. I was wrong, and you and your poor village paid the price for it."

"I still don't understand why Grimdale looks like a scene from a Salvador Dali painting?"

In response, Father Maxwell jerks his screen around, showing off the view out his window. I squint at the screen, making the shapes resolve themselves. Outside the church, the sky is the same dark gloom as here. Thunder rumbles from within the ominous cloud, and a moment later, lightning forks across the sky, sending a tree crashing to the ground.

Father Maxwell turns the camera back to his face.

"The Veil is now thinning in multiple places," he says. "It's been like this for several days over All Souls, and it's how the Soul-Eater got through and came after me. But I didn't know it could thin in different places at once. And it's getting worse, which means that any creature of the Veil might try to use this thinning to leap into our world, as the Soul-Eater did."

"And Jack the Ripper? He showed up on the night of the festival and tried to kill me and Edward."

Father Maxwell's face twists in pain. "I'm sorry I wasn't there to help. But if you're talking to me now, you must have triumphed against him."

"We banished him again, but I don't know how many times we can do that. I'm pretty new at this whole witchcraft thing. He killed an innocent woman before he trapped us in a cellar, and our senior witch ghost, Agnes, invaded his body, so when we sent him back beyond the Veil, he took her with him."

"And he didn't try to kill us," Edward says sullenly from behind me. "He tried to kill *me*, which I think is horribly unfair since at that point I'd been Living for all of seventeen minutes. He said that he intended to use Brianna for her 'true purpose'."

Ah, so Edward noticed that, too.

"Any idea what my true purpose might be?" I ask Father Maxwell. "I thought it was to travel the world, talk to ghosts, and drink all the coffee. But apparently, I've been mistaken."

The priest rubs his weary face. "From what little I've been able to gather from my sources, no one knows why we exist. Scripture tells us that Jesus said that he was the resurrection and the life, and he raised up Lazarus to prove this to his disciples. So from a purely Biblical perspective, we are here to glorify God."

I fold my arms. "I don't buy that, and from the way you're talking, neither do you."

Father Maxwell shakes his head. "There are accounts of Lazarii far older than the Bible, and many who are born with our gift are from different religions and cultures. Most often, we are depicted as psychopomps."

"Psycho-what?"

"Psychopomps are benevolent figures who guide the spirits of the deceased into the afterlife. However, they don't generally have any control over how or when a person dies. In Ancient Egyptian art, we are shown as servants of the jackal god Anubis, guiding souls to the afterlife where their hearts will be weighed against the feather of truth. There are the *shinigami* in Japanese mythology and the winged Vanth in ancient Etruscan art. This idea is supported in Saint Ekaterina's writings. She defines her purpose as a guardian of death. She believed that death is but one stepping stone upon a sacred pathway that each human soul must walk, and it was her job to ensure that souls passing over took their next steps along the pathway. Death is a vital part of the human experience – both the event itself, but also, the knowledge of it. Without death, humans would never have to face the limits of our abilities or the consequences of our actions. We would not value our loved ones, or our achievements, or the sanctity of our own souls, because we would never have to face the reality of losing them."

"I disagree," Edward says. "As a libertine, I've been terrified of death and yet still I worked hard to sully the sanctity of my soul."

"Of course, you may do what you wish with your own soul, Edward. That is the free will that we have been gifted. But even you acknowledge that death was supposed to be the end of life, the next step upon the pathway. But there are many humans, and many beasts and creatures, who wish to skip over death and upset the order of things. They wish to deviate from the pathway, and Ekaterina saw it as her job to ensure that every mortal soul stayed on the righteous path."

"But we can manipulate death." I gesture to Edward, Pax, and Ambrose. "I brought them back, and they never walked the pathway. And you saved all those people..."

Father Maxwell nods. "I suppose that as beings with one foot on the pathway, we must have some power over death – although not as much as the deities who control it, if you believe in that sort of thing. But that's only one theory. Other scholars believed a Lazarus is cursed, and those that say we are—"

"So basically, you have no idea?" I lift an eyebrow in what I'm coming to recognise is a very Edward-esque manner.

"None in the slightest. All I know for certain is that Lazarii can see and manipulate the soul-cords of humans, that we can help lost souls cross over, that our own soul-cords are black, instead of silver, and that if we use our magic too much, we create these holes in the Veil, and that we often ourselves die in mysterious ways. St. Ekaterina, for example, disappeared from the cell in her nunnery in the middle of the night and was never seen again."

I glance down at my chest. I can see the soul-cords of the

ghosts sticking out from my chest – those winding silver strings tinged with blue. Blue must be for a resurrected soul because the colour only appeared after I brought the ghosts back to life. But I cannot see my own cord. Come to think of it, I've never been able to see it.

Black cords...

I remember the cords that rose from the Order's cross pins when Father Maxwell and I pulled the Soul-Eater into the demon mark. He must see in my eyes that I recognise it, for he says, "When a new Lazarus joins the Order of the Noble Death, they bind their soul to the Order's mission. Even if their body dies, a piece of their soul is still connected to those amulets. It's what makes the Order so powerful, and so dangerous."

"So when you told me to snap the cords, I *killed*—"

"No. You didn't kill them. Remember, the owners of those crosses died by Björn's sword a long time ago. But their souls have been held in limbo by the Order, held back from walking the pathway so that they might serve the Order's purpose. I don't know for certain, but I think that their souls make it to the other side of the Veil, but they can be controlled by the high priests on this side. When we severed that control, their souls went back to their home beyond the Veil, finally at rest, and that force drew the monster back with them."

Even in death, the Order controls their priests from the other side of the Veil? But why? "What is the Order trying to do on the other side of the Veil?"

He shrugs. "They've never exactly been forthright with me about their plans. The only way to find out would be to walk the pathway to the other side of the Veil, but that's generally considered a one-way trip. Whatever the Order is doing there, I believe it's why they are so desperate to get to us. They want to put our souls to work for them."

This is so complicated. I can't even begin to comprehend the scale of what he's telling me. The Order isn't just after my life, they want my soul, too?

And what about Jack the Ripper? He must know something of the Order's plans from when he was controlled by them. That's why he talked about my 'true purpose'?

Why does a Victorian serial killer know more about my soul than I do?

I curl my fingers into a fist, longing to slam it into the wall or the computer or the Ripper's stupid face. Why can't I get any answers? Why does this have to be so big and scary and dangerous?

"I won't use my resurrection powers anymore," I say. "I don't care that I made a deal with Abberline and the three witches. From now on, I'll let the Grim Reaper claim whomever he wants. And you can't use it anymore, either."

"I will try." Father Maxwell blinks. "But that's the problem. Every time I swear it will be the last. You will find your own reasons for using your power, Bree. That is the curse of a Lazarus. It won't be long until the demons come for you."

I rub my temples. "We're getting nowhere. I'd like to know how we can *stop* the Veil from weakening and put everything back the way it was, thanks."

"I'm afraid I don't know." Father Maxwell pats the stack of books on his desk. "I've been searching, but everything I've found seems to say that the only being in the universe capable of fixing the Veil is the Lord of Death."

"And who's he when he's at home?"

"Again, there are numerous different depictions throughout history, but we're most familiar with him as the Grim Reaper – scythe and black cloak and crown of bones and all that jazz."

I slump my chin on the desk. "Great."

"I'll keep looking," he says. "I have my books. I have Saint Ekaterina's writings. I will find *something* that will help us to strengthen the Veil so that this cannot happen again—what's that?"

He looks up at something offscreen, and that's when I hear a faint noise. It's in the background, and I might've mistaken it for someone having music playing in the next room if I didn't know that Father Maxwell was all alone in a church with his pet Viking.

"Father, talk to me. Is that Björn?"

But he's still looking in the direction of the noise. It almost sounds like...chanting.

Latin chanting.

"Father? Are you having a clergy slumber party? We should have got an invite. I love playing "Light As A Feather, Stiff As A Board...""

He places his finger on his lips, then gets up from his desk and disappears from view. I lean forward, my fingers digging into my thigh.

"What's going on?" Ambrose whispers. "Who's chanting?"

"I don't know, but Father Maxwell has left to investigate—"

The words catch on my breath as a dark shadow moves across the window. Another dark shape appears, and another. The graveyard outside swarms with them.

Pax grabs the screen, angling it towards him. "What are those enemies? Are they Druids who have dyed their cloaks black? Where is Björn to rend their flesh with his axe—"

Father Maxwell cries out.

I muffle my scream with my hands as two shapes fly past the screen. There are sounds of fighting, and a sickening *CRACK*, and Father Maxwell whimpers.

"What's happening?" Ambrose asks. "Bree?"

I can just make out the edge of a black robe fluttering on screen. A deep voice booms, "I bring you a message, blasphemous priest. All-Souls Church is to be Re-Sanctified by the

Order of the Noble Death. Kneel before God and confess your sins, Father Maxwell, or face his wrath."

Father Maxwell says something that I can't make out, but his words break off into a scream that's abruptly cut short.

Something wet and dark splatters across the screen.

Then a white hand reaches out, and the entire screen goes black.

9

PAX

"I can't believe I'm doing this. Grimdale is being invaded by demons from beyond the Veil, and we're going down to the city for a shopping trip." Alice swerves around a black motorised horseless chariot blocking two lanes. "Watch where you're going, you wanker! I've got a bumper and I'm not afraid to use it!"

"Alice, my darling, are you sure you don't want me to drive?" Dani grips the windowsill.

"Are you implying that I'm no good at driving in London? Because I'll be perfectly fine if these jizzbiscuits would stop getting in my way!" Alice lays on the war horn and leans out the window to throw a rude gesture at an old lady whom she just cut off.

She would make an excellent chariot racer.

"Curse his parents to be turned into goats, and that his sister becomes ugly and unmarriageable," I offer. I am very good at cursing. I got an award for it at Centurion Scouts.

"He's gone, Pax." Beside me, Bree looks a little queasy.

We are back in London, which is much larger and noisier than it was when I first came here, back when it was still called

Londinium. It smells worse, too, and that's saying a lot since only richer Romans could afford indoor plumbing so most residents used to throw their faeces into the streets. Bree says that normally we'd take the train because only the mad drive in London, but we need to get to All Souls quickly, and Alice is the only one who has a motorised horseless chariot, aka a car.

Technically, it's not her horseless chariot—er, it's not her *car*. It belongs to the museum and it's an enormous beast of a thing with an entire small Roman villa fitted on the back that's filled with seats that fold down. According to Alice, the museum uses it to transport artefacts and run small group tours of Roman sites around Grimdale. This seems insane, since in the hands of the right general, my soldiers and I could have conquered an entire country with one of these. I call it the most remarkable siege engine I've ever seen.

Mike calls it a 'transit van.' Bree calls it a 'death trap.'

I don't know what everyone's complaining about. This is fun. It's like a chariot race! I hope there is a laurel wreath at the end for the winners, because it looks like we're going to win. We're certainly passing all the other cars on the road.

"The church is just up ahead," I say for the benefit of the rest of the passengers, since I'm currently the only one with my eyes still open. Bree grips my knee so hard that her knuckles are turning white.

"Do you mean, directly beneath that ominous black cloud? Why, I'm shocked," Dani says as she prises her eyelids open.

She's right. Up ahead, the skyline is smudged by a dark cloud. Unease trickles down my spine. I reach for the reassuring weight of my sword's hilt.

There is no need to panic. Björn is there. He is a mighty warrior, and his war gods will protect him and the priest.

But still, I worry.

"Great, there's no parking." Alice stomps on the brakes. The sleek black car behind us performs some impressive manoeuvring to avoid running up our backside. "I'm not moving for that damn Tesla. You lot, get out, I'll circle the block."

I have never seen two ex-ghosts and one Dani exit a car so fast. Bree is a little slower, but only because her legs don't seem to work properly. The moment my sandals hit the footpath, Alice takes off, throwing me onto the grass. Bree helps me up.

I dust myself up and straighten my scabbard. "If she were a Roman chariot racer, she would have many statues built to honour her skill."

"But we are not in Rome," Edward sulks. "And she is *terrifying*."

Even though the goddess Sol is high in the skies, it's so grim and gloomy that when I wiggle my fingers in front of my face, I can barely see them. We fumble about, making sure that all of us are here and have all our limbs attached.

"Which way to the church?" Dani asks.

"Follow me." I draw my sword. Bree holds my other wrist and links arms with Ambrose, who holds Edward, and poor Dani is forced to endure the full brunt of the prince's whining at the end of our merry line. I shuffle my feet along the path, remembering each step that I trod with my friend Björn last time we visited.

I train my senses on the world around me, listening for the sounds of enemies rustling in the graveyard. The thick, metallic scent of death wafts across my nostrils. Rising from the gloom, I can make out the shapes of the gravestones and...and other shapes.

Bodies cloaked in black robes lay slumped where they fell upon the battlefield.

Björn has triumphed.

But then why hasn't he come out to meet us?

Unease settles on me as I make my way slowly towards the

church. The doors yawn open, a great, blackened maw like the mouth of a beast ready to swallow us whole. I reach out with my sword hand and touch the wood, wishing to reassure myself that it is solid and real. My fingers brush something sticky. I raise them to my nose and sniff.

Blood. They're covered in fresh blood.

"I don't like this," Bree whispers, her fingers digging into my skin.

"Björn? Father Maxwell?" I boom as I drag Bree and the others into the church. My voice echoes off the rafters high above. I cannot see a thing except for two pale spots glowing in the distance – the candles lit on either end of the altar.

"Maybe we shouldn't be so loud," Bree whimpers as we move down the aisle toward the altar.

"Anything lurking in the shadows already knows we're here, and besides, a Roman doesn't skulk in the shadows like a coward. He announces himself so his enemies can come out and face him."

"Or, at least, his smell announces him," Edward mutters from the back.

We move between the rows of pews. I see more dark shapes strewn between the wooden benches. My heart squeezes in my chest as I check that each one wears the distinct black cloak of the Order. If one of the bodies belongs to Björn, I'll channel my inner Nero and start burning shit down.

My sandal scuffs a stone step. We reached the altar. Bree scrabbles in her pocket. She pulls out her magic rectangle and turns on the light.

The beam joins the candles still burning at the altar. The gloom sends to bend away from the light, revealing the width of the altar and beyond it, the carved figure of the Christian son of god nailed to his cross, his mouth open in a silent, hideous scream...

Wait a second...

That's no statue!

Beside me, Bree drops her magic rectangle. "No. please no..."

"Is that..." Dani's voice wobbles.

I rush forward, but I'm too late. Father Maxwell's body has gone cold. His hands have been nailed through, pinning him to the wooden cross. But it is the blow to his head that did him in.

As I yank out the barbs in his skin, I realise they are not nails at all, but the spiky crosses worn by members of the Order of the Noble Death. I gather the priest in my arms and kiss him lightly on his bloodstained forehead. His body feels so light in my arms. He will be honoured by his god for all the good things he did.

Crucifixion is a lot more fun when it happens to your enemies, instead of your friends.

Bree is crying softly. Edward's low voice describes the grisly scene for Ambrose as I lay the priest atop his altar. It's only then that I see the message scrawled on the stone in what looks suspiciously like blood.

A message that turns my red-blooded Roman heart to ice.

BREE MORTIMER, STAY AWAY FROM THE CROWN.

IO

BREE

This can't be happening.

The Order of the Noble Death *killed* Father Maxwell. They found a way through his wards and came inside and strung him up like one of his own saints.

They placed their crosses through his hands and feet. They took away his soul so that I cannot reach it.

They hurt him so badly that he bit through his own tongue from the pain.

Father Maxwell was a good man. He tried to use his powers for good, and he wasn't perfect, but he didn't deserve *this*.

He was our only chance.

He'd already given us so many answers. I now knew that the black cords twirling from those crosses were the souls of the Order's Lazarii who were on the other side of the Veil. *One, two, three, four.* I reached out and snapped all of the cords.

The Order has already taken Father Maxwell's life. They're not going to have his soul, too.

Bile rises in my throat, and I have to turn away from the altar. The message scrawled on the stone blinks in front of my closed eyelids.

BREE MORTIMER, STAY AWAY FROM THE CROWN.

It's a warning. A promise of what will happen to me and my loved ones if I don't comply.

If only I had any idea what it meant.

Stay away from the crown...

"Do you think..." Edward's voice wobbles as he comes to stand beside me. "Do they mean that you must stay away from me?"

My eyes fly open. In the gloom, I can just make out the outline of Edward's regal features. He holds his head high, with that haughty tilt of his nose that tells the whole world they should bow at his feet. But I've known this man all of my life. I can tell when he is upset.

I rest my head on Edward's chest, listening to his heart racing through his ribcage. He's alive, and he's a royal prince, and days ago, his chest was filled with only dead stars and broken dreams. He loops his fingers in mine and squeezes.

"I don't think they're referring to you," I say, holding him tight because his arms feel like home to me – the only place left in the world that's safe and secure. "You never technically wore a crown, did you?"

"Before my father disowned me, I sometimes wore one at royal functions." Edward lifts his regal chin, his anthracite eyes glinting off the flickering candlelight. "It was frightfully heavy and smushed down my hair in a most unflattering way. It did, however, bring all the countesses to the yard—"

"Yes, thank you for that insight into your princely sex life in the form of an early 2000s hip-hop song. I think if the Order wanted me to stay away from you, they wouldn't be so cryptic. Or are they being cryptic? Whatever this crown is, they must assume that I know about it."

What does it mean? What crown? Why did Father Maxwell have to die so they could keep me away from it?

A fresh wave of sorrow engulfs my body, and I cling to Edward as the grief bubbles over and leaks from my eyes. Father Maxwell was the only person I've ever known who has the same powers. Well, I knew Vera, but I didn't know she was like me until she died. And Quoth may be able to see ghosts, but he's not a Lazarus. Father Maxwell was able to answer the questions that had made me weak and afraid, and in turn, a little of his bravery rubbed off on me.

He made me feel as though I was...not *normal*, exactly, but *wanted*. He made me believe I was part of something bigger than myself, and that I carried within me a capacity to be so much more than just Bree the freak who talks to ghosts.

My tears splatter on Edward's shirt, and he strokes my hair with his long, soft fingers, and whispers, "I have read a thousand poems about grief, each one eloquent and profound, and yet not one can capture the raw beauty of a tear shed for someone you love. I am so sorry, Brianna."

I sniff. "You have nothing to be sorry for. And I'm—"

I cut off my words with a gasp as I hear footsteps scurrying through the nave.

Pax leaps up and draws his sword. "Who goes there? Don't come any closer or I'll gut you and place your intestines between your ass cheeks to make a delicious sandwich—"

"Whoa, easy, big guy." Alice's voice rises through the gloom. "It's just me. I found a parking space and ran in here. You should see the massacre outside. Creepy cultists strewn everywhere. But where's the—holy *shit*."

"You probably shouldn't say that in a house of God," Ambrose warns.

"Fucking cuntwipes," Alice curses, and then I hear a retching sound as she throws up all her road trip snacks.

So she's seen Father Maxwell.

"Well, as fun as this party is," Edward drawls as he tries to move me towards the exit, "I think I'd like to go somewhere slightly less depressing and filled with dead creeps. If anyone wants me, I'll be at the pub, and—"

BANG.

The door to the sacristy flies open, slamming into the wall.

I scream.

Pax leaps forward, sword drawn. "Show yourself and fight me like a real Roman."

"Only if you fight me like a true Viking," a familiar voice booms. "And we shall both drink mead together in Valhalla."

"Björn, I'm so happy to see you!" I cry.

The Viking drops the heavy black object he's carrying and runs to Pax. They embrace, and then Björn snatches me from Edward's arms to crush me against his chest. He smells of blood and honey.

"I'm so pleased you are alive, friend of Father Maxwell." Björn releases me and inclines his head to Pax. "And you, my brother."

"Björn, what happened? We were talking to Father Maxwell when..."

"The priest has gone to Valhalla." Björn crosses to the altar. Lovingly, he bends to one knee and places a kiss on the priest's bloodied forehead. He prays over the priest, calling down the vengeance of his warrior gods.

Fresh tears roll down my cheeks.

Björn gets to his feet and slides his sword back into his scabbard. When he turns to speak to me, he is a warrior once more. "The Order of the Noble Death swarmed the church. With the Veil weakened, it must also weaken the wards that protect this place. Or they simply overpowered them with sheer numbers. I have never seen so many of them, never knew their number was so great. They broke their ranks against our wards until the magic could no longer protect us. I killed as many as I could, but while I was overrun, they broke through and went for Father Maxwell…"

Björn nods down at the corpse splayed across the altar.

"We must give him the funeral rites," Björn says.

"A warrior's funeral," Pax agrees.

"But first, we have another battlefield task to attend to."

I brace myself for some grisly tradition. I remember that Pax once told me his general had him and his men cut off one hand from each of the dead so they could tally the day's efforts. Vikings have got to be worse…

Luckily, Björn doesn't take out his sword. He drags over the heavy object he'd been carrying and props it up against the altar.

I scramble on the ground for my phone. When I find it, I point the torch at the object. I gasp as I realize it's a woman in a black robe. She wears the pointed cross of the Order of the Noble Death. She's breathing shallowly and dried blood cakes the side of her face from a shallow wound above her temple. Her black-tinted soul-cord stretches from her chest, whirling around her at insane speed as the final threads of her life unravel.

Björn slaps her face roughly. "Wake up!"

The woman coughs. Her eyes flicker open, wide with fear. Pax kneels on the other side of her and places the blade of his sword at her throat.

"Pax," I warn. I don't want to watch him hurt her.

The woman's eyes narrow on me. "Bree Mortimer."

She says my name like it's a curse.

I remember that this woman helped kill Father Maxwell, and despite the grief weighing my veins, I find a smile for her.

It's a smile that promises vengeance. "Yeah, yeah, you're coming for me. I got your note."

Björn kicks her with his leather boot. "She is yours. A gift from the battlefield for my friends."

"Oooh, goody." Pax grins as he presses his knife harder against her throat. "Which punishment shall we inflict upon her? We could go for the classic crucifixion, handy since we have a cross right here. Or we could send her to fight to the death in a gladiator ring, or sew her inside a sack along with a dog, a rooster, a snake, and a monkey, and throw the sack into the Thames."

Björn rubs his hands together gleefully. "Or we could try a traditional Viking punishment, the blood eagle, where we separate her ribs from her spine, pull them outward to form wings, and remove her lungs from her chest."

"Blood eagle, you say?" Pax's voice rises with excitement. "I'm interested."

"Wait." I throw myself in front of them before they can detail any more horrific tortures. "We can't kill her yet. She might be the only person who can give us some answers. We're going to try and talk to her first."

"And *then* I can feed her to a lion?" Pax's face lights up.

"The only lions around here are at the London Zoo," Dani says.

"Don't give him ideas." I turn back to the woman. "Here's the deal. I've got a thinning Veil and monsters coming after me and until a few months ago, I thought I was the only one in the world who could talk to ghosts. I have no fucking idea what I'm doing, so can you help a girl out and tell me what the fuck the Order is up to and what this stupid crown is?"

She spits at me. "Why should I tell you anything?"

"Because I've got a Roman centurion holding a knife to your

throat, and one word from me and he'll gut you like a haddock on fish and chips night."

"I'm not afraid to die for my God." She juts her chin proudly.

"Fine, but are you willing to come back for him?" I raise my hands. "Do you forget what I am? I have the same powers you do, only I don't have some pesky Order telling me how I can use them. I can make sure you don't cross over, but walk the earth as a ghost for the rest of your days."

I have no idea if I can actually do what I described, but this priestess doesn't need to know that. The shudder that runs through her body tells me that I hit my mark.

Her eyes narrow as she scrutinises me. "What did you do to Father Bryne? He hasn't reported back to us in several days."

"He made me an offer, and I refused. He took it badly, and ended up in an argument with the business end of a rifle."

"It was an accident," Ambrose says defensively from behind me.

"You never should have refused Father Bryne," she chokes out. "It's been centuries since one of our own wore the crown. With you, we could have done great things. We could have transformed death. You should have been the shining star of the Order, a beacon of hope against the darkness of the Veil. Instead, you refused us. Now, we cannot allow you to live, not when you threaten everything..."

"*I* threaten everything?" I scoff. "I'm not the one strutting around with my little club, raising serial killers from the dead who kill innocent people."

"Nonsense. The Ripper will only kill a Lazarus. We command him..." she trails off as she realizes her mistake. "If you killed Father Bryne, then the Ripper is no longer under his control."

"I thought you would have known that."

"We thought he'd done his duty. We thought the last of the

original bloodline was wiped out..." she shoots back. "And now, thanks to you, war has come to the Veil."

"War?"

"You think you have killed them?" she roars, her eyes bugging out as she casts around at the corpses of her Order buddies. "You have done them a favour. They each longed for their chance at the crown. Once we're rid of you..."

"What's she talking about?" I look over at Björn, but he looks as confused as I am.

"The throne sits empty. It will be ours! You will not take it from us."

"What throne? What are you talking about? Just tell us how to repair the Veil!" I shake her.

She rolls her head to the side, biting at her collar. I have no idea what she's trying to do, but then her eyes suddenly roll back in her head. She lets out a little choking noise and goes stiff in Björn's arms. Her head collapses against Pax's knife, drawing a few droplets of blood before he yanks it away.

Pax shakes her roughly. "Don't play games. What sorcery is this!"

I grab her wrist and feel for a pulse, but there is none.

"No. You can't get away that easily."

Somewhere in the back of my mind, I know that I shouldn't do this, but we're already up to our ears in monsters, so a little more magic can't make things worse, can it?

The Order just killed the only man who might have been able to help us, so I think it's only fair I get my pound of flesh from them.

I call up my powers and search for her cord. The room transforms as the cords become visible — Pax and Edward and Ambrose, shimmering bright blue, Dani and Alice with their silver threads, and faint black cords of the members of the

Order of the Noble Death as their last vestiges of life slip from their slain bodies.

I focus on the priestess as her cord unspools from her body, but it's odd, different. My fingers catch on it, but I almost drop it again. It *feels* wrong – coarse and barbed. It hurts my fingers to hold onto it, but I need answers, so I grit my teeth against the pain, and yank.

A memory assaults me.

I'm the priestess now, only I'm younger – an acolyte. The Order of the Noble Death found me after my college boyfriend choked on a dildo during rush week and I accidentally brought him back to life. They offered me a full-ride scholarship if I joined them. So now, here I am, on my very first mission. I'm ready to prove myself.

It is not going well.

The demon we're trying to contain broke free of its demon mark. It tears into my fellow priest – an older man named Damien with greying hair and kind eyes – and rips out his intestines before the bishop steps in and sends it back beyond the Veil.

I run to Damien, my fingers grabbing for his cord, ready to reel him back to us before he begins to walk the pathway, but the bishop wraps his bony fingers around my wrist, staying my hand.

"But I can bring him back!"

The bishop shakes his head sadly as he plucks the cross from Damien's chest, shoving it deep into his pocket. The end of the black cord flicks through the air before disappearing.

"Damien does not wish to come back. He begins his true work now. Our sacred duty is as walkers between two worlds, Ada. First, we must exist in the world of the living, where we learn the beauty and the sorrow of death. Only once we die does the pathway open for us to the world of the dead, where we take up our rightful role as the guides of souls. Once we pass through a doorway, we cannot return, but but we are always connected to the Order." He taps his Lazarus cross. "We can reach Damien on the other side of the Veil if we need to. He will keep us apprised of what is going on, of what the Lord of Death is doing, and when we will have a chance to seize the crown. And in return, we—"

The memory wobbles and the priest's face melts away into a black blob. My ears ring with a loud, horrible buzzing.

Something's wrong. This isn't right.

I think she is using some kind of magical protection against me.

I cry out as the cord snags on my palm, and I pull *hard*.

There's a POP from somewhere in the universe. All Souls trembles on its foundations, the nave groaning above us.

"Oh dear," Ambrose says. "This is a bit of a pickle."

As one, every dead Order member's body jerks and sits up stiffly, like their shoulders are being yanked by invisible strings.

"Uh, Brianna..." Edward says. "Perhaps you could inform us mere mortals what's going on?"

"I would if I knew myself." I move behind Pax, who has his sword drawn but looks around anxiously, not sure where he's supposed to stab first.

The Order priests all open their mouths at once. My heart freezes in my throat. This is a different kind of magic – not the resurrection magic that a Lazarus has in the Living Realm, but something much darker. Something from beyond the Veil.

As one, they speak.

"The throne lies empty. Long live the Lord of Death."

Their mouths hang open, and they let out a *whoosh* of air that sounds like a sigh.

The priestess's cord slips from my fingers.

They all drop again, dead and silent and still.

"What. The. Fuck?" Alice gasps.

"My thoughts exactly," Ambrose agrees.

Dani snaps her fingers. "Okay, I don't know about puppet priests, but I *do* know about dead bodies, so let me see what's what here. Pax, get Bree away from that priestess. Be careful. Don't touch her saliva." As Pax lifts me away from the altar, Dani bends to examine the collar of the priestess' cloak. "I bet she had a cyanide capsule sewn in there. I read about spies doing that in case they're captured and don't have their hands free – they bite down on the fabric and BOOM, it's light's out and hello to the reaper."

Shit. This is what the Order does to their own priests? Forces them to commit suicide?

I think about the strange way Ada's cord felt in my fingers, and how I was pulled from her memory. They are using powerful magic to make sure someone like me can't see what they're doing.

"What do we do with her?" Pax asks Dani, obviously upset that his lion plans have been thwarted. "And the rest of them? I know! We pile them into a grisly effigy on the front lawn of Grimwood so that everyone knows not to mess with Bree. Do you think that's a good idea?"

Dani throws up her hands. "Why do you think I'd know?"

"You're the undertaker," Alice points out gently.

Dani rubs her temple and glares at me. "Bloody hell, why is it always up to me to bury the bodies?"

In the end, we bury the bodies.

We dig a grave in the cemetery behind All Souls and bury Father Maxwell. Björn places his sword in Father Maxwell's stiff hands. He pricks his finger and draws a rune on the priest's head in his blood.

"You were a true son of Odin," he whispers.

A single tear falls from his eye, splashing against the priest's still lips.

Pax pours a libation of communion wine and says his prayers to Mars, the god of war. He places a coin in the priest's mouth (nicked from the collection plate, but I don't think Father Maxwell's god will care), and I toss in a dog-eared, well-loved Bible I found in the back of a pew.

Pax and Björn fill in the hole while Edward recites his most famous poem, the one that Hugh stole from him. Ambrose sings a solemn hymn. He has a lovely singing voice. I lean in close and rest my head on his shoulder.

I want to cry. Father Maxwell deserves my tears. But the grief is too new, too raw. I'm still looking around our group, waiting for the kindly priest to show up and offer us a slice of chocolate log. But he's gone.

I think about what he said to me, that we Larazii might be psychopomps – guiding newly dead souls along the pathway through the Veil. Does this mean that another Lazarus will greet Father Maxwell, or does it mean that he must walk alone?

I kneel beside his grave, touching my hand to the cold earth. "I'm so sorry, Father. I wish I was walking with you right now. I wish I could be your guide."

In Ada's memory, the bishop said that a Lazarus is born on earth so that they can learn the sorrow and beauty of death. But I see no beauty in this...this *ending*. This cold earth and this life unfinished. Rage burns hot against my heart, making my chest feel as though my skin were peeling away, exposing my raw organs to the gloom.

"What about the bodies of the Order members?" Dani asks Björn. "We can't just leave them lying around. If the police find the bodies, being a centuries-old, badass Viking won't stop you going to jail."

"He could claim self-defence?" Ambrose pipes up.

"Do not you fear about the bodies," Björn pats his chest. "I shall take care of them in the way of the Vikings, by stripping the corpses of any valuables and using their blood to make a delicious cocktail—"

"Yup, definitely shouldn't have asked," Dani winces. Alice moves behind her, their fingers intertwined.

"I must show you something," Björn says when the last shovel of dirt has been placed on the grave.

He leads us back to the church. My stomach churns as we feel our way back through that gloom-filled nave, tripping over the fallen bodies of the priests of the Order of the Noble Death. I shudder to think that they might be the ones guiding Father Maxwell.

I wish I could find out what was going on beyond the Veil, and what the Order members there were watching out for, but I don't like Father Maxwell's path to getting answers.

Björn's head hangs as he enters Father Maxwell's little office behind the sacristy. He picks up an object from the desk and clutches it against his heart, smearing bloody fingerprints across the leather. "By the time I reached the sacristy and Father Maxwell's office, he had already been slain. The Order was ransacking his books. Those who got away took many precious tomes with them, but they did not get this."

Björn places the familiar dusty volume in my hands.

Ekaterina's gospel.

"Thank you," I breathe, knowing the risks he'd taken to get the book to me.

"Father Maxwell seemed to believe the answers lie in that book." Björn closes my fingers over the book and presses it into my chest, as if I might feel his heartbeat between the leaves. "I hope that you will find them."

"Björn, what will you do now? I mean, after you've enjoyed your blood cocktail."

"I shall continue Father Maxwell's work, of course." Björn cracks his knuckles. "The parishioners need me. Odin's blessings upon you, Bree Mortimer. If you need me, I will come."

The last thing I see as we pile into the van is the faint outline of a Viking bending on one knee and bowing his head to us.

"Well, fuck," Dani says as she slumps into the passenger seat of the van. "We came here for answers, and all we got was a dead friend and a creepy warning from a bunch of priestly meat puppets."

"We're not completely empty-handed." Alice takes the book from my lap. "We did get this giant tome of knowledge that's written in an obscure dialect of mediaeval Latin."

I lay my head in my hands. "Father Maxwell has been studying that book for years and didn't have all the answers. And we don't have any of his notes or research."

"Ah, but he didn't have an Oxford archaeology dropout and the ghost of a centurion," Alice opens the book to a random page. "We'll crack this."

II

BREE

"Stop here!" I yell as Alice swerves around the busy intersection, a chorus of horns blasting in our wake. "I have an idea."

Obediently, Alice slams on the brakes. The van lurches to a stop in the middle of the road. The horns have become a barrage of disgruntlement.

"What's going on?" Dani asks.

"I have to see a man about a Ripper."

I leap out of the van. Pax clambers out before I can slam the door behind me. He tosses me over his shoulder and carries me through the speeding cars, depositing me safely on the footpath in front of the Whitechapel tube station.

"I'm perfectly capable of crossing a road by myself," I say as I squeeze his arm. "But also, thank you."

Pax beams. "Alice must drive us everywhere from now on. Her bloodthirsty heart will make our enemies quake in their sandals."

"I believe you." I scan around the area where all the Ripper-ologists, t-shirt salespeople, and tour guides hang out. "There he is."

Abberline is blowing on a tour guide's stack of pamphlets, so they blow away as soon as she tries to hand them to unsuspecting tourists. He smirks as we approach. "Well, Ms. Mortimer. Now that you're here I can do what I've really wanted to do all day."

"And what's that?"

Abberline plucks a reusable coffee cup from a tourist's hand. "Hey!" the tourist yells. "How are you doing that?"

"I'm not doing anything!"

"My cup's floating in midair." The tourist jabs his finger at the cup. "Look at it! There's no string or anything!"

Abberline raises the cup high above his head as the crowd looks on. With a flick of his wrist, he dumps coffee all over the tour guide's head. She screams, dancing in wild circles as she tries to flick away the offending liquid. Her brochures flutter all over the street, causing a minor environmental catastrophe that we'll no doubt pay for when climate change comes for us all.

Given all the homicidal priests and monsters from beyond the Veil, I'll be happy if we even live until climate change comes for us all.

Abberline dusts off his hands and straightens his lapels. "Yup, that was even more satisfying than I predicted. Good day to you, Ms. Mortimer, Mr. Terrifying Roman. I hope you have come to make good on your promise."

"I have," I say. "That's why you need to come with us."

"Excuse me?" He clutches his belly, his laughter dripping with sarcasm. "I've not been able to leave Whitechapel for over a hundred years. Even with your powers, I don't see how you can move me away from the spot of my Living shame."

I lift a handful of moldavite stones from my pocket and shove them under his nose. "These stones in my hand will help you not just to leave Whitechapel, but to leave London. I made you a promise that I would grant you life once we defeat the Ripper. Well, now I know that to bring you back to life, we have to figure out your unfinished business. How convenient that I need the Jack the Ripper dead and your unfinished business is stopping him before he kills again."

Abberline pales. "I can't do that. I can't go after the Ripper."

"You can," Pax steps forward. He oh-so-casually slides his sword from the waistband of his trousers. I'm surprised no one in the street has commented on it. The blade is coated in dried blood. Pax grins manically. "It's simple. You follow Bree into the horseless carriage. Or I use your sinew to make a lovely macrame pot plant holder."

"I'm a ghost. You can't hurt me."

"Can't I?" Pax nods to the moldavite stones in my hand and cracks his knuckles again.

If it's even possible, Abberline grows paler.

"This is your chance to change your legacy." I gesture to the tourists surging from the tube station to make a beeline for the Ripper souvenir stands. "So many people die with regret in their hearts, and it stops them from moving on and being with the people you love. You get the rare opportunity to do something about it."

"Fine, fine." He shoves himself off from the wall. "I suppose I have nothing better to do."

I hold out my hand, and Abberline takes it. His face twists with wonder as he feels my fingers in his and the familiar surge of heat from my body. We shake, then Abberline floats out onto the street towards the van, lurching and cursing as the cars pass through his body. Pax throws me back over his shoulder and walks behind him, one hand on the hilt of his sword.

"Everyone, this is Detective Abberline," I say as I sit back down in the car and indicate the vague area of space that

Abberline's ghost inhabits. "Some of you can see him. Some of you can't. But he's going to help us destroy Jack the Ripper once and for all."

I2

PAX

We return to Grimwood, our pockets laden down with the crosses from the fallen priests – a parting gift from Björn. No one comments on Alice's driving. No one speaks to Abberline (except for Edward, who attempts to convince the Inspector that he must always address him as 'Your Majesty').

No one says much of anything at all.

Bree's brow knits in concentration. I know that she's thinking about all the things the priestess said. But none of them made any sense. Something about a crown and throne and the priests of the Order not being sad to be slain. I get that. Dying on the battlefield is an honour, but as far as I'm aware there's a balding king on the throne of England and he's very much alive (much to many people's disdain).

We Romans aren't very fond of kings, either.

As we pull up Grimwood's driveway, Mike shuffles outside and waves at us. His expression is grave.

Bree leaps out of the car before it even stops. "Dad, what's wrong?"

"You'd better come and see for yourself."

He steps aside to let us in. I hear voices from the kitchen. My hand flies to my sword, but I don't draw it out yet. I follow behind Mike as he leads us into the room.

The place is packed tighter than a Roman amphitheatre on two-for-one lion-feeding days. Who are all these people? I thought Mike cleared everyone out of Grimdale?

I glance around at their faces, and I notice something strange. No, two strange somethings.

Firstly, I recognise some of these faces from over the centuries. There's that nasty man who owned the house before Bree's family, and there's a Christian hermit who briefly made his home in a hollowed-out tree near the altar before he was chased away by a wolf.

The second something is that all these people are...*wrong*.

I can't explain it. When I look directly at one of them, they seem like normal humans I could stab if the mood so took me, but when I look away, their edges go all blurry, and I find I can't quite remember what they look like.

And they don't seem to know how to act like humans. I had to have lessons from Edward to know to drink my tea with my pinkie finger pointing out, but I do know that I'm not supposed to pour it into my ear, like that woman is doing. And that man over there is trying to cut off his hair with a bent fork.

They're all shuffling around the kitchen, talking gibberish and banging into things with this crazed look in their eyes that reminded me of Druids after they ate certain mushrooms.

I don't like it. And when I don't like something, I stab it until it goes away.

"I'm so pleased you brought me from my nice, familiar street corner to join this soiree," says Abberline as he backs down the hallway. "If anyone wants me, I'll have my head in a liquor cabinet."

I turn to Bree. She is my general. I need her orders before I pull out my sword. Beside me, Bree goes stiff. "Dad, who *are* all these people?"

I don't hear Mike's answer, because I see another familiar face in the crowd. A face I will *never* forget. A man with a neatly trimmed beard elbows a nun out of the way and rushes me. " Pax Drusus Maximus!"

"Marcus Cocceius Firmus, my good friend!" I throw my arms around him. "What are you doing here? I haven't seen you—"

"—since I died of asphyxiation in our camp after that prostitute sat on my face! By Jupiter's jolly janglies, what a way to go." Marcus thumps me on my back so hard that I nearly swallow my tongue. "Pax, old buddy, you look exceptionally well and virile for your age! Did you come up with the rest of us?"

I frown. "I don't understand. I have just come from London. Where did you come from?"

"Why, from the...other place, of course!" He screws up his face, as if trying to remember. "They said when we got up here, we wouldn't be able to remember it. I don't know why I remember that I can't remember it, but not what it is I can't remember. But never mind all that, I'm back now. What's happened? Did we beat the Druids? Where are the nearest public baths? Do you have any pickled fish? I'm *starving*—"

I glance back at Bree, who is staring at one of the strange people, her skin bone-white.

"That looks an awful lot like Sophie Henderson." Bree grabs my hand and squeezes. "But didn't she die when I was a kid?"

"She did." Mike takes a sip of his tea. "And now she's in my kitchen, doing that weird thing with her neck. And there's my old friend Pete, whose funeral I attended not two years ago. And he's banging his head against the wall."

"I see at least five of my previous clients," Dani says.

"But these people aren't ghosts!" Bree cries. "They've been dead, and suddenly they're alive again. How? Why?"

"I'm no expert," Ambrose says slowly. "But I think that hole in the Veil is letting out more than just ghosts. I think these are souls who have crossed over, and now they've come back to life."

13

BREE

When you have a house full of newly resurrected people who've forgotten how or why they're alive again, there's only one thing to do with them.

Pub.

We traipse down to the Cackling Goat as a loud, strange group. Pax takes up the lead, talking to his soldier buddy a mile a minute. They only stop their gruelling march to randomly slap each other on the back.

Abberline strides behind them, his eyes darting every which way, his hand constantly on his ghost revolver, even though it won't be able to save him. His policeman's instincts are still active, telling him that all is not right in Grimdale.

I hang back, watching in morbid fascination as several of the resurrected try to chew the bark off a poplar tree. My pockets are still filled with the spiked crosses we took from the dead Order priests, the faint black tendrils of their soul-cords spinning through the air around me.

I think Ambrose is right – these people are souls that have come through the hole in the Veil. If what Father Maxwell said is true, then the Veil is supposed to be one way. Unlike Pax and

Edward and Ambrose, these souls weren't stuck here as ghosts. They have already walked the pathway to the other side of the Veil. Going backwards like this must mess them up.

Ambrose grips my arm tightly, his pockets also jangling with crosses. Meanwhile, Alice flips through St. Ekaterina's book, frowning at the pages while Dani steers her around obstacles.

"They're called shades," Alice murmurs, licking the tip of her finger to turn a page. "Not ghosts. Not zombies. Shades."

Shades. It seems appropriate. They are but shadows of their old lives, and the world they have returned to is a figment they don't recognise.

We arrive to discover the pub is full to bursting, which makes no sense since Dad emptied out the village. Even the landlord and his employee Mr. Stibbens left town, which was probably for the best. But a quick glance around reveals that every single patron is a shade.

"How is the pub even open?" Alice asks, looking up from her book.

I point behind the bar. A girl who couldn't be older than me, wearing an extremely low-cut peasant shirt, wool corset, and layers of skirts, serves a pint to a Roundhead soldier, who promptly tips it down his breeches.

Lottie waves at us through the crowd. She and Mary hover near an empty table in the courtyard. We push through the crowd of newly Re-Livings and sink gracefully into seats. My pockets jangle.

"That's Esmerelda," Lottie says as she waves at the publican, who can't see her. "She used to be my best friend before I caught her with my husband behind the smithy."

"You should hex her," Mary whispers gleefully.

"What? During happy hour?" Lottie looks horrified. "I wouldn't dare."

Abberline gets to his feet. "If you don't need me to face the Ripper right at this moment, I'll be over there at the bar, making friends with Esmerelda's beer tap."

He strides away before I can stop him, howling in agony as several shades bowl right through him.

"This is completely insane." I slump my head into my hands. I can't even fathom what's going on.

Dad and Edward arrive at the table, their hands full of glasses. Dad spills beer on the table as he sinks into his own seat. "I must say, although that Esmerelda speaks like she's stuck in a Chaucer poem and she has no idea how to make a gin fizz, she's certainly a high-spirited, friendly lass."

"Not you, too," Lottie sighs.

Out of the corner of my eye, I see Abberline shove his head beneath the beer tap, but his proximity to me means the liquid bounces off his chin and sprays everywhere. Esmerelda shrieks and slaps his cheek. *Hard.*

"It's almost a pity Noel isn't around to run quiz night." Dad sips his beer with his good hand. "With this lot on our team, I think we'd have the history round in the bag."

THUMP. Alice slams the book on the table and sinks down behind it. She accepts something that might've been a gin and tonic from the selection on the table. She takes a sip and makes a face.

Dad leans forward. "Okay, Bree-bug, let's have your theories. Does the presence of Dani's ex-clients mean there's another Lazarus in town?"

I sink down in my chair. "I don't...I don't think so. These people weren't ever ghosts. At least, I've never seen them around before. And their cords look different. They're tinged with red, like the smoke that comes from the Ripper. I think Ambrose is right – if the souls walk a pathway to the other side of the Veil when they die, they're only supposed to walk one way. That's why they walk with a Lazarus, because it helps them find their way forward? But if the Veil is now thinning to allow beasts like the Soul-Eater back through to our world, then maybe these souls are coming back through, too? Do you notice how they're a bit...strange?"

"Why yes, I *have* noticed that a village full of people who are supposed to be dead is rather odd," Dani says without looking up from the page Alice is studying. "There's a couple in the corner who I embalmed two years ago."

"What I mean is, unlike when I resurrected the ghosts, these people have been beyond the Veil." I pause. "Whatever that means. I guess the whole point is that we're not meant to know until we die, and then once we do know, we can't go back. But these guys have come back, and that makes them all weird." With a stone sinking through my intestines, I remember what happened earlier today. "When I tried to resurrect that Order priestess and I saw her memory, everything felt *wrong*. And then when I grabbed her cord it was like barbs sticking into my skin. I wonder if when I tried to get to that priestess, *I* somehow yanked all these people back through the Veil."

Just another thing that I'm responsible for.

"It doesn't matter if you did," Ambrose says reassuringly. "You don't know how to control your powers. Once we fetch these poor souls a cup of tea and one of Esmerelda's infamous mutton pies, I'm sure they'll feel chipper again."

"And then we can get back to the serious business of finding this crown that you're supposed to stay away from," Edward says. "Because if there's a crown floating around out there going to waste, it might as well be on my head."

I glance out the window. The sky has grown darker, reducing the village to a gloomy Instagram filter. Across the street on the village green, a group of shades have started some kind of dance-off, their limbs jerking at strange angles as they sway and bop to a tune that only they can hear.

More shades wander over to join them. Those who aren't dancing gather together in stiff-legged groups, their mouths hanging open as they sing tuneless sounds. Here and there I catch snatches of recognisable songs – snatches of memories from lives they once lived – but something of death crawls over my skin as I watch them. These souls aren't like my ghosts – they are no longer the people they were in life. Death has changed them. Of course it has. Death *is* change. You can't go back. At least, you're not supposed to.

I understood something then, in that way certain things about my magic just hit me – knowledge that I didn't know I possess. Ambrose and Pax and Edward *never died*. Not truly. Their original bodies might have decayed and been lost to time, but their souls lived on just as they are and will continue to be, until they die for real.

That *terrifies* me.

Seeing those shifting, broken, hopeless souls, my heart aches at the thought that anyone I love might become one of them. I've spent far too much time thinking about death, about what it might be like once the beautiful white light engulfs you and you cross over. But if death mangles your soul so much that you become something different, I don't want it.

Is that why Father Maxwell's religion spends so much energy dwelling on the paradise that awaits you after death? Because they know that no one would follow them if they guessed the truth. Vera's drawings of hellbeasts and demons seem more accurate to me.

Death is a horror that our souls cannot endure and remain whole.

What is it like to experience that kind of horror, and then to be dragged up from it to return to your old life? To know in your soul that you're not supposed to be here anymore, that the world has changed and you have changed, but to not remember the outrages your soul has endured?

Lightning arcs across the dark.

A moment later, the shades' singing turns to screams.

I look over at the village green and see something made of shadow and teeth moving through the crowd. The night air fills with the scent of blood and the sound of bones crunching.

Another beast has found its way through the Veil.

I shove my chair back. Pax is already running towards the green, his sword raised. His friend the Roman soldier follows him. The beast turns towards them and—

CRUNCH.

Pax hollers as his friend is chomped within the jaws of the beast. "You give him back," he demands, stabbing his sword at the demon. The blade goes *CLINK* as it chips one of the beast's teeth, but it doesn't even slow it down.

It makes a wet smacking noise as it moves towards another shade – the sound of a thousand tongues flicking against teeth.

Panic seizes me as Pax reels for another swing and I'm brought back to the horrible moment at the fair when the Soul-Eater descended and I was powerless to stop it. Father Maxwell may have led the demon to us, but without his knowledge of demon marks, we never would have banished it.

This time we don't know the demon's name.

I scream as Pax swings again, and the monster catches his sword blade in his teeth and flings it away. Ambrose clings to me as Edward pulls my father behind a chair.

"Jolly good show." Abberline lifts his face from a mutton pie. "Better than an evening at the music hall. Can someone pass the gravy?"

"Bree, quick, we have to do something." Alice tugs my sleeve.

"Drat my luck, I left all my demon-slaying supplies back at the house."

"Not all of them." Alice holds up the book. "What did Father Maxwell do last time to defeat the demon?"

"He made a demon mark from vegetables," Dani says. "And that trapped the demon inside it so he could banish it."

I explain, "A demon mark is a way of writing a demon's name—"

"I know what a demon mark is. I've played Dungeons and Dragons." Alice flips through the pages of St. Ekaterina's book. "I think I saw...ah, here it is. This picture looks like our friend the tooth fairy's nightmare."

SNAP, SNAP, SNAP, CRUNCH.

I tear my eyes from the horror of the monster devouring another shade to focus on the page Alice holds up. "I think so."

Alice points to a symbol in the bottom corner of the drawing. "Here's your demon mark."

I don't want to do this.

It feels hopeless. Last time it took me and Father Maxwell and I had him guiding me. Every bone in my body is telling me to run. But Pax is in trouble, and all the shades, and everyone I love, if I don't at least *try*.

I thrust my hand into my pocket and clasp the spiky crosses. "But I don't have anything to draw it with."

"Here." Dani grabs sauce containers from the nearby tables. She piles them into my hands. "Go. We'll try and get the shades away from here."

Behind me, I hear Pax cry out – the brutal, reckless roar of a soldier who knows he's fighting a losing battle.

"Ambrose, Edward, my dad..." I say their names like a mantra as I grip the sauce bottles. Dani nods. "Go!"

I don't think. I run, the bottles jiggling in my arms.

My heart pounds in my ears.

I run towards the monster, even as my legs turn to jelly and my stomach lurches and I taste bile in my throat.

I stop in the centre of the road and start squirting sauce in a huge circle, dropping the crosses at random points, hoping and praying to gods I don't believe in that I'm doing this right.

I frantically try to remember the design Alice showed me. I glance back over my shoulder, and there's Dani, running towards me, the demon mark scrawled on a napkin in bright red tomato sauce.

My best friend, saving my ass as always.

I finish one sauce bottle and toss it away, then uncap the next one and get to work. I don't look up, even though the horrible noises of gnashing and crunching echo in my ears.

Pax, please be okay. Please...

As soon as I'm done, I leap back, careful not to smudge any part of the circle. Dani grabs me and pulls me behind a tree, where Edward, Ambrose, Alice, and my dad are already huddled. Edward wraps me in his arms and I finally dare a look across at the carnage.

It's bad. The green is littered with shades, their new, ill-fitting bodies torn and severed. The rest of them huddle in their small groups, moaning and swaying but not even trying to hide or escape. Pax leaps around them with the grace of a dancer, swinging with deadly accuracy as he severs tongues and jaws and rows of razor-sharp teeth. But as soon as he cuts off a piece of the monster, it grows back again.

My heart leaps into my throat as Pax swings his enormous frame up a lamp post. He places his blade between his teeth and hangs on with both hands, swinging his legs to build momentum. The creature barrels towards him, making that horrible *SLAP SLAP SLAP* of its tongues flapping against its teeth.

"Pax, you fool!" Edward yells. "Your prince commands you to stop hanging about and get over here."

If Pax hears him, he makes no acknowledgement. His thick forearms bulge as he strains to hold on. Pax lifts his legs just as the monster snaps its teeth right below him. He lets go and sails through the air, landing on the beast's back.

Those backyard sword-fighting lessons he gave me must be paying off, because immediately, I see what he's trying to do. There are fewer mouths and teeth on the monster's back, which might mean there's a weak spot. Pax plants his feet wide and, with a roar of defiance, drives his sword deep.

SSSNNNNNAAAAAIIIIIIIIIEEEEEEEE!

The noise the creature makes cannot be described as a scream. It shakes the earth beneath our feet. My ears ring. Beside me, Ambrose doubles over, clutching his skull, his beautiful features scrunched with pain.

And Pax...my Pax grips the hilt of his sword as the creature bucks, trying to throw him off. Red mist belches from hundreds of toothy mouths. The shades sob and cover their ears.

The monster bucks again and Pax's hands fly off the sword. His eyes meet mine, and for a moment, the world stills, and all I can see is that maniacal, blood-drenched smile. Pax offers me a thumbs up and mouths something to me. I can't hear him over the monster's wail, but I feel the words as they pierce my heart.

Goodbye.

"No," I breathe as the creature rolls, slamming Pax to the ground. He bounces hard, his sword sliding away, and the creature rounds on him for the kill—

And stops.

And turns.

A glass beer bottle hits it between several of its unblinking insect eyes.

It screeches as another bottle lands in one of its mouths, glass shards piercing its pink, lolling tongue.

"That'll teach you for eating my customers!" Esmeralda

yells, pelting the creature with more bottles. She has perfect aim.

The monster surges towards her, jaws yawning wide, teeth slick with gore. Pax rolls to his knees and lunches for his sword. Esmeralda stands her ground. She yanks a broom and brandishes it as the beast leaps into the road—

—straight into the centre of my demon mark.

"Yesss!" I cry as the beast slams into the force field thrown up by the mark. I wriggle out from Edward's grasp and sprint to the edge of the circle. I touch my finger to one of the crosses and call up my power.

Black, thick soul-cords dangle in the air, like a web holding the demon inside them.

I snap the cords.

The ground opens up, and Pax drags me away as the creature slides through the dark, cold void, snapping its teeth and slapping its tongues to try and gain a hold. Its cry pierces the world. But the Veil wants it back, and I am a Lazarus. I carry the magic of the Veil.

"Go back from where you came from," I yell, and the creature slips and jerks, and I realise that it's been pelted by bodies. All the shades are being sucked back through the Veil with it, their bodies sliding across the earth to topple over their edges. Their cries are a chorus of misery and happiness. They don't want to go back. They long to go back.

All they were supposed to know now is death.

The weight of the shades falling on top of it finally breaks the monster's hold. Its shriek cuts off as the void closes behind it.

I sink back into Pax's arms. We did it. I can't believe it, but we managed to banish that beast by ourselves, and send the shades back, too. We were lucky that Alice had seen the demon mark in the book, and Dani had thought of the tomato sauce, and Edward got everyone to safety, and Pax had fought so valiantly.

I stare around the green, at the broken bottles and trampled grass where hundreds of shades had stood.

Grimdale is empty. Not even a single duck on the pond.

"Well, that was exciting!" Mary claps her hands.

"And you got rid of that pesky Esmeralda, too." Lottie dances a jig.

"But who will make the mutton pies?" Abberline looks terrified at the idea of no mutton pies. I'm starting to think that our esteemed inspector isn't as altruistic as history led us to believe.

I run to Pax, arriving at the same time as Edward, who – in a most un-Edwardlike move, cradles our warrior's head in his lap. "You were so brave," he whispers. "I would compose a poem in your honour. 'His visage fair as marble stone, Chiselled by gods with artful hand, In his eyes a fire, deeply sown—'"

"Please," Pax croaks out. "I have just escaped death by the hairs on Mars' testicles. Don't torture me further."

"He wouldn't dare." I wrap my arms around him, laying kiss after kiss on his bloody brow. "Come on, let's get you home."

Edward and I thread our arms under Pax's shoulders and yank him to his feet. But as soon as I take his weight, I topple over, hitting the concrete hard on my tailbone.

"Owwwwww." I rub where it hurts. My head spins. Ambrose drops to my side, but when I blink, I see two of him.

"I think…" I gasp out. "I think banishing that demon used up my Lazarus powers."

Thunder cracks overhead.

Alice frowns at the book clutched in her hands as Ambrose helps me to my feet. "Grimwood is warded, right? We need to go there, now. I have a feeling that Toothy McSourbreath won't be the last demon of the Veil we have to fight."

14

EDWARD

Brianna forces us all to accompany Dani and Alice to their respective houses so they can quickly pack their things. Luckily, their parents left with the rest of the village, Dani's mother helping Alice's ailing father into a taxi to take him to a nurse in Argleton. This is just as well, because there remained only a few pieces of Pax's Raspberry and Chocolate Slices, and I don't want to share.

When we arrive back at Grimwood, we discover that the lights don't work.

"When you convinced me to join you on this lark, you never told me that I'd be roughing it in the dark with a bunch of half-dead clods," Abberline complains. I glare at him. The only one allowed to complain about the sorry state of affairs is *me*.

"The power must be out." Brianna flicks the switch up and down, but nothing happens. She slumps against the wall. I can barely make her out in the gloom, but her eyes glint at me through the darkness, weary from everything she's endured today.

"Don't look at me." I fold my arms.

"I wouldn't dare." She manages a little laugh.

"Why would we look at Edward?" Mike asks.

I puff out my chest. "If you were a ghost, Mike, I would show you such a trick, it would blow your hat off."

Abberline perks up. "I'm listening."

Brianna elbows me in the side as she slumps onto the chair in the foyer. "Suffice it to say that all those problems with the wiring were actually problems with a sexually frustrated royal prince."

"I think I've heard enough. I'll hunt out the candles." Mike shuffles off down the darkened hallway. A moment later, I hear him curse as he crashes into the sideboard. It's rather an imaginative curse, too. I make a mental note.

"Careful, Dad," Brianna gasps. She slides to the floor. "Ooof, I hate how weak I feel. I hope this wears off soon. Edward, you'll have to give up your boudoir so Alice and Dani can have the room."

"Excuse me? You can't ask a prince to sleep communally with the riffraff."

"I'm not asking you to sleep with the riffraff, I'm inviting you to join me in my bed with Pax and Ambrose."

I let out a long sigh, even though the thought of it makes my royal sceptre stand to attention. "Very well. If you insist. I shall try and bear this indignity with my usual noble forbearance."

Even in the dark, I can tell Brianna is rolling her eyes at me.

Mike returns with candles and a large mechanical instant lantern he calls a 'torch'. "But not the kind used for burning witches, Edward, and don't you forget it," he tells me as he shows me how to turn the light on and off.

A portable light fixture! Why didn't Brianna tell me about these before? I would have had such fun...

Now that we have light again, Dani and Alice run upstairs to drop their things in my boudoir, ignoring my *polite* instructions that if they move so much as one throw pillow out of place, it'll be off with their heads.

Abberline tries to claim the guest lounge as his personal domain, and everyone ignores him, mostly because the humans can't see or hear him, Brianna is exhausted, and as he is a civil servant, he is below my notice.

Brianna drags herself into one of the chairs in the foyer and quickly calls Mina on her magic rectangle. She asks if Mina and her paramours need to shelter at Grimwood as well. Thankfully, the cloud hasn't quite reached Argleton yet, so I don't have to share this house with that slobbering canine of hers. Mina wants to come running over, but Brianna tells her to stay put. There's nothing she or her fictional men can do from here, and Grimwood is already somewhat bursting at the seams.

Mike moves around the foyer, setting candles on the tables and fireplace. Ozzy swoops down from the chandelier and perches on the back of Brianna's chair. She pats his fuzzy head and he wraps his wings around himself, vibrating and letting out a little sound as if he's *happy* and not plotting our demise.

"Is that Ozzy?" Mike asks, staring at what must to him look like Brianna petting thin air.

"Yeah." Brianna turns around to face her dad. "And on the sofa over there is a new ghost. His name is Inspector Abberline. He tried and failed to catch Jack the Ripper back in 1888, so he's going to help us now. Try not to sit on him."

"I'll do my best. It's a pleasure to meet you, Inspector." Dad nods to the space next to Abberline, who merely sighs.

Brianna rubs her eyes. "Hey, I forgot to ask, if you can't see Ozzy, cuz he's a ghost, how did you know he existed? Mum says you're the one who named him."

"I may not be able to see the little guy, but we knew he was up in the attic. We hear all his comings and goings." Mike crouches down and holds his hand out near Ozzy's wing. The fuzzy beast sniffs it, then strokes Mike's finger with his tiny-but-lethal claws. "Always in the middle of the night, bangs and crashes and thumps and wings flapping. Sylv wanted to call an exterminator, but I convinced her that the attic belonged to Ozzy in the same way as the chair by the front window belongs to Entwhistle. I thought once I even heard a voice call out, 'winged spawn of Satan,' but I must've dreamed it—hey, that tickles! Is Ozzy touching my hand?"

"He sure is." Brianna sits back in the chair, smiling as she watches Ozzy dance back and forth over Dad's fingers. "He's such a cute little dude. I wish you could see him, but I couldn't even begin to guess what Ozzy's unfinished business might be. But this is odd, Dad. You shouldn't be able to hear Ozzy when I'm not around. And Pax and Ambrose and Edward said that they got more powerful, too, before I returned to Grimdale. Sometimes I wonder if it's not just me, but something about this house that's a little bit magical."

"Grimwood Manor is a special place." Dad holds out a finger for Ozzy to chew. He winces. "What now, Bree-bug?"

"As soon as I can drag my weary ass up from this chair again, I need to check the wards and strengthen them with these." Bree holds out her hand. The remaining crosses glisten under the flickering candlelight. "And then we need to take stock of our supplies. We don't know how long we're going to be holed up here. We need more candles and torches, batteries, water, loo paper, food...if there's enough wood in the box then we can light the Aga and brew a pot of tea—"

"Huzzah!" cries Ambrose.

"I'll help!" Pax leaps up. "I'll get us all some pudding."

Brianna looks as if she's about to argue, but then she seems to decide to leave the Roman to his own devices. She slumps back into the chair. "Sure, Pax. Pudding sounds lovely."

Everyone scatters to hunt down supplies. Except me. I know

where the important supplies are – the remaining bottles of wine we rescued from my cellar are hidden in the priest hole in the back of the closet that Ambrose used as a bedroom. Let others tend to the practical matters. I am needed here.

I move to Brianna and kneel at her feet. They haven't replaced the rug yet, and the flagstones are hard on my knees, but for once I don't mind a little discomfort. I gaze up at my Brianna, her features drawn gaunt, the hollows of her cheeks accentuated by the flickering candlelight.

I rest my head upon her thigh, wrapping one arm around her legs and reaching up with my fingers to clasp her hand.

I may be a spoiled prince, but I will kneel for my queen.

I slide my fingers from hers, moving down her leg, my breath hitching as I take in the exquisite plumpness of her thigh, the tantalising angle of her knee, the shapely curve of her calf. Lovingly, I cradle her foot and slide off the heavy boots she likes to wear. They hit the stone floor with a loud *THUD*, startling Ozzy from his position on the back of her chair.

"Edward, are you..." Her words trail off into a moan as I take her foot in my hand and press my fingers into the soft part of the sole, rubbing and stroking her toes until she is liquid in the chair before me.

Let it not be said that I, Edward the Poet Prince, don't know my way around every inch of my queen's body.

Lottie and Mary pass through the wall. "Oh, Breeeeee," Lottie calls, making a beeline for Brianna's chair. "We've come to stay with you and the handsome inspector, in case any of these rotten monsters are after ghosts. It's time your prince shows us his trick with the light fixtures—"

One look at Brianna's face and Lottie drags Mary off into the kitchen. I set down one foot and pick up the other.

"B-b-but you *hate* feet," Brianna shifts in the seat, throwing her head back as I hit a particular spot. "You said that everything below the ankle was an affront to poetry."

"I could never hate anything about you," I say honestly as I work my thumbs into her arch.

"You said that naked toes were like little piglets dancing at a trough, and they smelled even worse."

"If you lived with Pax and his stinky Roman sandals for five centuries, you'd agree. But, forgive me," I bend down and kiss the top of her feet, my lips brushing her soft skin, "I got off on the wrong foot."

"Edward—"

"I should know that you don't want any silliness. We are in serious trouble. All of us have one foot in the grave."

"Edward."

"Perhaps we can ask Pax to make us my favourite dessert." A slow grin creeps across my features. "Tirimashoe."

"*Edward.*"

There's that smile that lights up the dark. A smile that makes me believe for a moment that maybe I'm not completely useless.

"Thank you," Brianna murmurs as she melts into the upholstery. "Thank you, Edward. I'm so tired. All of this feels too big, too impossible. Everything's a mess. And now there's a crown involved. What crown? Whose crown? And don't say yours."

But I wasn't going to. I'm not even thinking about the crown. I'm mesmerised by the two simple words she uttered to me.

Thank you.

I close my eyes. Her words burn bright as the sun behind my eyelids. *Thank you.*

I've never given anything of worth to anyone. When I was Living, I had so much money that I never batted a perfect eyelid at the cost of the parties I threw and the lavish gifts I showered upon them. My poems might be more brilliant than any other poem composed before or since, but did they move people to act? To change their ways? To open their hearts?

Poetry is just pretty words. But my fingers in Brianna's soft skin, that smile on her face when once she was so sad and weary, that is *real*.

I am *needed*.

I think about the cat who crossed over in my arms, and how she got to experience a single moment of kindness before she walked the pathway beyond the Veil. How I wish I hadn't been so selfish in my life so I could have given her many more such moments.

I wonder if she is a shade now, her cat-soul corrupted by the desire to live again.

I wonder if my soul had crossed over the night that I died, out in the cold, all alone, with a wedge of glass in my posterior, if I would have come back as a shade. I had done everything I could to corrupt my spirit in life, would I not relish the chance to do it in death?

If not for my unfinished business, and Brianna...

Death may be closing in on us from all sides, but within the walls of Grimwood Manor, we are gloriously, beautifully, imperfectly alive.

Well, most of us. I nod begrudgingly at Ozzy. *And I will not squander this second chance. I will live every moment making sure that Brianna knows that she is loved.*

I will touch her feet and make her smile, and when the time comes, I will die for her.

15
BREE

"Something moves," Pax announces from his position at the window of the guest lounge, where we've all gathered for the evening.

"A worthy deduction, Sherlock," Abberline slurs, lifting his head out of the liquor cabinet to glare at Pax. "You probably saw a mangy fox."

"Don't talk down to cuddly, cute foxes," Pax shoots back without turning around. "That's racist."

My already tight chest constricts, and I struggle to breathe out. *Whatever's out there, it's no fox.* "What is it?"

"It's turned from the house," Pax whispers. "It's distracted. The wards are holding."

I let out my breath, but I can't ease the tightness in my ribs or the tension in my shoulders. It has been two days since we returned from London and banished the second monster. Two dreary, stressful, scary days locked inside Grimwood Manor while monsters of the Veil prowled around outside.

At least my magic seems to have recharged itself. Nothing gets Bree Mortimer going again like stuffing myself with Pax's baking (he has massively improved, unlike Edward, who valiantly offered to cook breakfast again and somehow managed to turn the hash browns green). I can now see and touch soul-cords once more, and simply lifting my head doesn't make me feel like I'm going to pass out.

The power is still out in the house, but the streetlights have come back on, and the solar floodlights Dad has dotted around the gardens are valiantly shining on despite the absence of sun. "They're supposed to keep shining through a nuclear apocalypse," Dad says proudly every time he passes a window. I don't have the heart to tell him that's not reassuring.

And most importantly, the wards are holding. I don't know how, or why, but as long as nothing gets inside the house, I call that successful magic.

"It's stalking something." Pax's voice rises with concern. "Moon? Entwhistle?"

"They're right here," Alice says from the sofa opposite mine, where she trying to read St. Ekaterina's book, but she's having trouble getting comfortable because she's weighed down by cat gravity. Opposite her, Dani spreads out Vera's drawings, entering details about each one into her computer. She and Alice are working on a catalogue of hellbeasts, which is so on-brand for both of them that it makes me smile.

Entwhistle opens one lazy eye and yawns at me.

"And Ozzy is here." Ambrose pats his fuzzy head. He nuzzles into Ambrose's hand. Ambrose's face melts a little, before he remembers the history between them that shall not be spoken aloud, and retracts his hand.

My hand goes to the sword at my side. I haven't been idle, either. Pax and I pushed the dining room table to the side and spend hours practising sword fighting. I'm not going to achieve my Gold Star for Stabbing badge at Centurion Scouts any time soon, but I'm getting better. I slide out of my chair and join Pax on the windowsill, fearing what I'm going to see.

I squint into the gloom of the street and gasp as I see the creature. With the floodlights in the garden on full blast, we can just make out the shadow of it lurching and wobbling through the trees at the edge of the cemetery. This creature has a vaguely octopus outline, but instead of eight tentacles, there are uncountably many, with vicious barbs extending along their length and toothy mouths on their tips. It moves as if the laws of physics don't apply to it, which perhaps they do not. It's not a thing that should exist anywhere but a nightmare.

But it's here, in Grimwood Crescent.

The hellbeast stops in front of a particular tree, wrapping its tentacles around the trunk. The barbs dig deep, scarring the oak that had stood there since Ambrose's day. It shakes the tree and through the quiet, dead night, I hear the faint snatches of someone screaming.

"Someone's in that tree!" cries Pax. He jabs his finger at the window, where I can just make out a figure in the highest branches, clinging to the trunk for dear life.

"That's a very silly place to have a nap," Edward says helpfully.

"Perhaps they're attempting to disguise themselves as a bird," Ambrose suggests. "Perhaps it would work better if they had a large egg—"

We have been stuck inside in the dark way too long. "Alice, do you see an eldritch tentacled beast anywhere in that database of yours?"

"We're looking!" Dani cries. Entwhistle howls in protest as the cats are unceremoniously dumped from Alice's lap.

I turn back to the window. The creature's tentacles peel back, like the petals of a flower unfurling, to reveal a black beak that opens into a round mouth like a gateway to hell. It yawns up at its victim as it shakes the tree once more.

"We have to save them. Do we have a name yet?" I call out.

"Just a second." Dani flicks frantically through Vera's pictures. "There's an awful lot of monsters here. This one has tentacles, right?"

"It is resplendent with tentacles," Edward says, peering through the window at the creature as though he were admiring a particularly vulgar painting.

"And it has a kind of beak? And lots of beady insect eyes?"

"I don't see insect eyes. The tentacles have barbs, and mouths on the ends."

"Whoever comes up with the designs for these creatures certainly has an overactive imagination," Ambrose says. "Mouths on the ends of tentacles, what an absurdly impractical—"

"I've got it." Alice yanks a page from the pile on the table and thrusts it in my face. "The beast is called...no, actually, we shouldn't say the name out loud. It might summon something even worse. Here's its sigil. Are you sure you don't want me to—"

"No." I glare around the room at my friends, and my father, as I shove the sword into my belt and grab for the bottles of spray paint that Mina left here after Edward's party. "This is very important. No matter what happens out there, you're all to stay behind the wards. I have my powers, but you don't, and I'm not losing one of you to a beast who looks like a bad D&D character. Got it?"

Dad looks miserable, but he reaches across and knits his fingers in Ambrose's. "We got it, Bree-bug."

"Let's go." Pax draws his sword. "By Jupiter's dribbling dong, we will spill the blood of the beast tonight."

For once, I'm not going to argue with the Roman and his sword. Pax and I leave the room and creep through the house. My Roman's sandals flap against the wooden floors. He reaches the front door. He nods to me. I nod back. We practiced this.

Everything will be okay.

Blood pounds in my ears.

"For Jupiter. For Bree! For Rome!" Pax yells as he flings open the door and charges into the darkness.

The creature rears up, letting go of the tree and swinging around to face Pax. It takes the beast quite some time to do this, as it appears that sending instructions to hundreds of tentacles takes a significant amount of brain power. By the time it starts globbing its way toward Pax, beak clacking and snapping, tiny tentacle mouths all going 'glub glub glub,' my warrior swings his sword down and cuts off the end of a tentacle.

My heart leaps into my throat as the beast makes a wild, wailing noise and lunges at Pax, but I can't watch. He's doing this to buy me time, and I won't waste a single moment of his sacrifice.

I charge down the driveway, heading for the street.

I feel it the moment I cross the wards – a rising sickness in my stomach that sends me doubling over, my hands gripping my knees as my stomach retches and heaves. That's what these creatures do – they suck out all the goodness from the air.

I push past the nausea and lurch to the middle of the street. I lift the can of pink spray paint. As I reach into my pocket for the drawing of the demon mark, I swear as the edge of the paper knifes across my skin, opening the world's longest paper cut that immediately blooms with blood.

Could this day get any worse?

I ignore the throbbing in my palm, hit the nozzle, and start to spray.

First, I draw a large circle, big enough to trap the hellbeast and all its tentacles. I drop the crosses around the path. Three parallel lines here, a half moon there, a thing that looks a bit like a spider on drugs, some dots that might be a constellation, a swirl and...

No.

Oh, ghost-balls.

So the day *can* get worse.

The spray can fizzes. Nothing comes out. I rap it on the ground but it's no use. It's run dry. Who knew that graffiting demon marks uses up so much paint?

Behind me, the grunts and squelches of Pax fighting the tentacle creatures move closer, and the never-ending shrieks of whoever is hiding up that tree pound against the inside of my skull. *Think, Bree.* How can I finish the mark so we can trap the beast?

It will take me forever to run back to the house and bring another spray can. All I need is something liquid...

Pax barrels out of the gloom toward me, obviously thinking that I'd finished the demon-mark. I glance down, my chest exploding with panic, and then I see the blood pooling in my palm.

I crouch down and smear my palm across the road, wincing as stones dig into the cut. My blood forms a crimson arch next to the fluorescent pink. It's only a thin trail, but it completes the mark. It's enough.

It's *more* than enough.

The air charges with magic as the demon mark activates. It feels a hundred times more powerful than the mark I made with Father Maxwell. Which doesn't make sense, since two Lazaruii should be more powerful than one.

My body hums and fizzes as the magic arcs through the air. Holding on to the circle is easier, too. I focus inward, pulling up my magic until the black threads of the Order crosses appear. Then I run back behind the wards just as Pax steps into the circle.

PLOP PLOP PLOP. The tentacles follow him. One grabs his ankle, but Pax hacks it off, yelling in triumph as the entire beast slithers and wobbles into the circle. Pax leaps out just as I snap the cords.

As if I've been trapping demons forever, the ground opens up into a yawning black maw, and the creature drops through. As the earth closes once more, red mist leaks from the hole and the Ripper's laugh echoes along Grimwood Crescent.

Pax bounds over to me and sweeps me into his arms. He cups my cheek as he kisses me. This kiss was like fireworks going off inside my mouth. It pulsed with the heat and light and fire of the battlelust that burned through Pax's veins.

"You were amazing," he groans as he eats the breath from my mouth. He pulls me closer, kissing me with such devastating fervour that my knees tremble like some heroine from a gothic novel.

"*You* were," I manage to choke out. "I didn't know Roman soldiers were trained to fight Cthulhu..."

"Gesundheit," Pax quotes a word he learned from the Moving Picture Box.

I sigh. "I didn't sneeze. That was a joke. I'll explain it to you when we're back inside. Or maybe I'll make Dani do it. She loves a challenge. That was so strange, though. Creating that circle was so easy. All I did was add a smear of my blood and—"

"Help, help!"

We both pull back, breathing hard. In all the excitement of banishing the tentacle monster, we forgot about the person still stuck in the tree.

Pax squeezes my hand and we both draw our swords as we run back across the street to stand under the oak tree. I peer up into the branches and stop dead.

Clinging to the top of the tree is...Kelly Kingston.

"Kelly? What are you doing here?" Kelly lives on the other side of the village in Riley Jenson's fancy townhouse (the one his parents gave him). "Why didn't you leave the village with everyone else?"

"Riley thought the gas leak story was a pile of nonsense," she sobs, clinging tighter to the trunk.

That's fair. It wasn't exactly very convincing. "Where is Riley now?"

"He's—" Kelly's body convulses. She points a trembling finger toward the street, where we'd banished the hellbeast only a few moments ago. "The creature got him. It tore him to pieces. I don't think—"

"It's okay." The words feel woefully inadequate, but they're all I have right now. "Pax is going to come up and get you down."

Pax looks confused. "But that's Kelly, your enemy. She is stuck in a tree. Why would I rescue her?"

"Because..." I try to think of a way to explain that he'll understand, but nothing comes to me. "Do you always question the orders of your general?"

Pax grabs the lowest branch and pulls himself up. He is a thing of beauty, his muscles rippling through his tight t-shirt as he leaps effortlessly from branch to branch. For an immovable wall of pure brawn, he dances up the tree with the grace of a ballerina. I try to focus on watching the street for more monsters, my sword at the ready, but by the time he drops a whimpering Kelly onto his shoulders and prances back down, I'm drooling a little.

Okay, more than a little.

Pax dumps Kelly unceremoniously at my feet. "Here she is. Can I behead her now?"

"No beheading."

"Good, good." Pax rubs his fingers together. "I agree, beheading is too good for her. It will be over much too soon. I'll fetch the sack, but I don't know where we're going to find a snake and a monkey—"

"Bree, wh-wh-what's going on? What's he talking about?" Kelly's shrill voice echoes down the deserted street.

"Ignore Pax. He's talking nonsense. Can you walk? We have to get you out of the street. Lean on Pax's shoulder."

Kelly glares at Pax's shoulder like a sword might leap out of it and cut her to pieces, which honestly with Pax is entirely possible. But then her legs wobble and she grabs him and allows him to help her hobble towards the house. "Where are you taking me?"

"Somewhere safe?" I can't quite form it into a statement. I hope we're safe.

I shove open Grimwood's front door and Pax drags a whimpering Kelly up the porch steps. In the light of the flickering candles Dad has placed all over the foyer, I can just make out Dani heading for the kitchen.

"Hey, Bree, Pax, nice job on the monster. I don't suppose you happened to stop at the shops for some milk while you were out, because we're down to the powdered stuff and Alice wants some in her tea—" Dani's face freezes when she sees who we're carrying. "Kelly?"

"Hold the door open," I call out. "She's heavy."

Abberline floats past. "That's it, bring another stray inside. We're not already packed to the rafters as it is."

Sometimes, Inspector, I wish I'd left you back in London.

Pax and I drag Kelly's half-conscious body through the front door. Kelly's eyes grow wide as she takes in the towering foyer with the sweeping carved staircase and the cobweb-infested chandeliers and the bloodstain that we still haven't washed out of the flagstones.

"Yeah, yeah, I know what you're thinking. Yes, I do live in the

Addams Family house," I sigh. I don't have time for this. I'm still trying to figure out why adding that tiny bit of blood to the demon mark made it so much more powerful. "But Lurch doesn't open the door anymore. He ran away, left us in the lurch. Ha ha."

"It's...big," she breathes.

"Yes. That's what this house is famous for. The bigness."

"Is that Bree back? Did she get any milk?" Dad appears behind Dani. He takes one look at Kelly and scurries off. "I'll get the first aid kit," he calls back. "Bring her into the lounge."

"I'll bring cake!" Pax shoves Kelly into my arms and scurries off, too.

Dani meets my eyes, and I nod. She smiles, a slow, sad smile that reminds me of where the two of us began our journey together, and how far we've come.

With Dani's help, I drag Kelly's dead weight into the lounge. We half plop, half shove her onto the sofa. She rolls over and sits up, regarding me with those cruel eyes of hers, although right now she doesn't look as terrifying as I remember. She looks afraid. I don't think I've ever seen Kelly afraid before. It's not as fun as I expected.

I hear a tapping behind me as Ambrose wanders in.

"Bree, the milk situation is a little dire. What do you think about sending Ozzy out to see if he can pick up a bottle from the corner shop? We could send him with a couple of quid in coins to pay for it, so it's not really stealing. The only flaw in this plan is that I don't know how far his ghost mojo will allow him to carry it—" Ambrose stops. "Is someone else here? This room feels unusually tense."

"Ambrose, I'd like you to meet my arch nemesis, Kelly Kingston," I say. "Kelly, meet Ambrose Hulme, the newly living ghost of a famous Victorian explorer who I bought back to life with my resurrection magic, and one of my boyfriends."

"Your *what?*" Kelly gasps.

Ambrose frowns, and my cheery, happy-go-lucky adventurer manages to look a little terrifying. "Why is she here?"

"Truthfully, I don't know." I collapse onto the sofa opposite Kelly, pulling Ambrose down beside me. I need him with me. Ambrose is the one who makes conversations like this easier. I regard Kelly across the table as I address my next words to Ambrose. "We saved her from being eaten by that hellbeast. But I don't know what she was doing in the street being chased by a hellbeast in the first place."

"I was afraid, okay! When I saw that creature eat Riley, I realized that the village didn't have a gas leak. This was something..." Kelly's face screws up as she searches for a word.

"Uncanny," Ambrose finishes for her.

"Right. Uncanny. *Supernatural.* And I figured the weird girl who talks to ghosts might be able to help. So I came here, but then it followed me and I got lost in the dark trying to find the house. I thought it wouldn't be able to climb a tree." She shudders. "What was it going to do to me?"

"It's probably better you don't know the answer," I say. "Why did you think I'd help you? You've been horrible to me for my whole life, and these last few months since I've been back I haven't exactly been civil to you, either."

Kelly shrugs. "I know Alice is here. I thought that maybe she'd talk you into it. She can talk anyone into anything."

"Not true."

We all whirl around. Alice leans against the doorframe, her dark eyes reflecting flickers of candlelight. She looks tired.

"I couldn't convince you to stop being awful to Bree and Dani. Not when we were at school, and not now." Alice shrugs, as if it all means nothing to her. "I spent too many years being afraid of you and what you might do to me if I dared to be myself. But I'm not afraid anymore, Kel. Take or leave me as I am, but don't hurt the people I care about."

Kelly whimpers. "Are you going to kick me out? There are *uncanny* things out there."

Alice shrugs again. "It's up to Bree. It's her house."

Kelly turns to me, face expectant. Ambrose squeezes my hand. I fix my eyes on Kelly. I can't help it. I may not choose to leave her outside in a tree for a hellbeast to eat, but I don't exactly want her staying in my *house*.

"Why did you come here?" I ask again. "Tell us the truth this time."

"Maybe I missed Alice, okay?" Kelly yells. "Maybe I thought you were nicer than I am. Maybe I don't even know why I was mean to you. Maybe I was jealous or something?"

"You, jealous?" I scoff. Alice meets my eyes across the room. In her flickering orbs, I see the shape of her friendship with Kelly over the years, and how precarious and unsafe she must have felt. I squeeze Ambrose's hand, and I suddenly wish that Dani was here beside me. But I also understand and respect that Dani can't be in this room right now.

That's true friendship.

"Not exactly. Maybe. I don't know." Kelly slumps back on the sofa and folds her arms. Her lower lip puffs out. "Look, if you're going to kick me out, just hurry up about it. I don't want to hear a whole lecture—"

Is this girl for real? I roll my eyes at Alice, who gives me a 'what did you expect' look.

I sigh. "Here's the thing. You've been horrible to me my whole life. It's not as if you didn't know your words had power at school. You made everyone hate us. They were too scared of you to do anything else. All those meetings my parents had with the school, with your mum, where you said that you'd stop being horrible to us, and then as soon as their backs were turned, you'd get even worse. And now you want me to shelter you in this house that you made fun of, and you want me to trust you with secrets that you've already used against me? I can't…I can't do that until I understand why."

"Why?"

"Why did you do it? Why did you hate me and Dani? What is it about me that's so—" my voice cracks, "—unlikeable."

"Oh, Bree." Ambrose lays his head on my shoulder.

Kelly sighs. "Fine. Whatever. You want the truth? In primary school, we were actually friends for a bit."

"We were not. I'd remember that."

"We *were*. We'd go to each other's houses for playdates. I used to listen to you yammer away to your invisible friends. I thought you were sad, but your house was cool and your dad helped us with fun art projects, so you seemed like a good choice for a friend. I can't believe you don't remember."

She sounds affronted, as if her so-called friendship is so memorable that it's impossible to believe I couldn't remember.

"I had an accident around that age that messed with my memory," I say. "So if we were friends, what happened?"

Kelly fluffs the cushions behind her. "We used to jump rope together on the playground. You were shit at it, but I would trip myself up so you wouldn't feel so bad being such a loser. But then one day you told me that my grandmother wanted me to find her diamond earrings. My grandmother died five years earlier. Ever since, my mother had been looking for her earrings. They were worth a lot of money, and she wanted to sell them off so she had the funds to leave my dad. You told me that my grandmother said the earrings were in an old cookie jar we kept in our knick-knack cabinet. I thought it was just one of your dumb stories, but I went home and stole the jar out of the cabinet and looked inside, and there were the earrings." Kelly's face scrunches up. "That's freaky, right? But it's also pretty cool. That's when I knew that all the nonsense you said about talking to ghosts was real. I guess…I didn't have a cool magical power like that, and I thought when people found out, they'd like you and not me. I didn't want you to take all my friends away and become the cool kid."

I don't know whether I wanted to slap her or hug her. "Let me get this straight, you tormented me for years because you thought I was a...a threat?"

"I guess so. If people found out you could talk to their dead relatives and shit, they wouldn't like me anymore." Kelly glares at Alice, and from deeper in the house, I can hear Dani laughing at something my dad said. "It's true, isn't it?"

Alice says nothing.

"If I'd been alive when you were around," Ambrose says. "I would have been your friend."

Kelly snorts. "Fat chance. Not after the way I treated your girlfriend. She probably told you all about breaking her science fair project, and pouring honey in her shampoo bottle at school camp."

"She didn't need to. I was there for all of it," Ambrose says. "I was the one whose shoulder she cried on when she came home to the safety of Grimwood. Well, a metaphorical shoulder. It wasn't nearly as corporeal as it is now."

"What-what does that even mean?" Kelly glares at Ambrose, trying to puzzle him out. But he's oblivious to her fear, and he keeps right on going.

"And I *may* have taken joy in our recent revenge efforts, but even so, I would have liked to be your friend, Kelly. I would have been a true friend to you. I would have told you when you were being cruel to Bree, because I don't think this cruel person is really who you are. I think that you envy Bree's adventurous spirit. If you weren't so afraid that people didn't like you, you'd probably get to have more adventures of your own."

Oh, Ambrose. You are too good for this world.

"Easy for you to say. You're—"

"An ex-ghost? A blind man?" Ambrose laughs. "Yes, very easy for me to say. Much harder to practice. Being brave is always the hardest path. But it's also the most joyful."

"Maybe...maybe I carried it a bit far," Kelly stares at her hands. "But...wait a second, did you get your ghosts to dump cotton candy on me?"

"And they haunted you at Riley's house," I grin. "And Pax *may* have pushed you into the duck pond. So maybe we call it even?"

My hand moves of its own accord. It sticks out across the table, dangling in midair.

Kelly stares at it for a long time. The grandfather clock in the corner ticks ominously. I'm just about to withdraw my hand when she grabs it and shakes wildly.

She sighs. "Fine."

"Glad that's settled." I sweep my arm around the room. "Welcome to Grimwood Manor. If you'd like to follow me, I can get you settled into a guest room, and then Pax the resurrected Roman warrior will serve tea and biscuits. I'm afraid we're out of milk."

"I'm so happy to have you here." Ambrose throws himself at Kelly and squeezes her in one of his famous hugs until she relents and embraces him back. "But just know that if you do anything to hurt Bree, I *will* eviscerate you, mash your organs into a thick paste, and serve it on my scones with a dollop of clotted cream."

As Kelly follows me and Ambrose into the hallway, I swear I hear her mutter under her breath, "What have I done?"

16

AMBROSE

After three slices of Pax's absolutely heavenly lemon drizzle cake, Kelly slowly begins to calm down.

If only *everyone* would calm down.

Edward is upstairs, yelling lines from a poem about deception at the top of his lungs. Alice hasn't moved from the doorway, and I can feel the heat of her eyes burning holes through Kelly's skin. Pax stomps up and down the hallway outside, muttering about feeding cake to one's enemies.

Abberline is drunk...well, as drunk as a ghost can be. And now that he's around Bree and can touch, smell, and taste more, he's gorging himself on all the sensory experiences he's been deprived of for the last hundred years. It's understandable – I myself had quite the indulgent few days when I first became Living again – but amid our troubles, it is a spot annoying.

All this racket is agitating Bree, who is sitting with Kelly until she's ready to go to bed in the guest room upstairs. Bree doesn't need any more excitement after banishing that monster already tonight. I can tell that performing that spell sapped her energy, and she'd like to go to bed herself, but Kelly seems content to keep sitting up and rehashing her harrowing day.

"—and I told Riley that we should leave with everyone else, but he never listens to me. It must be nice to have magical powers. If your boyfriends don't do what you say, you can just threaten to make them ghosts again."

"I don't think threatening to take away people's lives is the best way to get them to do what you want—" Bree sighs as Alice screams that Pax stomped on her foot. "Case in point. Ambrose, could you stay here with Kelly while I have a little chat with Pax?"

"Of course."

The sofa creaks as Bree gets up and drags Pax and Alice away from the doorway. I can overhear her saying something about blood. I debate moving over to sit next to Kelly, but now that she knows I was a ghost, I don't want to presume she'll want to sit next to me. I try to think of something I might say to her to cover up the loud conversation happening in the hallway.

"Terrible weather we're having, isn't it?" I say pleasantly. "It's almost as gloomy as the winter I spent in the Arctic Circle. Six months with no daylight and bitter cold, but the pickled herring was simply *divine*—"

"You saved her life," Bree says to Pax.

"Good." He thumps something with his fist. "Now I get to kill her."

Kelly whimpers.

"No, Pax."

"She is your enemy. If you were a Roman, you would—"

"—toss her in the duck pond tied inside a bag with a snake, a rooster, and a monkey, I know, I know. But we're not in Roman Britain anymore, are we? We're in Argleton in the twenty-first century, and we should try to forgive our enemies. I know that I haven't set a very good example since I got back, and yes, your revenge so far has been pretty satisfying. But Kelly's here now, and she needs us. And if I'm being honest with myself..." I hear Bree sigh. "I'm partly to blame for stirring up this old battle between us. I have to ask myself a difficult question. Why do I still care so much what Kelly thinks? I'm not a kid anymore. I'm twenty-three years old. Why do I want her to see me as more than the weird loser from school?"

"You're *not* a loser."

"I've spent five years of my life running away from my problems, and I have nothing to show for it. That's the dictionary definition of a loser."

"Then I will stab the dictionary!" Pax roars. "How dare it define you as anything other than a perfect goddess! I will burn its paper and doodle penises all over the margins. I will use its pages to wipe Zeus' buttocks—"

"Is it always like this?" Kelly asks me in a small voice.

"Pretty much." I lean forward. "Would you like a game of cards? It might take your mind off things."

"Aren't you blind? How can you even play cards?"

I remove the card deck from the little games drawer beneath the table and flip the top card over for her. "They have Braille on the corners, see?"

"Oh." Kelly doesn't move, but then I hear her reach forward and pick her plate of cake off the table. "Then sure. Let's play cards."

I deal out hands for a game of rummy. For a few minutes, there is no sound except the two of us shuffling our cards around in our hands and Bree and Pax arguing outside. Kelly says I should start, so I do, placing down a pair of twos and discarding a five I don't require. But as Kelly debates her turn, she blurts out.

"So you're Bree's...boyfriend?"

"I am." I beam at the word. I can't believe that I get to be Bree's boyfriend. It's an honour and a joy, and every day I want to pinch myself that it's real, that she's really mine. It took so long for Bree to decide she could use the word for us, for what we are to her, and I am prouder of being her boyfriend than I am of anything else in my life, including my manuscript.

"But what about those other two guys? The huge one and the sullen one with the nice hair?"

"They're her boyfriends, too."

I expect Kelly to say something rude, but instead, she asks, "How does *that* work?"

I don't really understand the question. "It works because we love Bree."

I hear a thump as Kelly flops back against the cushions. "I don't understand why she's letting me stay here. You all hate me. Everyone hates me. I wasn't nice to her."

"No, you weren't." I place down my discard. "Your turn."

"I wasn't lying before. I don't know why I picked on her and Dani." Kelly slaps down a set. "Three jacks. At home, my dad was super strict. He had rules for everything, and I always felt like I had to be super careful of everything I did or said, or I'd set him off. And then I got to school and other kids would listen to *me*. I liked being in charge, the one who made things happen, instead of the one they happened to. I could say who was in and who wasn't. I didn't have to be afraid of anything, not like when I was at home."

I nod. I know that fear all too well. My father wasn't a warm person, either. To him, I was a disappointment – a weak boy with a head full of silly dreams, which he reminded me of frequently. When he drank, his mocking anger would turn violent, but at least I never saw him raise a finger to my mother. As soon as I was old enough, I joined the Navy. He disapproved, of course – I was supposed to take over his shop. He jeered at me as I set off for my first commission. "You won't last a day out there."

But I was so used to being afraid of when the next blow

would come that I actually enjoyed the structure of the Navy. I learned the rules. I followed them. I didn't live in fear. I loved being on the open sea, heading on an exciting adventure far, far away from my father. But then I got sick and lost my sight, and they sent me back, but he wouldn't take me. He refused to give me a cent to help with my medical expenses. I was a newly blinded man completely on my own, with no money, no friends, and very few jobs open to me. It was the darkest time in my life – darker even than when I was imprisoned in Siberia on suspicion of being a spy.

It's not something I like to talk about, as it all happened so very long ago and I have met so many wonderful friends since then, but I tell all this to Kelly. I want her to understand. "What my father did and said left a mark on me, as yours left you. Those marks might not be visible, but they are with us always."

"I guess."

"I've been friends with Bree and Dani for a long time," I say. "The things you did to them left a mark, the way your father left a mark on you. Is that what you wanted?"

"No." Kelly sniffs. "I was dumb. Riley's dead, isn't he?"

"You saw him ripped to pieces, so, yes?"

"We're all going to die."

"*No.* Bree's going to close up the holes in the Veil, and everything will be fine again." *I hope.* "And you're safe here in Grimwood. But you have to trust Bree, even when strange things happen that you don't understand. In this house, we leave our baggage at the door, okay?"

"I've never met anyone as absurdly optimistic as you before." The cards shuffle as Kelly puts down her hand. "Full house. I win. Want another game?"

With the doors of the manor locked tight, our wards firmly in place and strengthened by the magic of Lottie and Mary, and every surface dancing with flickering candlelight, Grimwood stands as a beacon of light amidst the darkness of the village.

At least, I assume it stands as a beacon of light since I can't see the effect for real.

As far as we know, we're the only house in the village with still-living occupants, but we don't dare venture past the wards to find out.

Each day, we pore over St. Ekaterina's diary and the other occult texts Mina gave Bree, searching for anything about a crown or how to repair a hole in the Veil. Each night, foul creatures rattle the windows and howl at the chimneys, but they cannot penetrate Grimwood's walls. Pax stays up, standing sentry beside the windows or roaming the house with his sword drawn. The rest of us eat Pax's baking and play Settlers of Catan in the lounge. (A very interesting game when you play with a royal prince who keeps demanding everyone pay him tribute just for existing.) Bree helps me to add Braille labels to the cards so I can play, too.

It would be a lovely existence if not for the death surrounding us, closing in on us.

With every hour that goes by without a solution, Bree grows quieter. She carries the guilt of every death upon her shoulders. I hate being so impotent to help. I can't help decipher the books, although I am getting quite good at looking up things on Bree's magic rectangle—er, mobile phone with voiceover software. The internet contains knowledge of everything that was, is, and might one day be. Surely, it will give us an answer.

On the third night since Kelly came to live with us, she and Edward are out in the foyer, arguing over who gets the last piece of Raspberry and Chocolate Slice. Pax is in the shower, singing Roman drinking songs while he makes squelching noises with his armpits. Bree sits on the end of the bed with me, and the weight of her sorrow steals my breath.

I have to do *something*.

I take her hand and pull her to her feet. "Come with me."

"I c-c-can't." Her voice wobbles. "This house is so full of people, and they all expect me to figure this out. I can't get a moment to myself, and I'm somehow supposed to do battle against death itself..."

"I know. Come with me."

Something in my voice stirs her. She lets out her breath in a rush, and when her fingers find mine, it's as if she is touching me for the first time, the brush of her skin full of wonder.

I pick up my cane and with a few sharp raps on the floor to find my way, I lead her down the winding halls, into the wing where her parents live, the wing that's off-limits to B&B guests. I stop in front of a dusty door, my fingers searching for the handle.

"Ambrose, why are we going in here?"

I push open the door, and we step inside. My cane hits the edge of a stack of empty paint cans. I turn to the left, leading Bree between two towering stacks of extra table linens and cans of baked beans as large as my head.

"Ambrose, what do you want to show me in the storage room?"

"This." I tug her through the gap in the boxes. Bree gasps.

"Oh, I forgot about this place."

"I know." I grin. Memories come back to me as I breathe in the familiar dusty air and listen to the vast expanse of the space. *The ballroom.*

I attended many fine galas hosted by Cuthbert in the ballroom, decked out in my finest tails, the ladies resplendent in jewelled gowns that twinkled beneath the flickering light of a thousand candles. There was so much sparkle in the air that my eyes – so used to seeing only faint outlines of objects and pale squares of light – delighted in the visual display in a way I never normally could. I revelled in the noise, the shimmering flecks of light, the pleasant conversations, the music that lifted my soul.

I was quite the dancer back in my day. I amazed Cuthbert's friends – no one expects a blind man to be able to dance, but I memorised the steps, and the music gave me all the cues I needed to place my feet and twirl my partner. After the house fell to Cuthbert's descendants, balls went out of fashion and the room was closed off. Mike and Sylvie had big plans to renovate it and use it for weddings and events, but then they got a roofer to quote to fix the roof, and Sylvie's voice rose three octaves as she cried, "They want *how* much?" So now it's a storage room.

Bree's footsteps echo as she steps across the marble floor. I feel the air shift as she disturbs years of dust. "Remember when we used to play in here? Hide and seek in the supplies, and ice skating on my socks across the marble floor, and then roller skating after I got skates for Christmas, and you and Edward trying to teach me how to dance." She laughs, her voice lighter than it's been for days. "Thankfully, Edward never tried to dance with me the way he did at Alice's party."

At the memory of the three of us dancing at Alice's party, my body has a very different reaction. My cheeks flush with heat and I move towards her instinctively, my cane rapping on the marble floor. I didn't bring her here because I wanted to ravish her, but I cannot control my obscene thoughts around this woman.

"Here it is!" Bree's voice echoes from the far corner of the room. "Remember when I was roller skating in here and that piece of plaster came down! That was when Mum said I wasn't allowed to play in here by myself anymore. As if I was ever by myself. There's still a hole over here. I think it's even bigger now. I can see darkness and—Careful, Ambrose, I don't want you to trip on the plaster."

She slides her fingers through mine, and the touch rises a longing in my chest that makes me bold. I twirl her around, touching my hand to the small of her back as I glide her across the floor. I know exactly how many steps I can take before I hit a wall, and the echo of our footsteps tells me exactly where I am in space. I know that apart from that one corner, there is nothing in this room I can trip over or hit. The freedom and joy of it rushes my body, and I spin Bree under my arm, delighting in her laugh as I catch her and dip her low.

"You're amazing," she breathes as I pick her up again. Her arms go around me, which isn't strictly proper, but she lays her head on my shoulder and her heart thuds against my chest and I don't give a flying fig about what's proper.

"You're the amazing one." I stroke her hair, wishing I could hold her like this forever, that she didn't have to walk out of this ballroom and into the realm of monsters, that death didn't stalk her. But in this vast, empty space where it's just the two of us, I hope she can breathe again and find her way back to me. "We're going to figure this out. You'll see. Everything will be fine and dandy."

"Oh, Ambrose." Bree's fingers trace down my spine. "I don't know what to do. Out there, when I made the demon circle, I ran out of spray paint so I used my blood to finish the circle, and it made the magic super powerful. I didn't even have to try, not like with the Soul-Eater. So is it Lazarus blood that helps to trap the demons? But Father Maxwell was bleeding all over the other demon mark, so that doesn't make sense, either. And we can't ask him. Father Maxwell was my last hope. We're trapped in this house and if we don't figure out how to close the Veil or what the Order meant about this bloody crown nonsense, eventually the creatures will break through the wards and—"

"You speak as if this is all foretold. We still have hope." I kiss the top of her head, not wanting her to finish that sentence. I try to sound bright, but even I feel overwhelmed by the task before us. "We have St. Ekaterina's writings. And Father Maxwell can't be the only one who knows things. After all, the Order of the Noble Death has been around for centuries, and Lazarii have been around even longer. Surely, in that time, someone has abused their power and broken the Veil, and yet the world continued as normal. Which means that there must be a way to stop this."

"I just understand so little about my magic, and even less about the Veil. Father Maxwell said that Lazarii might be psychopomps, but I don't know how that's going to help us."

"Well, you do know one aspect of your power well – you talk to ghosts, right?" I say. "If no one living understands this stuff, find someone dead." An idea occurs to me. "Like your great-grandmother, Elsie. Isn't she a ghost? That's how she was able to visit you when you were a baby after she was dead."

"But Dad *saw* her," Bree reminds me. "And Dad can't see ghosts. So she can't be a ghost."

"But she can't be a Lazarus, either, right? Because the doorway is one way. Not even a Lazarus can come back once they cross over. So maybe she's a mix of Lazarus and something else, like a revenant or a shade? Isn't Lazarus' story that he becomes immortal after Jesus brought him back? That's why people keep seeing him everywhere. Whatever Elsie is, she might know what's going on. After all, she went to all that trouble to visit you when you were younger. Maybe that's important."

"I don't know." Bree sways gently with me. "But you're right. It's worth a try. Thank you. I needed this."

I squeeze her. "We can stay here a little longer."

"I'd like that."

We sway slowly, holding each other as our feet shuffle over the marble floor. I breathe in her pear and almond scent and I know that even if we don't manage to figure this out, even if this is the end for all of us, I will go to my grave happy because I love and have been loved by Bree Mortimer.

A gust of cold air from the corner where the roof is leaking catches us, making the skin on Bree's arms pebble. I pull her closer, spinning her away, trying to keep her warm. Windows along two walls usually let light pour in, but with the gloom outside, there is no break from unrelenting darkness.

"Ambrose," Bree murmurs against my shoulder. "If we ever get out of this alive, what do you think is going to happen to us?"

"We'll live happily ever after until the end of our days," I say with certainty. "That's what happened in all those stories you made me and Edward make up for you as a child. You used to scold us if our stories didn't end with a happily ever after."

"Yes, but...how can we come back from *this?*" Bree's voice rises in pitch again. "People have *died,* and seen their dead friends and relatives rise from the grave. Even if I do manage to put things to rights, my powers are dangerous. And that's aside from the problem of what you and Pax and Edward will do. You can't just keep mooching around Grimwood without jobs, bank accounts, or birth certificates. We have to make a *life.*"

"We'll figure it out together. We always do."

She pulls back to face me, her lips an inch from mine. My

chest aches from wanting her and wanting this life together that she believes is so impossible. "I can't think about it anymore. I feel as though I'm going to explode from worry. Please, Ambrose, kiss me until I don't have to think anymore."

"I'm always happy to oblige my lady." I stroke my thumb along her cheek, pulling her in close to capture her lips with mine. As my tongue ventures into the sweet depths of her mouth, I understand Edward's insatiable need to turn everything into poetry, Cuthbert's compulsion to collect and study all the mysteries of human history. I want to capture this moment, these sensations, the alchemy of this woman, forever.

As she sinks against me, her lips brushing mine with growing intensity, I swallow her fear, taking from her this burden that she shouldn't have to carry.

And as I lay her down on a pile of guest towels, spread her legs wide, and lap at her juices until she squirms and mews and begs, I hope that she knows that no matter what happens, I will love her until the stars blink out and the ocean dries up, maybe even longer.

I can't give Bree the answers, but I can give her this release, this moment to collect herself. I can remind her exactly what we're fighting for.

And perhaps, when I'm called to the front lines of this battle, I will give her the life that hums in my veins.

17

BREE

"Yo, witches." I bang a wooden spoon on the bottom of my mother's cast-iron skillet. "Where are you? I need to talk to you."

Kelly looks up from her coffee and makes a face like she's sucking on a lemon, but I'm through hiding my true self for her sake.

Dani grins at me over her stack of Pax-cakes. (Pax-cakes are pancakes smothered in caramelised bananas, bacon bits, and a drizzle of lemon syrup. Pax has spent the last two weeks perfecting the recipe, which is just as well because his first attempt – combining the fluffiest pancakes with a traditional Roman fish sauce – sent most of us reeling for the toilet.)

"You hollered?" Mary floats through the wall, yawning and stretching. Lottie comes in from the sitting room.

"This better be important. I was watching *Supernatural* and Sam and Dean are just about to figure out that Madison is really the werewolf—"

"EXCUSE ME," Edward booms from the other room. "Spoiler alert!"

"It's very important." I tap my nails on the skillet. "Say I wanted to find someone, but I didn't know where they were or if they were even still alive. Could your magic help me do that?"

Mary cracks her knuckles. "That's easy. Give us something difficult, like cursing a cheating husband's sausage to turn blue. In fact, let's do that – I love a good husband sausage curse."

"No one's sausage needs cursing," I say firmly. Kelly's eyes widen as she stares at the spot where Lottie and Mary are. I know that all she can see is me talking about sausages to empty air. But she doesn't run from the room or say anything nasty, which I consider progress. "Tell me how I might find someone using magic?"

"We perform a scrying spell," Lottie explains. "Scrying is a kind of mirror magic. The mirror is a way to look into another place, another location, sometimes even another time. You won't get a location on a map, but you will see the person where they are, and be able to talk to them. The landscape around them might also give you a clue."

"Once, we were scrying for Lottie's husband," says Mary. "And found him in a rather compromising position in the stables with—"

"Yes, thank you, Mary." Lottie shoots her friend a look that would chill the bones of any person who actually still had bones. "Mary raises an important point. You have to be very careful with scrying. It's the kind of magic that should not be taken lightly."

"Why? Isn't it just like a witch telephone?"

"Mirror magic is all about revealing truths. But that goes both ways. When you look into the mirror, you don't know who might be looking back at you, or what they might be able to see."

I nod. "Got it. So if I want to scry, what do I do?"

Mary dunks her head into Dani's stack of Pax-cakes. "Well, the first thing is that you need to be initiated into our coven."

I roll my eyes. "You can't be serious. We have literal monsters right outside. This isn't the time for pointless rituals."

"The initiation ritual is *far* from pointless, young lady!" Lottie waves her finger at me. I decide not to tell her how much she sounds like Agnes. "It binds our magic to a single purpose."

"Can't you just explain to me how to do the scrying? I'm good at following instructions."

"No can do," Mary's muffled voice says from inside the stack of fluffy goodness. "Successful scrying requires three witches."

"Can't we just..." A noise outside makes me lose my train of thought. I run to the window, but all I can see outside is the gloom of the Veil.

I train my ears, and I think I can hear something looming in the dark, growing louder as it gets closer to Grimwood.

It sounds like chanting.

Pax whirls around from the stove, the newspaper chef's hat he made himself toppling over one ear as he reaches for the knife rack block where he left his sword. Edward comes in from the lounge, his sardonic grin wobbling a little at the edges, the storms in his eyes betraying his fear.

"What *is* that infernal noise?" he demands, leaning against the doorframe and running his fingers through his tousled dark hair. "Dani, if you've developed a taste for bland Gregorian chants, could you keep it to yourself? *Some* of us are trying to watch our programme and lose ourselves in Winchester fantasies."

"It's not me—"

BANG BANG BANG.

We all freeze. I drop my spoon. Edward leaps about five feet in the air and dives behind Pax.

"What was that?" Dad asks, his coffee cup jerking in his hand.

"If I had to guess, I'd say it's the Order of the Noble Death, here to get the party started." I grip the edge of the counter as Pax moves toward the front door, where the banging was coming from.

BANG BANG!

The whole house trembles.

"I thought they couldn't get up to the front door?" Dani whispers as we tiptoe into the foyer. I can see shapes moving through the stained glass panels on either side of the door. Pax stands to the side, his sword ready, his jaw locked.

BANG BANG BANG!

The door's hinges rattle.

"I thought so, too," I whisper back. "Maybe they still have power over the Lazarus crosses. But we warded the door, as well, and the witches helped me make some protection charms, so hopefully that keeps them out for—"

"We know that you're in here, Bree Mortimer," a voice booms, making my heart leap into my throat. "If you open the wards and allow us inside, we promise that we will spare you and your friends."

"Like you spared Father Maxwell?" I yell back. Seriously, the *nerve* of these guys. "I don't think so. I don't trust the clergy. Push off, the lot of you."

"Let me at them," Pax growls. "I'll make holy water out of their eyeball juices."

"As tempting as that is," Dad says, "I think it's best we ignore them and go back to this business about the scrying—"

"We can help you," another voice calls from the other side, female, and distinctly softer and kinder than her fellow priest. "This hole you've created in the Veil, these monsters who are hurting the people you love, we can make it all go away. All you have to do is become a priestess of our Order. You'll see that we're actually the good guys. We'll teach you how to control your powers so this can't ever happen again. That's all we want – to help you stop this."

I drop Dani's arm and move towards the door. Edward steps in front of me, his anthracite eyes clouded with despair.

"Brianna, do not go with them."

"You may be a prince, but you don't command me."

"They are lying. They are murderers."

"They know how to stop this horror," I whisper, as the fear that what he's saying is true ripples through my body, rooting me in place. "What choice do I have?"

His fathomless eyes plead with me. "You are correct – they know how to stop this, and they haven't. They let innocent people die because they don't care about the monsters or the people of Grimdale. They only want *you*. Maybe they want to kill you, as they killed Father Maxwell, but I think they want you for the same dark purpose that Jack the Ripper has turned his eye to you. If they're telling the truth, and they can stop this, then it means that it *can* be stopped." Edward steps back and nods to the witches. "Do the scrying spell. It's our best hope."

I glance at the windows again, at the dark shapes moving in the gloom. They're surrounding Grimwood, just like they did to All Souls. I think of what I saw in the priestess' memories. I think Edward may be right – they don't just want to kill me because I'm a rogue Lazarus. They want something more.

Something only I can give them.

Something to do with this crown.

But until they tell me the truth, I'm the best chance this village has got.

I turn to Mary.

"I need to be initiated as quickly as possible. What do we do?"

"We need to go to the old stone altar in the forest, which is sacred to..." Mary's face falls as she watches the shadowed figures outside the window. "Oh. Yes, this is a problem. We can't go to a sacred site because we'd have to cross the wards."

"I might be able to help," Dad says. "There are some stones in the undercroft beneath the floor of the ballroom that are believed to be the remains of an ancient stone circle. It looks as if whoever built the house actually designed the ballroom around them, as the circular marble design on the floor fits the circumference of the stone circle exactly."

"Wait, this house has a ballroom?" Alice says. "Cool."

"The ballroom has a leaky roof, so we can't allow guests inside. We use it as storage. Alice, your father looked at the stones for us once, back when Sylvie and I were young and naive and thought we could renovate the room. He said they were part of a Late Neolithic structure that was even older than Stonehenge. We can access the undercroft from a hatch inside the downstairs linen cupboard. It's a bit dank and dingy."

"And filled with spiders?" I ask with a shudder.

"That's perfect!" Mary cries.

"Well, the spiders aren't ideal." Lottie makes a face. "But the stone circle will be the perfect place for our rituals. I've always felt a magical pull from this spot, and now I know why."

I glance at my father. "You're telling me that we have a literal magical stone circle under the house and you never even told me?"

Dad pats the mahogany panelling lovingly. "This house has all kinds of secrets. I wouldn't be surprised if the very walls form a gateway to the realm of Death itself. Come on, grab a light, I'll show you."

18

BREE

"I can't believe that I didn't even know this was here," I say, stooping in the low undercroft to take in the circle of large stones overgrown with moss and weeds standing in the middle of the dingy underfloor crawl space.

"You probably don't remember it. I took you down here a couple of times as a little girl, but you hated it." Dad passes me down my basket of supplies. "You told me there was a nasty witch who lived here and she screamed at you. I thought you were just afraid of the dark, but she was a ghost, wasn't she?"

"That's right," I remember now. "She was all bent and horrible. Like Agnes on crystal meth," I glance around the room, but I can't see the mean old witch anywhere. I start taking out candles and lighting them.

"You mean Black Annie? She crossed over a few years back," Lottie says. "It turns out that her unfinished business was to make Agnes cry. And she finally did by—"

"Shhhh!" Mary raises a finger. "We promised Agnes that we would never tell."

"Not even to coven members?" I lift an eyebrow.

"You're not a coven member until we complete the ritual."

"Fine." I roll my eyes as I place my final candles and start pulling out the supplies Lottie made me collect. "Just tell me what I need to do to be initiated as a witch. And make it snappy."

"I'll leave your ladies to your revels." Dad winks in the vague direction of Lottie as he climbs back up the narrow ladder. Pax, Edward, and Ambrose linger, Pax making a face as he stoops lower to avoid hitting his head on one of the beams.

Lottie instructs me to stand behind one of the stones. The two of them spread out, so we're each standing an equal distance apart around the outside of the circle. "Usually, casting a circle works better with four of us – the four elements, the four points of the compass. But three is also a powerful number in magic, so this will be fine. First, raise your arms to the heavens and focus your energy on imagining a protective wall rising from the earth to surround us."

I raise my hands, then lower them slightly after I hit my wrist on an old lead pipe. Mary does the same while Lottie walks around the circle, chanting in a language I don't under-stand and moving her hands in odd ways as she sprinkles salt on the ground.

"This circle is now cast," Lottie stands in her starting posi-tion behind the largest stone. "Now, take your kit off."

"Excuse me?"

Mary is already peeling off her dress. "We have to perform the initiation skyclad – that means clad only in the sky. So get your clothes off."

Pax rubs his hands together. "I like this ritual."

"Oh, no you don't." Mary shoos him away. "Witches only. Go and cook us some eggs or something."

"Yes, Pax," Edward points to the ladder. "Get out of here. Your impressively large shoulders are blocking our view."

"You're leaving too, Prince." Lottie plants her hands on his chest. Because I'm here, she actually manages to shove him a little. "And take this other gentleman with you."

"But I am your prince!" Edward plants his hands on his hips. "And I shall stay if I so desire, and I *very much* desire—"

"Don't make me possess your body." Mary lurches toward him menacingly. "I'll do it. I'll use your limbs and make you cut off your own todger if you don't—"

In a puff of smoke, the boys have escaped back upstairs, slamming the hatch behind them. Mary descends, brushing off her hands with satisfaction. "Now that's taken care of, let us get skyclad."

"How can we be skyclad when there's no sky down here?"

"You use your imagination." Lottie tosses her apron into the gloom.

"Can't I just use my imagination to pretend we're not wearing any clothes—"

"No," Mary and Lottie say firmly.

I sigh. I yank my clothes off and fold them neatly at the bottom of the ladder. I hope like hell that no spiders crawl inside them. I cross my arms over my tits as goosebumps pebble along my arms.

Lottie and Mary's clothes disappear as they fling them away – a side effect of being ghosts. Mary's skin is covered in a lovely smattering of freckles. Both of them have bruising around their necks from where they were hung as witches.

I focus my attention on a spiderweb in the ceiling rafters.

"Since Agnes isn't here, I'm the next oldest," Lottie says. "I shall perform the ceremony. Step into the circle."

I do. Lottie points to a gold curtain tie she made me bring down. "You'll have to wrap that around your own wrists, I'm afraid. These old ghost hands can't quite do it."

I tie a knot in the cord while Lottie murmurs some stuff about loyalty to the coven. I slip the cord over my hands. Then,

Lottie makes me smear some dirt across my cheeks (gross) and drink from a chalice of wine (less gross, but difficult to do when one's hands are bound by a curtain tie. We should have started with the wine).

BANG!

The hatch jiggles ominously.

Fear leaps in my chest. *Have the Order made it inside—*

"Brianna is naked down there," Edward cries. "As a prince of England, I demand to be let in."

"She also said it's witches only," Ambrose shoots back. "So we're to stay up here like good ghosts until they're finished."

"I'm with Edward," Pax growls. "I want naked Bree. Besides, she might need my sword and—"

"I can think of a few uses for your sword, Roman!" Lottie gyrates her hips lasciviously.

"Go away!" I yell up at the hatch. "We're busy!"

I hear several mumbles, and then silence.

I turn back to Lottie and Mary. "Am I a witch yet?"

"I don't know…" Lottie eyes the food container peeking out from my basket. "What kind of cupcakes did you bring?"

"Red velvet. Your favourite. Pax is getting rather good at baking."

Lottie plonks down beside the basket. "Then I officially declare that you're a real witch. Set out the sweet deliciousness and let us feast."

"Aren't you forgetting something? We've got to scry for Great-Grandmother Elsie?"

Mary sighs dramatically. "Fine. But I need a sniff of cupcake first. Sugar sharpens my sight."

"I'm sure it does." I open the container and let her dip her head inside, and then I set up the scrying bowl and candles in the centre of the circle according to Lottie's instructions.

Draughts from the far corners of the undercroft keep blowing the candles out, but Lottie says they're only for dramatic effect.

I place my great-grandmother's pink luggage tag into the bowl of water. We were lucky that Dad kept it after Elsie fled the house, and luckier still that he remembered which box in my old bedroom he threw it in, and triple lucky that Mum hadn't got around to making him clear out that room.

The tag sinks to the bottom with more weight than I'd expect from a flimsy leather square. The water glows with a faint pink hue. Lottie and Mary reach out, and I grip their hands in mine, my fingers sinking slightly inside them.

It takes me a moment to cast aside the images of their memories — flashes of their lives from centuries before — hard lives where they clawed joy from whatever small indulgences they could get away with, and were hanged as witches for it. When I return to the room, the witches are chanting in that strange old language. The waters shimmer and shift.

I don't know the words, but I don't think it matters. I go to my place of peace and call up my powers. Lottie and Mary's silver cords shimmer as they coil around the circle, lighting our ritual where the candles have failed me.

"Focus on Elsie," Lottie instructs. "Try to reach her with your mind. What do you see?"

I peer into the bowl.

All I see is water swirling on top of a pink luggage tag.

"Nothing. I must be doing it wrong. You try," I say.

"Scrying doesn't work like that," Lottie says. "The one who is searching must look into the water."

"But what am I supposed to see? Do I have to do anything or—"

"Stop being so impatient." Mary takes a break from chanting to sniff the cupcakes again. "Magic doesn't always happen on a schedule. You need to look with your heart as well as your eyes."

Ghost-balls. That's super useful. How am I supposed to do that?

I look back at the water, and I do what I always do when I try to use my powers – I go to the memory of me and Dad painting a soap-box racer in the garage. I focus on the details of the memory – Dad's low, rumbling voice as he sings along, the steady brush of paint on wood, and the contentment in my heart. Something in that memory unlocks a door inside me, and when I peer into the swirling waters, I see a shape that wasn't there before.

It's a face.

My breath catches in my throat. I lean forward, watching the image shimmer and shift. Eyes and nose and chin come into focus, as well as a cute little pink hat that's a little old-fashioned but rather stylish.

My great-grandmother Elsie.

The shock of seeing her in the water almost makes me pull away, but I don't want to break the connection. Not when I can feel the magic rising off the water, pulling my face towards her.

All I've ever seen of her is the photograph on the wall. I remember the way she sounds and smells and feels in my dreams about the day she visited, but I know that brains can't actually recall faces from dreams, so I couldn't say that I'd *seen* her. But seeing her reflection in the rippling surface of the water is something else – something both alien and familiar, like looking into my own reflection in a carnival funhouse mirror.

I can see that we have identical cheekbones and the same slightly turned-up nose.

"Elsie?" I whisper. I feel odd using her first name, but I don't know what I'm supposed to call her. 'Great-Gran' is a bit too informal when we've never actually spoken as adults.

But there's something wrong.

Elsie stares out of the mirror, but her eyes are glassy, unmoving. Her features are oddly slack. Her skin is pale – and not just a normal White British Person's complexion pale, but a sickly kind of pale that could be...

No.

Oh no.

Elsie's *dead.*

19

BREE

Tears spring in the corners of my eyes. After all this effort, we found my great-grandmother, but she can't help us—

Elsie's mouth falls open.

Before I have the chance to scream, rose petals tumble out from between her lips. They tumble down the front of her pink dress, staining it wherever they touch.

In my fingers, Mary and Lottie's hands hum with a low, steady rhythm.

"I found her." My voice trembles. Tears tumble from my eyes. "She's dead. Recently dead. But how can she be recently dead? She died decades ago from a tumor. She can't die twice, can she?"

"I don't know, love. In your world, death isn't always the end," Mary says. "What else do you see?"

"Nothing. There's nothing. Well, rose petals are coming out of her mouth. And..." I squint into the water. "She looks as if she's lying on stone...no, marble. A fancy marble floor, like the one in the ballroom, but not as dusty. And there's an object beside her head. It's got white spiky bits, like bones—"

I gasp as a black shadow falls in front of the image, obscuring my great-grandmother.

A pair of red, glowing eyes fix on me.

When you scry, you don't know who could be looking back.

The Ripper rasps, "Hello, Bree."

20

BREE

My blood turns to ice. What is the Ripper doing with my great-grandmother? We sent him back beyond the Veil, so how has he found her if she's died in the Realm of the Living?

Either he's back already or...or...Great-Grandmother Elsie isn't in the Realm of the Living.

But if she's beyond the Veil, in the Realm of the Dead...

How can she die if she's beyond the Veil?

The Ripper backs up a step. He grins, sensing what I've figured out. "Answer me this, Little Lazarus, where does a Lazarus go when her soul is destroyed?"

Elsie, no. I'm so, so sorry.

"Why did you kill her?" I ask. "*How* did you kill her?"

"I knew you'd come for her," he says, avoiding my question. "But I didn't expect you to be on the other side of a looking glass. How cowardly. You should come step through the doorway and face me in person."

He reaches up with a finger and taps. The surface of the water ripples, and it takes everything I have not to recoil in horror. I expect his finger to puncture the surface and reach up to claw out my eyes, but it doesn't.

"You know where I am, Lazarus," he snarls. "Come and get me. Come and take what's rightfully yours—don't you let him take the crown, Bree Mortimer."

The Ripper slaps his cheek. "Get out, foul woman—did you hear me? I said to stay away from the crown."

"Agnes?"

"Yes, of course it's me," the Ripper says. "Who did you expect, the bloody postman?"

"Sorry, it's just not every day that the ghost of a witch talks to me through the lips of a Victorian serial killer," I snap back.

"We don't have much time before he gets control again. You listen to me, and you listen good." she snaps. "He wants the crown, but you can't let him have it. You need to look at my memories."

"How do I—"

"Just get in there, and be quick about it." The Ripper raises a shaking hand to the surface of the water. On the very edges of his fingers, I see her. A silver shimmer.

"Bree, what are you doing?" Lottie cries. "Don't touch the water."

I ignore her, stretching my hand out and skimming my palm over the surface. The water feels odd, heavy. My vision swims, and then I'm inside Agnes' memories.

She must have selected a specific memory, because I see myself as a plump five-year-old, wobbling on my bicycle as I ride it through the cemetery, my dad chasing behind me. I'm watching from a spot in the bushes.

And I'm not alone.

"I can't believe you've convinced me to hide in the shrubbery like a peeping tom," Vera mumbles as she opens up her purse and withdraws a large brownie wrapped in greaseproof paper. "They're not coming after a little girl."

"They are," I say firmly. "I saw them."

Vera munches on her brownie. "Did you ever think that what you saw might be a result of sticking your head in my baking tin?"

"Nope. I've had these visions all my life and my afterlife, and they always come true. The Order will be here—Vera, look."

"Bloody hell," Vera swears, and darts from the bushes.

Vera drops the brownie and bolts from the trees. I turn and see...myself, little Bree, speeding towards a figure dressed in a black cassock. The figure holds a Cross of Lazarus in one hand and reaches the other into the air. I don't know what they're doing, but the magic humming in the air feels wrong. Dangerous.

"Get away from her!" Dad yells.

The priest doesn't get away from her.

Bree screams. Her feet slip from the pedals. Vera runs as fast as she can, her sensible shoes sliding on the slippery path. Bree's bike hits a gravestone and she topples over the handlebars, hitting her head with a *CRACK*.

She drops to the ground.

She doesn't move.

All I can do is watch in horror as the Order priest hunches over Bree's – *my* – prone body, winding their hands through the air. As Agnes, I can't see the soul-cords, but I know exactly what the priest is doing. He's trying to snap my cord and take my life.

Dad reaches my body and shoves the priest away. He cradles me in my arms, whispering my name, checking my pulse, growing more and more agitated. The priest looks down and nods, satisfied that he's done what he came to do. As Agnes, I feel a strong urge to go over there and walk through him, but giving him a chill doesn't seem like sufficient punishment for killing a child.

Vera swings her gaze between the retreating priest and my body. She runs over and crouches beside Dad.

"She hit her head," Dad's voice rises with panic. "She's not breathing. I can't feel a pulse. I...I don't know what to do."

"Get out of my way," Vera snaps. Dad sits back on his knees, looking so shocked and sick.

Vera waves her hands over me, her fingers snapping closed, and although I can't see the cords through Agnes' eyes, I know exactly what she's doing.

I didn't *almost* die that day.

I *literally* died.

Vera brought me back to life.

I watch as Vera breathes my soul-cord back into me and rubs my shoulder as I gasp and sputter. "She's breathing fine now," Vera says. "Call the ambulance and get her checked over. It looks like a nasty bump on the head. But whatever you do, don't tell anyone that you saw me here."

Dad's too busy hugging me to reply. Vera gives a curt nod, then wanders off into the tombs. As Agnes, I float off to catch up with her outside the cemetery gates.

"Did the priest see you?" Agnes asks, the words falling from my lips.

"They believe she's dead. They will stop hunting her," Vera says.

"Hmmph. She gets to live, but the moment she starts performing resurrection magic, they will sense her. They will know that Bree Mortimer still lives, that the bloodline still endures, and she will always be a threat to them."

"So I shall be here to protect and guide her," Vera says. "And you will help me, with your visions. We promised Elsie—"

The memory wobbles and fades, and I'm staring into the

bowl of water again. The Ripper glares back with a distinctly Agnes tilt of his chin.

I can't believe what I just saw. "You...you knew my great-grandmother? You knew about the Order of the Noble Death, and that I'm a Lazarus? Why didn't you tell me any of this?"

"Your great-grandmother left me and Vera clear instructions," Agnes snaps back. "If I told you about your powers, you might've tried to use them, especially when you became close to those three ghosts. And I was right, wasn't I? The minute you learned what you could do, you started resurrecting people left, right, and centre. That caught the attention of the Order of the Noble Death. They knew you were still alive."

"But why did they try to kill me when I was a kid? Father Bryne said that they wanted me to join them. I wouldn't have even known what they were asking me about when I was five."

"Why? Because you're not just any old Lazarus, are you?" the Ripper huffs. "You're the heir to the Crown of Bones."

"I'm what the *what?*"

"Why do you think that your blood can close a demon mark and ward a manor house for days on end? Now that Elsie's gone, you're the only living heir."

What? "That's absurd. I'm not heir to anything except a crumbling old manor house—"

The Ripper snorts. "Yes, and why did Elsie go to such great lengths to ensure Grimwood remained in your family? Why did she come back to check on you to make sure you shared her powers, hmmm? Because she knew it would come to this one day. You would need the doorway. The Veil is breaking apart and the Ripper is causing mayhem. You can't stop him from up there. You'll find everything you need in the rose garden."

"Agnes, stop giving me cryptic clues – I'm not Sherlock Holmes. Just tell me what's going on—"

"What's going on is that—" the Ripper growls, and he lunges at the mirror again.

This time, water splashes from the bowl. I leap back, breaking my grip on Lottie and Mary. The image in the bowl disappears, and the water settles back to a calm, clear surface.

I lean against the stone wall of the basement, my heart in my throat. "What was that? What happened?"

Lottie and Mary hold each other. Both witches tremble. "He tried to get through," Lottie says. "He would have done it if you hadn't broken the connection. He's too powerful. He's tearing the Veil apart. We *have* to close the hole in the Veil."

"What did you see?" Mary asks. "Did you find Elsie?"

"I did, but she's dead." I swallow. "I think...I think I found her in the world of the Dead, which means that somehow the Ripper killed her there. I don't understand any of it. I talked to Agnes inside the Ripper before he managed to suppress her, and she said a whole lot of things that make no sense. Like, apparently, Elsie asked her and Vera to watch out for me."

"I believe that," Lottie nods. "The two of them were always whispering together. And Agnes was always checking up on you. I thought it was her grandmotherly instinct finally kicking in."

"She said that I'm 'Heir to the Crown of Bones.' Normally, I'd stay well away from anything that sounds like a bad romantasy book, but we're running out of options. Does either of you know what that means?"

Both witches shake their heads.

"I thought so. Since the Order doesn't want me to get this crown, and it's probably got something to do with the Ripper's special interest in me, I'm going to guess we have to find it first. Which means going to the Realm of the Dead."

I try not to think about how much that freaks me out.

Agnes says that I'll find everything I need in the rose garden.

Elsie said something similar, in one of my dreams. I guess that's where this is all going to end."

We find the rose garden, we find the Crown of Bones (whatever that is), and we have a way to end the Ripper's reign of terror once and for all.

I hope.

21

BREE

"The thing is, Grimwood doesn't have a rose garden." Dad tries to stir his cup of tea, but his hand won't cooperate. Eventually, he fishes the spoon out and drops it on the floor before taking a shaky sip. "The soil at Grimwood has far too much clay in it for roses to thrive. I tried to plant some out front when you were a little girl, remember? But they were so depressing that I pulled them out and added hydrangea bushes instead. I think I still have a scar on my finger from the thorns."

"And if Elsie never lived in Grimwood, when would she have had the time to tend a rose garden?" Ambrose adds.

Dad waggles a finger at him. "An excellent point."

"Perhaps you misheard her?" Edward points out. "Maybe she said they're in her 'nose harbour' or her 'post ardour,' which sounds positively *devious*—"

I shake my head, but then remember that Ambrose can't see me. "First of all, that makes no sense. And second, Ambrose heard Elsie mention the rose garden in my memory for when she came to see me, and I heard her when I scried. We didn't both mishear."

"Maybe there *used* to be a rose garden, but it was gone by the time you moved in?" Dani asks Dad. He beams.

"Dani could be onto something. Grimwood has changed so much over the centuries, there could have been a rose garden at some point." Dad peers between my three guys. "The three of you have firsthand knowledge of the history of this house. Do you remember a rose garden?"

Edward folds his arms. "I'm a prince. It's not my job to know the names of flowers."

"Aren't roses a symbol of your family?"

Edward scoffs. "I tried to have as little to do with my family as possible. If Grimwood had roses when I purchased it, I probably had them torn out."

"I walked the gardens many times when I lived here," Ambrose says. "I do not recall the scent of roses."

"If Druids can't hide in them, and you can't get drunk off them, I wouldn't notice plants," Pax says. He yawns loudly. My poor centurion. He looks hagged, his shoulders drooping and his eyes bloodshot. He's wearing himself out trying to stay awake to patrol the house. Abberline has begrudgingly agreed to take the next watch so Pax can sleep, but Pax doesn't trust the inspector not to get drunk (truthfully, neither do I), so he's still awake.

Agnes says that I'm the reason why the wards aren't failing, but since I don't understand how, I can't tell Pax to step down.

"No offence intended, but on the off chance that your memories aren't perfect, I have an idea," Dad says. "I kept some of the old house blueprints, and paintings and sketches from around Elsie's time, and from the Van Wimples before her. Sylvie kept wanting me to throw them out, but I was positive they'd come in handy one day. Of course, I was thinking if we needed to locate an old pipe or something. But maybe a previous occupant will have conveniently labelled the rose garden on one of them."

"That's perfect. Where are they?"

"In the closet in your old room."

DAD STAYS DOWNSTAIRS and gets a pot of tea boiling (still no milk. It's a travesty) while the rest of us climb the stairs to my old bedroom. I push the door open tentatively. I haven't been in this room since the night Pax and I sullied my childhood bed and met a shapeshifting raven.

It's now filled with even more boxes and detritus from the renovations. Stacks of roofing shingles are piled beneath the window where my dollhouse used to be, and paint cans form a small fortification around the foot of my bed.

Kelly wanders around the room, picking up my old soft toys. My shoulders tense. I don't like her in here, pawing over the space that was once my sanctuary from her. She lingers over the old photographs pinned to my corkboard while Dani and Alice pull archival boxes from the closet.

We spread the stuff out all over the room and shuffle through it. Ambrose climbs up next to me on the bed. It takes me a long time to go through my stack because he wants me to describe every piece to him, especially when I get to several sketches done by his friend Cuthbert.

"Nothing in here." Dani closes the lid on one of her boxes. "I don't see anything about a rose garden."

"Sorry, were we supposed to be looking at this stuff?" Kelly frowns. She found a nail file somewhere and was giving herself a manicure. "No thanks, I don't touch gross old documents. I could get a disease."

"How were we ever friends?" Alice shakes her head.

"It's no good." I fall back on my old bed, sending up a cloud of dust. "There's no rose garden here. So what did Elsie mean? She wouldn't have given me this clue unless it meant something, and Agnes seemed to think it was important."

"Um...Bree?"

"Ambrose, what is it?"

He has his fingers stretched up, running over where I carved our initials into the plaster moulding.

$$B + P + E + A = 4EVA$$

"Bree, look!" His face is rapturous, but we don't have time to get lost in memories.

"I remember writing that, but it's not important now—"

"No, look! The roses."

I squint at his fingers. My heart hammers against my chest. How had I never noticed before that the mouldings in my bedroom were decorated with *roses*?

"Shit," Dani says. "I didn't even think of that."

"Wait, wait. I saw something." Alice scrambles through the papers strewn across the floor. She pulls one out and hands it to me. "Interior design ideas. I skipped past them because I thought we were looking for an actual garden. Here."

I glance down at the paper. It's a series of sketches of the room we're in. Some show the way it looked before – a dark, wood-panelled gentleman's billiards room – while others show designs for a light, feminine space. Alongside these sketches is a list of changes noted in slanting, loopy handwriting. The list is signed with the initials E and dated the year Elsie took possession of the house.

"It looks like some of your great-grandmother's renovations from when she was planning to live in the house," Alice says. "From what I know about Victorian houses, the billiards room would be where the man of the house went in the evenings for a drink and a cigar. He would have entertained friends there, too. But Elsie never married. My kind of girl."

"She turned it into her rose garden," Dani breathes.

We all get the same idea at the same time. Ambrose and I start pressing on the moulding above the bed while Alice climbs on Dani's shoulders to check above the windows. Even Kelly pulls over a stepladder and starts to feel along the moulding near the wardrobe.

Grimwood is a house of secrets. Of course Great-Grandmother Elsie would have left a secret of her own.

"I found something!" Kelly cries out.

We all rush over. Ambrose hits his leg on the bed and stumbles into me, but he's too excited to even cry out. I get up on the stepladder opposite Kelly and peer at the moulding.

"Look, this one turns." Kelly twists the rose in her fingers. Plaster dust rains down on both of us. "But nothing's happening."

"There's another one over here," Alice calls out.

My heart leaps. "Twist them together, maybe?"

It takes a couple of tries for Kelly and Alice to coordinate, but they both twist the roses a sharp left turn at the same time. There's a mechanical crunching sound, and a panel pops out of the wall beneath them, revealing a square, black hole.

Scratched into the wood beneath the hole, in what looks distinctly like Elsie's handwriting, are the words:

ONLY THE DEAD MAY PASS

"I can't believe I slept in this room for years and never knew about this." I turn on the flashlight on my phone and point it at the wall. The light doesn't seem to touch the sides of the space. "What is this?"

I step closer. An invisible hand reaches out from the hole and wraps warm fingers around my heart, tugging me closer. I glance down, and for the first time, I see my own black cord stretching out of my chest towards the hole and disappearing over the edge.

A soft voice calls my name. *Bree...don't be afraid...*

The weird thing is, I'm not. Unlike the creeping gloom outside, something about the darkness of this hole feels welcoming. Familiar. As if I've known it my whole life.

Which I guess, in a way, I have.

"What is that?" Edward recoils. "I don't like it. Brianna, make it go away."

"The voices don't seem malicious," Dani says. "They're telling me that they're...er, *proud* of me caring for the dead and for administering the medicine of grief to those left behind."

"I hear voices too," Ambrose says. "They're calling my name, telling me that I was supposed to have walked the pathway many moons ago, but they understand I'm needed here now."

Edward wears an oddly serene expression. "Mine says that the son does not have to follow in the footsteps of the father, and that I've been given a second chance to create a legacy I'll be proud of."

"Mine says that I have slain many enemies, and I will be greatly rewarded at the foot of Pluto's throne, but my greatest battle is yet to come," Pax declares. "And it also revealed who will win the next season of *Bake-Off*. The voice is wise, and all-knowing."

"I don't like it." Kelly clamps her hands over her ears. "It's horrible. Make it stop!"

She runs from the room.

I glance around my friends. They all wear strange expressions on their faces as they listen to voices meant only for them. The voice in my ears whispers my name once more.

Bree, the crown is waiting for you.

"Brianna, don't." Edward reaches for me, but I shove past him and walk right up to the edge of the hole.

I know.

I know things I shouldn't know.

I know what this hole is.

I thrust my head inside.

A rush of warm air sweeps over me, invisible fingers like a lovers' caress. *Bree, the crown is waiting for you. The pathway is open. You are needed to restore the balance.*

My own balance tips forward as my black cord spirals down into nothingness. I grip the edge of the hole to stop myself from falling in.

There are no edges, nothing of the interior of the house's walls. Nothing but a deep, dark, impossible void.

Hands grab me, yank me back. Edward wraps me in his arms, his princely features twisted with fear. "Brianna, you were about to fall. That secret passage is trying to lure you—"

I swallow. "It's not a secret passage. It's a doorway through the Veil to the world of the Dead, and I have to go through it."

<h1 style="text-align:center">22</h1>

BREE

"I went to the underworld once, I think," Mina says from my phone's speaker as we all settle back into the sitting room to figure out what to do next. "I'm still not entirely sure. But I had to drown myself to get there. And I had to bring a bottle of wine for Dante. He runs the place."

"Dante, the poet?" Edward looks interested.

"Yeah."

"You wouldn't really have been talking to the ruler of the Veil," says Lottie. "Only people like Bree, whose magic touches death, will see the reality of the place. A visitor such as yourself washing in on the waters of Meles would see what you wished to see."

"So basically, I'm no help?" Mina sighs.

"Basically." Lottie folds her hands across her lap.

"It seems pretty obvious," I say. "There's a hole in the Veil. The only way to fix it is from the other side. My great-grandmother left a pathway in our house to get there, so I go down and fix it, easy as pie."

"Speaking of pie, your plan has more holes in it than a blueberry flan." Mary frowns. "You can't just walk down this hole and expect to end up in the underworld. That's what Mina is talking about. She drowned herself. There has to be a sacrifice. Only the dead may pass. You have to die."

A sacrifice.

My breath stills as the idea nestles itself within me.

A sacrifice.

Some part of me knew it would come down to this.

I have been running all my life. Running from my powers. Running from the people I love most. Running from this house, my home. Running because my heart knew that if I stayed, if I got too close, if I embraced who I was, if I fell in love with three beautiful, impossible men, then I would have to say goodbye to them, and it would break me utterly.

But now I see that I was wrong to run. I should never have been afraid to fall in love. Because even if this fails and I lose them forever, I haven't lost at all. I've loved and been loved by them.

I always believed a home is a sanctuary – a building or a beach or a room where no one or nothing bad could touch you. I've searched the whole world and never found that place. Now I realise that home is someone holding you tight when you're at your worst.

And I have been my worst and most selfish within the walls of Grimwood, and Pax, Ambrose, and Edward have held me while I found myself again. Now I have a chance to be my best.

I'm not going to run. I'm not afraid to stay and fight this time. Now I understand how precious the gift is that I'm fighting for.

I'm not afraid of what's on the other side of that hole in the wall.

I'm not even afraid of losing them.

You can only lose someone if you've been blessed to be loved by them. And I'm so blessed to be losing everyone in this room. Not just the ghosts, but Dad, and Dani, and Alice, and Mina on the phone, and even bloody Kelly Kingston. Even if I lose them to the other side of the Veil, I will carry a piece of their souls forever in my heart.

I swallow. "I'm ready to be the sacrifice."

"That's not happening," Dad says. "Bree-bug, you're talking about *dying*."

"I don't have to die. I've already died once, haven't I?" I fix Dad with a knowing look. "When I fell off my bike when I was five."

Dad's mouth opens and shuts, his eyes wide.

"It's okay, Dad, I know it must've been awful for you. But it's true, isn't it? I died, and Vera brought me back to life. I can go through the doorway. That's what Elsie and Agnes have been trying to tell me."

"Bree might be right. I came back!" Mina cries.

Dad glares at the phone. "Only because of, what, narrative causation? Nevermore's magic is different to my daughter's. We can't guarantee that will happen again. I'm not letting Bree kill herself to save the afterlife. That's not her responsibility."

"Actually, as the heir of St. Lazarus, I think it *is* my responsibility," I say, aware of Edward and Pax staring daggers at me. "If I have to go to the other side of the Veil to fix this, that's what I'll do."

"Bree, you can't do this." Tears stream down Ambrose's cheeks. He flies to me, pulling me against him as if he can somehow trap me within his arms. I can't bear to look at him. I have never, ever seen him cry, or heard the kind of raw hopelessness in his voice that's there now. "Please. Don't leave us."

"Don't cry, Ambrose. Bree will not be the sacrifice. If the gods must have a sacrifice, I will go instead." Pax touches the hilt of his sword, and he sets his jaw in a determined line. "I too have died. I am a worthy sacrifice. It is decided."

"It is *not* decided. Pax, you have to stay here. I'm a Lazarus. I can come back. But I don't know about you. And there are monsters and the Order of the Noble Death right outside. The moment I'm gone, the wards are going to come down. You're our last line of defence against them. You can't allow them to enter Grimwood while I'm gone."

"But..." Pax's chin wobbles. I meet his pale blue eyes and am shocked at the fear swimming inside them. Pax doesn't know what to do with fear. It's completely new to him. The great Pax Drusus Maximus has one solution for every problem – stab it until there's no more problem. He's always been strong and brave for me, so I didn't have to be brave myself.

But this isn't a battle he can fight for me. He lowers his gaze. My heart skips as he regards me with the appraising eye of a general surveying his troops. He places a trembling hand on my shoulder, and when his gaze meets mine again, his eyes are filled with pride. "You will take your sword with you."

"Of course."

"You will stab anyone who gets in your way."

A lump rises in my throat. "You've taught me well."

He lifts a leather cord from around his neck, and loops it over my head. I reach down and brush my fingers over the small Roman coin tied to the cord. The coin Pax's soldiers placed with his body to pay the ferryman.

"Go, with the blessings of Bellona, goddess of battle and bloodshed." Pax yanks me from Ambrose's embrace and wraps his enormous arms around me, crushing me against him as if he might be able to hide me inside his skin so my destiny can't find me.

His lips crush mine, and his kiss is wild and brutal and sweet in a way that only a bloodthirsty warrior can be.

I manage to extract myself with only mildly crushed ribs, and I plant a kiss on his forehead. "I'll do you proud, I promise."

"You're still talking like this is happening, and it's not," Dad says.

For once, I ignore him.

I move to Edward, who is leaning against the fireplace, presenting his front as the remote, inaccessible prince.

"You're not coming, either," I say.

In response, he places a finger beneath my chin, tilting my head up to his so that his breath mingles with mine. His anthracite eyes peer at me with wonder, bright and clear. The dark mood that has settled over him in recent weeks lifts as he cocks the corner of his mouth up into a classic Edward smirk.

"Why aren't you sad?" I ask.

"I am *profoundly* sad." His finger brushes my cheek. "But I know that you have searched the world for your purpose, for a reason that you have been given this power, and now you have found it. I myself have been on the same search, for many more centuries than you have been upon this earth. And I believe that I, too, have found it."

Trust Edward to make this about himself. "What is that?"

"To love you," he says simply, his eyes filling with light.

All the air leaves my lungs.

Edward's finger drags over my lip, the corner of his mouth cocking ever more dangerously. "I cannot say it more poetically than that. I love you, Brianna, with every beat of my dark, wanton heart. I love you more than all the pretty words poets have found for love. I love you so much that you strike me mute. When I am around you, I have no rhyme for the way you make me feel. No couplet captures the fierceness of your spirit. I get all tangled up with longing to see you be strong and brave and kind and wonderful, and all the other things that you are. So even though I can't bear the idea of letting you go again, even though I feel I might bleed to death from the pain of it, I know that you have your purpose, and I have mine. We will hold the way open for you to return to us."

My heart kicks up like windswept leaves as I fall into Edward, my lips finding his to give him the goodbye that he understands. I kiss him with possession, claiming him as he has claimed me, this poet with his abrasive heart and his wicked mind, the one who sees inside my darkest fears as no one else can.

Too soon, Edward breaks the kiss. He pulls away, his long finger catching the edge of my lip, his eyes studying me as if he is trying to commit me to memory. "You'd better come back to us," he whispers, tucking a strand of my hair behind my ear. "Or else my poetry will become truly insufferable."

I nod and swallow, finding myself dangerously close to tears. But when I turn to Ambrose and allow him to hold me again, the tears fall freely, mingling with his to become a salty river. Ambrose buries his face in my hair and I dig myself into his shoulder, breathing him deep, wishing I could carry his heart with me.

"You are too brave and stubborn for your own good," he sniffs as he pulls back, his fingers tracing over my face, sweeter and softer than Edward's, but no less possessive.

"I'm only brave because of you."

"I want to come with you. It will be our last great adventure together."

"Ambrose, *no*. They need you here. *I* need you here. I think... this is something I have to do on my own."

"You'll never be alone, Bree. Not when our love is stronger than death itself." He kisses me then, so achingly soft and tender that I almost break right then and there. I can't bear leaving this man, who has such a zest for life that he's always been alive to me, a man who always believes I am better than I am.

Ghost-balls, but I'm finally ready to prove him right.

I break his sweet kiss, wipe my eyes, and turn away from the three of them. If I linger in their love for a moment longer, then I won't be able to go through with this. I find my best friend, my rock, and meet her eyes. "Dani, if I die, make sure my wishes are carried out. I want to be buried in Grimdale, in a mausoleum to rival Edwards, in a golden sarcohpagus, wearing my favourite Blood Lust hoodie and holding a plate of Pax-cakes."

"Why me?" Dani tugs on the strap of her skeleton overalls. "Why am I always the one who has to deal with the dead bodies!"

"That's *literally* your job," Alice says.

"Not you, too," Dani rolls her eyes at her girlfriend.

"We bury the bodies, remember?" I hold up my pinkie finger.

"Yes, but when I made that stupid oath, I didn't realise one of the bodies would be *yours*."

"It's not important, Dani, because she's not doing it." Dad folds his arms and glares at me. "Bree-bug, I've never been one to lay down parenting ultimatums, but you're *not* going to the Realm of the Dead. I forbid it."

"I'm not leaving for good." *I hope.* "My powers mean I can come and go." *I think.* "And if that doesn't work out, Dani's going to bring me back."

"Don't put that on my shoulders. I don't want it." Dani shakes her head so wildly that the skeleton earrings she's wearing do a little dance. "You're the one with the magical resurrection powers, not me."

"We might be able to help," Lottie says. "As you now know, Agnes has visions of the future. Sometimes she knows when someone might need something, so she makes sure they have it, even if they don't know why they need it."

Like the box of random things Vera left me. Agnes must have told her what to include.

Although it would have been easier if Agnes had just explained everything to me.

But then, perhaps Agnes didn't know if she'd still be ghosting around. It's possible that she foresaw that she'd end up inside the Ripper, but didn't know when it would happen.

Lottie nods, understanding what I'm now realising. "Agnes' power is quite remarkable. It's why she was hanged as a witch. She has all kinds of visions, but she usually doesn't know when they're going to happen, or how. But when she gets an odd notion, you have to go with it, because of butterflies flapping their wings and whatnot. Some years ago, Agnes told us that she'd be in a grand throne room, and a door would open, and on the other side of that door she could see our 'ugly mugs'. And she would push someone through the door. I think this is the way back from the Veil. So Bree has a way home. Another doorway."

"See?" I force a grin as I meet their terrified faces. "Everything's going to be fine."

"I don't like this," Dad says.

"Nor I." Edward wraps his arms around me. Ambrose rests his cheek against mine, his tears falling fresh and fast.

"Nor I." I gulp down the fear that bubbles inside me. "But it's the only plan we've got."

"I want it on the record that I am against this," Dad says as he shuffles into my old bedroom and sits down heavily on a box of music magazines.

Pax holds out his sword. "Want to stab something? It helps."

"Thank you, Pax. You may have a future as a therapist." Dad winces as there's a sickening crack from the direction of the front door, and the chanting from the Order of the Noble Death rises in pitch and fervour. "However, I won't deprive you of your sword. I have a feeling that you'll need it soon."

I stretch out on my childhood bed, staring up at the carving on the ceiling. B + P + E + A = 4EVA. But does 4EVA mean after death? What am I going to find beyond the Veil?

Pax bends over me and wraps the fingers of my right hand around the hilt of my own sword. He bends and kisses my knuckles, his lips leaving a warm tingle where they graze my skin. My heart stutters. He steps back, nodding at me.

I can tell that every fibre of his being objects to letting me go into battle without him at my side. But this is something only I can do. He's needed here.

I swallow hard, and step up to the hole in the wall.

I run my fingers over Elsie's words. ONLY THE DEAD MAY PASS.

Bree...don't be afraid...

I hope like hell I'm right.

"I can't let this happen." Dad's on his feet, rushing towards me as fast as his Parkinson's will allow him. I duck under his hand and, before he can stop me, I dive into the hole.

For a moment, I'm suspended in nothing. I can see my black cord again, ringed with a pale white light. It unspools from my chest at an alarming rate. That explains the winding sensation in my stomach, like all my stitching is being picked undone from the inside out. I try to reach out my hand to grip the cord, but my arm is made of lead. I can't move. All I can do is grip the sword in numbing fingers and watch my life unwind from me.

"Bree?" Dad shouts from somewhere behind me. At least I

think he's shouting. He sounds so far away, as if he's calling me from underwater.

"No." Ambrose cries. "We shouldn't have done this. Bring her back. Bring her back!"

"Brianna?" Edward's fathomless eyes bore into my back. I can't see him, but he's all around me, swimming with fear and uncertainty.

Somewhere in the distance, wood cracks.

But I can't contemplate any of it. As I topple into nothingness, white light explodes around me. It's so warm and beautiful that I sink into it, letting it pull me under until Grimdale and all my loved ones disappear from thoughts and time, and there is only me and the light...

23

BREE

The light is me and I am the light.

Warmth rushes me as my head swells with memories. It's as if I'm reliving all of the happiest moments of my life at once. I'm so joyful that I think I'm going to explode.

My dad giving me a red bike for my birthday. Dani and I meeting for the first time. Laughing at Pax's antics until I can't breathe. My mum taking me shopping because I got good marks at school. Ambrose telling me stories that make me believe the world is big and wonderful and waiting for me to explore it. Edward helping me write a speech about his life for history class.

Small perfect moments that mean nothing and everything.

And then, just as tears fall down my cheeks, the light fades at the edges of my vision and colours move inward, revealing the hazy outline of my old bedroom.

Huh?

I'm still in Grimwood Manor.

Ghost-balls. What's wrong *now*?

Everything is the same, but different. I'm looking at the world through a sepia film of fog. Through the haze, I can make out the shapes of the guys, my dad, my friends, Kelly. They're crowded around the bed, where they have pulled my lifeless body and laid me out. Their lips move but I can only hear the faintest whispers. Their silver cords are even more obvious now, curving through the air around me. But when I reach out to touch them, my fingers pass right through. I can't feel a thing.

I reach out and touch the table. At least, I try to touch it. My fingers fall through the wood, sending a jolt of pain along my arm.

Oof. That is unpleasant.

"Welcome to the ghost side." Lottie appears by my side. She embraces me. For the first time, her limbs don't go through me. We can touch.

She feels strong and solid, the only thing left in this room that is real to me.

No, not the only thing. I see Ambrose's features tight with worry, Edward's stricken face. Dani's mouth set in a firm, determined line.

Their love is real.

"Where am I?"

"I think this is the first test, to make sure you're ready to walk the pathway," Lottie says. "This is the bit where we choose to stay behind as ghosts or move forward. It's best not to look at them, dear."

Lottie tries to angle me away.

"I never wanted this, but it's lovely to meet you properly." Mary elbows Lottie out of the way and throws her arms around me. Her dress is coarse, her skin scented with wildflowers. She feels more alive than anything else in this room, which can only mean...

...I did it.

I'm a ghost.

Hooray.

I float around the room, trying to get the hang of moving. My feet keep dropping through the floor, making my ankles burn with agony. Mary and Lottie try to coax me into the hallway, but I find myself floating over to the sofa, trying to move into the circle of my friends, trying to see...

...myself.

There I am. I'm lying on the sofa, one hand flopping over the edge, the other held limply in Edward's long fingers. My eyes are open but glassy, my expression surprisingly serene.

I don't move.

My ghost throat tightens.

Ambrose lies down beside my prone body, pulling my back into his chest and wrapping his arms around me. Tears streak his cheeks. I reach out to wipe them away, but Kelly moves her giant head through my arm. I howl and stagger back.

Ambrose whispers something in my body's ear. I can't hear the words but I swear I can sense the waft of his breath against my earlobe, even though I'm hovering above him.

I can't stop watching those tears. I never, ever wanted to make Ambrose cry.

Edward paces behind the bed, wringing his hands, his lips moving, no doubt composing some ridiculous poem. All traces of arrogance have gone from his face, leaving behind a raw wound in his dark eyes.

Dad sits on his box of magazines, looking sickly pale. I can't hear a thing any of them are saying or doing.

What I can hear are thumps and hollers outside in the foyer as Pax valiantly attempts to hold back the Order.

I know in my heart that I have to hurry, that I have precious little time before the Order makes it upstairs and overruns this room. If they get to my body before I can get to that other doorway, I'm a goner. More importantly, I *must* keep them from discovering Elsie's secret portal. But I can't force myself to move faster or to leave my vigil beside the bed. I just want to linger, to watch. I'm drawn to the serene expression on my face, to the love of my family.

This is not a terrible way to die, surrounded by the people who love me, fighting to keep them safe.

Something hard slaps my cheek. I turn, and Lottie glares at me as she rubs her hand.

I touch my cheek. "Why'd you slap me for?"

"You can't become distracted by them." Lottie thrusts her hands on her hips. "It's difficult when you first start ghosting. You cling to those human connections that tie you to the world of the Living. Take it from an old ghost, you can waste hundreds of years existing in this *exact* moment. But you don't have time for any of that nonsense – you have things to do. You have to move past this."

I nod, but I can't stop my gaze being pulled back to the bed, watching my limp body as Ambrose strokes my hair. My ghost skin flushes with warmth at his love. Edward leans down and kisses my forehead and I can feel his lips on me, but when I brush my fingers against myself, I touch nothing.

"You have to stop," Mary tugs on my arm. "Hours and days and weeks will disappear in a blink of an eye."

This is how Pax passed so many years hunting invisible Druids in Grimdale wood. This is how Edward partied his way through centuries. They *yearned* for their old life with such ferocity that it took the only thing they had left from them... *time.*

Suddenly, I'm no longer in the bedroom. I'm out in the hallway, looking down over the grand staircase. Pax stands on the landing, facing down at the foyer. Grimwood's front door lies open, yawning into the gloom while priests and priestesses in black cassocks pour into the house.

A pile of dead and dying priests twitch at Pax's feet,

forming a wall that blocks off the staircase. He kicks them now the stairs with his Roman sandals as he strikes out at another.

"This is for Bree!" he cries as his blade slashes through the air, over and over again. Blood stains the newly repainted walls with crimson arches.

All this bloodshed...for me.

Pax's muscles ripple as he brings his sword arm down like a hammer of justice. I'm captivated by the raw power of him, by the beautiful way his lip turns up into a wild grin as he slashes and hacks. He moves with the grace of a dancer, and his enemies fall around him.

"Bree..."

I squeeze my eyes shut and turn slowly towards the witches. Only when I'm certain that I have my back to Pax do I open my eyes again. A concerned-looking Mary and Lottie peer back at me, while Abberline drags his head out of the upstairs liquor cabinet long enough to smile sadly at me.

"I have to hurry." I swallow. "I need to get out of this house."

"We know."

I see Lottie's hand flying towards me, but this time I manage to duck before I get another ghost-slap. "Will you cover my eyes? We have to go around Pax and I don't think I can resist him when he's like this."

"To be honest, that much raw masculinity in the room, I think we're all done for," Lottie grins. "But we don't have to around him to get to the hallway. We're taking the shortcut."

"What shortcut—ow!"

Lottie jerks my arm as she leaps into the air, zooming towards the wall that separates the bedroom from the landing. My feet leave the ground and I don't have time to contemplate the fact that I'm floating. I brace myself for the pain as we slam into it. Nothing prepares me for the sheer hell that is passing one's ghostly body through a solid wall.

I see inside the body of Grimwood – ribs of ancient wood, insulation like layers of muscle, wire arteries keeping the house alive. A mouse hurtles past my face.

Lottie drops my hand, and I tumble through the other side of the wall into my old bedroom. I manage to stop myself before I stumble into the bed. I hover, trembling, above the worn rug.

Ozzy looks up from where he's hanging in the corner of the room, shakes a wing at me, then goes back to sleep.

"That...that..." I hug myself. "That bloody *hurt!*"

"Probably not half as much as going in there." Lottie shudders as she regards Elsie's hole in the wall.

I step up closer and peer down into the void. This time, I can see a tangle of cords all bunched together at the entrance. Silver and black and red and silver tinged with blue, all tumbling down into the void.

Bree, come with me, a voice calls from below.

I can't believe I have to do this *again*.

My fingers graze the lip, just above Elsie's scrawled message. They manage to touch the edge. I very, very much do not want to get into that hole.

Bree, we must walk together.

A second ghost pops through the wall beside me. Abberline shudders, pulling his greatcoat tight around himself.

"I'm here to accompany you." Abberline's face appears pale. "It's only fitting that I face my greatest villains in the bowels of the underworld itself."

"And we're here to pull you back." Lottie wraps her hands around my own black cord and gives it a tug. I wince as it squeezes my heart. I'll definitely feel that. "If anything happens, tug three times on your cord and we will haul you back to this side. It's not all the way home, but it might be close enough."

"We believe in you." Mary pats my shoulder.

Abberline takes my hand, knitting his ghostly fingers in mine. He smiles down at me, and for the first time since I met him, it's a real, genuine smile.

I suck in a deep breath, and once more, step over the side of the hole.

24

EDWARD

Brianna's face is so lifeless, like a doll or one of Vermeer's paintings. (There, I said it. Take that, you swamp-dwelling Dutch flapdoodle who called my poetry 'a literary bodily function.')

Looking at Brianna makes my chest hurt, but I refuse to look away. Ambrose holds her, and I know I am watching his heart breaking as his tears stain her cold cheeks.

If she is dying a true death, then I suppose she should be a ghost now, stranded in that between-place where she's supposed to make her decision if she lingers or continues on. I don't look because I know if I see her as I used to be, on the other side of a divide that I don't know how to cross, I will lose myself utterly.

This is all part of the plan. But having Brianna become a ghost doesn't seem like a good plan. It is a very bad plan.

She has to come back to us. She *must*.

If anyone can stop this madness, it's Brianna. Brave, strong, impossible Brianna.

I believe it.

I *must* believe it.

Movement out of the corner of my eye distracts me for a moment. Dani has set out the spirit board on the table, and the planchette is flying around like mad. Kelly cowers behind the sofa.

"That's hardly the craziest thing you've seen in this house," Alice snaps. "Calm your farm."

"I bet it's Mary and Lottie," Ambrose sniffs. "They said they'd watch out for her."

"But can't you hear them?"

"Not in the place they're in right now. Can you read it?"

"It spells S H E S I N," Mike says. "Shesin? Oh, 'she's in.' Bree's gone to the other side of the Veil."

Brianna's father slumps back in his chair, his hand clutched to his chest. In his face, I read all the hope and the uselessness that I feel. I sent my love off to fight this battle on her own. What good is my princely title and all my education and my body like a Greek god if I can't do a thing when I'm needed most?

CRACK.

Kelly screams as something slams into the wall outside, sending several decorative plates and a portrait of Entwhistle dressed as a knight crashing to the floor. Pax yells something in Latin, and there's another CRACK, and a THUD.

Alice grips Dani's knee. "Are we being attacked by Batman?"

"It's the Order of the Noble Death. They must have gotten inside!"

I tear my gaze away from Brianna, although it pains me physically to do so. I pluck a sword from the coat rack in the corner. In a house like Grimwood, there's always a pointy weapon lying around.

I didn't like when I told Brianna that my purpose was to love her. To love her, means to fight for her, and to sacrifice for them. As a Living man, I have so little of worth to offer Brianna. But I have one thing I can sacrifice.

My life.

Dani calls out as I stride toward the door. "Edward, where are you going?"

"Pax is holding off those priests on his own." I test the sword in my hand, giving a few quick lunges. I'm rusty, having not practised much in several centuries, but I can still remember the fundamentals from my fencing lessons. And I have been tuning out Pax's lectures on proper Roman swordsmanship for a long time. Surely I know enough to bring down a couple of troublesome priests.

Moments count right now.

Ambrose's gaze flicks to me, his usually bright eyes swimming with fear. "Edward, you don't have to do that."

I grab the doorknob. "I do."

The knob turns beneath my shaking fingers.

I step into the hallway.

Brianna, I love you.

A dark shadow leaps at me, candlelight flashing on a blade. I raise the sword and step into my doom.

25

BREE

This time, I fall.

I fall until falling has no meaning. My cord unspools around me, winding through the air. I can feel the life being sucked away from me.

I fall.

And then I stop falling.

I land hard on my shoulder.

OW.

Ow owie *ow*.

Is the afterlife supposed to *hurt*?

My stomach feels like I swallowed a brick. I guess this is what it's like to be winded when you don't actually need to breathe. I try to move my limbs, but they're frozen in some kind of agonising yoga position on top of a lumpy pile of rocks. My vision swims and swirls, unable to focus and—

"Get off me. I'm already regretting this escapade."

The lumpy pile of rocks flashes me a disgruntled look and shoves me off him. I manage to haul myself to my knees as Abberline rolls over and straightens his hat.

"Well, this isn't quite what I expected."

I don't know *what* I expected, but after talking with Mina, I heard the afterlife was just an endless desert populated by poets. But I see no sand or sulphur.

I'm standing in Grimdale Cemetery.

My feet rest in the soft grass on the edge of Poet's Way. The concrete path has been swept clean of fallen leaves, and the graves stand to attention, each one scrubbed clean and bedecked with flowers in colours so vibrant my eyes hurt to look at them.

Ambrose's grave is to my right, the stone barely visible beneath a pile of bright flowers, the edges of the leaves shimmering with silver. Edward's mausoleum looms over me, the cherubs appearing even more lifelike beneath the strange, starless night sky. And to the left, where the Witches' Monument should be, is the ancient stone altar that marked Pax's grave, and a Roman funerary urn stands beside it, decorated with triumphant battle scenes.

"Bree Mortimer."

My name snaps through the air. I whip my head around, and for the first time I notice the figure standing in front of the mausoleum doors, hand outstretched towards me.

Vera.

She grips my black cord in her hand as if on the other end is a misbehaving dog.

"I'm here to walk the pathway with you," she says.

I stare at her hand, at the wrinkled fingers of a woman I met only in passing, who has watched over me my whole life.

I'm not an idiot. I take her hand.

She drops my cord, allowing it to unspool in front of us as we walk along the path. My boots fall lightly on the concrete. Vera is tiny, but strong, and she pulls me a little to force me to walk at her pace. Abberline follows behind us, muttering things under his breath that I don't care to hear.

Graves loom over us from either side of the path. Stone angels unfurl their wings toward me and gargoyles watch me with beady, monstrous eyes. I should be afraid, but I can never be afraid in Grimdale Cemetery. I've been so happy here.

With Vera's fingers wrapped around me, I am at peace.

"Am I allowed to ask questions?" I ask as we turn a corner onto another identical, grave-lined path.

"I suppose. Just don't be annoying about it."

"Where are we? Where are we going? What happened to Elsie? What's this crown that everyone's so excited about? How can—"

Vera sighs. "See, that's what I call 'being annoying.'"

"Sorry. It's just that I haven't had any real answers yet. I'm a little terrified that I've left my family behind to deal with a big mess without me, and I won't be able to go back."

Vera makes a disapproving noise in her throat. "I wanted to tell you everything, but Elsie refused. She said you deserved to have a normal life before she exposed you to your birthright. She didn't want you burdened by the responsibilities of your heritage until you were older. She believed that since the Order believed you were dead, you'd be free until she called for you. But she waited too long and the Ripper got to her first. Now everything is wrong here, and the Ripper and the Order are tying to unmake everything we have, unless you wear the crown."

"What about this crown—"

Vera holds up her hand. "Good goddess, you're annoying. This is supposed to be a sacred, sombre perambulation, where a psychopomps escorts a Lazarus along the pathway, and you're ruining it with your yammering."

"So this is the pathway? But why is it Grimdale Cemetery? And if you're a psychopomps, then why are—"

"You're right, she *is* annoying," Abberline pipes up. "What do you say we leave her here, Vera, and you and I go and get a pint somewhere?"

Vera turns around and glares at him. It's a glare perfected over hundreds of inconvenient and annoying customers, and it sends Abberline cowering behind me. Vera sighs and turns back to me.

"You know now that I am like you. I was a Lazarus when I was Living, and now I have a new job." She jabs her elbow at the path in front of us. "A Lazarus is a psychopomps-in-training. We are born on Earth, we learn about pain and suffering and grief and love and fear before we die ourselves, and then we are equipped for our role. Humans have such varied responses to their own mortality. It's our job to keep them on the pathway with grace."

I bite my tongue so I don't say that maybe Vera could do with a little more 'training.'

"The pathway is different for every soul. Often, it leads through a peaceful garden to the front door of a childhood home, or through the corridors of a prison, or down an elevator shaft. Once, it was underwater and the soul couldn't swim. I don't choose the pathway, The soul forms an image that reflects who they are. All I'm here to do is to get you where you need to go."

"And where's that?"

"To the boat." Vera yanks me around a corner. "Unfortunately, your days of being normal are over. Because I'm not quite like you, Bree Mortimer. No one is. You're the last in your bloodline. You've got your own job to do. It's right up here."

I gasp as the concrete path ends abruptly. The graves and trees and cherubs are no more. All there is ahead of us is sand, sand, and more sand.

"I should have brought along my Panama hat," Abberline says.

I sniff. The air is scented with water, sulphur, and desperation. I crane my neck to look up at the sky, or what I think might be a sky. Gone is the beautiful starless midnight of the cemetery. The sky is all wrong – a mottled mess of grey and purple clouds that don't float freely but seem to hang from some invisible ceiling, crisscrossed with lines of fiery flames.

On the horizon is a black void.

The hole in the Veil.

"Bloody Ripper, has to tear holes in everything." Vera makes an impatient noise and tugs me towards it. Abberline sighs, but he falls in step beside me.

I don't know how long we walk, kicking up sand beneath our feet, my ears never quite getting used to the way sounds hang in the air here, when I realise that the horizon is no longer simply sand and void. Ahead of us is a wide, raging river. The banks are crowded with people, all clamouring to get close to what looks like a ferry terminal.

Vera yells out to me as I drop her hand and break into a run. Abberline huffs along behind me. Footsteps pound the sand as more and more people emerge from the desert, all racing for the ferry terminal.

No, not people. *Souls*.

Their edges shimmer with silver that connects to their soul-cords, and the part of me that isn't merely human recognises them as those who have died, who have walked their own pathway with a Lazarus at their side. But they don't appear to be on the other side of anything. They're not in a 'better place.' They're running for the ferry, desperation clinging to them like Edward when the only thing he can think to rhyme with 'horny' is 'ignore me.'

I make it to the back of the crowd just as a small wooden boat pulls up. It's comically tiny for the amount of souls wishing to board, and people surge forward as they flood the gangplank. One woman ends up in the water, where she's carried away by the current.

"Don't all crowd on at once. Form an orderly queue!" A harried-looking man tries to direct the crowd as he ties up the boat.

"What's going on?" I ask the soul of a woman who sprints past me.

"What, did you die yesterday?" she frowns at me.

"About five minutes ago, actually."

But it was my second time.

"Oh, right." She jabs a finger at the gaping, terrifying hold in the Veil. "Some fool ripped a hole in the Veil, and without a Lord of Death to tell us not to, we're all going back while we have the chance. I want to see my grandkids again. They'll be grandparents themselves now, but I bet they'll be happy to see their granny again."

Don't count on it. I think of the broken, terrifying souls who returned to Grimdale. This must be how they did it. And more of them are coming.

But at least I know now that I'm not responsible for bringing those shades back through the Veil. At least, not directly.

"I just want to visit my house," an old man says as he shoves a boy into the sand and steps over him. "I lived there for fifty-three years and I want to know that the new owners are looking after the place. If they've dug up my prize-winning petunias, I'll haunt their arses."

"And I want to eat a piece of pizza," a teenager whoops as she elbows the old man out of the way. "Double cheese with all the toppings. The food down here is purgatory-level terrible."

The crowd surges forward as souls jostle to make it up the ramp and onto the boat. I try to shove my way through but it's like a mosh pit, surging and heaving. I lose sight of Vera. Abberline and I are carried along by the push of the bodies. Their silvery soul-cords tangle around me. Abberline grabs my arm and heaves me upright before I get pulled under.

"Thanks."

"Anything if we can get out of here." Abberline glares at the boat over the surging crowd, clutching his hat so he doesn't lose it. "If this is crossing over, I think that I'd like to stay a ghost, thank you very much."

"I don't think this is how things are supposed to be." I peer up at that hole in the sky, and I think that I can see the spire of the church and the duck pond through the churning gloom. Grimdale is on the other side of it. "Remember, we're trying to finish your unfinished business so you can come back to life."

Abberline smiles. "Sure we are. I'm not sure either of us is getting out of this place."

"You'd be right."

I whirl around. Vera's wrinkled face glares up at me.

I wrap my fist around the black cord protruding from my chest below Pax's coin. "I have a way back. Agnes saw a doorway—"

"That's nice, dear." Vera's voice drips with sarcasm. "But you have realm to save, remember? If we all ran away from death the way you do, nothing would ever get done around here. Get on the next boat."

"Why? Where does the boat go?"

Vera jabs a finger at the souls crowded on the ferry. "That boat is going straight through the hole you helped Jack the Ripper conveniently punch in the Veil back up to the Living Realm. But the next ferry is taking us to the Palace of Bones. You'd better have brought enough payment to get us there, because these old hips can't take a long walk."

"You're still coming with us?"

"It's my job to walk the pathway with you, and your

pathway doesn't end on the banks of the river of lamentations," Vera huffs. "Besides, if you want something done right, you'd better do it yourself."

As much as I do not relish Vera's negative attitude, I feel a rush of relief that she's beside me.

The crowd lurches back with a disgruntled sigh as the ferryman pulls up the ramp and pushes the boat away. The decks are completely full of people. They even bob about in the water, clinging to the edges as the ferryman directs his vessel through the turbulent waters. It floats along until it's swallowed by the mist.

The crowd of souls howl with anguish and frustration. Vera's hand on mine remains steady.

A moment later, another boat, empty this time, pulls in to the dock.

An identical ferryman steps off, shooing the souls back as he ties up. "Step right up!" he calls. "Next boat back to the Living Realm leaves in eight minutes."

"You'd better get moving," Vera hisses.

I draw up my inner metalhead, channelling Dani the time we went to see her favourite band, Blood Lust, and she was so desperate to get up the front that she elbowed her way through the sound desk and accidentally cut the power. I pull my elbows up to my face and angle my body, squeezing around and through people as I fight to make it to the front. I bite back the urge to apologise as one guy topples off the edge of the gangplank.

These people are already dead. I can't do anything to hurt them.

I cling to the end of the gangplank. Souls press against my back, trying to force me onto the boat. I look up at the ferryman, his face hidden behind a deep blue cowl. "I want to speak to whoever's in charge."

"That would be me."

"I mean, in charge of the Veil. The Lord of Death, that's what he's called, right? Will you take me to him? I can pay you."

I remove Pax's coin from around my neck. It still feels warm in my fingers. I don't want to part with it, this last piece of Pax that I carry with me, but I hold it out.

The ferryman stares at the coin. He nods as he grabs it, tucking it into his pocket.

"I can take you to the Lord of Death, but as to whether you get a word with him, that remains to be seen."

He steps aside, waving me onto the boat. I leap on board, and Vera drags a protesting Abberline behind me.

"Save a seat for me, dearie!" The grandmother tries to follow me, but the ferryman shoves her back. She falls into the water, flailing her arms as she's tossed about in the churning waves.

"You ungrateful bitch!" she yells. "You should respect your elders."

I glance at Vera. "Is she a friend of yours?"

"Please. My friends all have impeccable manners and much better hairstyles." Vera waves cheerfully at the woman as she's carried away in the current.

The ferryman starts to pull up the gangplank. The souls surge forward, some trying to cling to the end of the gangplank, others hurling themselves as the sides of the boat. The ferryman shoves them off with his oar. "This journey isn't yours," he yells at the crowd. "Another boat will be along shortly."

To my great relief, he pushes off and takes his place at the front of the vessel, steering the boat through the choppy waters. I sit on a cold wooden bench and stare down into the water below. Faces twisted in agony stare up at me through sightless eyes from the watery depths.

Mist envelops us.

I glance downstream at the hole in the sky. In it, I can see shapes moving – souls and monsters of the Veil returning to the Living World.

Edward, Pax, Ambrose, whatever's going on back at Grimdale, I hope that you're okay.

"—so strong, Bree. I know you can do this—"

Ambrose's voice fills my head. I touch my ear.

How is it possible that I can still *hear* him?

I rub my fingers where he is holding them. I realise that I can feel the weight of his arm around me. I draw in a deep breath, and his scent invades me, giving me strength. Somehow, his love is reaching me through the Veil.

I'm here, Ambrose. I'm doing this for you, for us.

Abberline paces across the deck. Vera kicks at his ankles. "Stop that. You're making me seasick."

"No, this godforsaken boat rocking every which way is making you seasick," Abberline mutters.

The ferryman rows along the river until he reaches another dock. This one is deserted, and there's a sign nailed to the jetty that says, "KEEP OUT. NO SHADES BEYOND THIS POINT."

This must be the place.

The ferryman sets down the ramp and Vera, Abberline, and I scamper off. I turn to ask the ferryman if he can return for us, only to find the jetty completely empty. It's as if the boat was never there at all.

Abberline stares up at the hole in the Veil. "Is it just me, or has that got even larger?"

Vera huffs and starts along the jetty. "I suppose there's nothing to do but to go in and meet my boss."

I follow her along the deserted jetty. Abberline drags his feet behind us. All around me, the desert sands swirl as the sky above us erupts with thunder. My skin itches, and I get the sense that from the darkness, we're being watched.

A faint silvery glow shimmers on the horizon. Vera storms off toward it, following a winding path that sparkles with silver light. The silver glow reminds me of the soul-cords, only much larger and brighter.

As we near the glow, I realize that the shimmering silver is coming from soul-cords. Thousands of them. *Millions* of them formed together into a castle that is as beautiful as it is impossible.

I gasp at the sheer majesty of the towering walls of shimmering gothic arches. In the centre, the building is perfectly symmetrical, each half a mirror of the other, but the eastern wing is much longer than the west, and the architecture there is more jagged and otherworldly. A countless number of silver cords bunch from the tips of the turrets and stream beneath every window of the castle, making the building so bright that I can't stare up at it. I have to take in only pieces of it at a time.

As I watch, a fork of lightning strikes one of the southernmost towers, and threads of silver untangle from the building. It's then that I realize that the castle isn't lopsided – the eastern wing stretches on into the distance. But the entire western wing has been consumed by the void, and all that remains is a skeleton structure held together with black tendrils.

Black like my own soul-cord.

Vera catches my eye, and nods. "Without anyone on the throne, the Lord of Death's kingdom is crumbling. Soon, it will be so weak that any riffraff will be able to claim the crown. An ineffective ruler is better than no ruler at all."

I place my foot on the first step and gasp as the silver cords hum beneath me. The pillars, the walls, the impossibly large doors – they're all made so silver threads. Souls built this palace. Souls keep it alive.

And something is devouring it.

Two scythes cross over the door.

"What is this place?" I whisper. "Who lives here?"

"You're supposed to be the clever one." Vera raps her tiny fist against the door. I swallow hard.

The doors fall open, revealing a long hall of towering columns, all shimmering with silver threads. Each column is decorated with words and symbols. One column I think is written in Egyptian hieroglyphics, another in German, another in Cyrillic, but some I don't recognise as languages.

Alice would go nuts for this place.

I peer behind the double doors, but there's no butler there, and no mechanism to automatically open them. "How did the doors open?"

"Good Goddess, it's not bloody important!" Vera is already miles ahead of me. I jog after her, passing between the columns.

"I'll just wait here," Abberline calls from the doors. "I'll guard the escape route."

"Chicken!" Vera calls from far ahead.

"I'm no chicken."

"Bwwwak bwak bwak!"

A few moments later, Abberline is back at my side, his face pinched with terror. He has his pistol in his hand, swinging it around every column. I don't have the heart to tell him that ghost bullets are probably useless here.

At the end of the colonnade, another set of silver doors throw themselves open. A clattering sound reaches my ears, a sound that is at once completely foreign and also eerily familiar, as if I have heard it before in my dreams. I step inside.

I gasp at the cavernous gallery that stretches out in all directions, so large that I cannot see the ends of it, so high that the ceiling is all in darkness. Spread across the space are towering looms, hundreds of them, *thousands* of them, and each loom clacks and clatters as silver threads pass through the warp and are wound on spindles. Great long tapestries of silver, shimmering light fall off the ends of the looms and curl over the floor.

"What is this?" I breathe.

"It is the work. The Work. Fate, life, whatever you want to call it," Vera shrugs. "No one's soul is ever alone. We're all interwoven."

I stare at the clattering looms, and I'm stuck again by the *knowing*. Something of this room lives inside me, a seed planted by my great-grandmother before I was even born. I was always meant to be here. I was always meant to understand.

I *know* that I'm witnessing the weaving of souls – souls born, living, and dying in a beautiful dance as they become part of the fabric of the universe. Souls entwined together with love and circumstance, each one affecting those they touch in ways that only make sense when you zoom out and see the patterns. And I see the patterns now, galaxies and nebulae splashed across the tapestries, symbols older than time and more beautiful than there are words to describe.

This isn't a factory of life, an assembly line for being human.

It's so much more *divine* than that.

"I need a drink," Abberline says. "My head's not made for this stuff."

"What happened here?" I point to the tapestry coming off the nearest loom. Huge patches of red mist mar the seraphic design. The edges around the rest mist are scraggly, unkempt. The tapestry gives off a faintly rotting odour.

"The Ripper happened." Vera strides off between the looms. Reluctantly, I follow her. As we near a large doorway on the opposite side of the room, I notice more and more of the red holes eating away at the tapestry.

I follow Vera through a set of doors carved with more

scythes into a wide reception room. I step inside, my boots making an echoing sound on the polished floor. My eye is drawn upward to the glittering ceiling of crystals, to the dramatic tapestries adorning every wall, and then to a dais facing me from the centre of the room. Atop the dais sits a throne made of bones and silver skulls.

The throne is empty.

"Look down," Abberline says, in a voice that implies I shouldn't.

I look down.

A body lies crumpled at the base of the dais. It doesn't move as we step into the room.

The body is wearing a pink dress.

Great-Grandmother Elsie.

No.

I roll her over. Her face stares up at me, perfectly still and serene. She clutches a spindle under her arm, but it's empty, the shaft cracked in two. She has no pulse, but I don't know if that means anything down here.

"What's this? Who leaves garden implements lying around?" Abberline kicks an object lying beside Elsie. I peer over at it, and my heart lurches.

It's a scythe.

"There are more bodies," Abberline says. "Look."

I look.

I wish I hadn't. Littered across the throne room are black-cloaked figures, their limbs bent at impossible angles, their hoods thrown back to reveal faces twisted in agony.

Priests of the Order of the Noble Death.

"Where are we?" The words babble out of me. I know I sound like an idiot, but I don't trust my own eyes, my instinct. I need someone else to say it.

Vera is only too happy to oblige. "You're standing in the throne room for the Lord of Death."

"Okay, so..."

Where is he?

As one, we all turn towards the throne that sits on the silver dais. It shimmers with silver light, the gossamer threads of thousands of cords twining together to form the intricate carvings on the back and arms. A black velvet cushion sits on top.

The throne is empty.

There's no one here.

26

PAX

"By Mars' mouldering man-meat, will you priests ever learn!" I swing my sword, drawing the blade across the belly of another priest and taking out one of Sylvie's beloved rabbit figurines on the sidetable. He topples to the floor, his guts spilling out like an upturned bowl of spaghetti. The priest, I mean. The rabbit bounces against my sandaled foot and rolls away.

I bend down and collect the rabbit. He's in two pieces. His ears have fallen off. Another casualty of this foolish war. I turn to the next priest, who is scrambling over the towering fort I've made from the corpses of his brothers and sisters.

I crush the broken rabbit ears beneath my foot. "You made me break Sylvie's favourite bunny. The one holding a little basket of strawberries. Now I'm annoyed."

The priest's eyes widen. "I think we should make a tactical retreat," he yells down to his comrades on the other side of my wall of bodies. "He's terrifying—"

He doesn't get to finish his sentence. I run him through, stuff the rabbit's bottom between his lips, and hurl him back over my wall onto the staircase below. I hear a satisfying *THUMP* followed by shouting as he lands on top of his comrades.

It's all going well, except that I can see through the bedroom on the left of the hallway to the window, where three priests have scaled the side of the house. One grips the stone ledge and swings his foot at the glass—

CRASH.

The window shatters. The priest swings himself inside and turns to help his two friends. Two of them carry large double-handed swords, while the first priest has some kind of spiked mace that I'd love to get my hands on. It looks great for crushing skulls.

I manage to avoid being sliced by the swords and duck under the first swing of the spiked ball. It sails over my head and smashes into the portrait of Edward on the wall, tearing through the canvas and shattering the frame into splinters.

Any moment now, my head is going to join it.

My arm is tired. I can't move fast enough. It's been fun maiming priests, but I know that I cannot hold out for much longer. Every precious second I'm still alive gives Bree more time to close the hole in the Veil. So I raise my sword again and turn to face the enraged priest.

He bears down on me with his spiked ball raised about his head and—

—cries out in horror as his arm is sliced off. The hand holding the spiked ball sails through the air, where it clonks a priestess on the head, sending her sprawling to the floor.

The priest's mouth opens wide as he gapes at the bloody stump that is his arm, but his cry cuts off abruptly as a sword runs him through.

"That's for ruining my portrait," an insouciant voice declares beside me.

Edward.

But it can't be Edward. His face is splattered with blood. He yells like a Roman marching into battle as he falls upon another priest, cutting the man down with a beautiful thrust.

It *is* Edward, a sword in his hand, thrusting and parrying, his footwork like a majestic dance.

The way he moves, it's almost...poetic.

He cuts down two more priests and reaches my side in the centre of the landing, his back against mine. He faces the broken window in the bedroom and I fix upon the pile of corpses blocking the staircase.

"I thought you said that you were hopeless with a sword," I say.

"I am nothing compared to you, Roman." Edward's jaw sets as he readies himself for the next wave. "The only moves I have were honed during philosophical debates with my good friend Hugh. When we debated the merits of Stoicism vs the Epicureans, things got a little bloody."

"You are quite remarkable, Prince."

I reach for him, pulling him close. I mash my lips to his. He tastes of blood and battle. My two favourite things.

His eyes widen, and he kisses me back. Behind his back, more priests clamber up the side of the house.

When we pull away, we are both smiling.

"What do you say, Roman?" Edward's face breaks into a

mischievous grin. "We will rid this house of all its troublesome priests so our Brianna can triumph."

"For Bree." I kiss the hilt of my sword.

"For Brianna." Edward tucks a strand of dark hair behind his ear.

We turn back to the horde and raise our swords for the last time.

27

BREE

I turn to Vera. "You said we were going to visit the Lord of Death. Where is he?"

"The Lord of Death is right here." Vera folds her arms and fixes me with a glare that could freeze a volcano. "You're deliberately being obtuse. I've told you, but you don't want to believe it."

"Believe what?"

"Bree, look." Abberline points to the tapestries that adorn the walls. The scenes are brought to life in vivid, jewelled colours, and shimmer with silver from the threads made of souls. One panel shows the ferryman shifting souls across a river, dropping the newly dead off at their respective locations across the Afterlife. Above him, a woman presides over it all. She wears a white gown, and a crown of bones, and silver cords unwind from her chest, spreading out to all the newly crossed-over souls like a tapestry. In the centre is a single, solitary black cord.

Not a Lord of Death.

A Lady of Death.

A Lazarus.

My heart leaps into my throat as I move to another panel. On the next wall, paintings done in a completely different style show the black-cloaked figure of Death riding astride a white horse, his scythe raised as he does battle with a horde of hell-beasts. Silver cords unwind from his flowing sleeves and his eye sockets, while his own black cord weaves around his weapon, protecting him.

On another panel, a wizened old woman hunches over a man tucked into his bed. On the other side of the door, the man's family huddles in a circle, their heads bowed in prayer. The old woman has a metal hammer that she swings back over his shoulder. The man's eyes are closed. He looks serene. His silver cord unwinds from his chest, the end flicking towards the woman as she reels him in with her own black cord.

I spin in panicked circles, taking in the images. There are hundreds of tapestries hanging in the vast room, each showing a different version of Death. A reaper. A warrior. A fiddler. An old woman. An angel. All of them with black cords.

Every version of Death depicted on these walls is a Lazarus.

It makes a crazy kind of sense. A Lazarus has control over life and death. We can touch the souls of those passing over, ease their journey, take them where they need to go, and bring them back if it's not their time yet. I guess these are qualifications for the job.

I think of something that Father Bryne told me – that numerous people have reported sightings of Saint Lazarus over the years – the white-shrouded figure standing watch over battlefields or the sickbed of a relative. But there have been other sightings, too – the grinning skull of the Grim Reaper, as he carries his scythe around, the winged Valkyrie carrying warriors off to the hall of Valhalla, the loyal dog who stands guard over his master's body, or the snazzy pink suit and matching case of my great-grandmother. The Lord or Lady of

Death makes themselves visible when required. They ensure that their legacy lives on, and that their work does not go unnoticed.

"I-I-I thought we were supposed to be psychopomps," I manage to choke out.

"That is the role of a Lazarus beyond the Veil, yes. But those who carry the blood of the First Lazarus have a different job. Death is big business, perhaps the biggest business there is," Vera says matter-of-factly. "Every business needs a CEO. And a Lazarus is uniquely qualified for the job. That's why the Crown of Bones is always passed down through the First Lazarus' bloodline. Only those who carry his blood and the Lazarus powers may wear it."

"You're telling me that—"

"Do I have to spell out everything like you're in bloody kindergarten," Vera snaps. "It's you, Bree. You're the last of the descendants of St. Lazarus' bloodline. You can wear the crown."

Panic rising in my throat, I run back to my great-grand-mother. I turn her over, almost losing my lunch when I see the vicious cuts slashed across her body, her head hanging onto her body by the merest thread. I smooth back her bloody hair from her face. My fingers catch in her small tiara. With trembling hands, I lift it from her head and hold it up to the light.

It's a crown of bones.

"Elsie was the Lord of Death," I whisper.

"And you're her successor," Vera says. "Agnes told her you'd be a good choice. Don't disappoint her."

Shit.

Shit on a spirit board.

As I stare down at the crown in my hands, so many things fell into place, as if I knew the answers already but they were locked away in a secret place inside my memory.

When Elsie came to see me at the house after she died, she

was the Lady of Death. She wanted to see if I had her powers because she wanted me to succeed her. That's why the Order of the Noble Death came after me when I was five. They wanted to get rid of Elsie's heir so they could weaken the magic and eventually take the Crown of Bones for themselves.

But Elsie hung on to her crown and kept me secret, until now.

The Order didn't know a heir of the Lazarus bloodline survived until I came back from my travels and started using my powers to resurrect my boyfriends. And when they raised Jack the Ripper to kill me, and I freed him from their bonds...

But who killed Elsie? Was it The Order of the Noble Death? But then why are their corpses littering the throne room? Why haven't one of them taken the throne—

"Hello, Little Lazarus," a familiar voice rasps behind me.

28

BREE

Ah, of course.

I whirl around. The Ripper stands in the entrance to the throne room, red mists swirling around him. He smiles.

"Agnes?" My heart soars with hope. "Are you in there? Can you hear me?"

"My little inner witch has been blissfully silent since the day you found me in the mirrors." Jack the Ripper nods to the mirrored ceiling. "She weakened herself getting her ineffective message to you. I think my depraved mind became too much for her."

Agnes, no.

The Ripper has taken far too much from me already. He shouldn't get to have her, too.

"You killed my great-grandmother." I think of the wounds on her chest. The vicious way she's been attacked. "She's your Mary Kelly."

The Ripper tilts his head to the side and runs his tongue along the edge of his blade. "Very clever. Yes, I did Mary out of order this time. She's supposed to be last, but as soon as I am king, I won't ever have to have a 'last' victim. Hello, Frederick, so nice of you to join us."

"Suck my dick, Jacky Boy," Abberline replies, but the wobble in his voice betrays his fear.

The Ripper chuckles. "Are you proud, Freddy? You caught me. I'll even admit that I did murder all those women, and I *loved* it. I wore their entrails as neckties, spread pieces of their hearts onto crackers, and made flaps of their skin into a fetching cravat. What do you plan to do with me—"

POP POP POP.

I jump as Abberline fires off his pistol into the Ripper's chest.

Jack throws his head back and laughs as the bullets topple from the holes in his waistcoat and clatter on the floor. "A human weapon won't work on me here, Freddy. I'm not made of the same stuff anymore, and soon, I'll be Lord over Death itself."

"Then why aren't you Lord of Death already?" Abberline shoots back. "Why are we all standing around an empty throne if you're so powerful?"

"Because his brain's the size of his dick," Vera cuts in. "And he doesn't think with either."

I stare at the crown in my hands, then back at the Ripper, and I realize why the throne is still empty. "Because you can't be Lord of Hell. You're not a Lazarus. You didn't know when you killed Elsie that you can't wear this crown."

"Ah, yes, Elsie did say you were brilliant." The Ripper's red gaze switches back to me, then focuses on the crown in my hands. "There lies the crux of the matter, Little Lazarus. Ever since my death, I have endured in this forlorn desert beyond the Veil. When I first arrived, the desert was practically empty.

Souls come here only when their psychopomps does not know what to do with them, which realm beyond death they belong in. We poor, rejected souls must remain here and wait for judgment as if we are not in a place where all souls become equal once more. How is that a fair system, I ask you?"

I glance at my great-grandmother's mangled body. "I think that seems too good for you, to be honest."

"Funny, Elsie said the same thing to me when she dropped me off here," he grins.

His smile turns my ghost bones to ash.

"That's right, Little Lazarus. When cancer did what Freddy here could not and felled me at the ripe old age of eighty-four, your great-grandmother was my guide to the underworld. We walked pleasantly through the streets of London as she told me that the current Lord of Death has finally convinced her to go into training for the big job, and that she has already ensured her succession and made sure that her new heir gets a real life before she learns about her powers, blah, blah, blah. All I do is do a tiny bit of ripping on a pretty young thing as we pass by, and Elsie loses her shit and drops me off in this wretched desert. She tells me that I can't travel any further until I've been forgotten by history. Our Elsie certainly had a flair for the dramatic." The Ripper chuckles. "As if I will ever be forgotten! So I have dwelt here ever since, waiting for my chance to cross the river to the next part of my journey, but the ferryman refuses my payment, and the other souls don't wish to travel with me, and the Order of the Noble Death constantly tear me away to dance for their amusement before banishing me back here. It is a miserable existence, and so I found myself in the company of those other poor souls forced to dwell in this between-place, souls deemed too dangerous to continue their journey until they have learned some twisted lesson. Many of those souls have been here so long that they have become the very things that our judges accuse us of being."

"The monsters," I breathe, shaking with the horror of it. Those horrific demons we sent back here were really once human? *How is that possible?*

"Oh yes, what you thought were creatures from the depths of hell were really poor human souls corrupted by the cruelty of the Lord's regime." The Ripper stares at the crown in my hands, his lips smacking together as if it were a delicious treat he plans to snack on. "And we have planned and plotted together for just such an opportunity as you gave us. You see, when a human takes a life, they lose a little piece of their soul. And you killed *me*, Bree Mortimer. You waited until I'd become mortal and then you drove my own knife into my chest. And so, when you sent me back to this wretched place, I was able to take a tiny sliver of your soul back with me. I found my way into the throne room, and by placing that piece of you in my blade, I finally had a weapon that could kill *any* Lazarus, including the reigning Lady of Death."

I stagger back, reeling from his words.

I did this.

It's all my fault.

I have never regretted killing the Ripper. He killed Pax. He had Edward inside him. He would have killed everyone I loved if I didn't stop him. But by taking up the knife myself, I'd given him the piece of my soul that he used to kill Elsie and leave the throne empty.

And without a Lady of Death...

"Yesssssss, Little Lazarus," the Ripper hisses. "You are getting it now. The Crown of Bones has been free for the taking all this time, but I cannot touch it, and I won't let the Order of the Noble Death anywhere near it. Without a ruler, the lands of the Veil have spiralled out of control. The Veil is consuming itself. With the Veil holier than a slice of Swiss cheese, my friends and I have been able to leap freely back into your world. And as soon as the Order got word from their psychopomps spies that the crown was free for the taking, they started sending their minions down here to try and claim it." He casts his arm around the room, indicating the broken bodies. "Poor misguided priests throwing themselves off buildings and drinking poison so they could come here and have a shot at taking the crown. But with my blade infused by your soul, I made sure they knew that they're not welcome. The Crown of Bones is mine and mine alone."

The full horror of what he's telling me hits me in the chest. The Order priests are killing themselves so they can cross to the other side of the Veil and try to get their hands on the crown. I remember the priestess screaming at me, 'You think you have killed them? You have done them a favour. They each longed for their chance at the crown.'

What would the pathway through the Veil be like if the Order of the Noble Death was in charge? I can't bear to think of it.

But the alternative might be even worse. I fix my gaze on Jack the Ripper. The crown in my fingers hums.

"Why do you even want this crown?" I ask, desperately searching for a way to get us out of this. "Isn't it a whole lot of tedious work you don't need? The Lord of Death is bound by rules and duuties. Won't it interfere with your chaos and mayhem?"

Worth a shot, right?

The Ripper merely laughs. "Oh, I have plenty of chaos and mayhem planned for when I am Lord of Death. It is said that only a Lazarus who has lived a mortal life can know how to truly honour the dead. My monsters disagree. The Veil should be ruled by those deemed too monstrous to move on to a proper afterlife, those who have been cast aside. You agree, don't you, Little Lazarus? After all, your whole life has been lived apart from other people. You were shunned because you're different, like me."

The crown trembles in my fingers. "I'm nothing like you."

"Aren't you?" He tilts his head to the side. "I suppose that's true. You murdered Jack the Ripper in cold blood. Not even I can claim that feat. Well, no matter. Soon we will be getting very cosy, Little Lazarus."

He steps towards me, his eyes glowing and a sadistic smile playing across his lips. Abberline steps in front of me. "Not a step closer, Jacky Boy."

The Ripper moves so fast I don't see him. One moment, Abberline is pressed up against me, shoving me back. The next moment, he's on the floor, rolling around in agony, bleeding from a deep cut across his abdomen. Red smoke curls from the edges.

Are ghosts even able to bleed?

How can he bleed in the Realm of the Dead?

It's the knife. The knife with a piece of my soul.

Double ghost-balls.

The Ripper blows on his blade, then turns back to me, beckoning me with his finger. "You and I are going to make a wonderful team. Divine law dictates that only St. Lazarus' bloodline can wield the scythe and wear the crown, but when your ghost boyfriend pulled his little stunt in the cemetery, I realised there was a loophole."

Oh. Oh *hell* no.

I understand exactly what the Ripper intends. He told me back in Edward's wine cellar, when he said he wanted to *consume* me.

I thought he meant to kill me, but his is a far darker plan.

He believes that if my soul is inside him, like Edward and Agnes, then he'll be able to use my powers as his own.

I snort. "I don't think you've thought this through. Agnes and Edward had to fight to stay inside you when they *wanted* to be there. No way are you going to be able to hold me inside you to use my powers against my will. I won't allow it."

"You won't have a choice," the Ripper growls. "You do it, or my beasts destroy everyone you love. You are doing an admirable job of holding back the Order, but they're a bunch of amateurs compared to the horrors I can visit upon you. They sent hundreds of their priests to their deaths simply for a chance to take over the throne for themselves, even after they knew you were still alive. They didn't know that they were walking into a rebellion. We cut them down before they could figure out how to take the crown, because we've been waiting for the only Lazarus weak enough to control. You."

My hands curl into fists. "I'm not weak. I've sent you back here three times now."

"Love makes you weak. Why do you think all those shades down at the docks are clamouring to return to Earth? Love. They leave so much they love behind that they cannot let go, even if paradise is waiting for them on the other side of the river. Why do you think your three boyfriends remained trapped in a lonely house for centuries? Love. Useless, foolish love. And you, my dear, sweet Lazarus, have waltzed across the Veil for love. But you don't seem to understand that you've bought yourself a one-way ticket. You're already dead. Climb inside me, and you will be immortal."

"I have no desire for immortality," I say. "I only want to save the world from you. I know, it's a lot to ask, but since you're on a whole supervillain 'let me tell you my life story before I kill you' soliloquy, if you could let me know how to defeat you, that'd be super."

"And deprive me of breaking you?" he says. "That way will be so much more fun."

He sweeps an arm above his head. The mirrored crystals on the ceiling CRACK like thunder – the same mirrors, I realise, that we used to scry into this place. Their surfaces turn to liquid, bubbling and wobbling as they flatten across the ceiling and an image appears on the choppy surface.

I cry out as I recognise Grimdale. The village is shrouded in black fog, deserted, many buildings damaged or on fire. The duck pond bubbles and emits a foul vapour. And right on the edge of the woods, a single house is lit up like a Christmas tree, glowing as a beacon of hope.

Grimwood Manor.

I try to hold back my emotions as the Ripper zooms in, cackling as he shows me the beasts crawling from the hole in the Veil to circle my house. A tentacled monster pulls up Dad's hand-carved letterbox. Another spits on Maggie's garden, and all the plants inside it wither and die.

"First, they will tear apart your precious house, and everyone inside it. They will enjoy breaking the Roman's bones one by one, and sucking the Pretty Prince's spinal cord out through his nostrils like a piece of spaghetti. They will flatten the blind adventurer like a pancake, roll him up with some syrup, and eat him. And then, they will move out across the land, taking the sadistic pleasures that have been so long denied them. They will lay waste to humankind, and then no one will be left for the Lord of Hell to rule."

"So what's the point?" I yell back, dropping to a squat beside my great-grandmother's prone body, my knee hitting the scythe still clutched in her hand. "If I get inside you and allow you to rule through me, you're going to do the same thing anyway."

"Oh, Little Lazarus, running away around the world when she should have been in her lessons, or she would know all this already. The Lord of Death has duties," he holds out his hand to me. "The tapestry must be woven. The souls must be escorted. The world of the Dead must be at peace. What better person to fulfil those duties than a master of murder? Because isn't all death murder in the end? Isn't it all a cruel trick of fate to take someone before they are finished? I will be a fine Lord of Death. I have many ideas for improvements. I want to make this place better for all souls, not just those who are deemed 'good' by some arbitrary standard. All I want is to do what I'm good at. You may have discarded your birthright and rejected the throne, but you and I together, Lazarus, will tame Death itself. Isn't that what you want? You who is so afraid of grief that you have tethered men who should have long since passed over. As the Lord of Death, you will never have to grieve again. But if you deny me, then your world burns. The world of the Dead will invade the Living. While the throne remains empty, I am free."

"Not on my watch."

My fingers close around the shaft of the scythe. I draw it up from the floor.

The wood grain of the handle lights up with a silver sheen. My hand feels as if I'm pulling an Edward and have stuck it in a light fixture. But I don't let go. The crown in my other hand hums louder.

The Ripper grins. "What do you think you're going to do with that, little girl? You can't wield it unless you are Lord of Death, and the crown is no longer yours to take. That is *mine*."

He advances toward me. I step away, darting beneath his grasping fingers. I stagger backwards up the steps as I struggle to maintain a one-handed grip on the scythe. The crown is now vibrating in my hand.

The backs of my knees press into the throne.

Bree, Ambrose's voice whispers my name. *I believe in you.*

I sit.

I fit the Crown of Bones over my hair.

I grip the scythe with two hands and grin at Jack.

"If you want this throne, Ripper." I raise the scythe. "You'll have to go through the new Lady of Death."

29

AMBROSE

Bree's body jerks in my arms. A faint hiss of breath escapes her lips.

"What's going on?" I cry. "Is she still dead? Is she waking up?"

"I don't know. I've never sent a friend through the Veil before," Dani snaps. "The planchette is moving. It just spelled out CORD DANGER."

"What does that even mean?" Alice cries.

"I don't like this. I want it to stop." Kelly whimpers.

"Well, maybe if you think happy thoughts," I suggest. "Rainbows. Sunflowers. Unicorns fucking carebears."

"Really?"

"No," Dani and Alice say at the same time.

I hold Bree tightly as her body fights. I don't know what's happening, but I know that she feels strange now, her limbs taut with tension, her body rigid but burning hot. I feel for her hand and link our fingers. When my palms press into hers, I feel a faint humming in her skin.

Bree. I don't know what you're doing down there, but I believe in you.

Come back to me.

I always thought love would be like a light in the darkness that I've lived with for so long. I thought love was having someone see what I couldn't and light the path for me to find myself again. But eyes are just eyes. A soul is what matters, and Bree's soul and mine have always been able to find each other in the darkness.

"Ambrose," Dani's voice cracks. "There's a terrible noise outside. I think—"

But I don't hear Dani anymore.

I hold Bree now, not just in my arms, but in my heart. I don't know how to let go. I just know that wherever she is, whatever she is fighting, she knows that I'm there with her, and that no enemy will ever be able to sever her soul from mine.

I press my mouth to hers and kiss her unmoving lips as the moon kisses the sea, my pale light to her storm. I kiss her, and I wish as I have never wished before that I can be her light, and she will find her way home to us.

30

BREE

The moment my ass hits that velvet cushion, I know I've done something I can't undo.

My head grows hot beneath the humming crown. And then, *BAM*. The magic hits me like a freight train, nearly throwing me off the throne. It feels as though every atom of me has been shot up with heroin.

As the fire in my veins pulls back a little, I *see* the cords. Not with my eyes. Those aren't even open, and I could already see them, anyway, but now I *know* them with another sense, a power long held inside me that recognizes my duty.

Not only do I see the cords as they wind their way along lives, but I see their beginnings. And their ends.

I can hear every soul as they move through their lives, as they are woven together into a beautiful tapestry of connections and love and friendship and grief. I know when each will take their next steps along the pathway. They have a kind of order to them, like the timetable at a busy international airport. Souls coming and going. And I am the air traffic controller in charge of it all.

I am the Lady of Death.

Well...*fuck.*

I clutch the scythe and reach out a hand, and I think about my loves. I *ask* for them. Their souls fly through the air, and suddenly, their three cords are in my hand. I can tell instantly that the thick, heavy one belongs to Pax, the sleek, smooth one belongs to Edward, and the vibrant one that seems to slightly pulse in my fingers is Ambrose.

They are still here. Their ends haven't come yet.

I know without knowing, in that strange way that has been happening to me ever since I returned to Grimdale, that if I were to hold the scythe to their cords and cut them, then they would be dead. For real this time. The thought of it makes me open my hand and release their souls back into the ether before I can see their endings.

They are alive right now, and waiting for me to return to them. But I'm still needed here.

I open my eyes. I take in Jack the Ripper's annoyed expression, the red mist leaking from his eyes, the gnarled red soul-cord twisting from his chest. And this time, I see that the cord has nearly wound out. It is ending soon.

I notice something else that I haven't seen before – two faint silvery soul cords wrapped around it.

Two cords?

Ah. Of course.

My scythe fits so perfectly in my hand. As if it has been made for me. My blood sings in my ears.

"You think you've won, don't you, Little Lazarus?" Jack laughs his evil laugh. "I've killed the Lady of Death once. I will kill her again. And while you sit for a few minutes on a forlorn throne, the beasts are pouring through the hole in the Void. You may rule briefly over the realm of death, but soon this place will be— oi, stop that!"

His hand flies out, slapping his cheek, where something tiny pushes against his skin from the inside. One of the silver cords jerks, dragging his red cord further from his chest, closer to his end.

"Don't you bite that OW!" The Ripper grips his ear as a puff of red mist escapes between his fingers. He hops on one leg as the bottom of his cape starts to unravel, and a black paw thrusts from the bottom of his trouser leg to play with the thread.

"Walpurgis!"

"Meow!" The paw disappears inside the trousers again, and a tiny bulge moves up the Ripper's leg into his torso.

The Ripper's head jerks, and when he comes to stare at me again, his face is a little lopsided. "Bree, I'm in here," he croaks out. "But he's too powerful. He's killed too many. You can't let him cut you. That blade can kill you, even here. But I can't—"

"Agnes?"

"Get it out!" The Ripper claws at his stomach. Of course, Walpurgis thinks this is a great game. I laugh as his little ghostly paws jab at the Ripper from inside. I can see his red cord spiralling from his chest, the end nearly here, but I don't know how we defeat him.

The Ripper reaches a hand between the buttons of his waistcoat, into the red mist that makes up his body. His mouth twists in agony, but he draws out Walpurgis by the scruff of his neck. The cat hisses at the Ripper's face, but the Ripper flicks his wrist and tosses him into the corner of the room.

"Meeeeow—"

Walpurgis' cry cuts off with an abrupt *THUD*.

The Ripper turns back to me, lips curled back in a snarl, his fingers wrapped around his knife. A jewel glints in the hilt of the blade, glimmering a deep, velvet black, and I know that is the piece of my soul that he took from me.

If that blade enters my flesh, it will kill me, even with this crown upon my head.

I duck as the Ripper lunges for me, but as I go to swing my scythe, I receive another knowing. I see where the Ripper will go at the end of his life. He thought waiting forever in this desert was the punishment for his crimes, but now I see the horror that awaits him in the next destination along the pathway.

And I can't send him there while Agnes is still inside him, or she'll endure it, too.

"See?" the Ripper snarls, swivelling back around as I stay my hand. "Love is weakness. You will not send me along the pathway, Lady, because you will lose the witch that lives inside me. Wherever I go, she's going, too."

"No, she's not."

Abberline leaps in front of me, his silver cord shimmering bright. "You and I have unfinished business, Jacky boy."

The Ripper slashes with his blade, and I gasp as he opens up a long, deep cut across Abberline's cheek. The detective flinches, but doesn't slow down.

"Good goddess," Vera breathes. "He's going to be a bloody hero, isn't he?"

Abberline clasps his hands together like a diver and plunges inside the Ripper, screaming the whole way. The Ripper's body jerks, red mist belching from his mouth and eye sockets. His limbs twerk and twitch, and he doubles over in pain as a wizened ghost topples out of his stomach, coughing as she crawls along the floor.

"Agnes."

"That stupid copper kicked me out," she gasps. "Where's Walpurgis—"

The Ripper shrieks. I turn back to see Abberline's silver thread blazing bright as it wraps around the red one, and the pair of them dance across the throne room floor as they fight for control of the body. The knife whips through the air, and I have to duck to avoid being cut.

"Do it." The Ripper jerks to a standstill as Abberline gains control. "I don't have much time."

My fingers hum against the scythe. "But it will kill you, too."

"I had one job – to rid the world of Jack the Ripper. Now, do it!"

A sob escapes my throat as I throw back the scythe.

I swing.

The scythe cuts both space and time as it slices through the air, and I don't feel a thing as it cuts cleanly through both the Ripper's and Abberline's soul cords.

The Ripper howls, and I don't know who is howling, but it is terrible. The throne room trembles. The looms rattle on their giant frames.

I drop the scythe.

The Ripper's clothes fall to the floor.

There is nothing inside them. Agnes runs over and kicks them, but they are only clothes. A black cloak, a spiffy top hat, a trim waistcoat, and, in the middle of them, a faded grey great-coat and a policeman's revolver.

The knife is gone.

"It's over," Vera says.

I slump against the throne, the crown heavy on my head. Agnes approaches cautiously, Walpurgis cuddled in her arms.

"Now you've gone and done it," she snaps. "You're the Lady of Death now."

"You're never happy, are you?" I roll my eyes at her. "What happened to, 'Thank you, Bree for saving the world.'"

"Hmmmph." Agnes nods to Vera. "I suppose it's nice to see you again. You took your sweet time getting her here."

I sigh. "You two deserve each other. Now, if you'll excuse me, I'm going back to the Living World."

I reach down to tug on my own black cord, but a ghostly hand shoots out and grabs my wrist.

"Where do you think you're going?" Agnes growls. "You're the Lady of Death now. You have duties."

"I'm not staying here." I gesture down to my cord. "I've got to get all those monsters away from Grimdale and back down here."

Agnes makes as if she's going to throw Walpurgis at me. I brace myself to catch a large, clawed beast. "I know you better than that. You're Elsie's blood, after all. You're going to shirk your duties because you want to go back to those three ex-ghosts."

"I *promised* them I'd come back. I've left them once before. I can't do it again."

"The crown doesn't care about your promise," Vera says. "The Realm of the Dead needs a ruler to set things to rights, and now you're it."

"Well, that's nice, but I all I wanted to do was fix the hole in the Veil. I saved the world. Isn't that enough? Besides, I have to die first, right?"

I look at Vera, who nods slowly. "Yes, but you're already dead. Twice dead, in fact. You died when you were five years old, and you're dead back on earth right now. That's what the doorway says. ONLY THE DEAD MAY PASS."

No.

I think of the guys, of my dad, of Dani, surrounding my lifeless body, hoping and wishing and praying that I'll come back.

"But I'm not qualified for the job. I don't know anything about being the Lady of Death. Maybe someone else could take over while I go up and enjoy the rest of my life with my hot AF ex-ghost boyfriends."

Vera turns to Agnes. "She's not getting it. I thought she was supposed to be bright. She has so much to learn, and unlike

Elsie and every other Lord or Lady before her, she doesn't have the reigning monarch to teach her. All she has is us. She needs to start *yesterday*."

"You're wearing the crown, Bree," Agnes explains. "The scythe belongs to you now. That's old magic, older even than magic itself. You can't just refuse the job and go back to the Living Realm."

"Can't I?" I point to the tapestries adorning the walls. "Other Lords and Ladies have done it. That's why there are so many recordings of Lazarus and Grim Reaper sightings throughout history."

Vera sighs. "Yes, but those are for ceremonial reasons. Appearing on famous battlefields, opening supermarkets, etc, etc. You have to do a little bit of PR to keep the brand alive."

"And Elsie coming back to see me?"

"Yes. That was to ensure the line of succession." Vera frowns. "It figures that her great-granddaughter would be exactly like her. Just as bloody stubborn and eager to run away."

"I'm not running away. I'm running *back* to the place where I belong. To my home."

"But you can't live among humans anymore. You're not one of them. The power the crown gives you will still be with you in the Living realm. That power isn't not meant for someone still Living. It will

I feel their cords tugging at me, their love drawing me back.

"I'm going back," I say firmly. "Will you both look after this place while I'm gone?"

"That's not how it works—"

"I'm in charge, right? I decide how it works."

Vera gasps as I reach up to the crown and snap off two long pieces of bleached bone. They feel warm and light in my hand, humming with magic that's older than time. I toss one bone to

Agnes, who manages to save it from Walpurgis, and hold out the other to Vera.

"Congratulations, you two. You're officially my regents. I'm going back to earth to have a *life*. Take care of things until I get hit by a bus. In the meantime, I just defeated the world's most elusive serial killer and now I'm going home to Pax, Edward, and Ambrose."

Vera snatches the bone from my hand. "We don't even know if this will work."

"Call me if there are any problems. Now, how do I get back?"

Agnes settles back into the throne. Walpurgis curls up into her lap and goes to sleep, his little body vibrating like a buzz saw. Agnes flashes me a rare smile and waves her hand. The tapestries on the wall part to reveal another doorway into the gloom, this one surrounded by bleached bones. The inscription above it reads:

ONLY THE LIVING MAY PASS

"You haven't thought this through," Vera says. "If you go back, you'll still be the Lady of Death. You'll have all her powers. There's a reason no Lord or Lady has stayed long back in the realm of the Living. You will be able to see when every person you love dies."

My heart thuds to a stop. "What?"

"The moment you touch those three men who've stolen your heart, you will see their deaths. You will never be able to unsee that. Death is not meant to be known by the Living. You will undo yourself with your own magic."

"It's never been done before, but maybe it's worth a try." Agnes stares at the piece of bone in her hand. "Bree has been practising her magic. Perhaps she will be able to hold back the visions of death."

Vera snorts.

"It's not only that. With things still unstable down here, and she is no longer an ordinary Lazarus. If she uses her powers even once, it could tear the Void wide open once more."

"I don't care what you think." I grip my cord in both hands and give it three tugs. "I won't use my powers, because I brought my three men back already, so I don't need them anymore. Now, if you'll excuse me, I promised them that I'd return to them, and I've broken enough promises in my life. I'm going *home*."

"This is your home now," Vera yells at me as I step towards the door. "Your great-grandmother lived the way she did because she knows that a Lady of Death must be alone. She did not die for you to waltz back to the Living World and leave the Veil bereft."

"You're not bereft. You and Agnes are in charge, and I trust the two of you implicitly. I'm sure you have improvements you'd like to make to the whole psychopomps thing. Maybe some annual leave, or a nice coffee machine in the break room." I wave at them both as my cord starts to drag me up towards the doorway. "Put your ideas to management and I'm sure we'll work something out. But I'm keeping the scythe. Toodles."

I heft the shimmering curved blade over my shoulder and step through the doorway, As I turn to wave goodbye to them, I gaze up at the ceiling, where the scrying mirror lies open. I can see the scene unfolding in my house. Pax and Edward overwhelmed by the Order of the Noble Death, Dad cups my cheek, his tears wetting my shirt. Ambrose's lips whisper to me.

Bree, come back to us. Come home.

"I'm coming!" I fly through the doorway. Grimdale Cemetery rockets past in a blur as I soar high above the pathway, back towards the shrinking hole in the Veil. I catch onto the edge of the hole, and with the black cord that protrudes from my belly, I pass through and stitch the hole closed behind me.

As the final stitch of my black soul cord pulls taut, sealing the hole in the Veil, I'm plunged into darkness, dragged under by the magic that pulls me in two different directions. And my mind goes still, and I succumb...

31
BREE

I open my eyes.

"Bree?" Ambrose's lips are on mine, hot and desperate and *alive*.

Before I have the chance to breathe, let alone shore up my magical defences, his kiss grabs my heart and twists, and his death appears in a vision before me. He stumbles on a rock on some faraway beach, falls, and hits his head. A great adventurer felled by a simple slip of the foot. His face relaxes into serenity as he stares, unseeing, at the sky, and he is young, far, far too young...

Ambrose, no.

I gasp and shove him away, reeling from the raw pain of it. I need to get some space. I need to call up my magic and—

"We thought we'd lost you," a dangerous voice purrs, and then Edward's lips are on mine, and his fingers tangle in my hair, and his death is in my heart, too.

No, no, don't look. Please, don't look...

But I can't turn my heart away. Edward lies face down on one of Grimwood's faded rugs, a pool of vomit around his mouth. Empty bottles and open poetry books surround him. A terrible loneliness emanates from his lifeless form.

"My turn, my turn! We have only seconds until they get in here."

"Don't touch me," I cry out, but it's too late. Pax gathers me into his arms, crushing me against him as he whispers prayers of thanks to his gods. And his death comes to me, too, fast and violent. The slash of a blade buried deep in his chest. His mighty form slumps forward as he falls upon a sword.

No, no, you can't go like that. You can't leave me. Please, Pax, please...

"Why are you carrying a gardening tool?" Pax looks disapprovingly at the scythe that's rolled onto the ground. "As a weapon, it will be useless in the hallways. Not enough room to swing it."

"Everyone, get back," Dani's voice penetrates my grief. "Give her some room to breathe."

Reluctantly, they let go, and the images recede from my consciousness. But they are burned into my memory. Vera was right – I'll never be able to unsee them.

This is a mistake.

But I can't let on to them, not when they are all staring at me with such hope and happiness on their faces. As Pax said, they have only moments left until the Order and the last of the Ripper's monsters burst through the door to the room. I roll off the bed and pick up my scythe. The wooden handle hums in my fingers.

The door bursts open.

"Step back!" I yell.

I *slice*.

Pax is right. There isn't a lot of room. I have to stop my momentum so I don't accidentally hit one of my friends. But this isn't an ordinary scythe and I'm no longer an ordinary girl.

Bright white light blinds me. The blade sings as it cuts space and time, and every single priest, priestess, and monster fighting in the hallway disappears.

Gone.

Obliterated.

The white light fades, and Grimwood's enemies are gone. Just like that.

Woah.

"Bree, you did it!" Pax barrels towards me, a huge smile on his face. He doesn't know anything is wrong, that if I touch him, I'll see his death again.

So I do what I should have done the moment I returned to my body, I call up my power and go to a place of calm. I pull up my magical shields and demand that no other deaths be let in.

Don't look.

I force a smile as Pax wraps his arms around me. This time, I don't see that sword sticking out of him. But it's too late. I can't unsee it.

"You're here!" Dani throws her arms around me. My defences hold. I don't see her death. "You came back to us."

"I sure did." I sit up, trying to force my heart back to normal as I struggle to figure out what I'm going to say. "Edward, you're holding a sword? And you're covered in blood? Are you okay? Do you have all your limbs?"

"He fought valiantly," Pax grins, slapping Edward on the shoulder. This time, Edward doesn't bite back at him. Instead, he smiles dopily, and I know that I cannot ever tell him about his death.

"What happened down there?" Dad asks. "Why do you have a magical scythe?"

"So..." I flop back against the couch, suddenly tired beyond belief. I can't find the words to tell them everything, so I settle for a piece of truth. *Don't look.* "I killed Jack the Ripper. Well,

Abberline did. And it turns out that I'm the Lady of Death now. But I left Agnes and Vera on my throne to act as regents, and I stitched up the hole in the Veil. As long as I act like a normal human and don't use my Lazarus powers ever again, the hell-beasts will stay on their side of the Veil, where they belong."

"Well, that's a relief," Dad leans down and kisses the top of my head. I can feel the crown humming there even though it didn't come back with me. "I knew you could do it, Bree-bug."

Don't look, don't look.

I slump back against the sofa. "It was a team effort."

"This calls for a celebration." Edward straightens. "Shall I go and get another bottle from my cellar?"

"We can't drink your whole unfinished business dry," I say. "You should keep some for selling, so you have money to live, to do things you want to do."

So you don't end up facedown on the floor, drowning in your own—

No, stop.

This is what Vera warned you about. No matter what you see, you can't interfere while you're in the Living realm. You can't bring them back again, or you risk opening up the Veil and letting out something worse than Jack the Ripper. You just have to accept that they're going to die in horrible, lonely ways, and you will miss them beyond measure. Love may be eternal, but grief is enduring, and...

"I don't think it was finding the cellar that brought me back," Edward says.

I blink, startled from my thoughts. "You don't?"

"I think it was when I realized that I could use the cellar for something good, something selfless." Edward grins. "We can sell the bottles and use the money to repair Grimwood Manor so that your parents don't have to sell it. That's what you want, isn't it? I've never done anything selfless before, but I like this. It feels good."

I look around at the faces of my father, my lovers, and my friends (and Kelly). I look up at the walls splattered with blood. I close my eyes and see three horrific deaths on the inside of my eyelids.

I came back for them.

I can't leave them again.

I have to *try*.

For them.

Grimwood Manor has been many things to me – a refuge, a prison, the place where I found myself again. And it has been so many things to people before me, too. For Pax, a battlefield. For Edward, a sanctuary. For Ambrose, a hearth. For Elsie, a portal to her throne room.

Maybe it was time Grimwood got to be the purpose it was built for – a home.

32

BREE

The next morning, I wake from a nightmare of lonely death to the scent of bacon, and the sound of my father humming.

Don't look. Don't look.

I shore my barriers up tight before I yawn and roll over, straight into Edward's waiting arms. "Don't you dare think about leaving this bed," he scolds me between kisses. "Don't leave me in desolation."

"As much as I hate to do it…" I manage, with great restraint, to untangle myself from him. "I need coffee."

I sit up and notice that we're the only two occupants of the bed. Edward takes advantage of my distraction to tug me down again, his lips hot on mine, his hands roaming over my naked body until I'm panting.

(I still sleep naked, because when you're surrounded by three hot AF ex-ghosts, why wouldn't you?)

All thoughts of coffee fly from my mind as he rolls on top of me, using his knee to push my legs apart. His lip curls into one of his devilish smiles as he shuffles under the blankets, kissing a trail of fire over my breasts and abdomen before plunging that rakish tongue between my thighs.

My back arches immediately as he laves his tongue over that sensitive bud. My muscles twitch violently, and I grab handfuls of bedsheets, desperate for him, starving for him.

Edward knows exactly what he's doing to me. He drags his tongue deliriously slowly, making me feel every moment, forcing all other thoughts but him from my mind. He dances lazily over my clit so that my pleasure rises like a slow-drip anaesthesia, settling into my bones and muscles until I am completely at his mercy.

"So much more satisfying than coffee," he murmurs, as he plunges his tongue inside me.

Now he begins to ravage my clit and pussy with abandon, his fathomless dark eyes regarding me from beneath the sheets, watching me as I come undone for him.

A sob passes my lips as the tension draws tighter, my belly tugging, my heart racing. I grind my hips into his face, and he makes these filthy gulping, slurping sounds that are more beast than man, and I am gone. Pleasure pulls me under, and I almost forget that I saw his death.

Almost.

When I come back to him, he is lying next to me, his legs tangled in mine, his lips pressing against my brow. "Every inch of you is something precious to me, Brianna. I could spend a lifetime between these legs of yours and never grow tired."

"Oh, poet prince, I bet you say that to all the girls."

"Nope." His eyes sparkle as he kisses me again, and I taste my own pleasure on his lips. "Just the girl I love."

Love.

That word that once made me break out in hives has a whole new anathema now, because Vera is right. I saw how he dies, alone and facedown in a pool of his own vomit. I can't save him, I can only hold him close as time marches us towards that tragic end.

I hate this.

"Where are the others?" I ask.

"Pax is fixing breakfast, and Ambrose fancied a walk around the cemetery in the sunshine." Edward's eyes glitter with mischief. "They have left us two indolent wastrels in bed for whatever carnal pleasures take our fancy."

"Why, my prince, whatever did you have in mind?"

Edward's grin widens as he pins my wrists with one hand. His shaft rubs against my thigh, hard and needy. He reaches his other hand between my legs, finding that bud he'd made so sensitive and stroking it gently.

"You saved the world," he whispers. "You saved me, and I thought I was quite beyond saving. You're remarkable."

I didn't save you. I can't save you. And I'm going to spend the rest of eternity grieving you.

But I can't bear him to know the turmoil in my heart. I want him to believe that everything is okay, that we have won.

"Why, thank you. But I didn't do all the saving by myself. You and Pax made quite the pair," I whisper as he rolls me onto my side and nudges my legs open to admit his hardness.

"It turns out that when those I care about are in trouble, I can be proficient with a sword. Allow me to demonstrate."

FOR THE SECOND time that morning, I make an attempt to get out of bed. Edward has returned to snoring away beside me. I slide myself out from beneath his arm and stumble around for clothes.

The curtains are still open, revealing a bright, summery day. Not a hint of a hole in the Veil. A couple of kids ride by the house on their bicycles, and Maggie is out in her garden, digging over her ruined beds. From somewhere deeper in the house, I can hear my dad singing along with the radio.

It's over. Everything is back to normal. The sun is shining through the window. Pax no longer has to stand guard for the monsters.

If I keep my defences up, I won't see any more deaths until I'm ready to take up the crown again.

So why do I feel jittery, as if I've had too much coffee, when I haven't even had a single drop yet?

Why does this peace feel so precarious, as if we're only one wrong move away from disaster?

Don't look.

I'm not even wearing the Crown of Bones here, and yet, it rests heavy on my head.

I turn back to the bed. Edward sleeps soundly, his hands clasped beneath his head. At rest, he looks so innocent, cherubic. His silver cord winds from his chest and dances through the air.

I remember holding the scythe in my hands, how that magic hummed through me, how with a single stroke of the blade, I could cut down a life.

I remember Edward's death.

All Lazarii see death too soon. We're seeped in the grief of the world from too young an age. Humans are supposed to fear death. It's supposed to be the great unknown. Our fear of death is what makes our lives worth living. We never know when our spindle will run out.

But I'm not supposed to fear death any longer. I'm supposed to master it. I'm supposed to be beyond grief, beyond human sentiment. I know that if I look again, I will see the end of everyone I love – my friends, my parents. I will know the date and time when I am to escort them along the pathway.

I don't want that knowledge. All I've already seen is tearing me apart at the seams.

How will I stop myself from trying to save them? How will I resist knocking bottles of wine from Edward's hands, or hiding Pax's sword, or leading Ambrose away from rocky beaches?

When will I ever be ready to say goodbye?

But if I don't resist, this could all happen again.

I can do this. I can stay away from my powers. After all, I still have time with all of them. I didn't see their faces clearly. I have no exact date. We could enjoy the time we have together.

Yes, I can do this. I just have to not look.

I pull on a Blood Lust band t-shirt and a pair of high-waisted black shorts and wander into the foyer. A delicious smell wafts from the kitchen and I can hear Pax in there, singing a Roman drinking song at the top of his lungs while he clatters pots and pans.

"Good morning, Bree-bug!"

I look up. There's Dad, kneeling on a drop cloth on the top landing, brushing stain onto the carved balustrade. He waves at me with one hand while the other splashes flecks of stain onto the front of his overalls.

Don't look.

I blink. "Are you seriously staining the balustrade the day after we saved the world?"

He shrugs. "Your mother called this morning. She's on her way home. I'd better get this finished or she'll have my guts for garters. Pax is making breakfast."

"Yoooo-hooooo." The front door bangs open, and Mum rushes inside in a cloud of perfume. She's weighed down by several shopping bags. "I'm home, and Mum and I got some decor items that I think Gwen will approve of. Bree, help me with these bags. Mike, how is that woodwork looking?"

"Excellent, my dear." Dad wipes his brush and gets to his feet. "I'll come and help you."

"I've got it, Dad." I pick up six shopping bags.

"No, no, I know your mother's fondness for shopping. There will be ten more in the boot." Dad starts down the stairs.

"Mike, careful—"

It happens in slow motion. Dad shuffles off the edge of the step, pitching his body off-balance. His mouth opens in an O of shock as he grabs for the balustrade, but it's his bad hand and the wood's slippery with wet stain, and he slides right off.

My heartbeat pounds in my ears, so loud that my dad's cry is only a faint squeak that cuts off with a sickening CRUNCH as he lands in a heap at the bottom of the stairs.

He doesn't move.

33

PAX

When Sylvie starts screaming, I drop my perfect Spanish omelette (odd, when I marched through Spain, or Hispania, as we Romans know it, I did not recall the breakfast food being so delicious), pick up my sword which I'd laid across the breakfast bar, and rush into the foyer.

At first, I'm confused. I can see no enemy to slay, no vicious hellbeast demanding its head be separated from its body. There is only Bree and her mother at the bottom of the stairs.

And then I see him.

Mike lies unmoving at their feet. His leg is bent in a way no leg should bend.

Bree kneels in a pool of his blood, her hands moving in the air while the desolation in her eyes makes me see red.

She's been broken since she returned from beyond the Veil. She won't tell us why, but I see it in her eyes. I may not be sensitive like Edward and Ambrose, but I know when a warrior has seen things on the battlefield that his heart cannot forgive.

I have rarely known fear in my life, but I'm terrified that this might destroy her completely.

I rush to Mike's side, but Sylvie holds me back. "You can't touch him," she scolds me. "It's dangerous to move someone who's had a fall."

A fall. It sounds so wrong. A great man like Mike should not be felled by something as silly as a fall. "But what am I supposed to do?"

"Comfort Bree. I'm calling an ambulance." Sylvie presses her magic rectangle to her ear.

Bree. I whirl around just in time to see her throw herself over her father. I grab her and try to pull her into my arms, but she holds onto him with a strength I didn't know she possessed.

"Yes, I'd like to report an accident. My husband has fallen down the stairs and we need an ambulance to Grimwood Manor—"

Bree kicks and bucks against me. I press her tight against my chest. "It will be okay. The doctors will come. They will make him better."

"No, Pax, you don't understand," she sobs. "His cord. His cord is unwinding."

Oh no.

No.

That's not happening.

Mike isn't dying on us. I do not give permission for this soldier to leave the battle.

I glance at Sylvie. She's clutching the phone, her lips moving but no sound coming out. Her face has gone pale. And that's when I know Bree speaks the truth.

I release Bree.

"I can do it. I can save him." Bree grabs something invisible in the air. She bites her lip as she moves her hands over her father's body. "Dad, please. Dad..."

34
BREE

I don't know how long I lie next to my father, my fingers locked in his, watching the faint rise and fall of his chest, before the ambulance comes and takes him away.

"You ladies did a great job," the paramedic says as she closes the ambulance doors. "You acted fast and you stayed calm. You saved your father's life, Bree."

Yes. I saved him.

I tore his cord from the air and pushed it back inside him.

I did the one thing I promised I'd never do again.

I hadn't even been in the world for a single day, and already I've used my powers. Already I've weakened the Veil.

It seems to be holding right now, but what about next time?

I didn't even think about what might happen. When I saw the cord unravel from Dad's chest, I just *acted*.

I'm supposed to be the Lady of Death. I'm supposed to answer to forces higher than my own selfish grief.

I can't do this.

As the ambulance pulls away with Dad and Mum inside, I stare up at the sky, searching with my eyes and with the sight granted to me as Lady of Hell for any sign that the Veil is weakened. All I see is bright, endless blue.

I close my eyes, and I see vomit, sword, and bloodstained rocks.

Pax wraps me in his arms. "It's okay. He's going to be okay. The healers will fix him as good as new."

"A course of leeches will see him right as rain." Edward pats me on the shoulder. But as he looks at me, his lip quirks. Edward always has a way of seeing right into the depths of my soul, into all the dark things I can't speak aloud.

I don't want him to see. Not this time.

I turn away from them and go inside.

"...AND I have this gnarly scar now. Want to see?" Dad tugs at the bottom of his hospital gown.

"Yes!" Pax exclaims.

"No!" I cry.

It's three days after the accident, and I'd like to burn down the hospital so I never have to see it again. Mum and I haven't left Dad's side since they brought him in. He broke his leg, three ribs, has a mild skull fracture (thankfully, no brain damage), and another fracture in his arm. But they've wrapped him up like an Egyptian mummy and we're just waiting for a doctor to come around and clear Dad to go home.

Pax, Ambrose, and Edward have been amazing, bringing us food, books, and blankets. Pax and Edward did a dramatic reenactment of their battle against the hellbeasts that Dad had to cut short because he was laughing so hard he was afraid he'd split his stitches.

Every kind thing they do makes my decision harder.

The doctor told us that falls are common for people with Parkinson's. "It's the most frequent cause of death. Mike was lucky this time, but as his condition advances, you might like to consider some adaptations to the house so he doesn't have to navigate stairs."

"Good news, Mike, you're sprung." Dr. Bakir writes something on Dad's chart. They exchange a few words about a local microbrewery Dad recommended the doctor try out, and then a nurse arrives with a wheelchair. Mum stands up to help her manoeuvre him into it, but Pax beats her to it, and plops Dad inside like he was a feather.

"With these nurses around you, you're going to be just fine," Dr. Bakir says.

We get Dad home, and as we wheel him up the driveway, he insists that we take a detour to admire the new flower beds Maggie installed after the monsters destroyed hers. Edward picks a couple of blooms so he can smell them, then tucks the flowers into my hair.

"I ordered a stair elevator for you," Mum says as Pax carries him up the porch steps. "It was supposed to be here today, but the postie hasn't been yet, so I guess you'll have to stay on the bottom floor until it arrives."

"We've taken care of that." Ambrose beams. "Follow me."

I exchange a look with Mum. We never discussed this. We follow Ambrose to the very end of the hall we use as the guest wing. The room here has been a mess – the furniture gone from when Gwen declared that we had to modernise.

But now, it's a finished bedroom, and it's beautiful. There's a lovely new headboard, painted in a soft blue with the faintest pattern of clouds and birds in the corners. Blue and white linens cover the bed. My feet sink into a soft sheepskin rug, and two old leather chairs that used to be in Edward's boudoir have been reupholstered in blue and white stripes and now sit beneath the window, looking out into the garden and the cemetery beyond.

"Pax made the bed," Edward says, with a touch of awe in his voice. "He tore the ends off that old bed and made the frame from a design he saw on one of Sylvie's magazines."

"Edward painted it," Pax says.

"I did the sewing," Ambrose adds proudly, pointing to a row of jauntily crooked curtains, and the clashing pillows on the bed.

"We didn't want you to think about the stairs for a while," Pax says to Mike. "If you need to go anywhere, I can carry you. I once carried a horse all the way across Gaul on a dare. You do not weigh as much as a horse, and you probably smell better."

"Probably?" Dad raises an eyebrow, but he smiles. Then his eye catches something. "What's this?"

He points at the wall behind us. I whirl around, and my eyes widen as I take in the beautiful mural of a country scene in the south of France. It reminds me a little of one of the pictures I saw in Mum and Dad's holiday photos.

But who did this? It must've cost a fortune to hire an artist to come in on such short notice.

"I painted it," Edward says sheepishly. He glances over his shoulder out the window, where a large raven sits on the sill, watching us with kind orange-ringed eyes. "Well, I had a little help from a friend. I heard that you like murals, so I thought I'd give it a go. It's a bit rudimentary, but..."

"It's beautiful, Edward," Dad says, his voice a little hoarse. "This is all so kind of you. Thank you."

A hard lump forms in my throat. I turn and try to wipe away my tears without anyone noticing.

"This is very nice of you boys," Mum says briskly, pushing Dad out of the room. This is her way of showing that she's deeply affected by what they did. "Now, Mike, I think the first thing I should do is settle you into the snug with an audiobook and—"

"No, no." Dad sits up. "I'm taking everyone to the pub."

"Oh, Mike, don't be ridiculous."

"I've been cooped up in the hospital for three days, Sylv, I need some fresh air. Besides, it's quiz night and we finally have enough for a family team, and I want to show off my scar." Dad wheels toward the door. "Let's go. Pax, help me down these steps!"

"I'm here!" Pax bounds off after him.

"The pub sounds excellent," Edward says. "Do you think the quiz will have a round about me? I am quite interesting."

Ambrose's fingers search for him. "I think it will be wonderful. We have so much to celebrate."

"You guys go ahead," I say with a shrug, stepping away from Ambrose before he can touch me, fighting every urge inside me not to burst into tears. "I'll catch up later. There's something I have to do first."

Ambrose's lip twists with concern. "Will it take long? We can wait for you."

"No need. I just want to do one little thing for Mr. Pitts that I forgot about, and I'll come and join you. Start without me. Round one is usually sports – I'll be useless then, anyway."

"Okay. We see you later!" Pax leans in and stage whispers, "The victory sex will be intense tonight."

I smile at him, and he's so happy that he doesn't notice how wobbly it is. "I believe it."

My lips burn to kiss them, but I resist. If I kiss them, I won't be able to go through with this.

I stand in the window of my bedroom and watch them walk down the driveway together. My mum and Ambrose walk with their arms linked, while Edward pushes Dad and loudly proclaims that everyone must make way for them, and Pax skips along in front, collecting more flowers for Dad to smell. On the corner of Grimwood Crescent, Dani and Alice wait, their smiles broad, their fingers knitted together.

My heart silently and quietly breaks.

The moment my family rounds the corner, I drag my suitcase from under my bed and throw it open.

I wrench open the doors to the armoire. No time to pack. I simply tip my entire wardrobe into the suitcase, stopping only to stuff my international adapter and a travel pillow down the side. I bounce on the lid until I get it shut, then check my passport and credit card are in my wallet, sling my purse over my shoulder, and pull out my phone to look over the train timetable. If I hurry, I can make the next one before Pax is even back with the first round of drinks.

I pause in the doorway, taking one last look at the bedroom that has been mine since I returned to Grimwood. My eyes move from the window where Pax watched over me every night, even many nights when he was human and needed to sleep, to the chaise lounge where Edward directed Ambrose and Pax to give me the best sex of my life, to the bed, where I lost my heart and found it again inside their chests.

I know that I'm going to break their hearts again.

I promised that I'd come home to them.

But I *can't*.

If I stay with them, they will die the way I saw in my vision. If I stay near them, I will use my powers to save them. But if I leave, then maybe that will change the future. It will change how they die. Maybe they'll get the lives – and the deaths – they deserve.

I can't be with them and wear the Crown of Bones. I thought I could, but I can't live with the knowing. I love them too much to lose them again. I can't know they will die and not step in.

My great-grandmother was right. The Lady of Death must be alone.

I think about walking back through the doorway. But I'm not ready for that yet, either. There's something I need to do first.

My suitcase is an impossible weight, but I manage to drag it down the hall and out onto the porch. I take one last look at the house that has shielded me and held me and made me who I am. Ozzy hangs from the foyer chandelier. He raises one wing, as if waving me goodbye.

I slam the door shut behind me.

35

EDWARD

"I can't believe we lost," Mike sulks as Pax helps him up the porch steps. "We should have wiped the floor with them. I had all the subject-matter experts on my team."

"Who knew that Edward would completely botch the 'Great British Poets' round," Ambrose says with a smile as he leans heavily against his stick, slightly swaying from the pints of cider he imbibed. Tipsy Ambrose is much freer with his tongue than normal, and I'm not sure I care for it.

"None of the questions were about me!" I growl. "I'm the only poet worth learning about."

The others laugh, which wasn't my intention at all. Mike unlocks the door. I race inside, eager to see Brianna. She said she would join us at the pub, but I suspect she lay down on her bed and fell straight asleep.

"Brianna?" I call out, heading in the direction of her boudoir. "We're home. You need to have a word with the quiz organiser about her lack of knowledge of British poetry—Brianna?"

I stop in the doorway. The bedspread is balled at the end of the bed, exactly as we left it. Bree's clothing is strewn across the floor – this is not unusual, but there appears to be less of it than there was this morning. The doors to the armoire are thrown open.

A hard lump rises in my throat.

I have sensed a darkness in Brianna since she returned, a vast chasm that I cannot hope to cross. She keeps a secret that is eating her inside, and I am about to behold the terrible consequences of that secret.

I check the bathroom. The large bottles of sweet-smelling toilette are still beside the bathtub, but all the tiny bottles of beauty elixirs Brianna kept beside the sink are gone.

"Brianna?"

"What has happened?" Pax storms into the room, his sword drawn. His lip curls back as he notices the armoire, the drawers tossed out, the clothes laid astray. "Someone has kidnapped Bree."

A fuzzy death cannon zooms through the door above Pax's head. Ozzy lands on the bed and starts doing a frantic dance.

"What is it, little guy?" Pax leans in, studying Ozzy's movement as he mimes opening some kind of box and throwing things inside. "Did they kidnap Bree in some kind of sarcophagus? Are they going to try and make her their Queen Cleopatra? But her nose is far too tiny—"

I shake my head. "Not even close, Roman."

I spy something white on Brianna's pillow. I pick it up, careful to ignore the cloud of her blazing almond and pear scent that wafts across my nostrils. I unfold the paper. My fingers tremble as I trace the words she scribbled to us.

Edward, Pax, and Ambrose.

I'm sorry.

I can't do this. I love you too much.

I'm sorry I couldn't tell you this to your faces. When I put on the Crown of Bones, I got a new magical power. I see when people die. I guess it's part of my job as the Lady of Death to know these things. But I'm not like any other Lady of Death. I came back to you. But it was a mistake.

Every time I look at you, I see your deaths. They are not noble deaths. They are horrible and cruel and unfair, and I can't bear it. But if those deaths are because of me, then perhaps me leaving will change them. I want you to have the lives you deserve, the lives that were stolen from you last time.

I am so afraid. I couldn't even go a day without using my powers to bring back someone I love. I won't be able to resist with you. Being near you puts everyone in Grimdale – everyone in the world – in danger.

There's a reason that the Lady of Death is supposed to be alone.

I'm going back beyond the Veil to take up my crown. This isn't goodbye forever. I'll be there to walk you along the pathway when your time comes. But before I do that, there's something I have to do in the Living Realm. Something I need to understand.

Know that I love you, and that you did nothing wrong.

Don't look for me.

Bree

36

BREE

"Excuse me? Hello?" A hand waves in front of my face. "Did you know that your phone's ringing?"

Reluctantly, I tear my gaze from the rattling window looking out across the industrial outskirts of London to the guy in a Chelsea cap opposite me. He's jabbing his fingers at my phone, which is vibrating so hard that it's wiggling across the table that separates us.

The guy catches it as it vibrates right off the edge of the table and drops it into my hands. "Sorry, I didn't mean to disturb you, but I thought you might like to know that it was making a break for it."

"Thanks," I mutter.

My head throbs.

I stare at the screen. My mum's picture appears as she calls me. I disconnect the call. My screen fills with screeds of messages. I scan them – they're all from Mum and Dani, but I recognise the words, the timbre, the raw panic. I never had the chance to get any of the ghosts a phone (or a 'magic rectangle,' as they prefer to call them).

I can't cry. If I let the tears fall, I'll get off this train in Paris and turn straight around and go back to them. That's all I want to do. But how long before Pax says the wrong thing to the wrong person at the pub and pulls out his sword? How long until Edward gets into one of his dark moods and I find him facedown on the rug?

And Ambrose...his was the only face I saw, and he looked so young, so much like he does now. And I'm supposed to stand here while he's taken from me?

I'm not good for them. Their deaths have made that obvious.

And how long until I use my powers to save them? How long until I decide to bring them back to me again and unleash all kinds of hell on earth?

I close my eyes and picture the looms. The gentle hiss and shuffle of the weft and weave echoes in my ears. Everyone I love is a single silver thread of those tapestries. They will be snipped off. I will lose them, and the closer I am to them, the more it's going to hurt.

I feel the Crown of Bones on my head. Even though it's not really there, I've worn it ever since I returned. Today it is too heavy to bear, but I must bear it. I have to do this.

Vera was right. No one should have this power in the Living realm.

One more job to do. And then I can go back to the throne.

Another message pops up from a number I don't recognise. I can't stop my finger from clicking on it.

> Edward: Bree, this is Edward. We have just procured a magic rectangle and Dani showed me how to use it. You must come back to us. We can work something out. We can figure out a way for you to not use your powers.

I screw my eyes shut. I shouldn't reply. If I reply, even to say what I need to say, I will give them hope. I need them to know that this is goodbye. I need them to move on, to have their beautiful lives with someone who will love them the way they're supposed to be loved. Someone who doesn't drive them to these horrible, lonely deaths.

I turn the phone off.

I FALL asleep on the Eurostar, but thankfully wake up before I miss my Paris stop. I get off the train and wander through the city in a daze.

The couples snapping lovey-dovey pictures in front of the Eiffel Tower make my stomach churn. I find a dive bar filled with loud college students chain smoking and singing along with French pop songs. I knock back glass after glass of cheap wine while I scour the lists of flights leaving Paris, searching for the cheapest deal to Malta.

Great-Grandmother Elsie ran away from the responsibilities of becoming the next Lady of Death, and she spent most of her life on the island. But something in Malta made her return to Grimdale and create the doorway. Something made her want to wear the crown.

I *need* to know what it is.

I book the earliest flight at 6:45AM. I lie awake in a bed with broken springs in a shared hostel dorm, the alcohol churning in my belly and my heart flayed open. I want to go home.

But I was kidding myself that Grimwood Manor is my home. It is many things – a portal between the worlds of the Living and the Dead, the place where I fell in love with three beautiful, impossible men, a curse that will haunt me for the rest of my life.

But it can't be my home. Not as long as I am the Lady of Death.

THE NEXT MORNING, I drag myself to the airport to catch my early flight. The plane is pretty empty, and thankfully I have a whole row to myself. Well, unless you count the ghost of a woman in an 80s power suit who wanders between the aisles clutching her hand over her heart and asking if there's a doctor on board.

I'm so tired that my defences fall down, and I see death everywhere. I see the pilot having a heart attack on the floor of an airport lounge. I see the smiling flight attendant in a hit-and-run. I see the woman in the seat across the aisle in a hospital bed as her heart gives out.

The weight of their deaths turns my bones to lead.

I touch down three hours later in Malta. My taxi driver takes me to a hostel in Valetta, the Baroque capital located between Marsamxett and Grand Harbours. I splurge on a private room that overlooks the towering fortifications of Grand Harbour.

Normally, when I touch down in a new place, I can't wait to get outside and explore. But this time, I sit at the window and look down at the bustling streets filled with tourists and street vendors congregating around the magnificent St. John's Co-Cathedral, and the only place I want to be is far, far away, in front of the fire in the Grimwood guest lounge, trying to stop Pax from throwing popcorn at Edward during his poetry reading.

37

BREE

Days become weeks, and weeks become months.

I don't get anywhere on my mission. It turns out finding someone who wanted to be alone in a foreign country is tougher than I thought. I ask around if anyone remembers Elsie. I look in old records. I go to places where I think she might have hung out and try and sense her. I even ask a few ghosts if they remember a woman who loved pink and could talk to them. But I can't find anyone, Living or Dead, who remembers her. I can't find her name on any official piece of paper.

Elsie was guided by the Lord of Death before her, but I don't have that. Jack the Ripper took her away from me. But something of her must remain on earth. She cannot be simply obliterated.

Even though I left it in the throne room, I feel the Crown of Bones on my head. It rests heavy, and sometimes I get shooting pains in my neck from wearing it. I know without knowing that the pain is a reminder that I'm bound as a servant of death, and I need to get back to my work.

I get better at shutting out the visions of death. I get

through most days without seeing death at all, but when I'm tired or hungover or sick, my defences go down and the visions rush in. Car accidents. Sickness. Murder. Suicide. Each one of them horrible and lonely and impossibly unfair.

I think about leaving Malta every single day, but I know that if I step foot in the airport, I'll find myself on a flight back to England.

So I stay.

I search for answers.

I get a job clipping tickets at St. John's Co-Cathedral, and handing out plastic modesty scarves to women who show up without their shoulders covered. I acquire a pokey flat down a narrow side street in Valetta, across the road from an ancient nunnery.

At night I eat by myself at one of the local restaurants. I can't taste the delicious local seafood without thinking of Pax, and the upmarket British-friendly tourist restaurants make me think of Edward, so I mostly pick at mediocre salads. A group of travellers I met at the hostel often ask me to tag along when they go out dancing or to one of the amazing beaches that dot Malta's coastline. Sometimes I join them.

Sometimes I catch myself laughing, having fun, and then I remember the three loves I left behind, and my smile falls away.

I'm in a literal paradise, and all I can think of is a grim, dark, crumbling manor, three impossible men, and the deaths that will come too soon.

It doesn't help that I'm haunted daily by images of what I am. Malta as a culture is deeply connected to death. Tourists line up to visit the catacombs and buy tacky sculptures of dying saints. Every time I wander through the cathedral, my boots clomp over the tombs of four hundred knights. Images of dancing skeletons and memento mori mock me, reminding me that I alone am responsible for all this. My time on earth is merely *waiting*, until I begin my new job as the Lady of Death.

I don't want to leave. I wanted to have a life with *them*.

I expect the pain of missing them to fade, but it doesn't.

Edward keeps texting me. He never says much, mostly sends snatches of poetry and complaints about Pax. I keep my phone turned off and locked away in a drawer, but sometimes, when it's late at night and my heart aches and I'm at my weakest, I pull it out and turn it on and read his latest updates.

> Edward: Now the Roman has fashioned a tiny chariot for Ozzy and has strapped it to Entwhistle to act as a noble steed.

> Edward: Entwhistle refuses to pull the chariot. He is washing his asshole. The Roman is unamused.

> Edward: I wish for you every night. Your body heat. Your scintillating mind. Your beautiful eyes beneath me.

> Edward: Come home or I will send you a hundred rhyming couplets about Pax's flatulence.

> Edward: Chariot update: Pax has recruited Moon as the noble steed. Moon took off so fast that we now cannot locate the chariot or either animal.

Sometimes, Ambrose or Pax will take over the phone and send me messages of their own. Ambrose tells me about all the innovations he's made to the Grimdale Cemetery tours, and sends links to articles he's found online about places he wants to visit. Pax sends blurry pictures of the ducks and his latest baking achievements. He says he's taking a cooking class over at the tech college in Crookshollow.

Their messages tell me that I made the right decision.

They have a whole life in Grimdale. They've made a home for themselves.

Without me.

It's exactly what I wanted for them, and reading about it makes me cry so hard that I can't breathe.

But they cannot be for me. I have to be alone.

I have to find my answers. I need to figure out where I fit in the world. Without them.

I never reply to the texts. Sometimes I go days or weeks without looking at the phone. But it's always there – the last vestiges of the life I wish I could have, the love for them that simply refuses to die.

When nothing else on this stupid planet endures, why must love? Why does doing the right thing have to hurt so much?

ONE DAY after the cathedral has closed for the night, my boss announces that the cleaners are stuck in the nearby city of Rabat because of a traffic jam, and could I stay a little later and help her clean up?

She takes the ticket office, while I begin the laborious task of cleaning in the nave of the church. It's a huge space filled with precious objects, and despite the efforts of the guards and guides, tourists drop rubbish everywhere, stick chewing gum to the pews, and dribble ice cream on the relics. I pick up a trash bag and start in the side gallery, where two Caravaggio paintings hang.

As I clean, Jessica – the church's resident ghost – pops out from her usual hiding spot in the old confessional and moves over to me. She mostly hides during the day, and I don't blame her. The church is one of the most popular tourist attractions in Valetta, and it's so full of people that unless she hides she's going to get walked through every five minutes.

When she's not hiding, she's playing pranks on the tourists – using her hands to make their ice creams melt and whipping their hats off their heads. I think she's enjoying having me nearby so she can cause more mischief.

I've seen her around several times, and I've even googled her. Twenty years ago, she got off a cruise ship and someone murdered her and left her body in St. Johns. The police suspected her partner, but they weren't able to make an arrest.

Jessica peers over my shoulder as I pick up a discarded ice cream cone. "Boo," she whispers.

"Boo right back," I say, looking her in the eye.

She leaps back in surprise. "You can see me?"

I nod.

The last time I travelled, I spent my days actively avoiding ghosts. But something has changed. Now I find myself seeking them out. They have the most interesting lives, and ever since I got to Malta, I've been helping as many as possible to cross over. I understand now that this is part of my training for being Lady of Death, and in some small way, it makes me feel closer to Pax, Edward, and Ambrose.

"Why didn't you say anything?" Jessica's eyes narrow, and I can tell that she's thinking back to all the silly antics she's pulled. "So you saw me twerking on the Pope when he visited?"

I nod.

"And are you the reason why I can suddenly touch people's hats?"

I remove a moldavite stone from my pocket and hold it out to her. "Yes, and also why you were able to make that priest's cassock fly up to reveal his polka dot underwear. That was particularly hilarious."

She cracks a smile, then bends to study the stone.

"You're one of them, aren't you? A Lazarus?"

I lean against the broom, searching her person for any sign of red mist. But no, she's just an ordinary ghost. "How do you know that?"

"There was a meeting in the church a few years back. Lots of self-important people wandering about in flowy black robes. They called themselves priests and priestesses, but I've never seen their type before. They talked about people like you, how you are dangerous, how they had to find every Lazarus who wasn't in their order before they brought more people back from the dead."

"I don't do that anymore."

At least, I'm trying not to.

Jessica waves her hand. "Pfft. Don't look at me. I wasn't going to ask you to make me a skinsack again. As if I'd want to go back to scumbag boyfriends and utility bills and spray cheese. I'm more interested in what's on the other side. Can you help with that?"

"Maybe."

As I explain to her about unfinished business, her face lights up. "I think I know what my unfinished business is."

"You do? Is it solving your murder?"

Jessica laughs as she shakes her head. "Oh, I know who murdered me. It was my scumbag boyfriend. No, but there is something else. When I died, I saw this light, and as I moved toward it, something grabbed my chest and yanked me back here. And I was staring up at the sky, a woman stood over me. She looked a little like you, and she was wearing this amazing bright pink two-piece suit. She said I'd been chosen to deliver a message. I told her that I wasn't a messenger, but she was quite insistent."

My heart hammers in my chest. *Elsie.* "What was the message?"

"'Tell her that I was wrong. Tell her that she doesn't have to do it alone. I came to Malta because my son deserved a normal life. I ignored the tug of the crown and the way my powers grew and changed. And then, despite how careful I was, I fell in love. And when my love died and the Lord of Death came for him, and showed himself to me again in my grief, he reminded me that when the crown sat on my head, I wouldn't fear death or grief any longer. That's why I'm going back to Grimwood. I'm making a doorway for her, because she deserves to have it all, love and grief and hope and eternity—Hey!" The ghost stares down at her hands, as the warm glow. "You did it! It's working!"

"I didn't do a thing." My chest tightens as the cord winds tight, and the end trickles through my fingers. White light surrounds Jessica. Her face lights up and she turns to me as the light spills from her, as she becomes the light.

"Thank you."

Jessica is gone.

I kick aside the sign that reads "DO NOT SIT ON PEWS" and slump down on the carved church pew.

Great-grandmother Elsie might not have left any trace of her Living life behind, but as Lady of Death, she left me this message shortly after she came to see me as a baby. In all likelihood, she had Agnes tell her that I'd end up here in the future, and she made sure that I heard her words now.

Tell her that I was wrong. Tell her that she doesn't have to do it alone.

But what does this mean?

38

BREE

On the weekend, I'm still thinking about my great-grandmother's message. The phone in my drawer buzzes. Edward is sending dozens of texts. But I'm in no state to look at it while my head is all messed up.

I need to get out of the house.

There is an archaeological site nearer the centre of the island called Mnajdra. It's a temple complex consisting of three circular temples of ancient megalithic stones that are supposed to be older than Stonehenge. I haven't gone to look at it yet, so I decide that today's the day to check it out.

Nothing like some old rocks to take your mind off a message from one's great-grandmother, the deceased Lady of Death.

I unlock my bike from the street outside my apartment and cycle through Valetta. It's still early morning so the cruise liners haven't disgorged their tourist hordes upon the city yet. I stop for a coffee and a *pastizz*, and then head out across the island.

I arrive at the temples shortly after they open. I pay for my ticket and wander through a museum, barely taking in any of the displays about the ancient people who built the megaliths or what they might have used them for.

This is good. I should get out of the house more.

It's already boiling hot by the time I wander down to the first circular megalith. There are two down the hill from the museum, and each is shaded from the elements by large tents. It's a relief to get out of the sun. I wander through a large hole cut into a piece of upright limestone and explore the stepped circular rooms that make up the structure, and try to wrap my head around Elsie's message.

Is she saying that I should go back to the guys? Is she saying that I shouldn't worry about living and instead go back down and sit on that throne?

Why does she have to be so damn cryptic?

Voices of nearby tourists intrude on my thoughts. A few voices in particular.

"I don't understand this place. They call this a temple! Where are the columns? Where are the statues of Jupiter? Where are the prostitutes selling their services at the gates?"

"I love it here. They actually let me touch the rocks—ow, hit my head."

"I must admit, I find it quite pleasing to the eye, also."

"Compose a poem to it, if you love it so much."

"Fine, I will! 'Each stone, a titan in its own right,
Reaching skyward with all its might.
Their girth so vast, their circumference so thick,
As if carved to resemble a giant's mighty prick.'"

"Oh, dear. Can't you make him stop?"

"They made me check my sword at the gate, remember?"

"'—Oh, how the peasants do marvel and gape,
At this colossal feat of ancient shape.
For though it may seem a mere jumble of rock,
'Tis a testament to the power of cock—'"

My heart thuds in my chest.

It can't be...

Can it?

My pulse races as I round the corner, and there they are.

Ambrose is happily running his hands along a stone, while Pax eats a giant *pastizz* and Edward stands on the highest platform, his arm extended dramatically in his poetical stance as he ad-libs another stanza about the phallic nature of the megaliths.

I rub my eyes. It must be the heat making me hallucinate. Because no way could they have found me. They don't even have passports—

Tears spring in my eyes and spill down my cheeks before I can stop them.

"Bree!"

Pax sees me first, but all three of them turn to me. Edward's sardonic features break into a smile so pure it makes the sun wobble. After Pax points him in the right direction, Ambrose grabs his stick and starts striding towards me.

I freeze in place. Every part of me tells me to run. But I can't. Not when Pax bounds over the mighty stones to reach me first. His arms go around me and he crushes me against him.

"It's Bree, it's Bree."

"Step aside, Roman, let us in." Edward elbows Pax in the ribs, and Pax reluctantly loosens his grip.

"What are you..." I can't get the words out, and not just because Pax is crushing my lungs. "How did you—"

"Are you surprised?" Ambrose's gleeful smile makes a fresh wave of tears topple down my cheeks. "Did we surprise you?"

I'm finding it difficult to breathe. "W-w-why are you here?"

Edward folds his arms. "I thought it was obvious."

"No, it's not. You should be back at Grimwood. That's your home now."

"Why would we, when you're our home?" Ambrose nuzzles his head into my shoulder.

Don't look. Don't look.

But I've already seen.

"Before we met you, Grimwood was our *prison*," Edward says. "You made it a home, Brianna. You with your silly games and your terrible Visigoth music and your attempts to teach us about modern life and feminism. You with your beautiful smile and ass that would drive men to ruination."

"I told you not to find me."

"You did, but you don't get to be the only one who gives orders around here." Pax curls his fingers into fists. "You ran away once before. You didn't give us a chance to take a stab at your problems. Well, we're here to take a stab at them now."

"He means that literally," Ambrose says. "He brought his sword."

"How'd you get a sword on the plane?"

Pax opens his mouth, but Edward presses his finger to his lips. "Now that is a tale worthy of the greatest poet, but Brianna only gets to hear it if she agrees to listen to us."

Three faces look at me, expectant, hopeful.

My poor heart can only take so much. My resolve, which was already balanced on a sword's edge, crumbles away.

Tell her that she doesn't have to do it alone.

"I can't do this here." I swallow. "Do you want to look at some ruins with me?"

WE WANDER DOWN A LONG, hot path to the second set of ruins. People mill around us as we climb through the stone chambers, and I take pictures on my phone of Ambrose posing like he's conquered a great mountain, one foot upon the stones, one hand gripping the end of his stick, his handsome features triumphant. In another photo, Pax squashes me against him for a selfie, and he smells amazing.

Even Edward is moved by the site. He reads aloud from the placards, and the next poem he composes is less phallic and more filled with awe.

All around us, tourists are taking their own pictures and frowning at their brochures. No one stares at us strangely. We're just a group of young people on holiday, laughing and joking and having a great time. We're perfectly normal.

I didn't realise how lovely that feeling could be.

It's everything I ever wanted.

It's everything I can't have.

The rug. The beach. The sword.

When the heat of the day gets too much, Pax starts begging for ice cream, and we decide to head back to Valetta. They'd taken a taxi here, so I call one to take us back to my flat. Luckily, there's one available with a bike rack.

My fingers tremble as I unlock the door to my tiny flat. They have untethered me by coming here. It takes me three tries before I get the key to turn in the lock.

"No," Edward announces as soon as I lead him through the door. "No, and no."

"Excuse me?" I fold my arms and glare at the tiny bed and faded chair crammed under the window, and the even tinier kitchenette slotted beneath the wonky ceiling.

Edward flops down on my narrow bed, and winces. "I'm a prince. I am used to a certain level of comfort. This lumpy bed of yours is not fit for these royal buttocks. That torn chair over there will not suffice for my grand and lordly thoughts—"

"Okay, okay, I get it. This place is a dump. But what do you expect? This is what I can afford until my Lady of Death salary kicks in."

Edward opens his wallet and pulls out a black card. "I will be paying for my girl to live like the queen she is. Call the fanciest hotel on the island. A hotel fit for a royal. Ask for the finest rooms for the four of us."

"I'm not your girl." I stare at the card. A gazillion questions float around in my head, but I settle on one. "But...but how do you have that?"

"Mina and Morrie helped me to apply for it. Did you know that paperwork is a fresh hell invented by sadistic bankers? If I were to be tortured by my father's soldiers, I'd choose the thumbscrews over bank paperwork."

I deflate a little. "You realise you can't just wave the card around like Morrie and expect people to give you things? You actually have to have a bank account with money in it, and a bank account requires identification—"

Edward looks offended. "I may be a royal prince, but I wasn't born yesterday. Morrie got us all passports, and he's been helping me sell off my wine collection. He has friends in high places who do not mind paying top dollar to keep their acquisitions private. You were right, Brianna. My wine *is* quite valuable. I'm not surprised, because given the piss you drink on a regular basis, I doubt anyone in this century has tasted a proper wine—"

"I have a bank account, too." Ambrose opens his wallet and shows me his own bank card. It's not a black one like Edward's, but it does have a blurry picture of Ambrose standing in front of Stonehenge, grinning with excitement.

"That's my thumb in the corner," Pax says proudly.

"I've been saving up my earnings from working at the cemetery," Ambrose says. "We pay your parents board."

"Wait, you still live in Grimwood?"

"Of course. We wouldn't leave. What if you came home and we weren't there?"

Home. A lump rises in my throat.

"But what about the sale?"

"You underestimate just how much Morrie's friends enjoy my wine," Edward says stiffly. "The repairs have been paid for."

I collapse into the torn chair. I think I might be having a heart attack, my chest feels so tight and achy. "You sold your wine to pay for the repairs to Grimwood?"

"Of course."

"We all helped," Pax says. "I lifted heavy things!"

"I held tools, and tripped over things," adds Ambrose.

It's too much. I picture them all helping with the roof repairs. Edward pretending that he's in charge while Pax helps my dad and the builders do all the actual work. Ambrose running back and forth, excitedly trying to be involved and bring everyone a cup of tea.

I wish I could have been there.

I turn to Pax, hoping for a distraction. "And what about you? Do you have a job?"

"I have something even better than a job," he grins. "A piece of paper!"

Sensing my confusion, Ambrose adds, "He means a special piece of paper saying that he has a diploma in pastry."

"After the graduation ceremony, he made us all call him 'professor' for a week," Edward grumbles. "I tried to explain that you need more than a pastry chef diploma to accept the title of professor, but he has a sword, so..."

"I worked at the Cackling Goat for a little while," Pax says. "But they fired me because they didn't agree with my policy for handling customer complaints."

"Let me guess, it involved a sack, a rooster, a snake, a monkey, and a river?"

"The boss said it was the most creative solution he'd ever heard," Pax beams. "He wrote me a reference to say I am a creative problem solver and I make the best date scones in all of England. Right now, I'm helping Mike fix things up around the house. With the increase in tourists visiting the cemetery, we've been busy."

"But enough about us," Edward says. "What have you been doing apart from ignoring my texts and living in squalor?"

I've been dreaming that you'd come.

I've been replaying your deaths over and over.

I've been missing you.

"I—"

Edward holds up a hand. "No. Not one word more until we have you out of this hovel and into surroundings befitting a lady."

39

BREE

All my protests fall away beneath the sheer force of their personalities. I find myself calling the fanciest hotel on the island and booking their finest suite. I call another taxi, one large enough to hold all of Edward's luggage this time (he'd piled it all in the ticket booth, which did *not* amuse the staff), and we pile inside.

Our hotel room is inside the ancient citadel walls of the old capital of M'dina, in the centre of the island. No cars are allowed inside the walls of M'dina, but there is a horse and carriage that gives tourists rides around the ancient city. From our enormous super king bed with enough pillows to construct a small Roman fort, we can see across the city below, and beyond the walls, the rolling hills and the ocean.

"I want to see the Hypogeum," Ambrose listens to his phone as it reads out. "And Fort St. Angelo, and the catacombs, and the Knights of Malta museum, and the old war tunnels beneath the Upper Barrakka Gardens—"

"How about a swim?"

The words fly from my mouth before I can stop them. I

know that we still have so much to talk about, but I don't want to do it here, in this palace that I don't deserve.

I want to do it by the water that reminds me of Ambrose's eyes, in a place where I come all the time to think of them.

Edward rings down to the front desk, and a concierge appears with a huge picnic basket filled with meats, cheese, pastries, and Champagne, as well as enough fluffy towels to wrap several Egyptian mummies. Pax carries the basket, as well as a small, waterproof bag, over his shoulder. Curious, I reach for the bag, but he swats my hand away.

I direct the taxi driver to take us to a spot that only locals know about, a private little cove I learned about from my friends. I've been here so many times I could navigate it in my sleep, but we have to go slow so Ambrose doesn't lose his footing.

We clamber down the rock-cut steps to the small patch of sand between sheer cliffs of jagged rock. I dump my towel and run into the azure water.

We've managed to make it this far without talking about the big, looming questions, but as I let the water cool my feet, I can't stand it a moment longer. I whirl around and face the three of them. "What's happened with Grimwood?"

Ambrose and Pax stop the rock sculpture they're building and go completely still.

The ocean roars in my ears.

"Since your father's accident, the sale has been on hold," Edward says as he kicks off his shoes and wades in to join me. "I've been helping them out when I can. They refuse to accept money from me, so I have to keep hiring people without your mother's permission. I'm not her favourite person, but at least the roof no longer leaks."

I swallow. "How's Dad?"

Edward's brow furrows.

"Please, tell me."

His dark eyes flicker with sadness. "He's been struggling since the fall. He can no longer get up the stairs, and his speech is slurred. He still insists on trying to do everything around the house, but if one of us isn't with him, he often injures himself or breaks things."

"Mike and I ride our horseless chariots around the village every morning," Pax says fondly. "But he's wobbly. I have to help him get on and off so he doesn't fall."

"He misses you," Ambrose says. "Your mum misses you, too."

"*We* miss you." Edward's eyes bore into me.

I stare defiantly down at my hands. If I open my mouth, I'll burst into tears. So I remain stubbornly silent.

"We didn't come here to make you feel guilty for leaving," Edward says. "We understand why you left."

"You do?"

"That's not true," Ambrose says softly. "We *can't* understand. We didn't travel into the Realm of the Dead with you. We don't know what it's like to wear the Crown of Bones. And we've never seen a premonition of someone else's death. We are just three ex-ghosts who are utterly in love with you."

"But you forget that we have been with you since you were a little girl making us play your games," Pax adds.

"We know you better than you know yourself," Ambrose adds.

"You're afraid, and when you're afraid, you run. This time, you weren't afraid of loving us. You were afraid of what you might do *because* you love us."

I sniff.

"The poets make love sound easy," Edward says. "As though it's this force of nature, like the ocean crashing ceaselessly against the rocks. It's something that happens to you, that wears away at your soul until you don't know where the ocean begins and you end. I used to believe in that kind of love, and in some ways I still do, because when I look at you I feel as though I'm being swept away out to sea.

"But real love isn't merely a force. It's also a choice. You choose to be vulnerable when you know that this person you love may be devilishly handsome with a wicked tongue," Edward grins, "but they are also deeply flawed, occasionally annoying, and they are made of stardust, just like you. Eventually, we all return to dust."

"You left because you didn't want to bring the monsters back," Ambrose adds as he too steps into the ocean, the water sticking his dress trousers to his legs.

Pax stomps in, sending up great waves. He still has that little bag slung over his shoulder. "We came to tell you that a little bit of monster is a fair trade for a lifetime of being with you."

The water crashes around me, heedless to the pain that stutters my chest. Looking at them is like bleeding out of my eyes. "It doesn't matter what you say, my mind is made up. We can't make this work. I'm not strong enough. I've seen you *die*. I can't spend the rest of my life with you knowing that I'm going to lose you."

Shaking, I turn away from them.

"You were always going to lose us, Bree," Ambrose cries over the roar of the ocean. "And we will lose you. That's what love is – being blessed to have someone in your life that you're afraid of losing."

"But I know exactly *how* I'm going to lose you, and when! And I could stop it, but I'm not supposed to."

For a long time, there's silence. I stare at the boats circling further out, the jagged cliffs on either side of us. I long to turn around but I know if I do, I will break.

Something moves in the corner of my eye. It's Edward. He wades out past me, his designer clothes clinging to his perfect body. He whirls around and grabs me by the shoulders, daring me to look into his eyes.

They are no longer fathomless. Those dark orbs are laced with a kind of grim understanding that terrifies me. Edward has always been able to see into the darkest parts of me, and now I fear he's seen too much.

"Is it truly so bad?" he whispers, his fingers drawing circles on my skin. "You saw our deaths, and they frightened you. You, my Brianna, who has seen so much death already, who know that death is only the first step along a pathway. Were they truly so awful that you think the way to save us is to flee us?"

I sniff. "You've come so far, Edward. You are no longer a depressed wastrel desperate for affection. To see you like that, alone, lonely, drowning yourself, I can't..."

Edward holds up his hand to me. "I think you should take another look."

I shudder at what he's asking me to do, but the desperation in his eyes is impossible to refuse. With shaking fingers, I raise my hand and press my palm to his. My head aches from the weight of my invisible crown.

I let down my magical defences.

His death floods in.

I see him face down on the rug again, the remnants of his desolation around him. But this time, I don't flee from the horror of it.

I let in his death.

I zoom out the image. I see me and Pax, much older, with grey in our hair and hunches in our shoulders, kneeling beside him, our arms wrapped around each other. We're in the ballroom of Grimwood Manor, only it's not the ballroom I remember. This room is bright and filled with the remnants of a blow-out party.

"It's exactly how he wanted to go," Pax says forlornly. "Before the cancer took his last pleasures."

I look up at Pax and smile. It's a smile tinged with great sadness, but I never thought I'd have occasion to smile at Edward's death. "He had so much fun last night, surrounded by all his friends. We guzzled the very last bottle from his cellar. He said goodbye to me a hundred times, and a hundred more goodbyes with his tongue in bed."

"Do you have to leave now?" Pax asks timidly, his arms holding me tighter. "He'll be waiting for you to walk him along the pathway."

I kiss his cheek. "I can hold you a little longer, my Roman. Edward always made us wait on him, this time he can wait for us to be ready."

I jerk back in surprise, my eyes opening to regard Edward's orbs of liquid darkness. "Well?" he cocks his lip in that arrogant Edward half-smirk. "Was I alone? Was I unhappy?"

Tears rain from my eyes.

"No," I whisper. "You were magnificent."

"Do me next!" Pax booms, nearly knocking me and Edward over with his tsunami as he bounds up to join us. Before I can protest, he slams his palm to mine and I'm transported to his horrific death by sword.

Only, I arrive when Pax is still alive. He sits on the edge of a bed in the master bedroom at Grimwood. And the person in the bed...

...is me.

I lie on my back, my torso propped up by a mountain of pillows. I am an old woman, my hair now completely grey, a pair of snazzy bat earrings hanging from my ears. My cheeks are sunken, and I think I have been very ill. My eyes are closed and my chest doesn't rise with breath.

I am smiling.

Although Pax's hair is grey, he is still a giant of a man, his muscles bulging as he holds my tiny hand between both of his and kisses my fingers. Tears roll down his cheeks.

Lovingly, he lays my hand down over my breast. He unclasps his leather sword belt, and slides his blade from the hilt. He holds it over his head and whispers a prayer to his gods, then he leans over and plants a small, perfect kiss on my forehead.

"I swore an oath to Jupiter that I will always protect you, my love. And now, as you walk your own pathway to take up the Crown of Bones, I will be there to slay your enemies and kneel at your feet. This is not goodbye, for I will be with you always."

He smiles as he grips the sword in his huge, loving hands. His breath rips from his throat with a sigh as he falls upon the blade. His body topples forward, so that the pair of us are skin on skin, as we leave together...

The image blurs and fades, and there is Pax, hopping about in the water with an expectant look on his face.

"Well?" he demands. "How do I die?"

"You die with honour," I whisper to him. "You die in my arms."

"Yes!" Pax thrusts a fist in the air.

Ambrose appears beside Pax. His hair is plastered to his face, and his jaw trembles. Salt crystals cling to his tangled eyelashes. He holds up his hand, and he tries to speak but his words won't come.

It doesn't matter. I know what he's asking.

I touch my palm to his.

He curls his fingers in mine.

And then, suddenly, I am on a different beach. The ocean is

cobalt-dark, choppy and dangerous. Stark, rocky cliffs rise around us. They make the beach I've taken them to look like a flat New Zealand shoreline.

He and I are filming something on a phone. I'm weighed down by all kinds of fancy, expensive equipment. I try to discern how old we are by our faces. I'm definitely older – there are wrinkles at the corners of my eyes – but Ambrose looks as young and vibrant as ever. It probably has something to do with the wide smile on his face and the excitement sparkling in his eyes.

He touches the microphone on his lapel and starts to speak about the remote island we're visiting for our latest travel documentary. A bitter wind gusts through the narrow cliffs, and he steps back on his foot to steady himself.

His foot slips.

I cry out as he skids backwards, his arms flailing wide as he scrambles for something to hold onto. But there's nothing but salt and air. He topples over the rocks, his head jerking as it hits with a sickening *CRACK*.

I jerk back to the present, tasting salt water as I lurch forward into the waves. Hands grab me, pull me out. Edward, Pax, and Ambrose hold me out of the ocean as I gasp and sputter.

Ambrose touches his hand to my cheek, and feeling the tears rolling hard and fast, tries to wipe them away. "My death makes you sad," he says.

"You're so young," I blurt out. "There's a terrible accident. It's not fair. It's not *fair*."

"But I'm with you?"

I nod, the tears coming in sheets now.

Ambrose wraps his arms around me, squeezing me as my body lurches with sobs. "Then I am not alone. Or lonely. I am happy. My only wish is that I will die in your arms, knowing that I am completely and irretrievably loved by you. The number of years don't count, Bree, only how you spend them. And if I get to spend them with you, then whenever and however I die, I shall die with a smile."

"Oh, Ambrose." I wrap my arms around him. He feels so good. I glare at each of them in turn. "How did you know? How did you see how you would die?"

"We didn't." Edward's eyes are black holes. "Only the Lady of Death has that power."

Pax pounds his fist to his heart. "All we know is that if we got to spend our lives with you, we would die happy."

Edward and Pax crowd in, joining our embrace. The three of them hold me as I sob and wail and scream. I howl my rage at the ocean, and my three lovers keep my head above water when I feel like I'm ready to drown.

Finally, I am spent, my body ragged from crying, my heart flayed raw. Edward kisses the top of my head. "Tell me, when you left us to come to this fair isle, were you able to turn your love off like a faucet?"

I have to fight hiccups to get out my answer.

"No."

"So then, what are you going to do?"

I sniff.

"I don't know."

"Well, that solves that," Edward says with his usual aplomb. "I'm glad we made the trip. I feel such closure."

I sniff again, holding them tighter as I fight to explain. "I told myself—hic—all kinds of lies about why I ran away when I was eighteen – because I wanted to be normal, because I was sick of living in a town where everyone knew my name. But—hic—the truth is that I was running away from love, because I was so deathly afraid of it. But then I came back, and the three of you were so...perfectly you, and before I even knew what had happened, my heart opened up and I was completely in love with you. And you're right, trying to stop loving you is like trying to turn off a tap to drain the ocean. I can't stop. I think about you all the time. I'm miserable, but that doesn't change the fact that when we're together, bad things happen to people. I understand what you're trying to show me with your deaths, but I love you so much that I can't control my powers around you. It's safer for everyone, for the whole world, if we're not together."

"You have learned so much control already. We have been with you all day and you didn't see our deaths until you touched us. And now that you know the *truth*, surely you must believe that together, we can solve any problem that the world throws at us, including death." Ambrose turns to me, and the blue of the ocean is the same colour as his eyes.

And I don't have an answer for him yet. So instead, I take his hand and pull him deeper into the water. Ambrose learned to swim during his time in the Navy, and he is excellent at it, graceful and natural as he keeps hold of my hand and allows me to pull him towards the rocks. "Come with me, all of you."

"Brianna, are you going to drown us out here? Because I must warn you that it is a foolish plan. I am very important. People will look for us. Well, probably not these two, but the authorities will spare no expense in finding my killer." Edward thrashes his arms about like a chicken as he attempts to follow us. "Brianna, your prince never learned to swim!"

"I've got him." Pax loops an arm around Edward's chest and dog paddles toward me. Edward protests, but he does stop flailing around quite so much.

With Ambrose's hand still firmly in mine, I swim around the cove until I reach a small hole in the rocks. The entrance to a cave. I pull Ambrose close. "The entrance is narrow, so hold on to my hips. Don't let go."

His wide smile could light the end of the world. "I wouldn't dare."

I wiggle my way through the cave entrance, dragging Ambrose behind me. On the other side is my favourite place on the whole island – a grotto formed from the cave, where sunlight streams in from an underground opening, turning the water a luminescent azure blue. Long niches are cut into the rock above us – the remains of ancient tombs.

I've always said that Ambrose's eyes remind me of the blue of the Mediterranean, but when I first came to this place, he is all I could see. And I know that he can't see it, but he gasps behind me, and I know he can feel the awe of this place, the way the cave hugs you, shutting out the world.

I pull myself up onto the rocky ledge at the rear of the grotto and help Ambrose out of the water. Locals who visit this cave leave behind supplies. I reach into a waterproof box and pull out a few towels and cushions and lay them down on the rocks. Ambrose sits on a cushion and pulls me against him.

"Where are we?" he asks, his voice echoing strangely in the circular cavern.

"This is part of a network of catacombs on the island," I explain. "Lots of them are open to tourists, but this one isn't. Rock niches are cut into the walls above us, and they were once the final resting places of people, although most of the bones have been stolen or washed away by now. And the light plays a trick on the water that makes it glow this beautiful blue colour. It's the same colour as your eyes."

Pax staggers from the water, dragging his tiny bag and a bedraggled Edward behind him. My mouth waters as I admire the way his clothing clings to his muscled frame. I have *missed* that arse. He pulls his dagger from his trouser leg (I still have no idea how he keeps it there without stabbing himself) and steps up to the wall. The lower walls are covered in all sorts of graffiti, most of it recent, but some more ancient.

Pax murmurs to himself as he carves something into the rocks. When he steps back, Edward reads out Pax's artwork for Ambrose's benefit.

$$B + P + E + A = 4EVA$$

Tears roll down my cheeks. I rest my head on Ambrose's shoulder and let them fall.

When I find the strength to speak, my words sound hollow and grave in the lofty cavern. "I came to Malta because it's where Elsie lived. The previous Lord or Lady of Hell is supposed to teach their successor, but Elsie's gone, so I don't have that. I thought that maybe if I could find some trace of her on this island, then I'd get to know her a little more. I was right. My great-grandmother left a message for me in Malta, probably at Agnes' behest. She knew I'd do exactly what I always do – I would run away from the crown. She knew because that's what she did. When she found out that she was supposed to be the next Lady of Death, she freaked out, and I can't say I blame her. She took my grandfather and got far away from Grimwood. She travelled for years trying to outrun her destiny, and she missed out on so much. She missed out on getting to live at Grimwood and getting to know you guys. I think she would have really liked you."

"We understand why you ran," Edward says.

"I don't!" Pax stomps his foot. "Death is inevitable. There's nothing you can do except face it, drunk and horny!"

Edward sighs. "Spoken like a true Roman philosopher."

I smile, thinking of Edward's death. "I don't want to be like Elsie. I don't want to miss out. I know I have to go away and be the Lady of Death, but I want us to have more days like this. I want to be with you, but after what I did with Dad, I'm so afraid that I'll mess up and break the Veil again. I can't be selfish. I can't just think of myself."

"We understand. You have responsibilities now. But does it have to be all or nothing?" Ambrose asks. "You're always talking about us having jobs. Couldn't being Lady of Death be your job?"

"Yes, royals don't do that much work," Edward says. "That why you have servants. Take it from someone who knows – I was a prince and I didn't do *any* work."

"I'm certain you'll put more effort in than Edward, but the idea is the same." Ambrose's face lights up. "You pick up your scythe and spindle on your shift and after twelve hours, you put it down and come back to the Living Realm and be our girl-friend? And Sundays are a day off."

"The standard work-day is more like eight hours now, and we get the weekend off." I squeeze his arm. "But I don't think that's how it works."

"Why couldn't it be? Aren't you the Lady of Death? Don't you decide how it works? You have the doorway that Elsie made you. I think this what she meant when she said she wanted you to have it all. You already left Agnes and Vera in charge as your regents while you came back here. I don't think anyone else has done that before."

"You broke a piece off the crown," Edward says. "My father would have had a heart attack if I'd done that. But *you* did it, Brianna. You never cared much about the rules. Perhaps there is a way that you can, as the modern poets say, have your cake and also eat it."

"Why have cake if you don't eat it?" Pax asks. "Is it to throw at Druids? That sounds fun. I wish I had a Druid to throw cake at right now."

I lie back on the cushions, tucking myself into the crook of

Ambrose's arm and staring up at the niches where centuries ago, people laid their dead to rest. Edward and Pax flop down beside us, our heads resting close, their breath warm in the air, their scents mingling into a memory of home.

People sat on this same stone that I sit on now, their hearts full of grief and love. They laboriously carved these special niches so their loved ones would have somewhere nice to lie, and even now, thousands of years later, their love endures in every tool mark and every ancient carving.

They had figured something out that I was only just realising. Life is a mad jumble of letting go and holding on. All this time, I've had them mixed up.

It's time I let go of that 'normal' life I've been pining for, a life that didn't fit me even when I chased it across the globe. And as for holding on...

"It could work," I say slowly. "I do have a two-way portal to the Realm of Death in my childhood bedroom. Being the Lady of Death sure beats cleaning hostel toilets and clipping tickets at the cathedral. Agnes could remain regent until I die and take over officially, but I could go down and help her, keep the afterlife ticking over, and learn more about my job until I'm ready to take over full time."

But I'll only be ready when the three of them can join me.

"As long as you give yourself plenty of holiday leave," Ambrose waves a hand around the grotto. "We need time to go on adventures like this."

"I think I can manage that."

"Does that make you a demigoddess?" Pax asks. "I've never been a boyfriend of a demigoddess before."

I laugh. "I don't know what it makes me, Pax, except crazy."

"I like crazy." Pax cups my face in his hand. He stares down at me, and that open, devout look in his eyes is the final straw. I might have passed beyond the Veil and returned again, I might have defeated Jack the Ripper and stopped a bunch of monsters from destroying my home, but I'm still only human.

And when a savage warrior looks at you like you're a mythological creature, you start to believe it.

Pax leans in and kisses me, and every doubt I have left is obliterated by the onslaught of his love. He takes my lips with a hardness that sends my head snapping back for him to catch in his huge hand. He drags me against him as he kisses me as if he were born for kissing me, as if this is his duty and he will perform it with all the passion and bloodlust that makes him Pax.

His teeth tug on my lip, drawing blood that he sucks away, eliciting a wanton moan from deep inside me. All these months without my ghosts, I thought my body had forgotten them, that they had become ghosts to me once more. But my body comes alive under Pax's touch, remembering every touch that came before.

Still kissing me, he pulls me up to sitting. His huge, rough hands roam over my body, squeezing my breasts so hard that I cry into his mouth. I love the possessive way he handles me. I may be a demigoddess to him, but I am *his* demigoddess and he has plans.

Pax's fingers skate beneath the strap of my bikini top, and then, POP, POP, the straps snap. He flings that material away as if it offends him, and his hands cup my breasts again with undisguised lust.

And then, all four of us are kissing. Chasing tongues and seeking lips, like moths drawn to an open flame. Fingers tangled in hair, clothes shrugged away, chests pressed to chests, heartbeats thudding as one, until we are naked together, four bodies feasting upon each other after being starved for so long.

When Pax lays me back down again, I'm no longer lying on the cushions, but on a warm and slightly damp body. Fingers trail over my skin, searching, seeking. Ambrose. He finds my nipples and rolls them expertly between his fingers, not rough like Pax, but with a gentle <> that makes my breath come out all ragged.

But for all Ambrose's gentleness, there's a fierceness in the way his hardness rubs between my thighs, and he whispers breathlessly in my ear, "Every day you were gone I wished for you. Wishes do come true."

"I wished for you, too," I whisper as his fingers map galaxies across my body.

"With every step along the pathway, in every realm before and after this one, I am always in love with you, Bree."

Well, *damn*.

"That's not fair," Edward growls. "Ambrose heard me say that on the airplane. He stole my poetry from me. That's plagiarism. Call the lawyers. Get out the beheading sword."

Ambrose chuckles, and the sound is a warm ache in my body.

"I have pretty words for you too, Brianna," Edward drawls as he crawls up my body, his dark eyes gleaming with mischief. "I think I shall write them down."

Edward pushes my knees apart. His eyes leave mine to fix between my thighs, watching Ambrose thrust inside me. My prince's smirk reaches his eyes, and my heart hammers in my chest at the way he's watching so intently.

I am aware in the stillness of the moment, with the only noise a hot, wet sound as Ambrose thrusts inside me, of just how exposed I am. At any moment a swimmer could enter the cave and see us, see me, laid out like this with a cock inside me and two other men naked and ready to ravish me. I am completely on display, and the way Edward's eyes are devouring me with primal lust makes anticipation curl inside me.

"*This* is poetry," he murmurs, his princely voice filled with wonder.

I shift my hips, allowing Ambrose to go deeper, enjoying the ache in my thighs as Edward holds them open. Ambrose fills me so good – not just my pussy, but my whole damn heart.

Edward runs his hands along the inside of my legs, flaring every nerve ending. He rests his elbows on the cushion, and as his gaze eats me up, his Adam's apple bobs. He lets out a sigh that is pure adoration.

"That's it," Edward murmurs, as if we need his approval. "Just like that. This is how my favourite dreams always begin."

He watches as Ambrose moves in and out of me, his lip curling back into that classic Edward smirk. I feel wanton with every part of me on display. A lewd rush of heat arcs through my veins.

When Edward finally, finally bends his head and makes contact, every nerve ending and synapse in my body flares to life, as if he has woken my body from a deep slumber. I bite down on my lip and press my head back into Ambrose's shoulder.

Having Edward drag his tongue over me while Ambrose is inside me is freaking unreal. I remember how much I used to love it when they were spirits and we did filthy things together, how their ghostly touch was *more* than touch. I was wrong, this right here...this is *perfection*.

Edward's warm, wet tongue moves in every direction, and I understand through the rising pleasure that he's writing letters with his mouth, spilling his dark soul to me. I can't discern the letters through the pleasure that tears through my body, but I don't need to. He says it all with the possessive way he holds me and that smoldering fire hidden in the depths of his anthracite eyes.

I reach out for something, anything, because if I don't hold on I'm going to float away. I gasp as Pax slaps his cock in my hand.

He groans as I close my fingers around his shaft. He's so huge that I can barely get my hand closed. I have *missed* this cock. I have had several dreams of it in our months apart. Pax's cock should be immortalised in art. He should have entire museums dedicated to it. Extremely large museums.

I pump Pax in a clumsy way while Edward ravages me with his tongue. All the while, Ambrose languidly plunges inside me, as if we have all the time in the world.

I know, better than anyone, that we don't. But after they forced me to witness their deaths, their *full* deaths, I finally understand, truly understand, the lesson that every Lazarus is here on earth to learn. That grief is merely love that endures. Love unspent, with no place to go. I am so lucky for every day I get to love them, and that one day I will grieve them.

For the first time since I placed it on my head, the Crown of Bones feels light.

A sob tears from my throat as the pressure inside me builds, and the warm flush becomes a river of molten lava pouring through my veins. But it's when Edward plunges a finger inside me, beside Ambrose's cock and I am so full of them that I cannot breathe, that I'm finally swept away.

I scream their names when I come.

I scream so loud that I'm certain the dead can hear me from beyond the Veil.

I don't care.

My loves came back to me.

I still can't quite believe it, not even when the lava gives way to a warm, undulating pleasure, and I roll off Ambrose and collapse against the cushions, catching my breath. Only when I look up and see their three faces tipped towards me, eyes bright with love and desire, do I dare to believe this is true.

"I want Bree's ass," Pax says.

I make a gulping sound.

"Pax, you can't say things like that," Ambrose scolds him. "Bree might not want to do that, especially not with your size—"

"Yes," I say quickly, surprising myself. "I want all of you. *Please.*"

The 'please' comes out needier than I intended, but it gets the point across.

I expect Edward to grumble, but he flashes Pax an obliging smile and lies back on the cushions, one arm behind his head, the other draped casually at his side. He looks like a Renaissance painting.

"Come, Brianna," he commands. "Your prince wants you on his cock."

I crawl to him, my body putty in that arrogant, baritone voice of his. How quickly Edward can undo me. Sometimes I think all the stories about him don't go far enough to explain his capacity for craven pleasures.

And he's mine. And I'm his.

I straddle him. A sigh escapes my lips as I sink down on his glorious cock. I have *ached* for this for months. I am so wet from Ambrose that he slides in easily, seating himself completely inside me. The tip of his cock jerks a little, and I gasp, but he doesn't seem in a hurry to thrust.

Ever the lazy, carefree prince, Edward leaves one hand behind his head. With the other, he grips my hip, guiding me as I raise myself slowly and lower myself down on him, making me control my own pleasure. His dark eyes are hooded with desires, and the way his smile twists, I know he has *plans* for me.

"Roman, remember what we brought in our bag of tricks."

"Yes." Pax heads over to the little waterproof bag that he's been carrying all day. He hunts around in it and pulls out a bottle of lube. My cheeks flush. How certain were they that this would go their way today?

Ambrose must sense my question. "We didn't dream that today would turn out like this, but we hoped."

"I love that you hoped." I crane my neck to see inside the bag. "What else do you have there?"

"Never you mind," Edward says. But when Pax drops the bag, it topples off the edge of the rock, and all kinds of things spill out. Handcuffs, a blindfold, a candle, things I don't even have *names* for.

"My new friend Morrie also introduced me to the wonders of online shopping," Edward admits. "And he and I share certain...proclivities..."

"You brought this bag of tricks with you from Grimdale? You were so certain that you'd get lucky?"

I slam my hips down on his cock, and Edward's eyelashes flutter. A low moan escapes his lips that almost makes me delirious.

"I have lived for several centuries and never been more certain of anything in my life." Edward tilts his chin towards me. "I am the luckiest prince alive."

"And I'm the luckiest centurion alive," Pax grins as he holds up the lube.

"You're the *only* centurion alive."

"Because of you." Pax's voice is right by my ear. He shuffles in behind me, his thick thighs straddling Edward's leaner legs. His cock nudges me in the back as he rubs lube along the shaft.

Edward's fingers dig into my skin as he starts to move his hips, doing some of the work for me. "We are going to fill you so, until you come so hard that we'll ruin you for any other man, and you'll never dream of leaving us again."

"Already done," I moan as I grind my hips down on him. He feels amazing inside me.

"Still, we have to make sure," Edward purrs, his hands holding me steady as Pax draws a lube-coated finger between my cheeks. It feels cold, but quickly warms beneath his touch as he circles it around my hole.

I reach out to Ambrose. "Please," I murmur. "I want to be full of you, too."

"Of course. I want all your wishes to come true."

Ambrose carefully steps over Edward. His fingers tangle in my hair, feeling where I am and lining himself up. He shudders as my lips close over his cock. I wrap him in my mouth, allowing my tongue to explore the textures along his length. He tastes incredible, like sunshine and limoncello tinged with the salt from the sea. He tastes like all the best parts of travelling – undiscovered places and amazing flavours and discovery and magic.

Ambrose isn't the kind of guy who fucks a girl's face, making her spit and choke for his control fantasy. He strokes my hair lovingly, circling his hip a little so that I don't have to do all the work. He glided in and out of my mouth with ease.

"You're so warm," he murmurs, stroking my head as if I were a kitten he wished to tame. "Your lips are like silk. Oh, Bree, I have missed you terribly."

I can't say anything with him filling my mouth, but we've spoken enough words already. I suck him harder, relishing the deliciously pained expression on his face as he fights his own body for control.

Pax pushes his finger inside me. I gasp around Ambrose, revelling in the rudeness of it. It feels tight and strange but then Edward thrusts his hips forward, driving so deep that my eyes roll back in my head.

"Don't worry, Brianna," Edward breathes. "Let go. We're here to catch you."

So I do.

I let go.

I let go of all the pain and fear and grief that I've been using to push them away.

I let go of my desperate need to be like everyone else.

I let go of *everything*, and they catch me. They hold me.

I allow my body to go slack. I tip my head back so my vision is filled with sky and tombs as my three lovers hold me and fill me. I let my invisible crown slip over one ear as I lose myself in their love.

The head of Pax's cock drives into me just as Edward thrusts again, and I suck and gulp around Ambrose's shaft at the delicious ache of them filling me.

Pax grunts as he drives a little deeper with every thrust. I'm dimly aware of Edward coaching him in his velvet voice, making him go slow, making sure that he doesn't hurt me. I'm so far gone that I can't even tell how deep Pax is when he and Edward begin their synchronised thrusting. All I know is that I must have gone back beyond the Veil, because nothing on earth feels as good as this.

My head swims, and fragments of light scatters across the sky and rock and graves.

I want them closer. I want them in my blood. I want their souls and mine to be woven together for eternity. And I can do that, I have the power, but for now, this, right here, is all I need.

I'm filled with them, filled with love so powerful that not even death can come between us.

The three of them *worship* my body, holding me between them, an altar where they lay in supplication. Edward and Pax work together in a relentless rhythm that drives me to oblivion. When I try to breathe, all I do is choke on Ambrose's cock. The lack of air only adds to the lightness that fills me, the sensation that I'm floating on some kind of cloud made of cocks that has me utterly paralysed with pleasure.

I come. I come with screams and cries of gibbering nonsense. I come begging and I come panting. I come so many times that my body is one continuous flow of pleasure.

I can't see them come because my vision has turned to light, but I feel them. Ambrose first, spilling his sweetness between my lips. Greedily, I swallow every drop. Pax is next, his huge hands squeezing me as he shudders through his release, followed by the bereft feeling of him sliding out of me, leaving me with Edward.

Of course he is last. Of course the Prince of Pleasure wishes to wring every last drop of my soul from our joining. His anthracite eyes are the first thing I see as my vision clears, and they shimmer with joyful, unwept tears.

"Come for me again, Brianna," he commands. "Come for your prince like a good girl."

I clench around him as his head tips back. His smirk transforms into a pained look of ecstasy as he spills himself into me. And it feels like the end of something. But I'm beginning to understand that not all endings are sad.

"That was…" I breathe as I let Ambrose gather me in his arms and pull me back down into the cushions. He kisses along the curve of my neck, as Pax hands Edward a towel to wipe away the sweat from his brow. "I have no words."

"Don't judge us on this one performance," Edward says as he rolls his trim, perfect body into the water to wash off. "We aren't finished with you, Brianna. Now that we have you back, we're not going to let you go until you're a quivering mess who will never dare to leave us again."

"It's true," Ambrose says with a smile. "We all agreed. It's 'quivering mess' or we haven't done our jobs."

Pax scoops me into his arms. "Where are we going now? We need to do this on every corner of this island. We have to go to every place that Bree has been without us, so we can make her forget that she ever felt alone."

"I like the way you think, Roman." Edward touches his finger to his lips, and his cruel smile only makes him more. "After all, we have barely dipped into my bag of tricks. But for tonight, I think we have more things to discuss with Brianna, back at the hotel, in that enormous bed."

40

AMBROSE

I wake in a tangle of limbs in the enormous hotel bed. The room smells of fancy bergamot and hibiscus soap, and outside the window, people talk and laugh, while horses *clop-clop-clop* down the narrow streets. I feel an odd tremble of timelessness, a sense that I'm not certain if I'm back in my first life or living my second, new, better life.

But then I lean over and my fingers graze Bree's naked skin, and I know exactly where I am.

I touch my hand to her cheek, feeling her soft breath and the steady rise and fall of her body. She doesn't stir. Our Bree doesn't do mornings. But even though it physically pains me to think of leaving her, I'm desperate to relieve myself.

Reluctantly, I untangle myself from the various limbs and find my way to the bathroom. My ablutions completed, I move to the window, heading for one of the overstuffed chairs.

Imagine my surprise to find the chair occupied.

"I'm sitting here!" Edward growls.

I leap back in surprise, narrowly avoiding toppling over a lamp. "What are you doing awake at this hour? You detest mornings almost as much as Bree. I assumed you were still in bed."

"I'm trying to get my new magic rectangle to work. I want to book plane tickets back to Grimdale."

"Already? But this place is fascinating. There's so much to learn about the history, so many new foods to try, and we haven't even had a carriage ride yet." I settle myself into the chair beside him, listening to the world pass by outside, the mix of languages, the CLICK of magic rectangles snapping photographs, and the cries of the carriage driver for tourists to get out of his way.

"Ambrose, the last time I was in a carriage was when my father banished me from London. It stopped too long on the wrong corner and I was nearly robbed, and upon disembarking my foot slid into a giant mountain of horse manure. I have no desire to repeat the experience. Besides, Brianna has been here for months. She will want to see her father. But if you want to stay behind for the knights and the horse dung, I won't stop you—"

"Don't be absurd. I want to be with Brianna. I can book the tickets." I whip out my own phone from my pocket and start to navigate through the screens.

Edward's chin lands on my shoulder as he watches the screen. "How are you doing that? And why is your magic rectangle talking to you?"

"It's telling me what's on the screen so I can hit the right buttons. Yours won't do that, but Mina set it up for me and showed me how it works. I love how this new world tries to make things easier for people like me."

Edward huffs. "Don't get used to it. One thing I've learned in four hundred years of existing on this mortal plane is that nothing is easy except drunkenly falling out windows."

"I shall just have to avoid being near windows while inebriated, then. Flights booked." I grin at Edward as I turn the rectangle toward him so he can see the tickets on the screen. "Now, do you have any other plans for this glorious morning? Only, I have an idea."

"I sense trouble," Edward says, but there's a smile in his voice. "I *adore* trouble."

"Speaking of trouble," I turn my body towards the bed. "Hey Pax, are you awake?"

"Only if you possess the golden nectar of the gods," comes the grumbly answer.

"We can get you a coffee on our adventure. Can you bear to leave Bree sleeping for a couple of hours? Edward and I are going shopping. We thought you might like to join us."

"Without Bree?" Pax sounds confused. I hear shuffling as he extracts himself from the linen sheets.

"I thought we could bring her back some coffee." A slow, cheeky grin spreads across my face. "And a ring."

"I can't believe you got a taxi driver to take us all the way to Grimdale," Bree says to Edward as she leans her head against my shoulder in the backseat of the cab.

"I told you," Edward says, somewhat snippily. "I have a superpower. In my day, people would fall over themselves to be able to drive my carriage anywhere in the country. Once, a man even knelt at my feet so I could use his back as a footstool."

"That's because you were a royal prince and he was afraid of being beheaded. I'd hardly call that a superpower."

"Actually, beheading someone in one clean stroke *is* a skill," Pax pipes up. "Lots of bone and bits of stuff that get in the way. Personally, I'm from the 'hack-and-slash' school of beheading. Makes more mess but is infinitely more satisfying."

"Yes, thank you for that, Pax." I can't see, of course, but I know from her tone that Bree is rolling her eyes. Old Ambrose might have secretly worried that their bickering would mean that Bree is thinking of all the reasons why she'd be better off without us, but not anymore.

Not when she could soon be wearing our ring on her finger.

Pax, Edward, and I scoured the shops around M'dina and we found the perfect one for her. Three silver strands twisted and knotted together with a black titanium thread, with a tiny piece of moldavite in the centre of the knot. On the inside we had the jeweller engrave the words, "Four souls as one."

Three silver and one black strands. Four soul cords woven together for all eternity.

I smile to myself as I tune back into the conversation. Bree is still berating Edward for his excessive taxi spending. "—you have to be careful with your money, learn about compound interest—"

"Mmmm, sounds positively filthy," Edward purrs.

"Here you are," the taxi driver yanks on the brake so hard that my head bounces off the roof. "Is this the place?"

"Yes," I say immediately. I can't see where we are, but with the window rolled down, I can *smell* it. The gardenias and hyacinths Mike has planted beside the gate, the crispness of Maggie's vegetable garden, the faint whiff from the tour buses that are stopped at the cemetery.

I step out of the car. My stick raps against the familiar concrete driveway. I hear a meow and turn to greet Entwhistle, who has decided to welcome us home by howling about how much he's been mistreated in our absence.

I turn to help Bree. "I can't wait to have a shower and go for dinner at the Cackling Goat," she says as she heaves her suitcase from the trunk. "The food in Malta was great, but they can't do a decent steak pie. I'm dying for a steak pie at my favourite pub."

"There's just something we have to do first." I link my arm in hers. "Follow me. Leave your case behind."

Gone are the days when Bree needed to lead me around. I spent almost every day since she left us at Grimdale Cemetery. I know every inch of that place from the high iron gates to the remembrance garden we recently installed. All the plants have a tactile experience or lovely scents, so the garden can be enjoyed by blind people, too.

But I'm not showing off my garden. Instead, I tread a familiar path, my feet leading me to the steps of Edward's gaudy mausoleum. I know that only twenty feet away is my own humble grave, and the altar where Pax's men buried him looks down on us from higher up the hill.

This is it. This is the place – the crossroads where our real lives with her began.

"Here?" Edward asks me.

"Here." A broad smile plays across my face.

"Guys, what's going on?"

I drop to one knee. Beside me, I hear a loud THUNK as Pax hits the flagstones.

"Do I have to do that?" Edward sighs. "These trousers are silk."

"*Edward,*" I hiss.

"Fine, fine." A moment later, Edward's hand rests on my shoulder as the poet prince lowers himself before his queen.

Bree's voice quivers. "Ambrose, what...what is this?"

I grip her hand in mine. Pax places his huge fingers on top, and Edward on top of Pax.

I open my mouth to ask the question, and I find myself suddenly overcome.

"Bree..." I prepared a speech this morning, filled with all sorts of lovely words about Bree and what she means to us. Edward the poet even blessed it. But now, with her fingers wrapped in mine, the words fly out of my head. "We...that is... we wish...erm..."

"We want to marry you!" Pax blurts out.

Bree gasps.

"We want to be your husbands," I add hastily, words coming out in a rush. "We want to be yours today and every day hereafter. We want to shower you with gifts and kisses and orgasms. We want to live inside your heart until the sun falls from the sky. We want to bring you your morning coffee and let you use our chests as pillows even when you drool in your sleep. Pax wants to stab your enemies and bake you cakes. I want to cheer you up when you are down, and Edward wants to worship your body and your mind and do chores around the house—"

"We never agreed to that," Edward interrupts. "But the rest of it is true."

"Ambrose?" Bree's voice wavers. "You really want this?"

"It would make me the happiest man who has ever lived if you would be my wife, and we could have adventures together for the rest of our days, and perhaps even beyond."

Bree starts to speak, but her words dissolve into a sob. My heart stutters, and for a moment I think that she has forgotten everything that happened in Malta, that she still believes we cannot be together, that she has to endure both the Living and the Dead worlds alone.

But then she wraps her arms around me, pulling me to my feet and pressing her body close. Her heart thuds against my chest. "Yes, a thousand times yes."

"By Jupiter's jaunty joy-stick, I was getting worried there!" Pax booms. "She's going to marry us."

"As long as we agree that the chore thing isn't legally binding, I am pleased," Edward says. "Ambrose, you should do the honours."

I pull the ring from the box I've kept safely in the pocket of my frock coat. I take it out and carefully slide it onto Bree's finger. She gasps. "Ambrose, it's perfect. Three silver cords and one black, and is that moldavite?"

"We didn't think you were a diamond kind of girl."

"I love it. It's absolutely perfect." Bree's voice cracks as she hugs us each in turn. "You do all realise that legally, the four of us can't get married. Anything we do is strictly ceremonial. And bound to cause a stir."

"Good," Edward says. "I enjoy being the subject of gossip."

"But we can have a wedding, right?" Pax's voice lights up. "I love weddings. The pomp! The dresses! The drinking songs! The sword fights over who gets the biggest slice of cake!"

"We already have the wine sorted," Edward adds.

"And I can plan the honeymoon." I think of the long list of places Bree and I have talked about visiting together. I got a taste of what it will be like to travel with her in Malta, and my feet itch to explore this world together.

Bree threads her fingers through mine. The cool metal of her ring touches my skin, and my heart has never felt so light. "Let's not get ahead of ourselves. We have to tell my parents first. And Dani. And we're not in any rush. We are young. We have our whole lives ahead of us. For now, I just want to *be*."

I rub the pad of my finger over Bree's knuckle, feeling the knotted strands and the tiny stone that glitters for me if I hold it near a bright light. Any time I worry that this is too good to be true, I can touch that ring on her finger and remember that today and every day afterwards, she is ours and we are hers.

Edward slides his elegant hand through my other arm, and Pax tugs us along on Edward's other side. We move back out the main gates – Mr. Pitts repaired the hole in the fence after the senseless defacing of the Witches' Monument, so our shortcut is gone – and up Grimwood's driveway. Bree stops every few feet to exclaim over the new flowers and odd sculptures in the gardens.

"Ambrose and I have been helping in the garden," Pax declares. "I made the sculptures."

"They're very...interesting."

"They're cubist," Pax says proudly. "Mike says that's when you do art that's made of simple shapes. So I did the shapes of body parts I have chopped off our enemies, so everyone will know not to attack Grimwood Manor ever again."

"I..." Bree's voice chokes. I don't know if she's struggling not to laugh or to cry. "I have no words."

"Do you like the garden?" I brush my fingers over a fragrant lavender bush. I never thought I would enjoy gardening. I've always loved to sit in nature, to listen to birdsong and to smell the heady scent of flowers, but to garden, one must stay in the same place long enough to plant a seed and wait for it to bloom. All my afterlife, I've itched to be moving, but now I'm ready, at last, to put down roots.

We've all bloomed here at Grimwood Manor. Pax has learned that he is so much more than his strength and his bloodlust. Edward's dark heart has grown so large that he can no longer contain his feelings within it. He has learned to forgive others, and to forgive himself.

I have learned that adventures are better shared with people you love.

And Bree? The girl who spent her life running from who she is, the woman who gave us our life and our hearts, she has learned that the price of love is grief, but that price is always worth it. And that being 'normal' is highly overrated.

"I love the garden. I love everything about this place." Bree squeezes my arm as we walk up the steps. "This is our home."

EPILOGUE
THREE YEARS LATER

"That was an amazing trip," Ambrose says as we step out of the Uber onto the concrete driveway. He clutches his cane in his hand, but he doesn't use it. He knows this place by heart.

And so do I.

"My favourite bit was when you challenged that burly Italian plumber to an arm wrestling match," I say as I slide out of the car, my carry-on backpack thumping my hip. "And the entire pub got in on the act. I've never laughed so much in my life."

"I'm so glad you caught it on video." Ambrose flexes his biceps. "Otherwise, there's no way that Pax would believe I beat that fellow. It was our best trip ever."

"You say that after every trip." I smile at him as I take the handle of my suitcase from the taxi driver and turn toward the house. "I loved it, but I'm so happy to be home."

Home.

Just saying the word feels strange and wonderful.

Ambrose collects his suitcase, and the two of us start wheeling our way up the driveway. Flowers burst from the garden beds, and the sweet scent of hyacinth and honeysuckle flavours the air. Framed in ivy like a postcard of old English grandeur, Grimwood Manor looms over us. She has never looked more beautiful, with the grey clouds converging overhead.

"Stop dallying, you two," Mum scolds as she pulls up behind us in her runabout. She turns the wheel to back the car into the narrow garage. "There's too much to do. I have a list stuck to the corkboard in the kitchen. Get a wiggle on! It's not as though those other two will have things under control."

"Of course, Sylvie!" Ambrose links his arm in mine. We ascend the steps together. My heart hammers in my chest. It's been two weeks since I saw them, and—

The door flings open before I even reach for the knob. "Bree!" Pax barrels toward us. He's wearing a pink frilly apron and his face and arms are dusted with flour. A glob of purple icing is stuck to his cheek.

He wraps me in one of his bone-crushing Pax hugs. I bury my face in his shoulder and breathe in his scent. Pax still smells like the bloodthirsty Roman I adore, but these days his scent is usually tinged with the delicious smell of baking.

"Come and see what I made." He grabs both our hands and drags us inside. I barely have a moment to glance around the newly remodelled foyer. So much has changed since Ambrose and I left for Italy. The walls have a new coat of paint and some luxurious gold-flecked wallpaper accents. Most of the heavy gilded frames and swords have been taken down and replaced with more modern artwork, but Cuthbert's old gun still has pride of place on a wall opposite. A bold, modern rug covers the dark stain by the fireplace where Father Bryne met his maker. The space looks light and airy, but also retains its character. All of this is Edward's doing. Our prince has quite the eye for interior design. His little touches all over the house have transformed Grimwood's decor into a modern pleasure palace.

But I don't have a moment to take in Edward's latest changes because Pax drags us into the kitchen. He makes a triumphant gesture at the island, where a seven-layer tower of purple icing flowers and tiny candy skulls reaches nearly to the ceiling.

"Pax, it's beautiful!"

The couple on the top of the cake are dancing skeletons. It's *perfect*.

Pax beams. As I struggle to describe the majesty and details of the cake to Ambrose, Pax shyly produces a tiny cupcake iced in the same design and hands it to him. Ambrose gingerly touches the petals of the icing flowers and nibbles on a skull. "This is amazing."

"Don't give the Roman a big head, or he'll use it to smash through a door again."

I whirl around. Edward leans against the doorframe, looking suitably princely in a crisp pair of tailored trousers and a black silk shirt. His dark curls flop over his face, and a slow, easy smile spreads across his features.

"Edward." I run to him and throw my arms around him.

He kisses me – one of those dark, sinful Edward kisses that burns through me like a forest fire.

"Don't ever leave me in desolation again," he whispers against my lips. I laugh despite myself. He says the same thing every time we come home, as though Ambrose and I have died instead of sat on a beach in Italy for two weeks.

"You were hardly in desolation. You and Pax have been having loads of fun without us. I saw the videos. And you've done an amazing job on the foyer. But what about—"

"Come." Edward grabs my wrist, tugging me into the hallway. "I must show you the preparations."

"But Mum said she had a list—"

"Sylvie forgets that *I'm* in charge of this party."

Edward leads me down the hallway. He throws open the doors to Grimwood's ballroom.

I gasp. The place is gorgeous. Edward has been lovingly restoring the room ever since he took over the house from my parents. He's resurfaced and polished the marble floor until it gleams, repaired the leaking roof and broken windows, and installed working chandeliers to replace the ones he blew as a ghost.

The windows on the end look out over the cemetery. In front of them, a wooden gothic archway is bedecked with purple and red flowers. Rows of seats face the windows, the first two rows hung with velvet rope and 'reserved' signs. A red carpet aisle scattered with rose petals leads down the centre of the room.

Edward turns to me, beaming. "What do you think?"

I have no words for how perfect it is.

With the money from the sale of Edward's wine collection, he purchased the house from my parents, paying off the mortgage and giving them a nice nest egg for their retirement. I didn't expect my poet prince to embrace the B&B business, but even five-hundred-year-old poet princes can surprise you.

All his life, Edward had been told that he was worthless and useless, but no one had ever given him a chance to prove them wrong. Now that Grimwood is his, truly his, he's found a new love for the house, for making it beautiful and for sharing it with people. In many ways, it's an extension of the parties he used to host here when he was alive the first time. Instead of his libertine friends, it's paying guests whom he now charms with his dark eyes, long lashes, and witty conversation until they agree to listen to his poetry recitals.

We converted a wing of the downstairs guest rooms into a

self-contained apartment with its own entrance. Mum and Dad live there. It's much smaller and easier to maintain, and we installed ramps and other accessibility features so Dad can get around easily. He even has a small garden patch and a workshop.

Edward and Pax co-own the B&B business. Pax was never going to last working for someone else, but he's an excellent handyman. And his baking talents are renowned the village over. He's even taken the Grimdale Bake-Off trophy from Maggie.

Ambrose and I have started our own project – we make travel videos. Ambrose mostly does the talking. He's a natural storyteller, and now that his book about Ambrose Hulme the blind adventurer (who we're calling his ancestor) has come out, our growing social media presence is helping to sell copies and increase his profile. We show off awesome locations but also talk about some of the joys and pitfalls of travelling with a disability. We're doing small trips around the UK and to Europe for now. I don't like being away from Grimdale for too long.

And I have my own job to think of.

Being the Lady of Death is a pretty crazy schedule. I've kept the title because, if I'm being honest, nothing sounds quite as cool as being Lady of Death. But I've done away with a lot of the stuffy rules about how the job has to be done. The realm of the Dead shouldn't be run by one person, nor should anyone feel they have to run away from the afterlife so they can be normal.

Being Lady of Death or a psychopomps or a Lazarus doesn't have to define you. It's just a job. It's not etched on your soul the way certain people can be.

Mostly, I've trained Agnes and Vera to deal with the day-to-day matters, but I'm often required at unsociable hours for ceremonial appearances, escorting celebrity souls along the pathway, and to fix the soul loom whenever it decides to start weaving curse words. Those closest to me understand and they're always here for me when I get back with a hot bubble bath and freshly baked Pax-cakes.

Over the last three years, we've hunted down several acolytes for the Order of the Noble Death, and convinced them not to join the order but to work for me instead. I'm trying to teach people about their powers so they don't have to feel alone and afraid, which is how the Order sucks them in in the first place. Grief and loneliness make people do dumb things. I know from experience. It will take a long time to dismantle the damage the Order has done to the business of death, but I'm working on it, one soul at a time.

Not this week, though. I'm officially on leave. I have a hot date with three sexy AF ex-ghosts, and a wedding to attend.

I turn back to Edward, taking in his glittering anthracite eyes and the way his mouth quirks. He's trying to pretend he doesn't care if I like what he's done, but he cares too much. I stand on tiptoe and brush my lips across his alabaster cheek. "Everything looks amazing. Dani and Alice are going to love it."

A COUPLE of hours later the guests arrive, their cars quickly filling the parking spaces at Grimwood, then the cemetery, and then spilling down the street. Dani watches them from behind the curtains in the master guest suite, her brow furrowed. She smooths the front of her Vera Wang dress (a wedding gift from Edward) over and over again.

"Stop doing that. You'll fling all the beads off and I'm not sewing them back on," I grumble as I try and pull her hair back into a passable up-do.

"Whatever happened to burying the bodies for me?" Dani grins.

"Bodies, yes. But I draw the line at domestic labour."

"Ha, ha, laugh all you want at me, but it's going to be your turn next." Dani unclips the pearl necklace she chose an hour ago and puts on a heart-shaped locket instead.

"Maybe."

"No more maybes. It's time. You and those ghosts have been written in the stars since the day you met. It's time you stood still long enough to let them in, Miss Lady of Death. You're only young and hot for your wedding photos once."

"Well…" I grin.

Dani slams her fist on the antique dressing table. "Tell me!"

I can barely contain my happiness. I've been waiting until after her wedding to tell her because I didn't want to steal her thunder, but I can't bear keeping the secret a moment longer. "We set a date. It's the anniversary of the day I came home to Grimdale, at the start of summer. We're going to have the ceremony in Grimdale Cemetery, in front of Edward's mausoleum. I checked with Mr. Pitts that it's okay, that it wasn't disrespectful, but he's given us the go-ahead. Which is good, because I want to be married before I have the baby."

I touch my hand to my chest. The baby just started kicking the other day. I haven't told everyone yet, because the moment Mum knows she'll make me slow down, and I still have so much to do to prepare for her arrival, and get get the throne ready for my maternity leave.

We're having a baby. I can't believe it. I peek down at the tiny soul cord protruding from my stomach, noticing the black colour that matches mine. A descendent of St. Lazarus bloodline. My successor.

My *life*.

I'm not going to let my child grow up afraid of being

different or wondering about their powers. They will get to live and fall down and scrape their knees and fall in love and experience the grief of loss. When they're old enough, I'll take them through the doorway and show them that there is a whole world after death, and even when we feel grief, we can know that the souls of our loved ones are well-looked after.

Unless they get on Agnes' bad side.

"A baby? EEEeeee!" Dani leaps up from the chair, causing me to scatter hairpins across the floor. She throws her arms around me. "I'm so happy for you all. And then we can be married ladies. Alice wants babies, too. We can have tea parties and complain about the laundry and go shopping for vacuum cleaners and get our pilot licences and other things married ladies do."

"Sure, we can do that, but first, you actually have to *get* married." I nudge her towards the door. "You look amazing and you'd better get out there. Your future wife is waiting for you."

"Do you think I need to change back to the pearls?"

"Go!"

Dani gives me a shaky fist bump. The two of us link arms and head down the hallway to wait in our secret spot beside the ballroom entrance.

All the guests are seated. I can hear them talking. Suddenly, the background music stops. Dani squeezes my hand so hard I swear I hear things popping.

"Careful, that's my scythe hand."

Dani grips the doorframe instead. Her knuckles are as white as her dress.

The music starts, and everyone falls silent. Dani and Alice have chosen the Type O Negative song, 'Black Number 1,' which perfectly suits their sense of humour. Hopefully, the guests appreciate grim and sexy goth music as much as we do.

I might have the same song at our wedding. It would be

appropriate. If I hadn't already chosen Blue Oyster Cult's 'Don't Fear the Reaper.'

I straighten the black chiffon and lace bridesmaid dress that luckily still just fits over my tiny baby bump and take my first steps towards the aisle. Edward is at the doorway, muttering something into his earpiece. As I pass, I distinctly hear him mutter, "Pox-ridden Romans," but I don't have time to linger and find out what Pax has done to piss him off. Edward looks up as I pass and the way his dark eyes devour me with such naked heat makes me stumble.

I recover before anyone notices and make my way up the aisle to meet Kelly at the altar. She walked in from Alice's side. My ex-nemesis offers me a shaky smile. "You look good, Bree."

"You, too." I smile back. Kelly and I will never be close – too much has gone down between us – but we have a grudging truce and I no longer dream of elaborate revenge scenarios. Besides, she's still terrified of Pax, so I feel safe.

The music swells, and the guests stand as Dani and Alice enter from opposite sides of the hall. Dani's billowing gown makes a dramatic entrance, while Alice beams in her tight fishtail dress. They meet at the altar in front of Pax, who has managed to get himself ordained as a celebrant, because that is the most Pax thing ever.

Dani was ready to call the whole thing off a month ago, after the registry office had a kerfuffle over using her deadname in the official documents, but after Pax went in and very nicely 'suggested' they pull heads from assholes or he would make the condition permanent, everything got straightened out.

Having a bloodthirsty Roman in your corner is helpful.

"Friends, Romans, countrymen," he bellows. He doesn't need a microphone to be heard in every corner of the ballroom. "Lay down your swords and listen. Dani and Alice are getting married."

There is a smattering of laughter. Pax, serious-faced, slides his blade from his pants and lays it reverently down on the makeshift altar. The laughter abruptly halts.

"Where I come from, a wedding ceremony would begin with the couple sacrificing an animal. They would cut it open and study the entrails to ensure their union had the approval of the gods."

Several people in the audience made faces.

"And then the groom would pretend to kidnap the bride from her mother's arms, so that the household gods wouldn't think that the bride was willingly leaving them. She'd be carried in a procession to her new house, while she held aloft a torch made of whitethorn to honour Ceres, goddess of fertility. Then, the wedding party would break a loaf of bread over the bride's head, and throw wheat sheaves at her. And then the couple would climb into their marital bed and..." Pax starts performing a rude gesture, but Alice fixes him with her devil eyes and he manages to contain himself.

Pax lets out a breath. "But I am very far from my home, and I have slaved over the stove for hours to make the bread loaves for dinner, so no one is throwing them. We are at a different kind of wedding today, a Dani and Alice wedding. There can only be one of these, because there is only one Dani, and only one Alice. I have been honoured by the gods to be able to call these two my friends, and I have gotten to know them over the years as two of the most passionate, amusing, clever, and kind people. So I like that they're getting married, and that hopefully, after this ceremony, we still get to be friends!" He beams, and everyone laughs.

He's going to make an amazing father. They all will.

Dani and Alice read their vows to each other, and then we sign the marriage register. I'm so busy trying to stop my tears from ruining my makeup that I barely notice what box I'm signing. Before I know it, that's all done and we're back in our places and Pax is speaking again.

"May Jupiter's blessings rain down upon you." Pax claps his hands together. "May Mars strike down your enemies. May Bacchus keep your cups filled with wine and your hearts filled with each other. And may Ceres bless you with many children, and love everlasting. Now kiss, before we start throwing bread!"

Dani's eyes meet mine over Alice's shoulder. They are glistening with tears, which mirror the tears in Alice's eyes. She smiles as she leans in and kisses Alice, softly and sweetly, as if they have all the time in the world to savour each other.

I can see their soul-cords and I know this is not true. But I also know that even if you only get to hold someone you love for a short time, it is never, ever a waste.

Grief only chases love, and everyone gets to live forever in someone else's heart.

Their recessional music begins ('No One Lives Forever' by Oingo Boingo, because of course it is), and Dani and Alice link arms and headbang their way out of the ballroom as everyone cheers and throws rice.

My best friend is married. Dani and Alice look so happy and so perfectly themselves. That's all anyone ever wants, isn't it? To be accepted for who they are.

Ambrose steps in from his seat in the front row, and links his arm with mine. He smiles like a Cheshire cat. Pax dances in front of us. He picks up Dani and Alice under each arm and crushes them to his chest. I have rice all through my hair and between my boobs. Today is the perfect day.

"Can I get the wedding party over here?" The photographer drags us away to the cemetery for the portraits.

We laugh our way through those as we drape ourselves all over Edward's mausoleum (He gave Dani permission). When we finish, we walk the long way around the cemetery so Alice can lay her flowers on her father's grave. He died last year. I escorted his soul to the Veil personally. He spent the entire journey talking about his daughter and how proud he was of her. Alzheimer's cannot take everything from him – it never touched his soul.

It's my favourite part of my job, actually, to escort the souls of those who have been trapped inside their bodies or their minds by cruel diseases. Released of the bonds of their bodies, their souls are free. They are so happy. They have so much love in them, even in death.

It makes it easier when I return to the Living Realm and see Dad. He's getting worse. His speech is so slurred that he's hard to understand, and the rigidity in his body means he can't do a lot of tasks now. But no matter what happens, I know that inside his soul is the same.

I can't wait for him to meet his grandchild.

When we return to Grimwood, Edward and his team have already converted the ballroom into the reception venue. The banquet tables glimmer with tall silver arrangements. The buffet table groans beneath the weight of Pax's feast.

"You'll save a dance for me?" Edward simpers as he strides past, a plate with two cupcakes on it. "I just have to deliver these."

"Who are those for?"

"You didn't think we'd miss this party." Lottie and Mary float through the wall to appear beside the DJ booth. Mary licks her lips. "Dani and Alice both look lovely."

"They'll be glad you guys are here, too." I point to a small gallery over the doorway, roped off so no guests can go up there. "We've made a special area for ghosts. You can dance up there all night and no one will walk through you. Edward will even have platters of food sent up there for you to sniff." I wink at Mary. "Maybe your new boyfriend the Squashed Navvy will take you for a spin around the floor."

"You're the best." Mary jumps up and down gleefully, accidentally knocking the DJ's coffee cup off his table. Edward rushes to clean it up.

I shrug. "I don't know about that. Are you sure that you don't want to be Living again? I have the power. I can do it. Or I could help you cross over and you could hang out with Agnes and Vera?"

Mary makes a face.

"Don't worry about it." Lottie waves her hand. "It's actually quite fun being a ghost. I think I'd miss it too much. Now, if you excuse me, I'm going to whisper lascivious things in the air of that beautiful man over there."

"It's time to throw the bouquets!" Dani calls out as the DJ winds down the last song of his set. She and Alice stand on chairs and all the unmarried people, no matter their gender, crowd around them. I stand right at the back to give someone else a chance, since I technically have a ring on my finger and a date booked. But Pax barrels his way through the crowd and plucks one of the bouquets from the air before it even gets close to the crowd of women.

"I got it!" he cries, thrusting the bouquet in the air as though it's a chariot-racing trophy. "I am the winner. I shall be married next."

"I wonder who the lucky man will be," Dani says, with a smile in Edward's direction.

The DJ starts up again, and the dance floor fills up. I rest my head on Ambrose's shoulder, swaying gently as I watch Edward try to twirl Pax under his arm. My heart is so full of love.

What's next for us? Will this peace we've fought so hard for remain?

I have no idea.

And I'm okay with that.

As Ambrose spins me around the room, chattering brightly about our upcoming trip to Turkey, we pass by a tall, familiar man talking to Dani on the edge of the dance floor. Dani meets my eye, her expression panicked.

What's going on? Why does Dani look so freaked out?

It's my duty as her maid of honour to save the day, so I dance Ambrose closer. "Hayes!" I wave at the detective inspector. "Why don't you join us for a dance?"

"I can't right now, Bree." Hayes pops one of the mini dessert Pax-cakes in his mouth. "I'm just telling Dani here about an interesting new case we're working on."

Dani's eyes widen with fear. My heart thuds in my chest. "Oh yes, what's that?"

"The council are draining the duck pond to do some environmental testing." Hayes wipes the edge of his mouth with his napkin. "On the bottom was a pile of Ralph Sommersby's golfing trophies. And the funny thing is, Ralph's widow says they were supposed to be buried with him. Since Dani was Ralph's undertaker, I'm just asking her what she knew about that."

"Er..." Dani shoots me a terrified glance.

Ghost-balls.

"Dani's very responsible," I say quickly. "She would have done everything to make sure those trophies went to rest with Ralph. I'm sure it's some teenager's idea of a joke, or perhaps Ralph's wife threw them in there herself. She certainly didn't like him very much."

Hayes reaches for another glass of bubbles. "That may be true. We're exhuming the body next week. If there's any sort of funny business going on, we'll find it. But you wouldn't happen to know anything about the trophies, would you, Bree?"

"Who, me?" I wink at Pax across the room as he touches the hilt of the sword hidden in his trousers. "I'd never ghoul around like that. I hope whoever threw those trophies in the pond is prepared for some grave consequences."

EPILOGUE
MANY YEARS LATER

I *am the light, and the light is me...*

Warmth rushes me as my head swells with memories. All of the happiest moments of my life play at once. I'm so joyful that I think I'm going to explode, but I'm familiar with this feeling now. I grit my teeth and brace myself for impact—

"Ow." Pax yells as he hits the ground hard. I look up from where I've landed perfectly on my feet, and thrust a hand towards him. He grips me and I brace myself against a gravestone and pull him to his feet.

"Sorry, the landing is always a little bumpy. I told Agnes to fix it, but she's been busy trying to settle a pay dispute with the Soul-Tormentors."

"Where are we?" Pax glances around. "It looks like Grimdale cemetery."

"It is, and it's not." I squeeze his hand, pulling him along the path. "This is the pathway. Come on. Let's go. I've got some souls who can't wait to see you."

As Pax and I walk, he talks about our daughter, Aurora. She's living in Berlin right now, as an aerialist in part of a performing circus troupe. When I told Edward last time I was down here, he nearly choked. But even so, I could see the pride in his dark eyes. To all of them, Aurora can do no wrong.

Pax is worried that Aurora will be so bereft that it will dull her spirit. He worries that she'll give up all her Living dreams now that she's alone. Of course, he should know her better than that, but he's a father. They always worry.

"Aurora will be fine." I squeeze his hand. "She told me all about her plans to turn Grimwood into a retreat for all her artist friends and her favourite ghosts. She'll fill the house with people who celebrate life, and she'll come and visit us sometimes while I'm training her."

Pax nods happily. Aurora is always surrounded by people. She makes friends easily, both with the living and the dead. She never worries what people think of her odd habits, odd parents, and odd way of talking to thin air. Honestly, I could have done with someone like her in my life when I was a kid. She'll make an amazing Lady of Death one day.

But not anytime soon. Aurora has a whole life to live first. And the current Lady of Death likes her job too much to give it up.

At the end of the pathway, we step beneath the open doors of Edward's towering mausoleum. Only instead of entering the prince's tomb, we step into my glittering throne room. Pax whirls around in awe. He's never seen it before, except in the scying bowl I taught him to use when I'm down here, but it's much more impressive in person.

"Is that my daughter, and my favourite Centurion?" Dad grins as he emerges from the hall of looms, clutching a screwdriver in his hand. "Welcome. I hope that you're ready for some hard work, because these machines are older than time itself and twice as temperamental."

"You made it, Roman," Edward drawls. He rises from the golden sofa he's set up in the corner, pushing aside the painting he's working on. "It took you long enough. The food down here is dreadful. Will you make some Pax-cakes?"

"Pleeeease?" begs Ambrose, doffing his hat to Pax as he enters from the Hall of Looms. "We miss your baking."

"I haven't been dead five minutes and you're already putting me to work." Pax stares down at the sword in his hands. "I thought that Hades would be non-stop brawling with demigods and feasting and bending Bree over the back of her throne—"

"Oh, there's plenty of that," Edward grins. "And what's great is that any sexy toy you can imagine just pops right into existence. Why, the other day, Ambrose had this brilliant idea to—"

"How's Aurora?" Ambrose interrupts, his cheeks flushing as he hugs Pax. "Did you see her before you—"

"She's in Berlin. I imagine she's heard the news now, and will be on her way home." Pax looks sad for a moment. "I feel bad for ruining her performance. I'm going to miss her."

"We all do," Edward's eyes turn pensive. "But when she's ready to begin her training, she'll be back down here. And in the meantime, we can bend Brianna over her throne and—"

"As tempting as that is," I toss my scythe at him and sink down onto my comfy velvet throne. The Crown of Bones slips over one eye. "I've only got time for a round of Pax-cakes. I have to get ready for my next personal appearance. My favourite author of kooky, spooky romance novels is about to die by poison, and I want to see if I can talk her into not becoming a ghost so she can come and hang out with us instead. We've got work to do."

THE END

What do you get when you cross a cursed bookshop, three hot fictional men, and a punk rock heroine nursing a broken heart? Read book one of the Nevermore Bookshop Mysteries – A Dead and Stormy Night – to get the story of Mina and her book boyfriends.
http://books2read.com/adeadandstormynight

(Turn the page for a sizzling excerpt).

Can't get enough of Bree and her boys? Read a free bonus scene from before Bree left on her travels, as well as her playlist, along with other bonus scenes and extra stories when you sign up for the Steffanie Holmes newsletter.

http://www.steffanieholmes.com/newsletter

EXCERPT
A DEAD AND STORMY NIGHT

Uncover the secrets of Nevermore Bookshop in book 1, *A Dead and Stormy Night*

http://books2read.com/adeadandstormynight

Wanted: Assistant/shelf stacker/general dogsbody to work in secondhand bookshop. Must be fluent in classical literature, detest electronic books and all who indulge them, and have experience answering inane customer questions for eight hours straight. Cannot be allergic to dust or cats – if I had to choose between you and the cat, you will lose. Hard work, terrible pay. Apply within at Nevermore Bookshop.

Yikes. I closed the Argleton community app and shoved my phone into my pocket. *The person who wrote that ad really doesn't want to hire an assistant.*

Unfortunately, he or she hadn't counted on me, Wilhelmina Wilde, recently-failed fashion designer, owner of two wonky eyes, and pathetic excuse for a human. I was landing this assistant job, whether Grumpy-Cat-Obsessed-Underpaying-Ad-Writer wanted me or not.

I had no options left.

I peered up at the towering Victorian brick facade of Nevermore Bookshop – number 221 Butcher Street, Argleton, in Barsetshire – with a mixture of nostalgia and dread. I'd spent most of my childhood in a darkened corner of this shop, and now if I played my cards right I'd get to see it from the other side of the counter. It was the one shining beacon in my dark world of shite.

I don't remember it looking so... foreboding.

Apart from the faded *Nevermore Bookshop* written in gothic type over the entrance, the facade bore no clue that I stood in front of one of the largest secondhand bookshops in England. A ramshackle Georgian house facade with Victorian additions rose four stories from the street, looking more like a creepy orphanage from a gothic novel than a repository of fine literature. Trees bent their bare branches across the darkened windows and wisteria crept over grimy brickwork, shrouding the building in a thick skin of foliage. Cobwebs entwined in the lattice and draped over the windowsills. There didn't appear to be a single light on inside.

Weeds choked the two flower pots flanking the door, which had once been glazed a bright blue but were since stained in brown and white streaks from overzealous birds. A pigeon cooed ominously from the gutter above the door, threatening me with an unwelcome deposit. Twin dormer windows in the attic glared over the narrow cobbled street like evil eyes, and a narrow balcony of black wrought iron on the second story the teeth. A hexagonal turret jutted from the south-western corner, where it might once have caught sun before Butcher Street had built up around it.

When I used to hang out as a kid, the first two floors were

given over to the shop – a rabbit warren of narrow corridors and pokey rooms, every wall and table covered in books. The previous owner – a kindly blind old man named Mr. Simson – lived on the remaining two floors, but for all I knew, the new owner used that space as an opium den or a meat smoker.

At least the flaccid British sun peeked through the grey clouds, which meant I could make out these finer details of the facade. The buildings on either side of it were cloaked in the creeping black shadow that now followed me everywhere. I squinted at the chalkboard sign on the street, hoping for some clue as to the new owner's personality, but all it had on it were some wonky lines that looked like chickens' feet.

This place is even more drab than I remember. It could use a little TLC.

That makes two of us. I squinted at my reflection in the darkened shop window, but I could barely make out the basic shape of my body. At least I knew I looked fierce when I left the house, in my Vivienne Westwood pleated skirt (scored on eBay for twenty-five quid), vintage ruffled shirt, men's cravat from a weird goth shop at Camden market, and my old school blazer with an enamel pin on the collar that read, 'Jane Austen is my Homegirl.' Combined with my favorite Docs and a pair of thick-framed glasses, I'd nailed the 'boss-bitch librarian' look.

That is, if you ignored the fact that I pushed my nose up against the glass to see my reflection, and twisted my head in order to see all the details of my outfit because of the creeping darkness in the corners of my eyes.

Please, Isis and Astarte and any other goddess listening, let me get this job. I can't deal with any more rejection.

I smoothed my hair, sucked in a breath, pushed open the creaking shop door, and stepped back in time.

As the shop bell tinkled and the smell of musty paper filled my nostrils, I became nine years old again – the weird outcast kid whose mother was banned from school events after swindling the chair of the PTA with a Forex trading mastermind program that was really just a CD-rom of my mother comparing currency trading to doing the laundry. (It was his own fault for getting swindled. Who even uses CDs anymore?)

As soon as the school bell rang I'd sprint into town, duck through this same door and escape into another world. I'd curl up in the cracking leather armchair in the World History room with a huge stack of books and read until my mother finished her shift and came to collect me. Books became my friends – characters like Jane Eyre and Dorian Grey the perfect substitutes for the kids who were horrible to me. When I was older and the guys at school sneered at me and fawned over my best friend, I fell into books again – this time to fall in love with the bad boys, the intelligent boys, the boys filled with anger and lust and pain. Dark horses and anti heroes like Heathcliff and Sherlock Holmes, and melancholy authors like Edgar Allan Poe spoke directly to my soul.

Mr. Simson barely said a word to me, but he never seemed to mind the fact that I read every book in the shop but couldn't afford to buy any. Sometimes he'd even let me riffle through the boxes of rejects before he sent them away for recycling. People would come into the store and try to sell Mr. Simson stacks of airport books – James Patterson and John Grisham paperbacks that no one buys secondhand. When he refused their generous bounty, they'd creep back at night and shove the volumes one by one through the mail slot, so Mr. Simson always had stacks of them lying around. I would smuggle the books home to our housing estate – If Mum caught me reading she'd lecture about how men didn't like smart girls and we'd have a big row – and read them under the covers at night or hidden in my textbooks during class.

It was in Nevermore Bookshop where I first discovered punk

music. I found a box of battered 1970 zines in the Popular Music section, and I lost myself in faded photographs of bored teenagers with bleached mohawks. None of them fit in, and they didn't give a shit. I was in love.

The memories flooded back as I stepped into the gloomy interior. My boot landed on a thick carpet in the wide entrance hall, flanked on either side by tall shelves crammed with books. A small line of taxidermy rodents peered down at me from tiny wooden shields nailed along the moldings. *I don't remember those.* The new owner sure had strange taste in interior decor. But then, he had written that acerbic job ad...

I ran my fingers along the spines of the books, moving carefully to avoid tripping over the stacks of paperbacks littering the floor. Must and mothballs and leather and old paper caressed my nostrils. The air practically *sweated* books.

"Hello?" I called, coughing as dust tickled the back of my throat. *Was the bookshop always this dusty?*

Hello, beautiful. A voice croaked from behind me. I whirled around, a retort poised on my lips. But no one was in the doorway. I twisted my head to peer into the corners of the room, but I couldn't penetrate the shadows.

Where did that voice come from?

"Hello?" I called out. *The first thing I'm going to do if I get the job is brighten this place up a bit.*

Something rustled in the dark corner above the door. I glanced up. My eyes resolved the shape of an enormous black bird perched on the top of the bookshelf. At first I assumed it was stuffed, but it unfurled a long wing and flapped it in my face.

"Argh!" I flung my arm up, slamming my elbow into a stack of books, which toppled to the ground. The raven croaked with satisfaction and folded its wing away.

What in Astarte's name is a raven doing in here? It'll poop over the books. I wonder if it's roosting in the roof somewhere? We'll have to find that if we want to chase it out...

"Croak," said the raven with an accusatory tone, as though it had heard my thoughts.

"I guess you kind of suit the place." I glared at the bird as I bent down and fumbled for the books. "A raven in Nevermore Bookshop. Once upon a midnight dreary—"

"Croak." The raven's yellow eyes glowed. Something in that croak sounded like a warning.

"Fine. Fine. I didn't come here to quote poetry to a bird." I stood up and rubbed my throbbing elbow. "I want to talk to the boss. Do you know where I might find him?"

As if it understood the question, the raven dropped off the shelf, swooped past me, and flew around the corner, disappearing through an archway on the left. I followed it into what would have once been a drawing room and was now a jumble of mismatched shelves and junkstore furniture. In the middle of the room were two heavy oak tables – one holding a large globe, the other a taxidermy armadillo. Books stacked so high it looked as though the armadillo was building itself a border wall. Old cinema chairs and beanbags under the window formed a reading area, and the large lawyer's desk that had served as Mr. Simson's counter still took pride of place beside the grand fireplace, although the brass plaque on the front now read "Mr. Earnshaw."

The raven swooped around me and perched on the desk lamp, its talons clicking against the metal. It took me a few moments to register the man hunched over the desk – the dark, wavy hair that spilled over his shoulders obscured his face, and his black clothes faded into the wood behind him.

"We're closed." A gruff voice boomed from inside the hair.

"Your sign still says open."

"Well, flip it over for me on the way out," the voice managed to sound both exasperated and uninterested.

"Um, sure. Mr. Earnshaw, was it?" I waved. He didn't even look up from his paper. "I saw the job ad you posted on the Argleton app, and I wanted to—"

"App?" The head snapped up. Eyes of black fire regarded me with suspicion from beneath a pair of thick eyebrows, deep set in a dark-skinned face of such remarkable beauty I sucked in a breath.

The new proprietor was younger than I expected him to be – Mr. Simson had been an old man even when I was a girl – and far too handsome to be working in a bookshop. His exotic features and sharp cheekbones belonged on the cover of a fashion magazine. The defiant tilt of his chin and twitch of his haughty lips concealed a storm raging inside him.

Danger rolled off him in waves. Danger... and desire.

Thick muscles bulged at the seams of his shirt. He'd rolled the sleeves up to his elbows, one thick forearm graced with the tattoo of a barren, gnarled tree and some words in cursive script below.

Even though he was an Adonis, this Mr. Earnshaw also looked like a complete wanker. He scrunched up that perfectly-sculpted nose, his lips curling back into a sneer. "What the devil is an app?"

What kind of weird question is that? "Um... you know, an application for your phone, so you can get the bus timetable or talk to your mates or—"

"Don't talk to me about *phones*," Earnshaw snapped. "People spend too much time on their phones."

Right. I'd forgotten the part in the job ad about hating ebooks. *This guy must be one of those weirdos who eschews technology.* "Oh, I agree. I mean, phones should only be used for calling people. And checking social media. That's it. I would never read on mine," I blubbered, shoving my phone behind my back. "I mean, studies have shown it can cause long-term eye damage and—"

"No matter how long you keep talking, it's not going to change the fact that we're closed. What do you *want?*"

"I'm applying for the assistant's job." I fumbled in my purse for the envelope I'd carefully sealed, trying to avoid accidentally showing him the ereader tucked behind my makeup case. "I've got my resume in here for you with all my qualifications and—"

"I don't need that. If you want the job, tell me why I should hire you."

"Right, well..." This was the weirdest interview I've ever been to. Earnshaw's eyes stabbed right through me, turning my insides to mush. I opened my mouth, but then he blinked, long black lashes tangling together over those eyes – they were like black holes, gobbling whole universes for lunch. A shiver started at the base of my neck and rocketed down my spine, not stopping until it caressed me between my legs.

Now I wanted the job more than ever, just so I could stare at this specimen all day. Bloody hell, I always did have a thing for surly bad boys. I blamed Emily Brontë. The brutish and untamable Heathcliff ruined me for nice guys.

"If your answer is to gape at me like a bespawling lubberwort," he growled, "then you can take the job and shove it where the sun don't shine—"

"That's *not* my answer." My cheeks flared with heat. *Who even is this guy? Adonis or not, how'd he get off talking to customers and potential employees like that? No wonder the place is deserted.* "I was just collecting my thoughts. You should hire me because I'm a hard worker. I'm punctual. I have some retail experience, as well as design expertise so I can do graphics and window displays—"

"I don't care. Why do you want to work *here?* No one wants to work here. That was the whole *point* of the ad."

I racked my brain for an answer to that question. *What does he want from me?* "Um... I guess because I used to hang out in the bookshop all the time as a kid. I know where all the books go and I've personally helped Mr. Simson fix that till on at least two occasions." I pointed to the ancient contraption the raven was pecking.

Earnshaw glared at me, his eyes flicking over my face as though searching for something. He didn't say a thing. The silence stretched between us until even the raven got bored of hunting for worms in the credit card machine and stared at me, too.

Is he waiting for more?

"And... um, I have all sorts of useful skills." I scrambled for anything that might endear me to this strong-chinned man. "I have a fashion degree, so that's probably not useful. But I am a Millennial, so I can do the store's social media. I could build a website—"

You can see it, can't you? That strange voice said. *It's obvious. She's the one he told you about.*

Earnshaw grunted. I narrowed my eyes at him. *Does he hear it, too?*

Just hire her already, that voice said again. *She's pretty.*

"Hey!" I glanced over my shoulder, looking for the owner of the voice so I could kick them in the nuts. But there was no one else in the room.

Was it Earnshaw? But the voice didn't sound like him, and judging by the way he was still staring at me, he already thought I was nuts. *Maybe he didn't hear the voice after all?*

Besides, the voice sounded like it came from *inside* my head.

Please, don't tell me that on top of everything else, I'm now hallucinating voices—

I like her, the voice interrupted. *I bet she'll bring me treats. Berries, smoked salmon, maybe even a hard-boiled egg.*

I peered over my shoulder again. *Are they hiding in the hallway? Behind the beanbag stack?* "Who's there?"

Earnshaw's head whipped up. "Who are you talking to?"

"You didn't hear that? Someone prattling on about salmon and eggs."

Earnshaw's eyes narrowed. He reached out and clamped an enormous hand around the raven's beak. "You didn't leave the door open, did you? We're supposed to be *closed.*"

"No. I..." My shoulders sagged. *Who am I kidding? This is hopeless.* "I guess I'll just be going now. Thank you for your time and—"

"You start tomorrow," Earnshaw glowered. "We open at nine. Be here at eight-thirty, but don't let anyone else in. If you're late, the bird gets your paycheck. Welcome to Nevermore Bookshop."

TO BE CONTINUED

Uncover the secrets of Nevermore Bookshop in book 1, *A Dead and Stormy Night*

http://books2read.com/adeadandstormynight

BOOK BOYFRIENDS MAY DO IT BETTER...
...BUT THEY'RE MORE TROUBLE THAN THEY'RE WORTH.

After being fired from my dream fashion job, I return home to my village under a cloud of failure and take a job at the quaint Nevermore Bookshop. I'm hoping for an easy few months while I get my life together.

But this is no ordinary bookshop.

A mysterious curse on Nevermore brings infamous fictional villains from classic literature to life in the real world.

My "easy" job involves rescuing customers from a 6foot4, grumpy, tattooed Heathcliff, drinking tea and evading the authorities with suave villain Moriarty, and making art with Edgar Allen Poe's shy, cheeky, raven shifter, Quoth.

As if that isn't crazy enough, my ex-best friend shows up dead with a knife in her back, and I'm the chief suspect.

I'm going to have to Agatha Christie this shiz if I want to clear my name.

OTHER BOOKS BY STEFFANIE HOLMES

Nevermore Bookshop Mysteries

A Dead and Stormy Night

Of Mice and Murder

Pride and Premeditation

How Heathcliff Stole Christmas

Memoirs of a Garroter

Prose and Cons

A Novel Way to Die

Much Ado About Murder

Crime and Publishing

Plot and Bothered

Grimdale Graveyard Mysteries

What do you do when three hot AF, possessive ghosts want to jump your bones? Find out in this spooky, kooky paranormal romance series set in the same world as Nevermore Bookshop.

You're So Dead To Me

If You've Got It, Haunt It

Ghoul as a Cucumber

Not a Mourning Person

Kings of Miskatonic Prep

Shunned

Initiated

Possessed

Ignited

Stonehurst Prep

My Stolen Life

My Secret Heart

My Broken Crown

My Savage Kingdom

Stonehurst Prep Elite

Poison Ivy

Poison Flower

Poison Kiss

Dark Academia

Pretty Girls Make Graves

Brutal Boys Cry Blood

Manderley Academy

Ghosted

Haunted

Spirited

Briarwood Witches

Earth and Embers

Fire and Fable

Water and Woe

Wind and Whispers

Spirit and Sorrow

Crookshollow Gothic Romance

Art of Cunning (Alex & Ryan)

Art of the Hunt (Alex & Ryan)

Art of Temptation (Alex & Ryan)

The Man in Black (Elinor & Eric)

Watcher (Belinda & Cole)

Reaper (Belinda & Cole)

Wolves of Crookshollow

Digging the Wolf (Anna & Luke)

Writing the Wolf (Rosa & Caleb)

Inking the Wolf (Bianca & Robbie)

Wedding the Wolf (Willow & Irvine)

Want to be informed when the next Steffanie Holmes paranormal romance story goes live? Sign up for the newsletter at www.steffanieholmes.com/ newsletter to get the scoop, and score a free collection of bonus scenes and stories to enjoy!

About the Author

Steffanie Holmes is the *USA Today* bestselling author of kooky, spooky paranormal, cozy fantasy, and gothic romance. Her books feature clever, witty heroines, secret societies, quirky villages where nothing is as it seems, creepy old mansions, and alpha males who *always* get what they want.

Legally-blind since birth, Steffanie received the 2017 Attitude Award for Artistic Achievement. She was also a finalist for a 2018 Women of Influence award.

Steffanie lives in New Zealand with her husband, a horde of cantankerous cats, and their medieval sword collection.

STEFFANIE HOLMES NEWSLETTER

Grab a free copy of *Cabinet of Curiosities* – a Steffanie Holmes compendium of short stories and bonus scenes – when you sign up for updates with the Steffanie Holmes newsletter.

http://www.steffanieholmes.com/newsletter

Come hang with Steffanie
www.steffanieholmes.com
hello@steffanieholmes.com